MY NAME IS MEMORY

"Brashares's fantastical romance hopscotches between the present day, where Daniel and his love, Lucy, meet as students in Virginia, and their former lives, where they've always been mismatched by time and circumstance. . . . An inventive, romantic, **highly pleasurable ride through time.**" —*The Washington Post*

"It's pure romance!" —*New York Post*

"A page-turner that combines a beautiful story of love and fate with the elements of the supernatural." —*Woman's Day*

"Calling all Twilight fans! You'll fall hard for this story of a cosmically tormented couple: Daniel can recall all of his previous lives, and he pursues his great love, Sophia, through the ages."—*Glamour*

"Literature is filled with lovers that not even death can divide. Heathcliff and Cathy, then Edward and Bella; now in Ann Brashares's entrancing new romantic saga, readers will be swept away by Daniel and Lucy, whose love is truly one for the ages. . . . A potent mix of *The Time Traveler's Wife*, *Twilight*, **and something entirely new**, *My Name Is Memory*. . .will remind readers that when it comes to love, hope springs eternal." —*BookPage*

"We all like to believe in the constancy of love. And then along comes Ann Brashares to take the concept to a whole new level." —*Minneapolis Star Tribune*

"In *My Name Is Memory*, Ann Brashares . . . offers an adult novel that **takes readers on a tour of cosmic coulda-beens**, romantic rendezvous,

Praise for *The Last Summer (of You & Me)*

"[Brashares] weaves a tale full of delicious plot twists and revelations that will surprise and enthrall you. . . . A glorious novel of unrequited love, longing, and the meaning of friendship."

—Adriana Trigiani, *New York Times* bestselling author of the Big Stone Gap novels

"A vivid elegy for youth, and Brashares is wise as well as sentimental. She sagely remembers just how it feels to be young, lost, and in love. If you don't grow misty there's something a bit shifty about the state of your heart."

—*The Miami Herald*

"Natural, insightful, and affecting."

—*Entertainment Weekly*

"Get out your handkerchiefs."

—*The Vancouver Sun*

"*The Last Summer* is as much a treatise on loyalty and letting go of childish ways as it is on a summer of love."

—*USA Today*

"An unputdownable beach book calls for love, deceit, and sex. And *The Last Summer (of You & Me)* . . . has all those elements." —*Cosmopolitan*

"Would do nicely under a beach umbrella."

—*The New York Times*

"Compelling . . . steeped in the familiar longings for lost time that readers seeking the carefree pleasure of a summer will enjoy."

—Kim Edwards, *The Washington Post*

"[Those with] a hankering for a breezy summer read will easily relate to Brashares's restless threesome of lost souls."

—*People*

"Ann Brashares's new book will delight all of her *Traveling Pants* fans— now grown-up and ready for this very adult novel of love, loss, and the beauty of intense family bonds."

—Anita Shreve, *New York Times* bestselling author of *The Pilot's Wife* and *A Wedding in December*

MY NAME IS

Memory

✳ ✳ ✳ ✳

Ann Brashares

RIVERHEAD BOOKS

New York

RIVERHEAD BOOKS
Published by the Penguin Group
Penguin Group (USA) Inc.
375 Hudson Street, New York, New York 10014, USA
Penguin Group (Canada), 90 Eglinton Avenue East, Suite 700, Toronto, Ontario M4P 2Y3, Canada
(a division of Pearson Penguin Canada Inc.)
Penguin Books Ltd., 80 Strand, London WC2R 0RL, England
Penguin Group Ireland, 25 St. Stephen's Green, Dublin 2, Ireland (a division of Penguin Books Ltd.)
Penguin Group (Australia), 250 Camberwell Road, Camberwell, Victoria 3124, Australia
(a division of Pearson Australia Group Pty. Ltd.)
Penguin Books India Pvt. Ltd., 11 Community Centre, Panchsheel Park, New Delhi—110 017, India
Penguin Group (NZ), 67 Apollo Drive, Rosedale, Auckland 0632, New Zealand
(a division of Pearson New Zealand Ltd.)
Penguin Books (South Africa) (Pty.) Ltd., 24 Sturdee Avenue, Rosebank, Johannesburg 2196,
South Africa

Penguin Books Ltd., Registered Offices: 80 Strand, London WC2R 0RL, England

This is a work of fiction. Names, characters, places, and incidents either are the product of the author's imagination or are used fictitiously, and any resemblance to actual persons, living or dead, business establishments, events or locales is entirely coincidental. The publisher does not have any control over and does not assume any responsibility for author or third-party websites or their content.

First Riverhead hardcover edition: June 2010
First Riverhead trade paperback edition: June 2011
Riverhead trade paperback ISBN: 978-1-59448-518-3

The Library of Congress has catalogued the Riverhead hardcover edition as follows:

Brashares, Ann.
    My name is memory/Ann Brashares.
        p.   cm.
    ISBN 978-1-59448-758-3
    1. Man-woman relationships—Fiction.   2. Reincarnation—Fiction.   3. Memory—Fiction.
I. Title.
    PS3602.R385M92   2010   2010000276
    813'6—dc22

PRINTED IN THE UNITED STATES OF AMERICA

10   9   8   7   6   5   4   3   2   1

For my dearest Nate, who has a gift for remembering

Not asking the sky to come down to my good will,
Scattering it freely for ever.

—*Walt Whitman, "Song of Myself"*

I HAVE LIVED more than a thousand years. I have died countless times. I forget precisely how many times. My memory is an extraordinary thing, but it is not perfect. I am human.

The early lives blur a bit. The arc of your soul follows the pattern of each of your lives. It is macrocosmic. There was my childhood. There have been many childhoods. And even in the early part of my soul I reached adulthood many times. These days, in every one of my infancies, the memory comes faster. We go through the motions. We look oddly at the world around us. We remember.

I say "we" and I mean myself, my soul, my selves, my many lives. I say "we" and I also mean the other ones like me who have the Memory, the conscious record of experience on this earth that survives every death. There aren't many, I know. Maybe one in a century, one born out of millions. We find one another rarely, but believe me, there are others. At least one of them has a memory far more extraordinary than mine.

I have been born and died many times in many places. The space between them is the same. I wasn't in Bethlehem for Christ's birth. I never saw the glory that was Rome. I never bowed to Charlemagne. At that time I was scratching out a crop in Anatolia, speaking a dialect unintelligible to the villages north and south. Only God and the devil can be counted on for all the thrilling parts. The great hits of history go along without the notice of most. I read about them in books like everybody else.

Sometimes I feel more akin to houses and trees than to my fellow human beings. I stand around watching the waves of people come and go. Their lives *are short, but mine is long. Sometimes I imagine myself as a post driven into the ocean's edge.*

I've never had a child, and I've never gotten old. I don't know why. I have seen beauty in countless things. I have fallen in love, and she is the one who endures. I killed her once and died for her many times and I still have nothing to show for it. I always search for her; I always remember her. I carry the hope that someday she will remember me.

SHE HADN'T KNOWN him very long. He'd shown up there at the beginning of eleventh grade. It was a small town and a small school district. You kept seeing the same kids year after year. He was a junior when he came, the same as her, but he seemed older somehow.

She'd heard many things about where and how he had spent the previous seventeen years of his life, but she doubted any of them were true. He was in a mental institution before he came to Hopewood, people said. His father was in jail and he lived by himself. His mother was killed, they said, most likely by his father. He always wore long sleeves, somebody said, because he had burns on his arms. He'd never defended himself against these stories, as far as she knew, and never offered any alternatives.

And though Lucy didn't believe the rumors, she understood the thing they were getting at. Daniel was different, even as he tried not to be. His face was proud, but there was a feeling of tragedy about him. It seemed to her as though no one had taken care of him and he didn't even realize it. One time she saw him standing in the cafeteria by the window while everyone else was jostling past him with their clattering trays, yakking a mile a minute, and he just looked completely lost. There was something about the way he looked at that moment that made her think he was the loneliest person in the world.

When he first appeared at school there was a lot of commotion about him because he was extremely good-looking. He was tall and strong-boned and self-possessed, and his clothes were a little nicer than most other kids'. At first the coaches were sniffing around for him to play football because of his size, but he didn't pursue it. As it was a small town and a bored town and a hopeful town, kids talked and rumors started. The rumors were ennobling at first, but then he made some mistakes. He didn't show up at Melody Sanderson's Halloween party, even though she invited him personally in the hallway, and everybody saw it. He talked to Sonia Frye straight through the annual junior/senior picnic, even though she was an untouchable freak to people like Melody. It was a delicate social ecosystem they lived in, and most people got scared off him by the first winter.

Except Lucy. She herself didn't know why not. She didn't respect Melody or her posse of yeah-girls, but she trod carefully. She had marks against her to begin with, and she didn't want to be an outcast. She couldn't do that to her mother, not after what she'd already been through with her sister. Nor was Lucy the kind who liked difficult boys. She didn't.

She had the weird idea—kind of a fantasy, actually—that she could help him. She knew what it was like on the outside and the inside at this school, and she knew what it took to maintain yourself through both. She sensed that he bore a heavier weight than most other people, and it gave her a strange, aching empathy for him. She honored herself with the idea that maybe he needed her, that maybe she was the one who could understand him.

He showed no sign of sharing this view. In almost two years he hadn't spoken to her once. Well, one time she'd stepped on his shoelace and apologized to him and he'd stared at her and muttered something. She'd felt nagging and uneasy afterward, and her mind kept going back to it, trying to figure out what he'd said and what he'd meant, but she finally decided that she hadn't done anything wrong and it was his problem going around with his shoe untied in the senior hallway at three in the afternoon.

"Do you think I'm overthinking this?" she'd asked Marnie.

Marnie looked at her as though it took restraint not to claw at her hair. "Yes, I do. I think you are overthinking this. If there was a movie about you it would be called *I Am Overthinking This*."

She'd laughed at the time and worried later. Marnie wasn't trying to be mean. Marnie loved her better and more honestly than anyone else in the world, with the possible exception of her mother, who loved her intensely if not honestly. Marnie hated to see her spend so much of herself on someone who didn't care.

Lucy suspected he was some kind of genius. Not that he did or said anything to let you know. But once she'd sat beside him in English class, sneaking looks when the class was discussing Shakespeare. She'd seen him, his big shoulders huddled over his notebook, writing sonnets from memory, one after the other, in beautiful slanting script that made her think of Thomas Jefferson drafting the Declaration of Independence. He had a look on his face that made her believe he was as far as he could be from the small, boxy classroom with the stuttering fluorescent light, the gray linoleum floor, and the one tiny window. *I wonder where you come from*, she thought. *I wonder why you ended up in this place.*

One time she'd asked him, in a fit of boldness, what the English assignment was. He'd just pointed to the board, where it said they were supposed to prepare for an in-class essay on *The Tempest*, but he looked as though he'd wanted to say something else. She knew he could talk; she'd heard him talk to other people. She prepared to give him an encouraging look, but when she met his eyes, which were the color of canned peas, she was suddenly swept away by an awkwardness so confounding that she cast her gaze to the floor and didn't pick it up again until the end of class. Usually she wasn't like that. She was a reasonably confident person. She knew who she was and where she fit. She'd grown up mostly among girls, but between student government and the ceramics studio and Marnie's two brothers, she had plenty of friends who were boys. None of them made her feel the way Daniel did.

And then there was the time, at the end of junior year, when she was cleaning out her locker. She was aching at the thought of not seeing him for the entire summer. She had parked her dad's rusted white Blazer badly, with two wheels up on the curb a couple of blocks from school. She had left piles of papers and books from her locker and a cardboard box of her pottery on the sidewalk while she tried to gentle the door open.

She saw Daniel out of the corner of her eye at first. He wasn't walking anywhere or carrying anything. He was just standing still with his arms dangling at his sides, gazing at her with that lost expression on his face. His face was sad and a bit remote, as though he was looking inside himself as much as he was looking out at her. She turned and met his eyes, and neither of them jumped away this time. He stood there as if he was trying to remember something.

The ordinary part of her wanted to wave or make a comment that seemed clever or memorable, but another part of her just held her breath. It seemed that they really knew each other, not simply that she had thought of him obsessively for a year. It seemed that he was trusting her to just stand there for a moment, as though there were so many important things they could have said to each other that they didn't need to say any of them at all. He looked uncertain and walked away, and she wondered what it meant.

Later she tried to explain it to Marnie as evidence of a true connection, but Marnie tossed it away as another "non-event."

Marnie felt that she was in charge of taming Lucy's expectations and had even adopted a special mantra for the purpose: "If he liked you, you would know it," she said constantly, a phrase Lucy suspected she'd read in a book.

It wasn't just that Lucy wanted to help him. She wasn't as selfless as that. She was madly attracted to him. She was attracted to all the normal things and then weird things, too, like the back of his neck and his thumbs on the edge of his desk and the way his hair stuck out on one side like a little wing over his ear. She caught his smell once, and it made her dizzy. She couldn't fall asleep that night.

And the truth was that he offered her something that no other boy in the school could: He didn't know Dana. Dana had always been a "handful," as her mother decorously put it, but when they were young she had been Lucy's hero. She was the smartest, fastest-talking person Lucy knew, and she was always brave. Brave and also reckless. When Lucy got in trouble for something, even for something dumb, like tracking mud into the house or spilling ketchup on the floor, Dana would take the blame. She did it even when Lucy begged her not to, because she said she didn't mind blame and Lucy did.

Dana became notorious when Lucy was in fifth grade and she was in ninth. Lucy didn't understand what all the whispering among the older kids and grown-ups meant at first, but she knew there was something to be ashamed of. "I had your sister," one or another of her teachers would always say significantly. Certain kids wouldn't come to her house anymore, or even invite her to theirs, and she understood that her family had done something wrong without really knowing what it was. Only Marnie was her unwavering friend.

By seventh grade Dana was the "Go Ask Alice" of the school, the cautionary tale, and her parents were the ones people endlessly speculated about. Did they drink? Were there drugs in the house? Had the mother worked when the girls were young? The speculation usually ended with somebody saying, "They *seem* nice enough."

Her parents took it all with heads bent so low it was like an invitation for more. Their shame was boundless, and it was easier getting blamed than doing nothing at all. Dana held her head high, but the rest of them walked around with a black eye and an apology.

Lucy tried to be loyal sometimes and other times wished her last name was Johnson, of which there were fourteen in the school. She tried to talk to Dana, and when it made no difference she convinced herself she didn't care. How many times could you give up on someone you loved? "Lucy's a different kind of Broward," she overheard her math teacher say to the guidance counselor when she entered high school, and she felt horrible for how fiercely she clung to it. She thought if she tried hard enough she could make amends.

Dana fell back a few grades for lack of attendance and every other possible crime that wasn't academic: drugs, violence, giving blow jobs in the boys' bathroom. Lucy once saw the envelope on her father's desk declaring Dana a National Merit Scholarship finalist based on her SAT scores. It was strange, the things Dana chose to do.

She dropped out for good on the second-to-last day of school, just a week before she would have graduated. She appeared again on graduation day and in the midst of "Pomp and Circumstance" made her dramatic exit. Daniel was possibly the only boy Lucy knew who hadn't seen Dana tearing off her clothes on the school's front lawn, surrounded by medics trying not to get their eyes scratched out as they carted her to the hospital for the last time.

Dana overdosed on Thanksgiving that year and went into a coma. She died quietly on Christmas. She was buried on New Year's Eve at a ceremony attended by the family and Marnie, her two surviving grandparents, and her crazy aunt from Duluth. The single representative from the school was Mr. Margum, who was the physics teacher and the youngest member of the faculty. Lucy wasn't sure if he came because Dana had aced his class or maybe given him a blow job or both.

Among the complicated legacy of Dana, the most tangible thing she left was a four-foot corn snake named Sawmill, and Lucy got stuck with it. What else could she do? Her mother wasn't going to take care of it. Week after week she thawed the frozen mice and fed them to him with abiding discomfort. She dutifully changed his warming light. She thought maybe Sawmill would die without the animating spirit of Dana in his life, and one time she saw a desiccated, inert version of him in his glass box and for a moment believed—with a mixture of horror and relief—that he had. But it turned out he had only molted. He was lounging in his hollow log, looking fresher than ever. Lucy suddenly remembered the dry gray skins Dana had thumbtacked to her wall, her only effort toward home decorating.

Eleventh grade was the first year Lucy allowed herself to be something other than Dana's sister. Because she was pretty, the boys forgot faster than the girls, but they all came around eventually.

Lucy was elected junior class secretary in the late fall. Two of her clay pieces, a vase and a bowl, were chosen for a statewide art show. Every moment of freedom or success was outmatched by a moment of guilt and grief. She hated that she wanted anything from them, but she did.

"You know, Lu, I don't have a single friend at that school," she remembered Dana telling her once, as though that was a real surprise.

"HE'S PROBABLY NOT even going to show up," Marnie announced over the phone as they were both getting ready for the Senior Ball, the final event of high school.

"He will if he wants to get his signed diploma," Lucy pointed out before she hung up the phone and went back to her closet.

Marnie called a second time. "Even if he does show, it's not like he's going to talk to you."

"Maybe I'll talk to him."

Lucy carefully took her new lavender silk slip dress out of her closet and undid the plastic. She laid it with care across her bed while she changed from a regular bra into a lacy cream-colored one. She painted her toenails pale pink and spent a full fifteen minutes at the sink trying to clean the clay and gardening soil out from under her fingernails. She used a curling iron, knowing the curls would fall out of her straight, slippery hair within the hour. As she drew black eyeliner along the edge of her top eyelid, she pictured Daniel watching her and wondering why she was stabbing herself in the eyeball with a pencil.

She often thought of that. Embarrassingly often. Whatever she was doing, she would imagine Daniel there with his thoughts and opinions. And though they'd never really spoken, she always had a clear idea of what he would think. He wouldn't like a lot of makeup, for instance. The blow-dryer would strike him as loud and pointless, and her eyelash curler like a torture device. He liked her sunflower seeds but not her Diet Pepsi. As her iPod shuffled her songs, she knew the ones he liked and the ones he thought were stupid.

He liked her dress, she decided, as she pulled it carefully over her head and let the delicate fabric settle over her body. That's why she'd picked it.

Marnie called again. "You should have gone with Stephen. He asked you nicely."

"I didn't want to go with Stephen," she said.

"Well, Stephen would bring you flowers. He'd pose for good pictures."

"I don't like him. What would I want those pictures for?" She didn't mention the main trouble with Stephen, which was that Marnie obviously admired him.

"And he'd dance with you. Stephen's a good dancer. Daniel's not going to dance with you. He's not going to care if you are there or not."

"Maybe he'll care. You don't know that."

"He won't. He's had a lot of chances to care, and he hasn't."

After Lucy hung up the phone for the last time she stood in front of the mirror. She did rue the lack of flowers a little. She clipped three small violets from the pots on her windowsill, two purple and one pink. She attached them to a hairpin and tucked them an inch above her ear. That was better.

Marnie came to the front door at a quarter to eight. Lucy could read the expression on her mom's face as she came down the stairs. Her mother had been guardedly wishing for some version of Stephen, a handsome guy in a tux wielding a corsage, and not just Marnie again, in her ripped black stockings. She'd had two lovely fair-haired daughters and not one eager boy in a tuxedo to show for it. To look like Lucy had been enough in her day.

Lucy felt the old pang. Now she knew what she wanted those pictures for. Her mother could use them to remember a better outcome than she'd had. Lucy appeased herself with her usual litany of guilt reducers: She wasn't taking drugs. She wasn't piercing her tongue or getting a tattoo of a spider on her neck. She was wearing a lavender dress and pink toenail polish and violets in her hair. She couldn't do everything right.

"Oh, God," Marnie said when she looked Lucy over. "Did you have to do all that?"

"All what?"

"Never mind."

"All what?"

"Nothing."

Lucy had tried too hard. That was it. She looked down at her dress and at her gold shoes. "This might be the last time I see him," she said plaintively. "I don't know what will happen after this. I need to make him remember me."

"I HATE THIS SONG. Let's go outside."

Lucy followed Marnie out of the school auditorium. Marnie hated every song, and Lucy creaked back and forth on her gold shoes, watching the dark red ring of lipstick on the filter of Marnie's cigarette. Marnie hunched down to relight, and Lucy saw the tender yellow roots at her part, pushing away the dyed-dark hair.

"I'm not seeing Daniel," Marnie said, more grumpy than triumphant.

"Who'd Stephen come with?" Lucy asked, meaner than she should've been.

"Shut up," Marnie said, because she had her disappointments, too.

Lucy did shut up for a while, watching the smoke climb and dissipate. She thought of Daniel's diploma left on the table along the wall of the gymnasium, and it felt like a rebuke to her. He really wasn't going to come. He really didn't care about her. Lucy felt as though her makeup was stiffening on her face. She wanted to wash it off. She looked down at her dress, which cost her an entire semester of Saturdays working at the bagel shop. What if she never saw him again? The thought gave her an almost panicked feeling. This could not be all there was.

"What was that?" Marnie turned her head abruptly.

Lucy heard it, too. There was shouting inside the school, and then a scream. You hear plenty of screams in the vicinity of a high school party, but this was one that made you stop.

Marnie stood with a look of surprise Lucy rarely caught on her face. People were piling up at the main doors, and you could hear the shouting. Lucy startled at the sound of glass shattering. Something was really wrong.

Who do you think of when glass is breaking and people are screaming real screams? That was a telling thing. Marnie was right there and her mother was home, so Lucy thought of Daniel. What if he was in there somewhere? The crowd was piling up thick and wild at the main doors, and she needed to know what was going on.

She went in through the side door. The hallway was dark, so she ran toward the shouting. She stopped as she intersected with the senior hallway. She heard more glass breaking in the distance. She saw dark streaks on the floor and instinctively knew what it was. More blood pooled and rolled down the senior hallway, and she would have thought, she observed numbly, that that floor was flat. She took a few steps and froze. Somebody, a boy, was lying there mostly in the dark and everybody else was running away. It was his blood that was creeping down the hall. *"What is going on?"* she shouted after them.

She felt for her cell phone in her bag with shaking hands. By the time she'd opened it she heard the sirens, and there were many of them all at once. Somebody grabbed her arm and pulled at her, but she shook him off. The blood crept toward the toe of her gold shoe. Somebody stepped in it and ran away, making shoe prints on the linoleum, and that just seemed wrong.

She made her way toward the body on the ground, trying not to walk in his blood. She leaned down to see his face. It was a boy in the junior class, a face she recognized but didn't know. She crouched beside him and touched his arm. He was groaning with each breath. He was alive, at least. "Are you all right?" It seemed obvious he wasn't. "Help is coming," she assured him weakly.

Suddenly she heard an explosion of shouting and footsteps coming toward her as the police arrived. They were yelling at everybody. They blocked the doors and told everybody to calm down, though they themselves were not calm.

"Is there an ambulance?" she said. Not loud enough, so she said it again. She hadn't realized she was crying.

Two policemen rushed to the boy, and she stepped back. There was another eruption of shouting into radios. They made way for the EMS guys to get through.

"Is he okay?" she asked, too quietly to make any difference. She backed up farther. She couldn't see anything anymore.

At that moment a policewoman pulled at her roughly. "You're not going anywhere," she commanded, even though Lucy wasn't going anywhere. She directed her down the science hall and pointed to a door on the right. "Go in there and stay until we can get a detective in to talk to you. Don't move, do you hear me?"

She pushed open the door to the chemistry lab where she had done experiments on the Bunsen burners in tenth grade.

Through the windows she first saw all the red from the lights of the police cars. She waded through dark chairs and tables to see out. There were probably ten police cars parked at odd angles on the patch of grass at the back of school where they spent free periods in good weather. When the lights flashed over it she could see how the tires had chewed up the grass, and that seemed like a further dire thing.

She made her way to the classroom sink more by memory than sight. She could have found the light switch, but she didn't feel like exposing herself to all the people bustling outside the windows. She turned on the faucet and bent forward, washing away makeup and tears. She dried her face with a stiff brown paper towel. Her violets drooped. She'd thought the room was empty until she turned around and saw the figure sitting at a desk in the corner, and it scared her. She walked closer, trying to adjust her eyes to the darkness.

"Who is that?" she asked in a voice just above a whisper.

"Daniel."

She stopped. The red glow filled in parts of his face.

"Sophia," he said.

She came closer so he could see who she was. "No, it's Lucy." Her voice shook a little. There was a boy bleeding in the hallway, and she felt a gathering disappointment that he still didn't know her.

"Come sit down." He wore a stoic expression, a look of resignation, as if he would rather she were Sophia.

She skimmed along the edge of the room, picking over chairs and jackets and bags kids had stowed there. Her dress felt insubstantial for this kind of night. He was sitting back against the wall in one of those desk/chair combinations with his feet crossed as though he was waiting for something.

She wasn't sure how close to sit, but he pulled a desk/chair toward him so the two right-handed desks faced each other like yin and yang. She shivered as she got close. She felt the goose bumps on her bare arms. Self-consciously she pulled the violets from her hair.

"You're cold," he said. He glanced at the little flowers on the desk.

"I'm okay," she said. Most of the goose bumps were owing to him.

He looked around at the piles on the stools and chairs and desk-tops. He pulled out a white sweatshirt with a falcon on it and held it out to her. She put it over her shoulders but did not contend with the sleeves or zipper.

"Do you know what happened?" she asked, leaning forward, her hair brushing past her shoulders so it almost touched his hands.

He spread his hands out flat on the desk as she'd seen him do many times in English class. They were the hands of a man and not a boy. He seemed to be steadying them for something. "Some juniors crashed and vandalized the senior lounge and hallway. A couple of them had knives, and there was a fight. I think two of them got cut and one kid got stabbed."

"I saw him. He was lying on the ground."

He nodded. "He'll be all right. It's his leg. It'll bleed, but he'll be all right."

"Really?" She wondered how he knew.

"Did EMS get there yet?"

She nodded.

"Then yes. He'll be fine." He looked as though he was thinking about something else.

"That's good." She believed him whether he deserved it or not, and it made her feel better. Her teeth were chattering, so she closed her mouth to make it stop.

He leaned down and lifted something from a bag on the floor. It was a bottle of bourbon, half full. "Somebody left their stash." He went over to the sink and took a plastic cup from the stack. "Here."

He was pouring it before she said yes or no. He put it on the desk right in front of her, leaning so close she could feel his warmth. She felt breathless and light in her head. She put her hand to her warm throat, knowing it was turning red, as it did in moments of deep agitation.

"I didn't realize you were here," she said, forgetting to think how she revealed herself by saying so.

He nodded. "I came late. I heard the screaming all the way from the parking lot. I wanted to see what was going on."

She would have taken a sip of the bourbon, but her hands were shaking and she didn't want him to see. Maybe he understood this, because he leaned away from her toward the counter, where he switched on a burner. She watched the dots of fire flicker around the rim before the flame took hold. It reflected off the glass door and made a faint quivery light through the room. She took a quick sip and felt the sting and burn of it in her cold mouth. She tried not to wince at the fumes. It wasn't exactly her custom to drink whiskey.

"Will you have some?" she asked when he'd settled back into the desk/chair contraption. His knees brushed against hers. She didn't think he'd been intending to drink any. But he looked at her, and he looked at the cup. He reached for it, and she watched in amazement as he put it to his lips just where her lips had been and took a long sip. She'd imagined he might pour himself a cup but never that he'd share hers. What would Marnie say to that? This was intimacy she couldn't quite believe. She was sitting with him, talking with him, drinking with him. It was happening so fast she couldn't quite take it in.

She took another sip, recklessly. If he saw the shaking, she didn't care. Her hand was where his hand was and her lips over his lips.

Do you have any idea how much I've loved you?

He sat back again. He tipped his head to the side and studied her face. Their knees touched. She waited for him to say something, but he was quiet.

She squeezed the plastic cup nervously in her hand, bending the circle to an oval and back. "I thought the year would end and we would all go our separate ways and we would never have talked to each other," she said bravely. She felt like her words echoed in the silence, and hated being stuck with them for so long. She wished he would say something to cover them over.

He smiled at her. She thought she had never seen his smile. He was beautiful. "I wouldn't have let that happen," he said.

"You wouldn't?" She was so genuinely surprised she couldn't help asking. "Why not?"

He continued to study her, as though he had many things to say and wasn't sure he was ready to say them. "I've been wanting to talk to you," he said slowly. "I wasn't sure . . . when the right time would be."

In a completely juvenile and heady way, she wished Marnie could have heard him say that.

"But this is a strange night," he went on. "Maybe not the best time. Tonight I just wanted to make sure you were all right."

"You did?" She was worried her face was so eager as to be pitiful.

He smiled in that same way again. "Of course."

She took another sip of bourbon and giddily passed it to him as if they were old friends. Did he have any idea how much time she had spent thinking about him and fantasizing about him and parsing his every glance and gesture? "What did you want to talk to me about?"

"Well." He was trying to measure something about her; she didn't know what. He took another long swig. "I probably shouldn't be doing this. I don't know." He shook his head, and his face was serious. She wasn't sure if he meant drinking bourbon or talking to her.

"Shouldn't be doing what?"

He looked at her so hard it almost scared her. She wanted nothing more in the world than to have him stare into her eyes, but this was too much to take in. It was like buckets of water spilling off of parched soil.

"I've thought about this a lot. There are so many things I've wanted to say to you. I don't want to"—he paused to choose his words—"overwhelm you."

She had never had a boy talk to her like that. There was no cover of bullshit, no flirtation, no added charm, but his look was searing. He was different from anyone she had known.

She swallowed hard to keep herself down. She felt she could turn inside out and show him her kidneys if she wasn't careful. She would hold herself together, but she wouldn't leave him out there on his own. "Do you know how much I've thought about you?"

They were sitting knees to knees, pressing them together, so when he split his legs hers went right through until they were practically joined. Her knee was nearly in his crotch, and his was in hers. Her knee was bare, and his knee was deep under her dress, pressed against her underwear, and her nerves were thrumming. She had a feeling of disbelief. She was suspicious that her imagination was choreographing this out of pure desire and that it wasn't really happening.

"Have you?" he asked. She suddenly knew, just knew, that he was soaking her in, that he was as parched as she was.

He reached out and put his hand on the back of her neck and pulled her forward. She drew in her breath, astonished that he would put his mouth on hers. He kissed her. She lost herself in his breath and his warmth and his smell. She leaned so far forward that she felt the edge of the desk cutting into her rib cage under her breasts and her heart slamming against it.

His arm hit the cup of bourbon, and it fell to the floor. She vaguely felt the liquid splash and puddle under her foot and didn't care. She meant to stay in his kiss until she died if necessary, but she felt something strange, a strange sensation barreling toward her, a heavy foreboding. She was able to ignore it for a while, until it crashed into her all at once.

It was a sensation of feeling and remembering at the same time, two explosions colliding and expanding. It was like déjà vu but far more intense. She felt dizzy and suddenly afraid. She opened her eyes and pulled back from him. She looked into his eyes. She felt tears on her face, wholly different from her earlier tears. "Who are you?" she whispered.

His eyes seemed to dilate and refocus. "Do you remember?"

She could not make herself see in front of her. The room spun so violently she closed her eyes and he was there, too, behind her eyes, as though from her memory. He was lying on a bed and she was looking down at him, and she felt an undertow of despair she didn't understand.

She felt him now holding both her hands, she realized, and hard. When she opened her eyes his expression was so intense she wanted to look away. "Do you remember?" He looked as though his life depended on her answer.

She felt scared. She had another scene invading her mind that she couldn't place. It was him, but in a strange setting, not anywhere she knew. She felt as if she was fully awake and dreaming at the same time. "Did I know you before?" She felt sure it was true, and also that it couldn't be. She had a terror of not knowing quite where she was.

"Yes." She saw that there were tears in his eyes.

He pulled her out from the desk and held her standing up so her whole body was clutched to his. She felt a rocking against her chest, and she didn't know if it was her heart or his. "You are Sophia. Do you know that?" Her head was pressed into his neck, and she felt dampness on top of her head.

If he wasn't holding her, she didn't think she could stand up. She felt herself slipping. She didn't know where she was or who she was, and she didn't know what she remembered. She wondered if the bourbon was acting as some kind of hallucinogen or if she was just losing her mind.

Is this what it was like? Dana had loved to be out of control, but Lucy hated it. She pictured an ambulance coming to get her. She thought of her mother.

She pulled roughly away from him. "There is something wrong with me," she said tearfully.

He didn't want to let her go, but he saw the whiteness of her face and the fear. "What do you mean?"

"I have to go."

"Sophia." She realized he had two fistfuls of her dress, and he wasn't letting them go.

"No, it's Lucy," she said. Was he crazy? He was. He was confused and thought she was someone else. He was having some kind of psychosis. He was so crazy he was making her crazy, too.

She suddenly felt an overwhelming sense of danger. She cared about him too much, and he was a dangerous person to love. He wouldn't love her back. He'd suck her into pure confusion where he thought she was someone else. And she would want so much to believe him that she wouldn't know who she was anymore.

"Please let go."

"But. Wait. *Sophia.* You do remember."

"No. I don't. You're scaring me. I don't know. I don't know what you are talking about." She sobbed between the words.

She felt his hands shaking. She couldn't look at the despair in his face. "I wish I could tell you everything. I wish you knew. Please let me try to explain."

She pulled away so hard her dress tore down the front. She looked down and then at him. He looked surprised and horrified that he was still holding the fabric in his hands.

"Oh, God. I'm sorry."

He tried to put the sweatshirt around her to cover her up. "I'm so sorry," he said. He wouldn't take his arms from her. He wouldn't let her go. "I'm so sorry. I love you. Do you know that?" He was holding her, pressing his face desperately in her hair. "I always have."

She wrested herself away from him. She caught the desk with her leg and sent it backward. She tripped over chairs and bags to get to the door. She couldn't be loved like this. Not even her. Not even by him.

"You don't," she said without turning around. "You don't even know who I am."

She didn't remember getting to the front doors of the school, but a policeman found her there. She was crying and couldn't find a way out because all the doors were locked. That's what the cop told her mother when she came to get her, but Lucy honestly didn't remember any of it.

HE SAT CROUCHED in the room by himself for a long time after she left. He could still taste her on his lips and feel the warmth of her body against his, but they were a reproach now. He stared at the three wilted blooms on the desk where she'd sat. He still had a piece of her dress in his hand.

There was only regret left over. And disgust at himself. He

didn't want to move for fear of opening more cracks and letting all that in, and worse. He wished he could bathe in the touch and smell of her rather than in his failure, but the failure overwhelmed him. He'd destroyed all hope of her. He'd hurt her and upset her. How could he have done that to her?

She remembered me.

That was his worst weakness, his most toxic drug. He was so eager for her to remember, he would tell himself anything. He would do anything, believe anything, imagine anything.

She did. She knew.

In a daze he left the school long after everyone had gone. There were a few security guards left over, cleaning up the mess. Nobody bothered with him. His failures were private and invisible.

But not to her.

He'd pushed her. He'd scared her. He'd besieged her. He'd vowed he wouldn't, and he did. He'd kept himself together so scrupulously for so long, but when he came apart he did it with the force of centuries. He hated himself and every intention and desire he'd ever had. He hated everything he'd ever planned or wanted.

I love her. I need her. I gave away everything I had for her. I just wanted her to know me.

He walked until he was away from the sights and sounds. He found a clearing past the soccer field and lay down in the damp grass. He couldn't go any farther. There was no place to go, no one to see, nothing to want or hope for. He had built up his vision so patiently for so many years and wrecked it in a matter of moments.

She is my doing and my undoing.

She always had been. And what a price she had paid for it, too.

He couldn't stay there. He still saw the red of the police lights beating against the heavy June sky. He got up, and his back was wet with the ground. He walked down the hill away from the school. He was done with it, never to return, leaving it in the state of ruin in which he seemed to leave everything. He should have left the world alone.

He realized he'd forgotten to take his diploma. He pictured it sitting on the long picked-over table in the gym, alone amid the crepe streamers and sinking balloons. They were for the people who cared, who'd treasure it as though it was their first and last. He knew better. What did one more matter to him? So there it would sit, with his name written in careful calligraphy.

Why did he keep going when everyone else got to start over? Why was he still here and she would always go? Sometimes he felt like the only one on earth. He was different. He always was. His attempts at living in the regular world seemed stupid and false.

I've lost her again.

It would seem that someone who had been around as long as he had, who'd seen as much as he had, would have a longer view and some amount of patience. But he was too pent up, too full of need. She was right there, and he couldn't control himself. He tricked himself into thinking that she would look into his eyes and remember, that love would conquer all. The bourbon was tricky, too.

Nobody remembers but me. He kept that thought locked in its place, but this night he let it out. The loneliness of it was unbearable sometimes.

HE WALKED THROUGH fields and along a two-lane road. He walked along the river, and it felt good to be close to something older than he was. This river had a long memory but, unlike him, wisely kept it to itself. He thought of the Appomattox campaign, the Battle of High Bridge. How much blood had soaked into this river? And yet the river flowed. It cleansed itself and forgot. How could you cleanse yourself if you couldn't forget?

I don't want to want this anymore. I don't want to do this to her anymore. I want to be done.

He had no one to keep him here. He had no real family. In the life before this one, he'd lucked into one of the truly great families, and he'd recklessly given them up to follow Sophia. It was no wonder he got what he got in this life—an addict who left before he turned three and a foster family every bit as bad as he deserved. For the last two years he'd been on his own, living narrowly on hope. He'd given up blessings he hadn't been worthy of for the chance to be with her, and now he'd lost that, too.

What would it be like if you didn't come back? That was one of the few corners of experience he hadn't looked into. Would dying be different? Would you get to meet God finally?

He sat at the edge of the river, minding the cold, muddy soak of it, and wondering why you couldn't free yourself from those small inclinations. No matter how long you lived. Like the death-bound convict glancing at the clock. You could never quite fit the small rotations to the big ones, could you?

He pulled mud-covered rocks from the riverbank, small enough to fit in his pockets. Bigger ones he threw blindly into the riverbed, listening for the hollow crack of stone hitting stone or the merciful slap of soft water. He pushed rocks and mud into the pockets of his good pants, just daring his dumb autonomic brain to resist him. He stuffed a jagged few rocks into his breast pocket, a little abashed at his own stagecraft in a moment like this. There was no moment so momentous that it strangled all the little notions.

Except when you kissed her.

Decisions like this were more dignified in the future or the past, or when they occurred in the lives of other people. The petty workings of your birdlike mind brought you down, and forgetting was your only salvation. It was his curse to remember lifetimes of those moments.

Appropriately burdened, he trudged to the road and followed it onto the bridge. The dark air moved cooler and faster over the water. Headlights of a car appeared and grew on the other side of the river but passed without crossing. He got to the highest point, climbed onto the guardrail and sat on it, facing the river, dangling his legs over the water, feeling strangely young. He observed the rocks cutting into his skin as though they hurt someone else.

He climbed up to standing, balancing the guardrail under his stiff-soled shoes. He waved his arms to keep from slipping. Why did it seem important to jump and not to fall, when it came to the same thing? The heavy moisture in the air made his face feel wet. Another car passed.

Of all the millions of possible things he could take with him, he had a piece of Lucy's soft purple dress balled up in his hand and the sour taste of bourbon in the back of his throat. In his mind he held the look of fear on her face as she tried to get away from him and he wouldn't let go, ruining centuries of carefully nurtured hope, knowing he was ruining it, and still not being able to stop himself from ruining it.

That was enough to make him hold his balance and jump.

I was once a perfectly normal person, but it didn't last long. That was in my first life. The world was new to me then, and I was new to myself. It began in roughly the year 520 A.D., but I am not sure of the exact point in time. I didn't keep track of things in the same way then. It was long ago, and I didn't know I'd be remembering them.

I consider it my first life because I don't remember anything coming before it. I guess it's possible that I lived lives before that. Who knows, maybe I've been around since before the time of Christ but something happened to me in this particular life that led to the formation of my strange memory. Doubtful but possible, I guess.

And the truth is, some of the very early lives are murky. There were one or two when I think I must have died young from ordinary childhood diseases, and I'm not sure how they fit into the larger order of events. I keep a few bits and pieces from them, the expansive hotness of fever, a familiar hand or voice, but my soul was hardly situated before I moved along.

It's painful for me to think about that first life and to try to recount it to you. I would have done better to die early of measles or pox.

Since I first began to understand my memory, I've considered my actions differently. I know that suffering doesn't end with

death. That's true for all of us, whether we remember or not.
I didn't know it then. Maybe it helps explain how I did the things
I did, but it doesn't mitigate them.

I WAS FIRST born to the north of the city that was then called
Antioch. The first indelible notch in my long record was the
earthquake of 526. I had no perspective on it then, but in the
years since, I've read every account I could find to compare to my
own. My family survived, but it left many thousands dead. Our
parents had gone to the market that day, and I was alone with
my older brother, fishing in the Orontes, when it happened.
I remember falling on my knees as the earth rolled under us in
waves. For reasons I can't explain I got up again and walked
unsteadily into the river. I can still remember standing in water
up to my neck, feeling the syncopated roll of one surface under
the other, and then suddenly ducking under, my eyes open wide
and my arms out at either side for balance. I lifted my feet from
the ground and stretched out until I was parallel with the river.
I rolled until I was face up and saw the sky through the water.
I saw the way the light lost its certainty under there, and I felt
I understood something about it. I have known a true mystic well
enough to be sure I am not one, but for a moment the ticking of
time was silenced and I saw through the fabric of this world to
eternity. I didn't process it then, but I've dreamed it a thousand
times since.

My brother shouted curses at me to come back and then
followed me when I didn't. I think he meant to pummel me and
drag me back to shore, but the sensations were so peculiar he
stood a few yards from me, his face suspended over the river in a
look of abstraction. I came back up to the surface, and we waited

for the shore to go back to normal. And even when it did,
I remember walking home, keeping a wondering eye on the
ground as it passed under my feet.

WE WERE PROUD subjects of Byzantium then. Belonging to a
great empire made little difference in our small domestic life,
but the idea transformed us. It made our hills a little grander
and our food a little tastier and our children a little prettier
because we fought for them. The able-bodied men in my family
fought, albeit distantly, under the famous general Belisarius.
He, more than anyone, gave the glory and shape to our lives,
which were otherwise not glorious. My uncle, whom we revered,
was killed on a campaign to put down a Berber uprising in North
Africa. We had only enough information about his death to
demonize North Africa and every soul contained therein. I later
discovered my uncle was most likely stabbed to death by a
comrade for stealing his chicken, but again, that was later.

I sailed with my brother and a hundred other soldiers of the
empire across the Mediterranean Sea to North Africa. We were
inflamed by vengeance. Like many new souls, I was never better
suited to being a soldier than I was in that life. I obeyed orders
with absolute literalness. I didn't question my superiors, not even
in the privacy of my mind. I was fully committed, ready to kill,
ready to die for my cause.

If you had asked me why this or that Berber tribe, who shared
none of our culture, religion, or language, had to die or remain
part of Byzantium for a few years longer, I wouldn't have been able
to tell you. We weren't the first to conquer them and wouldn't be
the last, but I was a young man of faith. I didn't need to know
exactly the cause of my fervency. The fervency itself was the cause.

And just as blindly as I believed in the rightness of my side, I believed in the black heart of my enemy. This is characteristic of a very young soul and evidence, though not proof, that it really was my first life. I hope so. It would be an atrocity to have stayed that stupid.

In every life since that one, I've known from early on that I was different. I've known my interior life was something to hide. I have always kept apart, always shared little of myself except in the rarest cases. But that's not how I was when I started.

I was swelled up with eagerness for my first soldierly assignment, but we spent weeks, it seemed, making a camp civilized for our commander. We went to great and arbitrary lengths to make an African desert as comfortable to him as his hilltop home in Thrace. These are not the kinds of reflections I made at the time. I don't know if I reflected on anything at all. Little did I know then how long I'd have to reflect and how long I'd be saddled with my regrets.

Even exciting places are boring most of the time. Wars. Movie sets. Emergency rooms. This was yet another war when we mostly sat around gambling, bragging, getting drunk, and watching the meanest drunks pick fights—usually my brother in this case. It was almost identical to every other war I have fought in up to and including the Great War. The memorable parts, as in when you kill or get killed, take a very short amount of time.

At last our assignment came. We were making a raid on an encampment a day's march west of Leptis Magna. As the mission grew closer it became clear it wasn't an army encampment so much as it was a village. A village, we were told, where the army was being quartered.

"Is it a village of the Tuareg?" I asked with a shiny thirst for blood. It was the tribe I held responsible for killing my uncle.

My direct superior was a good motivator. He kne[...]
I wanted. "Of course."

I embarked on the raid with a knife and an unlit t[...]
I remember carrying the knife in my teeth, but that's an emotional
memory and not an actual one. I try to sift those out as well as I can,
but there are exceptions, some more pleasurable than others.

When I see myself in that life, it's mostly from the outside in.
It feels to me as though, without the awareness of my memory,
I wasn't me yet. This was an ordinary person who would become
me, and I look at him from a distance. Maybe that's what I do to
live with it. I contrast the scraggly, pimply, incapable exterior of
that young man to the storm of ferocity and self-importance
I know was going on inside his head.

My fellow raiders were like me, the youngest, the lowest, and
the most expendable. We could be counted on to see in black and
white and come back whole or not at all. We fanned out across the
valley, ready to make war.

At some moonless hour of that night, roughly a quarter of
our troop took a detour for water. My brother was put in charge
of the splinter, and I went with him. We found the water, but
afterward we couldn't find our troop again. There were about
twenty of us roving around in the dry scrub. I could tell my
brother was flummoxed, but he didn't want to show it. He was so
susceptible to power it corrupted him instantly.

He gathered his group. "We'll march directly to the village.
I know where to go."

He did seem to know where to go. There was only the suggestion
of dawn when we first saw the village on the horizon. "We got here
first," my brother crowed. We came together for a moment to light
our torches from a common flame. I remember the greedy eyes in
the firelight. We all wanted to do our share of living.

Ann Brashares

The village was no more than a shadowy cluster of simple structures and thatched roofs. I could picture the enemy soldiers crouching inside, sinister. I put my torch to the dry roof of the first domicile I came to. The thatch was made to burn. I felt a jab of satisfaction as I watched the fire catch and spread. I made my knife ready for any man who would come out and confront me. I went on to the next hut and laid my torch. I heard screaming somewhere behind me, but my ears were muddled by my own roar and thrill.

By the third house, certain smells in my nose and sounds in my ears began to penetrate my thinking mind, burrowing in like worms. The fire had made a false, manic dawn, but now the sun endowed a true one. I could see the house directly in front of me. By rote I surged toward it with my torch and lit a clump of roof, but it didn't take right away, as the others had. I went around back to try another spot, and I stumbled against a taut rope. I had visions of enemy traps, but as I stepped back I saw there were clothes hanging from it and from a line strung above. The wind lifted up and brushed the smoke away for a moment, and I could see it was a garden laced with clothing lines and small clothes drying in the gray air.

I went back around to the front of the house, confused and angry at the small clothes that hung on the line and the roof that sputtered and wouldn't burn. The torch that seemed so brilliant in the dark looked weak and false as the sun came on more brightly. The wind blew the smoke away, and I saw that many of the gardens had clothing lines. They weren't hiding soldiers; they were growing squashes and melons and drying laundry. Some of the gardens were already burning.

I didn't know what to do then other than get the house to burn. I couldn't have any other ideas. I confronted confusion with action. I lit the house from the bottom, a well-constructed wooden frame. Inadvertently I thought of the wooden frame we'd labored over for our house. I hurried around to the other side and found a scraggly fistful of roof to light. At last the fire took what I gave it, and the flames licked and popped. I thought I heard the sound of a baby's cry from inside.

The fire took all right. I couldn't tell if the emotion that filled me was horror or pride. I could barely move. I could barely force myself away from the blurring heat.

I saw the house as a head with wild, burning hair. The two windows were eyes, and the door was the mouth. To my astonishment the mouth opened and there was a person. It was a young person, a girl, wearing a nightgown.

When I think of it I try to picture her distantly, as the stranger she was then, and not as the girl I love. I change her a little in my memory; I know I do.

Her hair was long and loose, and her face turned to mine with the strangest expression. She must have known what I had done. I stood in front of her burning house with a torch in my hand. The torch had gone out. It had been enough to destroy their home and take their lives, though it was nothing now. I could hear the baby crying behind her.

I wanted to get the girl out of there. I wanted her to run. She was as beautiful as a fawn. Her eyes were large and green, with orange flames sparking in them. I felt panic. Who was going to help her?

I had changed sides. I was horrified. I wanted to put the fire out. There was a baby who would die. Maybe her sister or brother. Was her mother in the house? *You have to wake her up,* I wanted to shout. *I'll help you.*

I no longer seemed to know who had done this terrible thing, but she knew. The flames roared. The wind whipped them and spread them. They were dancing all around her.

"You've got to run!" I shouted.

Her eyes were puzzled and sorrowful but not fearful, darting, and crazy, as mine were. Her face was as calm as mine was contorted. I took a step to her, but the heat was uncrossable. Flames curled and spat between us.

She looked out at the burning houses and gardens of her neighbors and then at me. She turned her head and looked behind her into her burning house. I prayed she would step out, but she didn't. I couldn't imagine this would be the end of her. She stepped back in.

"Don't go!" I cried to her.

The mouth of the house was empty again. Within seconds the structure heaved and caved, but the flames stayed and fed on.

"I am sorry," I heard myself shouting to her. "I'm sorry." I repeated the words in Aramaic, because I thought that was a language she might understand. "I'm sorry. I'm sorry."

I WAS NEARLY insensible on the march back to our camp, but I did look up long enough to observe heavy smoke on the horizon. I remembered, distantly, that we hadn't rejoined the larger group, and as we got closer to the smoke I understood why. I was too numb to think or check my words.

"It was the wrong village," I said.

Only my brother heard me. He must have seen what I saw and known what I knew as well as I did. "It wasn't," he said stonily.

At that moment my anguish was too overpowering for me to think about anything else. "It was."

"It wasn't," he said again. I saw no guilt, no self-doubt, no regret. What I did see was wrath toward me, and I would have done better if I'd marked it and never said a word about that night again.

I HAVE WITNESSED many deaths and tragedies. I have caused a few since then. But I've never taken perfectly innocent lives again. I've never destroyed such beauty or felt so much shame. I try to keep my distance, but I still feel a sickness in my soul when I think of it, and the feeling doesn't lessen over time.

The stench of burnt wood and tar and flesh in my nostrils was so thick I believe it took a permanent place there. The blur of gray smoke got in my eyes and altered my senses forever.

CHARLOTTESVILLE, VIRGINIA, 2006

"YOU'RE SUCH A doubter, Lefty. Just come."

"I haven't slept in two nights," Lucy argued. "This place is a dump. I need to clean up."

Marnie looked around their small dorm room. "You can't clean it up without me, because then I might feel guilty. We'll do it tomorrow. Come on. Jackie and Soo-mi are downstairs already. We have to celebrate."

"What if I don't feel like celebrating?" Lucy was in fact a doubter and a lefty, and she was also superstitious about celebrating before she got her grades back. "What if Lawdry notices I turned in my paper two days late?"

Lucy's resistance was barely a sigh in Marnie's typhoon of will. "Here. Here are your shoes." Marnie chucked them one flip-flop at a time. "Bring some money."

"I have to pay for this thing I don't want to do?"

"Twenty bucks. People pay for a lot of things they don't want to do. The dentist. Wars in Iraq. Dead mice for Dana's snake."

"You aren't making it sound any more inviting." Lucy got her bag and put on shoes. Not the flip-flops Marnie threw at her. She had the energy for only small rebellions.

"Don't worry about Lawdry. He loves you." Marnie opened the door of their room and ushered Lucy out.

"No, he doesn't."

"I'm afraid he does."

"Whose car are we taking?"

"Yours."

"Oh, I see."

On the way out on Route 53 toward Simeon the sun was sliding into the flat roof of a Bed Bath & Beyond. Marnie put on one of her brother Alexander's terrible rap mixes and cranked it up while Jackie and Soo-mi started opening beers in the back. "Who is this person we're going to?" Lucy asked over the din.

"Madame Esme," Marnie said, studying her handwritten directions in the darkening car. "Two miles and turn onto Bishop Hill."

"Don't you two want to be sober for your twenty-dollar psychic reading with Madame Esme?" Lucy asked, glancing at Soo-mi's face in the rearview mirror.

Soo-mi held up her Miller Lite. "Not particularly."

"Is this really where we're going?" Lucy asked, turning onto a gravel road dotted with trailers and rusting carcasses of trailers.

Marnie was trying to figure out addresses. "Do you see any numbers?" she asked. "We want Twenty-three thirty-two."

"I think it's that one." Lucy motioned ahead to an aging mobile home surrounded by trellises woven through with roses. It might have had wheels once, but it didn't look like it was going anywhere anytime soon. "Are those roses real or fake?" she asked.

Marnie squinted. "I think real."

"I think fake," Lucy said as she pulled into the driveway.

Madame Esme met them at the door. Lucy saw more or less what she expected to see. Long green robe. Hair piled up. Lots of rouge. Oversized gestures.

"Who goes first?" Madame Esme inquired.

"Marnie, you set this up. You go," Jackie said.

"You three can sit in there." Madame pointed to a tiny living room/kitchen. There were a painted wooden table and four mis-matched chairs. "You follow me," she said to Marnie.

We watched Marnie follow her through a door into a dim room pulsing with candlelight. Madame closed the door after them.

"What are we doing?" Lucy asked, sitting on a metal folding chair.

"Alicia Kliner said she's supposed to be really amazing," Soo-mi said in a whisper.

Lucy didn't know what was potentially amazing in this. Her mother went to psychics every couple of years and was amazed when they said things like "You are at peace by the water. Books feed you. You cannot help but nurture." Her mother was also amazed by polarity, chakras, foot massage, and many items featured on the Home Shopping Network. Lucy suspected she had a higher threshold for amazement.

LUCY WAS FINE with waiting until last for the great Madame Esme, but it was hard to keep herself awake. Especially after Marnie emerged with a look of bursting smugness but claimed she couldn't talk about it until they had all finished their readings.

"Oh, come on."

"I can't. Seriously."

"Who do you care about more, me or Madame Esme?"

"Don't make me choose."

Lucy shook her head and put it back down on the table.

At last Madame Esme emerged for the third time and let Jackie out the door. "I'm ready for you," she said to Lucy.

Lucy yawned and approached. The small room was dark but for three fluttering candle flames on a card table. Two more folding chairs were pulled up to the table. As Lucy's eyes adjusted, she saw the open shelves of clothing. Sweaters and piles of pants and a mound of socks. It was more than Lucy wanted to know, and it badly undercut the veneer of mystery. Along the wall was a twin bed with one pillow. There was a poster, but Lucy couldn't make it out because it was mostly behind a shelf.

Madame Esme closed the door and sat. Lucy sat in the chair opposite. Esme closed her eyes and put out her hands facing upward. Lucy wasn't sure what she was supposed to do.

"Give me your hands," Esme said.

Lucy did so awkwardly. Madame Esme's hands were warm and clutched hers with surprising intensity. It was hard to tell with all the makeup, but sitting close and feeling her hands, Lucy sensed that Madame Esme wasn't much older than she was. How had she found her way into this profession? Lucy wondered. It took a certain amount of nerve.

Esme closed her eyes and rocked back and forth. As for acting, Lucy decided, it was only so-so. This was what you got for twenty dollars. She tried to shut down another yawn.

Esme opened her mouth as if to say something and then closed it again. She was quiet for an uncomfortably long time. Lucy strained to hear the voices of her friends on the other side of the door. "I'm seeing a flame, red lights, a lot of noise," Esme finally said. "Is it a school?"

"I don't know," Lucy said. She knew she was tired and grumpy, but she didn't feel like doing the work here.

"It feels like a school," Esme said. "A lot of people rushing around, but you are alone."

Lucy was ready for this. *You feel alone in a crowd. You are shyer than people think.* This was your basic psychic bait.

Madame Esme's eyes were twitching under her lids, but they became still. Her expression changed.

"You aren't alone. He is there with you."

"Okay." Lucy wondered if they were getting to the romantic wish-fulfillment part.

"He has been waiting for you. Not only now, but for a long time."

Esme was quiet for a while. The silence stretched out, and Lucy wondered if maybe that was it. But then Esme spoke again, and this time her voice was different, lower and more intense.

"You wouldn't listen to him."

"I'm sorry?" Lucy said politely.

"He was trying to tell you something. He needed you then. Why didn't you listen?" The voice was higher now, and plaintive.

"Listen to who?" Lucy cleared her throat. "I'm not sure what you are talking about."

"At the dance. The party. Something like that. I feel that you were scared. But still." Esme was squeezing her hands a bit harder than Lucy liked.

Lucy didn't especially want to know what Esme was talking about. Esme didn't know what Esme was talking about. She was just fishing. Saying standard stuff and trying to get Lucy to bite on something.

"You should have listened."

"To what?" Was a psychic supposed to be giving opinions?

"What he told you." Esme's voice was deeper and stranger. Her trance was getting more convincing. She was warmed up, obviously. Lucy had a sadistic impulse to kick her under the table. "Because he loved you."

"Who loved me?" Psychics never named names. They waited for you to tell them.

"Daniel," she said.

Lucy sat back. She made herself breathe. "Who?"

"Daniel."

"Okay," she said slowly. She sat up straight and felt the chair creak and reset. What did this woman know about her? Did she know them from school, somehow? Had Marnie somehow briefed her?

"Daniel, wanted you to remember. He kissed you, and you did remember for a moment, didn't you? But you ran away."

Marnie couldn't have told her that. No one could have. Lucy felt a wave of fear followed by a wave of nausea as her mind raced to find a rational explanation. She didn't want to say anything more. She wanted it to be over, but Esme had not finished with her.

"You said you'd try. When you were Constance you promised you'd remember, but you turned your back on yourself. You wouldn't even try."

Lucy felt tears burning in her eyes. Two years ago she'd packed that night away. She'd sealed it up carefully and tightly. How could anyone have known about it?

"He was lonely. You know that. And you are Sophia, his great love, and you said you'd try."

"What am I supposed to try to remember?" Lucy asked. It was a voice she hardly recognized. It escaped from some part of her, she couldn't tell where, airy and thin and hissing like a leak.

"You were supposed to remember . . . *him*." Esme said it loudly and with indignation. "You were supposed to remember how you loved him. He said he would come back, and you promised you would remember him."

Esme's head was almost vibrating, and though she held Lucy's hands, Lucy had the distinct feeling the rest of the girl's body was going somewhere else.

"In the war. You took care of him. He couldn't breathe. You knew he was dying. He didn't want to leave you, but you said you would never forget. You forget and he remembers. He told you what he was. He trusted you. You know, don't you?"

Lucy felt herself recoiling. She felt bitten and criticized. "I don't know." This girl had circumvented Lucy's defenses.

"You know what he is. You understand."

"I don't. What is he?"

"Please. You are Sophia, and he needed you."

"Stop! Who is Sophia? Why do you keep talking about her?" It's what Daniel had done, too. It had scared her then as it did now.

"I'm talking about you."

"No, you're not. I'm Lucy," she said hotly. She'd once seen a movie about a girl with a split-personality disorder. The way Esme talked, it was as though there were somebody else inside Lucy listening and even responding, and the thought of it terrified her.

"Now you are Lucy. But before."

"Before what?"

"You should find him if you can."

"How can I find him? I talked to him once. I don't even know him."

"Yes, you do. Don't tell me that lie."

Lucy yanked her hands away. "Can you stop this, okay?" Lucy heard the tears of her own confusion, the sound of herself betraying herself. Since when did a psychic scold you? She wrapped her arms around her body. She had to stick together.

Esme opened her eyes and looked at Lucy as though surprised to see her there. She blinked a few times. She and Lucy stared at each other as strangers. "You should find him because he loves you," Esme said faintly, coming back in stages.

It was worse with Esme's eyes open and fixed on her. Lucy didn't want the words to land where they landed. But they did.

"I don't even think about him anymore," Lucy said, half hoping Esme would be willing to make a deal and forget everything that had just happened. It was weird for both of them, she knew. And Lucy had yet to pay her.

Esme looked at her with a sharp reproach. She didn't look like a twenty-something-year-old person with too much green eye shadow and a desire for her payment. She looked like the oldest judge in the world. "How can you even say that?"

Lucy shook her head. She wished she weren't crying. She wished she could keep pretending that she had no fear and no faith in any of it.

"I don't know," she said, and she really didn't.

I told you about the girl in the village near Leptis in North Africa in my first life. My second life started roughly thirty-one years later in another part of Anatolia. Lives tend to cluster, you know. This second life was uneventful in external ways, but in my mind it was extraordinary. It started normally enough. I didn't know yet what I was.

But as soon as I was old enough to think—or old enough to remember the thoughts—I thought of the girl in the little thatched house. I saw her face in the doorway. Later I saw the flames and I understood what was happening to her and what I had done.

I thought of her every time I closed my eyes. I screamed at night. I cried in my dreams. I began to think of her in the daytime, too. I was probably only two or three years old and not old enough to understand my guilt or shame or the significance of her face to me. But I experienced the pure horror of it every day, almost as if it were happening to me.

I had a kindhearted mother in that life, but even she got tired of me. I lived in another world. I couldn't let it go.

The kind of memory I have is extreme, but many people have some small degree of it. I once knew a boy in Saxony whose family lived a few doors down from mine. One day when he, Karl, was very small, his mother came by with him to deliver

something or borrow something—I wasn't paying attention to
that part—and he saw my knife, my prized possession. I was
probably ten or eleven at the time, and he was not even three.
This tiny kid could barely talk yet, but he followed me into the
garden, desperate to tell me how he was stabbed three times
through his ribs by a thief, a footpad, who accosted him on the
road to Silesia. He saw my confusion and wanted very badly to
make me understand. "Not now, but before, when I was big,"
he kept saying, holding up his arms to make the point. "When
I was big."

He lifted his shirt and sucked in his belly to show me the
jagged birthmark along his rib cage. Needless to say, I was
fascinated and astonished by all this, and I asked him many
questions. I thought I had discovered a kindred mind. When his
mother came to fetch him she saw his animation and gave me a
long-suffering look. "Did he tell you about the thief on the
road?" she asked wearily.

Soon after that I went away. I began my apprenticeship with a
smith in a village several miles outside of town. I didn't see Karl
again for five years, but I thought of him hundreds of times.
When I did see him I immediately asked him about the stabbing.
He looked at me with interest but only the faintest recollection.

"The thief on the road to Silesia," I reminded him. "The
scar on your chest." This time it was me who was desperate to
convince him.

He looked at me and shook his head. "Did I really tell you
that?" he asked before he ran off to play with his friends.

I've learned since then that it's not that unusual for very
young children to have memories from their old lives, especially
if they suffered a violent death the last time around. Or maybe
the violence gives them a more urgent need to communicate.

Typically they express old memories as soon as they can talk and keep pressing them for a couple of years. And typically time passes and they get further away from their death and their parents get spooked or just fed up. The memories fade, and they put them aside. New experiences fill in. By the age of reason, at seven or eight, all but a few have forgotten and moved on.

This is fairly well documented, and I've followed the research carefully. There are scientists who have compiled thousands of interviews and case studies of this kind. But the good ones are naturally reluctant to say what it really means, and who can blame them? I, of all people, know how futile it is to try to make rational people believe.

My case was different. In my case, as I grew older my memory grew stronger and filled in. The more capable of reason I became, the more I remembered—little things and big things, names, places, sights and smells. It was as though my death was a long sleep, and when I woke up and reoriented myself, it all came back. I didn't remember these things as happening to someone else. I remembered them happening to me. I remembered the things I'd said and the ways I'd felt. I remembered myself.

By the age of ten I knew I was different, but I stopped talking about it. I knew I had been alive before. I didn't need to convince anyone else to know the truth of it. Mostly I was sorry that other people didn't remember the way I did. I wondered if they had old lives to remember, or if it was only I who came back again. I wondered if I was an error of God's planning that would be fixed at the end of my life.

I guess I still feel like an error of planning. I'm still waiting for it to be fixed.

With every life it starts more or less the same. My mind is a blur of infant's murk and then, sooner or later, I see her face in the doorway. She becomes clearer and more present, and then I see the flames. I try not to get so upset anymore. I know what's coming, and I think, *Here I am again.* Every life I start with her, my original sin. I know myself through her.

"WHAT'S GOING ON with you?" Marnie whispered to her on the way out of the trailer.

"Nothing." Lucy wouldn't look up. She shut the door carefully behind her, making sure the lock caught and sealed the strange air of that place behind her. Jackie and Soo-mi were standing by the car.

"Was it really that bad? Why won't you tell me what she said?"

"It was nothing. Just a lot of nonsense." It was difficult to lie to Marnie. There was no possibility of it if she met Marnie's eyes. She kept her head down.

The sky was dark, but the light coming through the window from inside the trailer illuminated the roses. There were plastic ones wound through the grubby white trellis, and as she studied them Lucy realized there were real ones, too, beautiful pink Celestials crowding against the plastic ones for sunlight and space.

"What kind of nonsense? Are you upset?"

Marnie wasn't just pestering her. She knew Lucy and sensed the real disturbance. It made it harder to push her away but also more necessary.

"So it turns out I love the water," Jackie reported. "And also I am my own best guide."

"Hey, I'm *my* own best guide," Soo-mi said.

Marnie was trying to remember. "I think I might be my own best guide, too."

"Is that worth twenty dollars?" Jackie asked.

"Maybe not, but does your energy run deep?" Soo-mi asked.

Jackie laughed. "Oh my God! My energy *does* run deep. What are the chances?"

Marnie was staring at her, and Lucy realized that it would be appropriate to laugh. Or smile at least. She tried. "Do you mind driving back?" she asked Marnie.

"No." Marnie plucked the keys from her hand. Marnie was agreeing to let her hide for now.

Lucy sat in the front passenger seat and leaned her warm head against the cool glass as they drove.

"So, Lucy, are you your own best guide?" Soo-mi asked her, aware that she had fallen out of the conversation.

"No," Lucy said, so tired she could barely lift her head. "I don't think I am."

LUCY SLIPPED OUT of Whyburn House after they got back. She drifted around the dark campus. Most people were at parties or packing up their rooms. Some people had already left. A few were probably still finishing papers. She walked up Jefferson Park Avenue to the Academical Village. She passed over the lawn and into her favorite of the west gardens and climbed up onto a serpentine wall built by her oldest crush, Thomas Jefferson. She yearned for a breeze or a few drops of rain. Something to change her.

She unfolded herself and lay down on the top of the wall, curved. She was tired but scared to go to sleep. Daniel had a way of finding her in her dreams, and she felt almost sure he'd do something to unsettle her tonight.

No dreams tonight, she instructed herself. That worked surprisingly well. From the time she was nine and watched a terrifying show about sharks, she'd warned her sleeping self off nightmares, and it had worked. Beginning at the age of sixteen, writing her term paper on *Jane Eyre*, she asked for dreams to bring her ideas or understanding. It worked sometimes.

Sophia again. A war. A hospital, where she cared for him. These were some of the bits and pieces that lay deep in the middle of her, disconnected from experience or conversation or memory. It seemed wrong that they could exist outside of her, too.

Was she crazy? Had she imagined the whole thing? Madame Esme had said absolutely standard things to the other three girls. Had she said standard things to Lucy, too, and Lucy had conjured them into something fantastical? And while she was questioning her sanity, Lucy had to ask herself, was Daniel a real person? Or was he the romantic fiction of a girl who'd been desperate for a handsome stranger to come along?

If you worried you were crazy, was that any indication that you were not crazy? Or less crazy? She'd settle for less crazy at this point.

Later, in her dorm, Lucy took a shower. Sometimes that could change you.

"Will you talk to me?" Marnie asked, as Lucy perched on her bed that night, still wrapped in her towel.

"I'll try." Lucy picked the orange polish off her nails. It was fun to pick if you had two or three coats of it on, but Lucy had one thin coat, and she dug and scratched at the nail bed with no satisfaction.

"Is Daniel a real person?" Lucy asked.

"Daniel? Your old flame Daniel?"

"Yes."

"I think so."

"You remember him, right?"

"I more remember you talking about him."

"Do you ever wonder what happened to him?"

"Not much. I recall some weird rumors. But I did wonder what happened to you at the last party and why you stopped talking about him."

Lucy nodded. She looked around the room. Although it was a different room from last year's, it was essentially the same room. Blocky pine furniture, same bedspreads and pillows and filthy, fuzzy rug and mugs on desks and chairs and mess everywhere. Different books but in the same places. Same Pink Floyd paraphernalia on Marnie's side, and on Lucy's side the same couple of old clay pieces from high school, Sawmill's terrarium, and the same two framed pictures: one of her and Dana when they were little in front of the Boat Pond in New York City and one of her parents in black and white, standing in front of the rotunda on their wedding day.

"After that you switched your love to Thomas Jefferson," Marnie recalled. "And though long dead, he's actually given you a lot more in return."

Lucy didn't disagree.

"I thought maybe you finally gave up on Daniel and decided to move on, but now I'm suddenly thinking that's not the whole story."

Lucy shook her head. "I saw him that night. I talked to him."

"Talked to him?" Marnie looked doubtful. "You shared words? More than two? He said some of them?"

"Yes. Many words. He said most of them."

"Really." Marnie sat up cross-legged on her bed. She put her pillow in her lap. She didn't look tired anymore. "What did he say?"

Lucy didn't have the wherewithal to untangle it and present it straight. But she needed to let some of it out. "Can you promise me something?"

"I don't know," Marnie said honestly.

"Can we put this back in its box after we talk?"

"We can try."

Lucy sighed. "He kissed me."

"You are kidding."

"No. I can't really believe it, either." She put her hand to her head. "Sometimes I think back and I wonder if I remember it right."

"You couldn't forget that, could you?"

"No. No. But it was a strange night. I felt like I was losing my mind. He said there was something I was supposed to remember. He kept calling me Sophia."

"Maybe he didn't know who you were. Was he drunk?"

"Well, sort of. Probably. I was a little bit drunk, too. And I kept asking myself that question—did he know who I was? In one way I felt sure that he did. I felt like he knew me better than I did."

"How do you mean?"

"Well, it all seemed familiar to me. Some of the things he said were things I have thought of before. Or dreamed about."

"Lucy, I can't believe you didn't tell me this."

Lucy shook her head. "It really scared me. I didn't want to think about it, and telling you would have made it real. I started having terrible panic attacks that summer—do you remember?"

Marnie nodded. "I still wish you'd told me."

Lucy dug at her thumbnail. "I knew you thought I was wasting my time with him. The way I acted was irrational to begin with. I admit it. But this was a bit much. I felt like my fantasies detonated and my head exploded. I still wonder if it even happened. That's how strange it was. Either he's crazy or I am."

"I vote him."

"I know." Lucy leaned back. Marnie knew how to give her a hard time, but she also knew how not to. Lucy rubbed the back of her head against the wall, knowing the tangles were going to get tanglier. "And then tonight, this Madame Esme. I really wanted her to be a fraud."

"I really wanted her not to be."

"Maybe she was a fraud. Maybe our energy runs deep, and that's that. I hope so. But she said other stuff to me."

"Like what?" Marnie's face was gentle. Lucy knew she wouldn't push.

"That name again. Sophia. She was talking about Daniel and that night and kind of judging me for not listening to him and trying to understand what he was saying."

"How do you know she was talking about Daniel?"

"Because she said so."

"She said his name?" Marnie's face gave away the slightest alarm.

Lucy nodded. "I know."

"They don't usually do that. Do you think she could possibly know him?"

Lucy shook her head against the wall. "Who knows? Maybe."

"It would be a weird coincidence. But maybe that explains it."

"There were other things, too."

"Like what?"

"She said things about Daniel that were familiar to me. Images I've had or things I've dreamed for a long time. Even longer than I've known him. Like about him not being able to breathe. I had this picture of me leaning over him and knowing that he is dying. I never told Daniel any of that."

Marnie shook her head slowly, thinking. This was their spot, facing each other across the small, crowded room, each sitting cross-legged on her bed. This was the perch from which they ran their world.

"She said I should find him."

"You should find Daniel? Why?"

"Because . . . she said he loves me."

"She said that?"

Lucy nodded. It gave her some significant feeling to say it, but the feeling was not the same as pleasure.

"God, that woman was selling me deep energy, but she was selling you crack cocaine."

"You don't think I should?"

"Try to find Daniel?" Marnie thought some more. She shook her head. "I don't know." She bunched her pillow between her hands. "Do you want to?"

"I don't know."

"You look miserable."

Lucy nodded.

"There are two possible things to do."

Lucy nodded again. She didn't trust herself to say anything more. She liked that Marnie could take over.

"You could try to find Daniel, and see if there's anything going on there. Or you could put this whole conundrum back in its box and try to forget about it."

Lucy didn't think very hard. "I'd like to forget about it."

My third life began and ended in the great city of Constantinople, and though it was poor, brutal, and short, it contained one momentous first: I recognized someone other than myself from an earlier life. And of course it was the girl from North Africa.

People had been familiar to me before that moment. I had begun to think I probably wasn't the only one coming back around. There were certain people I felt sure I knew from before. A much younger brother of mine reminded me naggingly of a dead neighbor. But I hadn't learned how to recognize a soul yet or even understood that you could.

I was about eleven years old, and I was standing at a vegetable stall in a market near the Bosporus. I was poor then. I don't think I once wore shoes in that life. There was some commotion a few stalls over. I saw a procession of strong-looking servants carrying a thing like a litter. I ambled over because it was exciting. I followed them at a little distance. I knew if I got close they would swat me away like a roach. But I wanted to see.

The curtains were delicate, and the wind gusted. With each gust I saw a knee or a hand or the rich fabric of a sleeve. It was a woman, I could tell. I believed she was a princess. I couldn't comprehend finer distinctions than that.

At some point the servants turned a corner, the curtain

rippled, I saw fingers, and then I saw a face peering out. I knew instantly and viscerally who she was. I might have gasped or made some noise, because she looked at me. The pose of her neck, her round, dark eyes staring out at me. It wasn't the same face, exactly, but it was the same girl. Now she was older than I was, probably twenty-five at least.

I can't tell you how I knew it was her. In the years since then I've gotten to be very good at recognizing souls from one life to the next. I find it puzzling myself, so it's hard to explain how I do it. But I am not the only one who can. It's not so different from the way you can know a person when she is twenty years old and recognize her again when she is eighty, though every cell in her body has changed in the meantime. There is almost nothing you could program a computer to do, by observation alone, that would allow it to recognize a person at such disparate ages. But we can do it. Animals can do it.

What is it we recognize? The soul is a mysterious thing. It's no less mysterious for me, though I've seen my own and others' refracted through hundreds of bodies over time.

One thing I can tell you from my unusual perspective is how powerfully our souls reveal themselves in our faces and bodies. Just sit on a train sometime and look at the people around you. Choose a person's face and study it carefully. All the better if they are old and a stranger to you. Ask yourself what you know about that person, and if you open yourself to the information, you will find you know an overwhelming amount. We naturally guard ourselves from the obvious truths of strangers around us, so be warned. You can get overstimulated and uneasy if you really start to look. One of the skills of living is simplifying as you go, so when you let your guard down, the complexity is troubling. There are certain rare people you find—usually they are healers or poets or people who work with animals—who live their lives in this state, and I admire them and sympathize with them, but I am not like them anymore. I've done a lot of simplifying in my life.

As you look at this stranger's face you will be able to guess pretty accurately at age, background, and social class. And as you look longer, if you let yourself see, the subtleties will clamor to show themselves. Doubts, compromises, and disappointments little and big—those usually reside around the eyes, but there are no rules. The hopes usually lurk around the mouth, but so do bitterness and tenacity. A sense of humor is easy to spot around the eyebrows, and so is self-deception. Add to your observation the set of the head on the neck, the carriage of the shoulders, the posture of the back, and you know a lot more.

These are the accumulated qualities of the soul, and they are expressed in life after life. By the time a person gets really old, the soul has worn in its body so completely that she probably looks almost exactly as she would if she had reached that age in one of her other lives. She need barely have bothered with the new body at all. Which isn't to say that souls don't change and evolve over time, because they do.

The first time you see a familiar person in a new body is a strange and even haunting sensation, but you get used to it. You start recognizing the telltale places where the soul asserts itself: the eyes, of course; the hands, the chin, the voice. The pathos is in how much of ourselves we hold out to any passing eye that takes an interest.

It was indeed haunting to see the woman in the market on the Bosporus. I ran toward her without thinking. I grasped the curtains with my grubby hands and yanked at them as I ran alongside. "I–I—I was—you were—I want—" I couldn't think of how to convey our connection. "Do you remember me?" In a childlike way, I didn't differentiate my experience from hers.

I don't know why I said that. If I could have thought a moment, I wouldn't have wanted her to remember me.

I doubt she understood me. I can't even remember what language I used. Anyway, it took less than a second for one of those bulky servants to put his hands on me. I was skinny and small, and he picked me up and threw me across the alley. Then he strode over and kicked me in the ribs and again in the chest.

"Stop!" she cried out. She threw the curtains aside.

His foot was already cocked, and he kicked me again in the face. "That's the wife of the magistrate, you insolent rat," he muttered at me.

She got out of the litter, to the surprise of her servants. People were crowding around now. "He's just a boy!" she said. "Do not touch him again." She spoke an elegant Greek.

"I'm sorry," I said, also in Greek. She leaned down and put her hand on my cheek. I felt blood leaking out of my nose. I owed her so much, and she owed me nothing but disgust, but she was kind to me. I wondered, feebly, how I was going to be in a position to make anything right for her.

"I am sorry," I said again, in the old Aramaic, the same words I used to apologize to her the first time. If it sparked a memory in her, I don't know. I am always hoping. She looked sad.

"I'm sorry to you," she said, and she stood up. "Take him home to his mother," she ordered a female servant. She disappeared behind the curtains.

I had no home or mother by that point, so I fled the servant before she could kick me, too.

Every day for a year or more I waited by that same stall in the hope of seeing her again. I concocted elaborate plans of what

I would do when I saw her. I scripted the things I would say if I
could get close enough. I found a job hefting bags at a spice stall
nearby and bought her small treasures with the money I made:
an orange, a piece of honeycomb. But I never saw her again.
I died of cholera before I had the chance.

From that moment, as I look back, I can trace the beginning
of a few unlucky themes that would carry on for centuries. Our
lives being mismatched in time. Her being someone else's wife.
Her forgetting me.

In spite of getting beaten, seeing her was the best moment in
my life. I was bewildering to myself, honestly, and I was looking
for patterns. Even if she was only an idea, the idea was comfort.
She had come back. She was alive again, in spite of what I had
done to her. She was beautiful again. She prospered. I could see
her again. Not that I would see her, but at least I could. In some
way that's when I first understood the regenerative power of life.

I clung to the idea that there was a point to my living over
and over, and to my strange memory. I thought it would give me
the chance to cure my sin and make it right. Little did I know
how long and fraught a road that would be.

People sometimes talk about the power of first impressions,
and believe me, there is truth to it. The path of your life can
change in an instant. Not just the path of your life but the path
of all your lives, the path of your soul. Whether you remember or
not. It makes you want to think hard before you act.

What if I hadn't burned down her house? How many times
have I thought that thought? What if I had seen the insanity of
what we were doing and put a stop to it? What if I had saved her
and her family and the rest of the village as best I could? I would
have gotten killed, but so what. I got killed a few years later,
anyway, and didn't accomplish anything by it.

If I had saved her instead of murdering her, we might have come back into the world together with ease and harmony, time after time. I don't mean to suggest there are simple formulas. But certain souls cohere. It's rare but possible. Certain souls pair up eternally, not unlike geese or lobsters. I've witnessed it a few times. But it takes two powerful wills to make it so, and mine accounted for one. It wasn't enough for me to want to find her again. She needed to want to find me, too, and she had every reason to stay a long way away.

DEATH IS AN UNKNOWABLE PLACE, but I have learned something about it over time. My state of consciousness after death and before birth is not like the normal state of waking and living, but I do have perceptions and memories from those times. It's hard for me to gauge how time passes in those dark transitions. I can't tell if it's one month or ten. Or nine, maybe.

Being as I am the custodian of this long, strange memory and one of the few people on earth who can report back from death, I've felt a sense of responsibility to keep track of how it works and try to understand it better. I'm not sure who will be the beneficiary of this long study of mine, or whether it will ever be any benefit at all, but it's what I do. Recording is not the same as doing, my old friend Ben would tell me, remembering is not the same as living, but the older I get the more it seems to me the best of what little I have to offer.

I can tell you the feeling of dying into a community of souls. It's when you understand you are no longer alive but you feel other beings around you, and it is profoundly comforting. People you might have known to some degree or other, who know and care about you, are with you. You don't talk to them or communicate in any explicit way, but you know you are not alone and that they will somehow keep you. You aren't capable of asking questions in this state, but there is a condition of knowing.

I also know the feeling of dying into emptiness. We all die alone, but this is different. You apprehend nothing and nothingness. You have the sense of wandering, and it can go on for a very long time. You find yourself yearning, almost hungering, for the presence of another being.

There's a pattern in it. Your death is the shadow of your life. If you have strong and loving attachments in your life, you will cohere to your community of souls. You will probably come back to life quickly and among your own people. Your lives will occur in clusters geographically and ethnically. When you go to a new place, you'll often migrate among your loved ones. If your community is ethnically mixed, you're more likely to change race, and if not you probably won't.

If you are distant and misanthropic, selfish or cruel, you will find yourself alone in life and death. You'll die into nothingness and come back among strangers or very occasionally among enemies. And you'll stay alone and at odds until you don't want it anymore. It takes a long time and a lot of effort to find any kind of community, much less a desired one. As I see it, this effort is both the penance and the rehabilitation. You will come back, but it takes a while. You will remain among strangers until you've made yourself some kind of family. It won't happen until you want it to.

I don't know about heaven and hell, and I haven't met God yet. But I have to admire the design.

Your will is operative between lives, but not in the way you are accustomed to. In death I think you tune in to the highest frequency of your will, and it's a sound you rarely hear in life because it is drowned out by the noise of living—by your particular place in the world and the short-term desires of your body. In death you are temporarily free from the rough grip of time. Your slate is wiped clean, you've got no stake anymore, so your will operates without pull or prejudice. Somewhere expressed in your highest will is a desire to pay your debts and balance yourself out. And though this balance is deeply salubrious to the soul, it doesn't necessarily bring any comfort or pleasure to a living body.

There are limits to your will, of course—like the expression of other people's wills. Which is why my story would be a lot shorter and more cheerful if I had simply loved Sophia from the start and found some way to make her love me. I wouldn't have spent more than a thousand years waiting for her and searching for her and trying to hold her close enough for long enough to overcome our first encounter.

Part of my punishment was that I didn't see her again for another two hundred years. But when I did, it set the course for the rest of my days.

LUCY SAT IN her backyard with the thick smell of newly cut grass in her head. It was nearly seven o'clock in the evening but still so hot she was sitting with her feet in a pot filled with cold water.

Now that she was grown up and fresh off the wonders of Jefferson's gardens on campus, she could see that this yard was nothing special. But when she was small it had been her pleasure dome. From her earliest memory she'd loved digging in the grass and making puddles with the hose. As with clay, she yearned to get her hands dirty. It was a tactile pleasure and another of her small-bore rebellions.

She'd made a vegetable garden in fifth grade and produced her own cucumbers, but the rabbits and deer got to it after seventh grade, when she'd spent a July in Virginia Beach with Marnie's family.

She'd planted her raspberries in ninth grade. Her mom complained about the rotten compost Lucy amassed and the fact that the canes took over the entire back of the yard. It was true that Lucy was generous to fertilize and slow to prune. But they had fresh sweet raspberries all through the late summer and fall, not to mention raspberry jam and raspberry sauce and frozen raspberries the rest of the year. "You pay four dollars for a stinky little half-pint of them in the supermarket, and compared to ours they have no taste at all," her mother acknowledged with a certain amount of pride.

Lucy's first act of landscape design had been their swimming pool when she was sixteen. The neighbors on both sides and in back of them had built pools, and her father had proclaimed they would build one, too. She'd made hundreds of drawings of it in her sketchbook. She didn't want a big bright turquoise rectangle like the neighbors had. She designed a small pool in the shape and color of a pond with a natural bank of grass and flowers that went right up to the water. You wouldn't even see any concrete unless you peered over the edge. She'd tried to figure out the kinds of materials they would need, investigated the drainage issues, priced it all to the best of her ability, and written out her order for the nursery.

But the time for the pool was never now. She'd pestered her dad year after year, presenting him with new and refined drawings until one night she saw him writing checks at the dining-room table and realized he was still paying off Dana's hospital bills. She didn't say anything more about it after that. And anyway, she told herself, a built pool would never have turned out as good as the one she'd imagined.

This summer Lucy had been eager to get home from school to her room and her raspberries and her nothing-special yard. She'd been feeling anxious since the end of the semester, sleeping little and badly, and waking up from terrible dreams. She'd told her mom it was the stress of exams. She had chasing dreams, burning dreams, beating dreams, and the wracking and crying dreams, which often featured the absurd Madame Esme trading off with Dana. And Daniel was a presence, seen or felt, in nearly every one. Lucy's body ached from the strain of them.

She'd hoped that being home would soothe her and bore her, as it usually did. She thought if she just changed the rhythm of her nights and days, the dreams would stop. And here she was at home, and exams were over and Madame Esme was far away, but the dreams persisted. She couldn't leave her brain at school. That was the problem. If she could have, she might have enjoyed a perfectly happy summer vacation.

She heard the screen door open and turned to see her mom. She had her pink suit on.

"Did you show a house?" Lucy asked.

"I had that open house on Meadow."

Lucy could see the sweat seeping into circles under the arms of her mother's pink linen jacket. "How'd it go?"

"I laid out food and flowers and cleaned that dump up myself. Four brokers showed up, not a buyer in sight, and those vultures had the nerve to eat my snacks." Her tone was so dramatic Lucy wanted to laugh, but she didn't.

"I'm sorry to hear it."

Her mother hated being a realtor. She said she'd prefer to sell underwear at Victoria's Secret, but her father thought that was unseemly for a graduate of Sweet Briar College. Lucy always had the feeling her mother couldn't rebel against her native prissiness, so her daughters did it for her.

"Well." She surveyed Lucy's sundress. "Are you going out?"

"Kyle Farmer is having a party."

"Kyle from chorus?"

"Yep. That one."

"Fun. I'm glad you are going to see your old friends."

Her mother took so much heart from simple social interactions that Lucy felt bad she didn't have more of them, or at least make it seem like she did. She wondered if she should have stayed in Char-lottesville for the summer with Marnie and spared her mother her true mood. She mostly avoided parties of old high school people. They had a depressing air of unearned nostalgia. Kind of like reunions but premature, where no one had gone out and done anything yet. But tonight she had a motive. Brandon Crist was going to be there, and he was the closest thing to a friend Daniel ever had at that school.

"Can I use your car?" she asked.

Her mother nodded, but her face showed reluctance. "You need to help pay for gas this summer, okay?"

"I know. I'll fill it up. I put in two applications today."

"Good girl." Her mom always wanted to be pleased. She didn't want to give Lucy a hard time. Dana had broken her so hard that Lucy's shortcomings were almost like gifts.

I'm skipping ahead to one of my most consequential lives, which was my seventh, and it began in Pergamum in Asia Minor in roughly the year 754 by our modern calendar. You've heard of Pergamum, probably. It was a great city once, though past its prime by the time I was born there. It was one of the loveliest places I've ever grown up.

It grew famous as a Hellenistic city with a giant and magnificent acropolis and a massively steep theater seating ten thousand bodies. It transitioned easily into a Roman town when they gave themselves to the empire without much incident in the second century B.C. It had one of the great libraries of the ancient world, with more than two hundred thousand books. Parchment was invented there after one of the Ptolemys stopped exporting papyrus from Egypt. If you know your ancient history, you know it was the library that Mark Antony gave to Cleopatra as a wedding gift.

A few of the glories of the city stood intact in my childhood, though some had crumbled, and most of the temples and shrines had been wrecked or converted to Christian churches by then. The marketplace stayed almost the same.

When I lived there you could see the Aegean from our doorstep. Now the city overlooks a valley fifteen flat miles inland from the sea. I went back there a few lives ago, when the German

archaeologists were just getting going on it, and saw the ruins of
the old city again. I knew the columns. I knew the blocks of stone
under my feet. I had touched those very ones before. I felt closer
to them than I feel to most other human beings. We stood still
while the world changed shape around us.

I'm not often nostalgic anymore. There's too much behind
me. I know that gradual change is the easiest to take, and the
giant leaps and losses can overwhelm you. My home and every
trace of my life and family from that time were long erased. But
that wasn't what got to me. It was the look of that ancient city,
once mighty and perched on a sea of commerce pushed farther
and deeper into dry remoteness and strangled off.

It was back then, as a child in the eighth century, that I
allowed myself to suffer how jarringly destructive the present
feels and how fragile the past. The present is over quickly, you
might say, and it is, but man, it goes like a wrecking ball.

I would sit at a certain crumbling altar overlooking the sea
and try to imagine our city as it had been before the degradations.
You wanted to think that history was a story of progress, but
seeing what remained of Pergamum and the direction we were
going, you just knew it wasn't so.

The first momentous occurrence of that life was the
reappearance of my older brother from my first life in Antioch,
returning to the role of older brother once more. That kind of
thing occasionally happens, family members repeating from one
life to another. Usually it's devotion that keeps people together
through lives, but the soul's basic yearning for balance and
resolution can sometimes bring a person back to confront a
previous torment. I recognized this old brother with a sense of
unease from when I was quite young. Every association with the
burning of the village in North Africa was harrowing to me, but

added to it was the enmity that had burst out between this old brother and me long ago, when I'd confessed to a superior—and later a priest—that we had raided the wrong village. It was my own relentless guilt that drove me to it, not hostility or vengeance, but my brother didn't see it that way. From that first moment of recognition, when I was not more than two or three years old, I knew I needed to steer clear of him.

He was called Joaquim now, and he stayed true to his early passions to become an enforcer of iconoclasm under Constantine, leaving our home and family in Pergamum at the age of seventeen. His mission was the destruction of religious art, the invasion of monasteries, and humiliation of monks. It's no mystery how the old and beautiful works came to be destroyed.

I was called Kyros then. In those days I struggled to consider myself by a new name each time. Later, I would answer to the name my parents gave me but think of myself by my old name. This was more disorienting than you can know. It's hard enough to maintain your identity through a single life in a single body. Imagine dozens of lives and dozens of bodies in dozens of places among dozens of families, further complicated by dozens of deaths in between. Without my name, my story is no more than a long and haphazard tangle of memories.

At times I wanted to give up the thread of my lengthening life. It felt too hard to hold on, to keep myself together as one person. I felt as though the past and the future, cause and effect, patterns and connections, were a huge complicated artifice, and it was only by my efforts that they kept going. If I gave up it would all dissolve into the raw chaos of the senses. That's all we really have. The rest is romanticism and storytelling. But we need those stories. I guess I do.

Sometime after the turn of the last millennium, I began

naming myself. Whatever my parents named me, I asked them to
call me Daniel, the name I had at the very beginning. Some
resisted, but all came around in some way at some time, because
I didn't really give them a choice.

THE NIGHT I want to tell you about took place about 773. There
are so many things I've seen that I could tell you about. But I am
telling you a story, a love story, and I will try, with limited
digressions, to hold on to my thread.

This particular night I remember distinctly. I hadn't seen my
dreaded brother Joaquim in two years, and he was coming home.
He had sent word a few weeks before that he had taken a wife and
would bring her to us when he came. Our household was in a
stir, as you might imagine. My brother was my parents' eldest
son, and though he was an awful person, he was gone so long we
all thought better of him.

Apart from my older brother, it was a good family I had then.
I've seen quite a range in my time, and there haven't been as
many of those as a person would hope. It's been an error of mine
to think there will be more, and I forget to cherish them as I
should. My father was a kind man, though distant, and my
mother was a deeply loving soul, probably too much so for her
own good. The worst I can accuse them of is parental blindness,
and that is something they share with nearly all those who love
their children. My two younger brothers, especially the
youngest, were sweet-natured and quick to trust.

I guess I was better at loving then, too, and also better at
being loved—the two go together. It was a long time ago. Back
then the past didn't stretch out nearly as far, and the present

seemed much more vivid—not, as it came to seem later, like an ever-tinier fraction of all there was.

Our family was not rich—my father was a butcher—but we were prosperous and had two servants. I'm sure my father had no meat to sell in the market that day. He slaughtered the fatted calf and every other creature with foot or flesh he could put a knife to for our "welcome home" feast.

My anticipation held as much dread as excitement. I hoped an improved version of my brother would come home with his wife that night, but I knew that the arrogant sadist who'd left would probably be the one to return.

The house and courtyard were laid out as if for an emperor. After all the scurrying preparations, we waited there in eager silence, my parents, my two younger brothers, my uncles, my maternal grandfather, several cousins, the servants. We couldn't eat or converse because of all the suspense.

It would not have been my brother's style to arrive when the food was freshly prepared, the meat and sauces were perfectly cooked, and the waiting was still new and enjoyable. It was his style to arrive after the food was wilted and congealed, and the thrill of anticipation had turned to restlessness and worry.

As we waited, the rain began. I remember my mother's attempts at buoyancy, her happy talk. We spoke Greek then. Not the language of Sophocles but a distant corruption. I can still remember most of the conversation word for word. I try to hold on to the old languages, but keeping them in my head isn't enough. They are built to communicate, and no one else speaks them anymore.

My brother arrived not on horseback in glorious regalia, as we imagined for him, but on foot, underdressed for the weather and irritable. He came from the darkness into the candlelight first. I looked at him, wondering what had become of his military career, but then his wife entered the room. From the moment she lifted her hood and uncovered her face, I didn't think about him again. This is the part I wanted to draw your attention to. This is the part that matters.

Seeing the girl from North Africa only in memories and dreams for a couple of centuries, I looked at my brother's wife and, to my astonishment, saw her made flesh again. To this day, there is no soul I recognize more immediately or more powerfully than hers. Whatever her age or her circumstances, she makes a strong impression on herself and on me.

First out of confusion, then out of shock, and then out of exhilaration, I stared at her too long. My brother was expecting to be greeted with proper bowing and scraping, and my eyes were fixed in almost painful rapture on his wife. A lot of trouble can be accounted to my foolishness that first night.

It wasn't his displeasure that finally penetrated my fat skull, it was hers. She was confused and embarrassed by all my attention. Her head was down, and her eyes, which had projected so much certainty the other times I'd seen her, were uneasy.

I tried to resume the normal kind of behavior. I embraced my brother. I stepped back to let the other family members take their turns. I watched my parents welcome their new daughter, Sophia.

I orbited her in a strange haze that night. I tried not to, but everywhere I stood and everything I did was in relation to her. I tried not to stare at her too long.

She looked burdened enough as it was. Instead of eating she glanced around at us, her new family, sparing every other glance for her husband. The rest of them feasted and drank while she sat delicately on her hands. My brother was several cups of wine in before he seemed to notice. "Is our food not good enough for you? Eat something!" he roared at her, and finally she did.

That night, I lay awake in wonder. At first I was moved just at seeing her, at knowing she was still alive and now close to me. It took longer to sink in, the injustice of how she happened to turn up. I didn't know all the ways I loved her yet.

But when I overheard my brother's voice through the wall I had to recognize what was going on. She was his wife. She belonged to him and never to me.

It wasn't jealousy. Not at first. I was awed by her and by the role she played in my mind. I longed for forgiveness. I didn't presume to want her or deserve her in that way. If my brother had been kind to her and she had loved him, I would have taken joy in her joy and just been happy to get to be near her sometimes. I think that's true.

But he wasn't kind to her. The voice through the wall rang with abuse.

I couldn't hear all of it, but he called her a whore. I heard my own name more than once.

I COULD BARELY glance at her the next day; I felt ashamed and guilty. Why could I never do her a good turn? Why did I only add to her suffering? But I did glance at her, eventually. I saw some misery, to be sure, but also pride. And when Joaquim spoke to her across the table I saw disgust in her face. By that look alone I knew she had not chosen to be his wife. His power over her was limited, because she didn't love him.

I avoided her for a few days out of consideration, but then my brother left. He disappeared for weeks at a time. He came home,

usually drunk, when he ran out of money. So over time I
discovered that Sophia gravitated to the garden as I often did,
and I allowed myself to say a few halting words to her, and then a
few more. Over the course of time I got her to tell me about
growing up in the city of Constantinople, which seemed magical
to me. Her father had been a master mason and builder of
several churches. He'd made repairs to the great dome of the
Hagia Sophia. But her parents died in a fire when she was nine,
which helped explain why her grandmother gave her to the
highest bidder when she was fifteen, at a moment when my
brother was flush from one of his few big victories at cards.

At the time I was apprenticed to an artist who had been
commissioned to design mosaics for the baptistery of our church.
I took Sophia to the work site and showed her the plans. Over the
weeks, and with some reluctance, I showed her carvings I'd made
and some verses I had printed on a piece of parchment. These
were things I had learned in earlier lives—languages, reading and
writing, carving and design. I hid them from most people,
because they were foreign to my upbringing and pretty much
inexplicable, but I didn't hide them from her. We had things in
common. She loved stories and poems as much as I did. She knew
many that I didn't. I opened up to her in a way I had never done
with anyone before.

That was the first time I knew her and loved her. I loved her
innocently then, I promise you. Even in my mind.

My brother never saw us speak, I'm sure, but he probably
heard about our friendship. Three months after the night he
brought Sophia home, he arrived at the house drunk and angry.
He'd lost a huge sum of my father's money gambling and earned
himself a beating and a threat against his life. On the other side
of the wall that night I heard him shouting, but I knew his insults

didn't matter to her. Then I heard another kind of sound.
A heavy crack against the wall and a scream and a muffled strike
and the sound of her crying.

I got out of bed and made my way into the room. Good as my
memory is, I don't remember how I got from one place to the
other. The door must have been locked. I remember the splinters
and pieces of it on the ground afterward. She was lying on the
floor, hair all tangled, her nightdress ripped apart and the sticky
shine of blood and perspiration on her face. Two centuries
before, in the doorway of her burning house, she'd stared at me
with strange equanimity, but now I saw distress.

I paused for a moment and saw my brother crouched and
glaring like a wolf. He was waiting for me, daring me to come
after him, trying to lure me into some game of his. But I didn't
think about him at all. She was the one who mattered to me.
I closed my fist and hit him in the face as hard as I could.
He went down. I watched him get up and then I hit him again.
I remember the look of astonishment in the middle of his
fury. I was the younger one, the smaller one, the weird one, the
artist. I punched him again.

His nose and mouth were bleeding. He was still drunk,
disoriented, sputtering and heaving, throwing ineffective fists.
The deeper violence was on its way but taking longer for him to
gather.

I wanted to hold her and comfort her, but I knew that would
only make it worse for her. She sat up, covered herself, and
backed against a wall.

If he wasn't so drunk and I didn't care so much, he certainly
would have killed me. It was the only asymmetry between us that
ever came out in my favor. I loved his wife, and he didn't.

I left him on the ground in his own blood and vomit.

I packed my few belongings. I woke my father and begged him to take care of her. I left my home and family with the idea that if I were gone, she might be safe.

Fighting Joaquim in front of his wife was one of the pivotal decisions of my long existence, and I've tried and retried myself for it in the years since. It was the spark for hatred and violence and enmity over many lives, and I ask myself how I could have averted it for her sake and mine and even his.

But in retrospect, it wasn't really a decision at all. Looking back, even from this great distance, I don't think I could have done anything else. Wrong as it may have been, I would do it again.

LUCY DIDN'T GIVE herself over to the party. She essentially waited on the couch for Brandon Crist to show up. She didn't even realize she'd snubbed the mighty Melody Sanderson until her friend Leslie Mills told her so.

"Melody is telling everybody you won't come out back to the tap because you think you're too good for Hopewood."

Lucy felt herself sifting down through layers of pettiness to make sense of that. Maybe it was true. "Excuse me?"

"She thinks all the kids who go to fancy schools up north act snotty now."

"Up north? I'm in Charlottesville."

"Right. I know."

"I just didn't feel like fighting through the crowd for a beer," Lucy said.

"I'm just telling you in case you, you know, want to go out there."

Lucy seriously considered going out there, but she stopped herself. She remembered a simpler time when she went to all lengths to stay on the right side of those girls. She also remembered when she and her parents could lay every trouble and pain and failure in one location. But Melody's term had expired, and she must have known it.

Still, Lucy chastised herself and walked into the crowded kitchen instead. It was true that you shouldn't go to a party if you couldn't be friendly. When Brandon finally did arrive she went right over to him. It was awkward, she recognized, but she felt strangely driven.

"I'm Lucy," she said. "We were in chemistry together."

"Of course," he said. "I know who you are." He sloshed his drink around in its plastic cup.

"I have a question for you," she said directly. He used too much gel in his hair, which for some reason led Lucy to consider that he probably thought she was trying to ask him out.

"Okay." His eyebrows were raised into flirt position.

"You knew Daniel Grey, right?" It seemed reckless and even thrilling to just say his name right out as though it was just any other name.

His eyebrows floated back down a little. "Yeah. Somewhat. Not well."

"Well, do you have any idea what happened to him?"

Brandon looked uncomfortable. "I don't know for sure. But you know what Mattie Shire and those guys said."

Lucy heard the bleakness in his voice, and a slow thumping started in her throat. "No. I don't. What did they say?"

"The night of the last party and the knife fight. You heard about what happened."

"A lot of things happened," she said warily.

Brandon looked around the crowd in the dining room. He didn't see Mattie Shire, but he saw Mattie's friend, Alex Flay, and hailed him over. "You remember Daniel Grey, don't you?"

Alex nodded, looking from one of them to the other.

"Were you there with Mattie when he saw him jump off the bridge?"

Lucy stared at Brandon. *"What?"*

"I wasn't there," Alex said. "But Mattie told me about it. I don't know if Daniel drowned or what."

Brandon nodded. "He was an unusual dude, rest his soul."

"You're saying he is *dead*?" Lucy asked.

Brandon looked at Alex, and Alex shrugged. "I have no idea. That's what Mattie thought. Nobody really knew. I never heard anything more after that. Everybody went off in different directions after that."

"He couldn't be dead," Lucy said fervently. She felt a burst of outrage, and she couldn't keep it off her face or out of her voice. "Wouldn't everybody have heard about it? Wouldn't it be in the newspaper or something?"

Neither of them wanted to argue with her. It wasn't personal for them. "A lot of people did hear about it," Alex said a little defensively. "I don't know where you were, but Mattie wasn't keeping it secret."

"And anyway, newspapers don't go out of their way to report suicides," Brandon told her. "Especially not teenage suicides."

Turning slowly away from them, she walked back to the sofa and sat on it, staring blindly at the window and seeing Daniel's face as he'd looked that night. She remembered her own fragile state in the days after, so beset by panic she didn't leave her house or talk to anybody.

She was vaguely aware that Brandon and Alex were still standing there, that her social graces were a failure and her mother would be ashamed. Brandon said something to her, something like "I thought everybody knew," but words were no longer making their way into her brain.

Daniel couldn't be dead.

Numbly, she fished around for her keys in her purse and walked out of the party to her car. She got in it and drove. She drove aimlessly along the darkest streets, in spite of her mother's constant exhortations to save gas.

Finally it was late and dark, and she drove to the bridge. She left her car on the grassy shoulder and walked out onto it. She stared down at the Appomattox. It was a mythic name and place for her because of her father and grandfather. She once asked her father why they always talked about the Civil War, whereas it seemed like Yankees never did. "Because we lost," he said. "You forget your victories, but you remember the losses."

She put her chin on the rail and watched the water flow darkly. This was a river of loss, and here was one more. She wondered how it would feel to jump.

My long absence from Pergamum was not enough to keep Sophia safe. I first heard reports from my youngest brother and then from my mother.

In three years, Joaquim's temper had deteriorated, as difficult as that was to imagine. My father died, and I mourned him and missed him terribly. Joaquim took over the butchery and drove a profitable business into the ground. I was horrified to discover he sold the family house and sent my younger brothers out into the world before they were teenagers. He left his wife with my mother in a room of a public house for long stretches while he ran away from creditors or ran up more debts. Sophia managed, mercifully, not to have his children.

When I got the message from my mother, I made another momentous decision. I borrowed a horse and rode thirty-some miles toward Smyrna to a remote cave I had last looked upon a hundred years and two lives ago. There had been a lot of wind and sand in those years, but I could still see the tiny markings I had made on the limestone walls. With my torch and my secrecy I felt like a tomb robber, but the tomb was my own and my bodily remains, thankfully, were not to be found there. I wove through the passages, descending into dank earth as I went. I didn't need the markings; I remembered how to go. I was relieved to see the pile of rocks I'd constructed completely intact. I moved them carefully, one by one, until I'd exposed the misshapen little portal. I squeezed through, realizing how much bigger I was in this life than in the one when I'd dug it.

I twisted my torch into the dirt floor of the chamber and looked around. The larger things sat on the ground covered in a century of dust. There were a couple of beautiful Greek amphorae, one with black figures depicting Achilles in battle and the other red-figured, showing Persephone borne down to the underworld. (I gave the first to the archeological museum in Athens in the 1890s, and I still have the second one.) There were a few good pieces of Roman statuary, some early and exquisite examples of metalwork I bought from a bedouin trader who claimed they came from the Vedic Kings in India. There was the beginning of my collection of feathers from rare birds, a number of wood carvings (the worst of which were made by me), a gorgeous lyra I learned to play from my patient father in Smyrna, and a bunch of other things.

The smaller and most valuable things I had to dig for. Less than a foot under the hard dirt were bags of gold coins: Greek, Roman, biblical, Byzantine, and a few Persian. Other bags held precious stones and a few pieces of jewelry. I tried not to linger over any of it. I had a sense of urgency and grief that day. But my fingers came upon the gold and lapis wedding ring worn by my first bride, Lena, who had died young and whom I had tried to love. I held it for a few moments before I put it back in the ground.

In my fourth life, I had been a trader. I used my experience and knowledge of languages to put myself at the hub of several profitable trade routes. I wanted to get rich, and I did. In part it was a reaction to my bruising and humiliating life in Constantinople. I hated being hungry, and because I knew other ways of living,

I hated it worse. I decided that if I was going to lug this memory around, I might as well be smart about it. I would use it to insulate myself from the whims of birth. For each life that I made money, and I did get good at that, I put most of it aside for leaner times. And I remember fantasizing that the girl from North Africa would see me when I was rich and powerful, and that she would want to know me then.

My fifth life, in Smyrna, I had the fortune of being born into an educated and well-connected family. As I grew up, I built on what I had learned from my previous life, and became a merchant of consequence. Beyond amassing piles of gold, I started to collect with a particular eye to the past and future. That's when I established my cave, and I used it for nine lifetimes before the traveling became too onerous. I moved my stash to the Carpathians about 970 A.D.

By now, more than a thousand years later, I've accrued a huge collection of property and currency and artifacts, though the feelings of power and pleasure that once came from owning it have faded significantly over time. The few things I've added to it in recent years have no objective value at all. I've found ways of giving pieces away without being recognized and also of entailing it to myself: Wherever I turn up, I always know my name. And these days, bank vaults and numbered accounts make it all a lot easier.

That night in the eighth century, I put everything in my cave back to rights and took with me a bag of fairly recent and homogenous gold coins—I needed money rather than treasure. I gathered supplies, made a few arrangements, bought a magnificent Arabian horse from a rich bedouin, and rode back to Pergamum the following afternoon. I found Sophia and my mother living in one room off an alley. My mother's spirits were in ruins. She was still trying to find a way to love my brother; her heart would not allow her to give up on him. Sophia's face was bruised, but her pride was mostly intact.

I set my mother up in a pretty village a few miles away. I tried to give her as little money outright as possible, knowing where it would end up. But I made sure she was comfortable, and I promised her I would return and bring my younger brothers back to her house.

I set off with Sophia that night on the back of my horse. It was a selfish thrill to have her there so close, but that was not the point, I told myself. If I left her there, she would be killed. Neither she nor my mother protested or asked a single question as we rode off. They knew this was her only chance.

The ride across the desert with Sophia on that fine horse was one of the happiest times in all of my many lives. I confess I've relived it so many times, I hardly remember it anymore. My feelings are strong enough to refract and distort the truth of that journey. But then, as my friend Ben might say, my feelings are the truth of that journey.

It took us four and a half days to get to Cappadocia, deep in the interior, and I wished, as we went, that the distance would lengthen and the horse would slow down. And I'll admit to you at the start that something changed in those few days. What had been an innocent and uncomplicated devotion on my part turned into something deeper and more problematic.

The first night was awkward, as you might imagine. I stretched a piece of blue fabric across four wooden stakes to make us a roof and laid blankets under it. I was good at making fires and preparing food. These were some of the many skills I had accumulated over my lives. (Some skills are in the mind and some are in the muscles, and I have spent lifetimes learning the limitations of the first and the value of the second.) But that night, it was like I had never done anything before. My hands shook as she watched me. Nothing felt familiar.

With my heart laboring in my chest and a feeling of satisfaction like a mother, I watched her eat rice and bread and chickpeas and lamb. She was as slender as could be and at first ate slowly. But as she began to relax, she demonstrated an impressive appetite. I barely ate any of the food I'd packed after that. I wanted there to be enough for her.

When she reached for things I could see the bruises going up her arms. She never talked about them, which somehow made them sadder to me.

We lay on our blankets at a safe distance. I didn't know how to talk to her right then. We were too close, and there were none of the social structures to make sense of us. I didn't want to presume. We both stared upward, and it dawned on me that the only function of my roof was hiding the stars. So without really discussing it, we crawled with our blankets out from underneath it and bathed in the sparks. I still look up at the sky most nights and never quite believe it's the same sky as that one.

I didn't want her to think I needed anything from her. I didn't want her to be afraid. I didn't know how close or how far to be. How much talking was burdensome? How much silence was lonely? How much attention was unsettling? How little attention was cold? I wanted her to know she was safe with me. She yawned and I wondered. She slept, and I watched over her.

The second day we rode I was more aware of the feeling of her arms on me, the particular impression of each of her fingers, her chest against my back. Her cheek pressed sometimes, her forehead. My nerves even felt out for the tip of her nose as we galloped through the dry, brown hills. But I didn't want anything from her. I didn't need anything. I wanted to make her

well and keep her safe. I didn't want anything else. To say it was
to make it so.

When we stopped for the evening she ate with more heartiness
and less urgency. I saw how her bruises yellowed and faded into
the lovely landscape of her face. I felt her basic knack for living,
her resilience, and I knew how it would serve her on the long
road. That was something you took with you from life to life. She
wouldn't know that about herself, but I would remember.

That second night was much colder, and I could no longer
find enough wood to keep a fire going. The blankets were thick
but not thick enough. She couldn't fall into a true slumber in
that cold. I watched her shiver, going in and out of sleep. I tried
putting my blanket over her. My eagerness, the intensity of my
purpose, kept me warm, but she shivered.

I went closer to her without quite deciding to. I didn't want
to overreach, but I had heat to share. I curled around her, a few
inches away, trying to give her some of it. She must have felt my
warmth in her sleep, because she gravitated toward it. I didn't
make the contact, much as I was yearning for it by that point.
I got under the blankets with her, and, childlike, she wound her
limbs in and around my warm surfaces. I felt the bare skin of her
ankles and feet wrapped around my calves, her back burrowed
into my chest; my arms went around her. She sighed, and
I wondered who I was to her in her sleep.

I didn't want to move. I was too happy, and the moment was
too fragile. My arm fell asleep, but I didn't want to take it from
under her. There are short periods of joy you have to stretch
through a lot of empty years, me more than most. You have to
make them last as well as you can.

On the third day as we rode I felt the way her body relaxed
into mine, and that was a gift. When we stopped to eat in the

midday, she spilled rice on my knee, and she smiled. I wanted her to spill a thousand things on me, lava, acid, bricks, anything, and smile each time.

That night she got under the blanket and curled against me without a word. "Thank you," she said as she fell asleep, her hair against my neck, the top of her head under my chin. My arms pressed against her breasts, and I felt her heart beating and mixing with the pulse in my wrist. I tried to keep my lower regions at a safe distance, as certain organs weren't complying with overall discipline.

Sometime in the night I must have let down my guard and fallen into a deep sleep. I had been dreaming, I guess, of older versions of ourselves, and I was disoriented. I had gone all the way back to the first time I saw her, for only a glimpse, but it must have jarred me. When I woke she was right there, her face in front of mine. I didn't understand exactly what she was doing there or where we were in time. The sight of her face filled me with regret.

"I am so sorry," I whispered.

I wasn't sure if she was awake or asleep, but I guess she was awake. "What could you be sorry for?" she whispered back.

"For what I did to you." I was certainly disoriented at that point, because I thought she would know what I meant. My connection to her felt so strong, I couldn't hold on to the idea that she could know anything less than I did. It was a strange, illusory moment of believing our experiences were the same. I don't understand where it came from. If there's one sad thing I know, it's that nobody's experience is ever the same as mine.

Confusion set her quiet face in motion. "What you did to me?" She sat up. "You didn't do anything wrong. You protected me. You saved my life. Not just now but many times. You've been kind to me at your own peril. I don't know why. You haven't asked anything from me. You've made no demands. You haven't been lustful toward me. What other man would do this?"

It was getting on morning, and I was as aroused as could be at that point and felt ambivalent about her innocence.

I sat up, too, trying to orient myself better. I wanted to explain, but I didn't know how much I could say. "I've tried to protect you. I have. But a long time ago, I did something to you that I—"

"To me?"

"To you." I couldn't stand the look of wariness. "Not to you, Sophia, as you are now. But long before. In Africa. You don't remember Africa." This was a reckless turn. What was I expecting? That she would suddenly sprout a memory to match mine?

Her eyebrows came down in a particular way she's always had. "I haven't been to Africa," she said slowly.

"But you have. A long time ago. And I—"

"I haven't."

There she sat, tiny under the giant dawning sky in that strange lunar landscape near Cappadocia with only me to look at. If my desire was to make her feel safe, this was not the way to go.

"No. I know. Of course. I was speaking in metaphor. I meant . . ."

Though I was looking for expiation, I wasn't going to take it at her expense. "I didn't mean anything." I shrugged and looked east, where the sun was puncturing our private night. "It's a strange memory I have." My voice was so quiet it probably drifted away before it reached her. I don't know.

She kept her eyes on me for a long time. There was uncertainty, but I could see the warmth, too. "You are a good man, and I do not understand you."

"Someday I'll try to explain," I said.

We got down under the covers again together, both of us

facing east. She pressed herself fiercely against me, so my body's ungovernable parts were made known to her. She didn't pull away but turned her head to look up at me again, sort of curiously.

I buried my face in her neck and felt for her ear with my mouth. I lifted up her skirts and put my hands on her bare hips. I opened her dress and kissed her breasts. I pulled her underclothes away and entered her with a pent-up passion that could only be imagined.

And imagined is all it was. That's not a memory but a fantasy I've enshrined alongside my memories so that it's almost become one. And I relive it in preference to the other version of events every time. My memory, as I've said, admits a few distortions. I try to cultivate it as a reliable record, and it's rare when my emotions are strong enough to bend the facts. But here I bent the facts wide enough to push myself inside her and stay there forever.

But let the record show the truth: She looked at me and licked her lips with an unmistakable passion, and she said, "I am your brother's wife."

"You are my brother's wife," I said, and mournfully, miserably, rolled a few inches away from her.

No matter how brutal my brother was, he couldn't take down the sanctity of marriage. Not the idea of it. He didn't respect it, but he didn't have the power to nullify it. I guess because we believed in it. We couldn't help ourselves.

I watched her carefully, and she watched me. A kiss, a real one, and all that would inevitably follow would transform our errand of mercy into a tawdry betrayal. No matter how I loved her. No matter how much I wanted to.

No one will ever know but her and me, the lower part of my body was urging.

But the brain in my head took a longer view. No one would

know but us, and my brother would be proven right in all his ugly suspicions, and we would always know we were wrong. When you live as long as I do, always is a crippling distance. I know she was thinking the same. In that moment my belief in our common mind was not a delusion.

ON THE LAST full day we rode slowly. A hot breeze covered us with sand and grit bound to us by sticky sweat, and I stank worse than our horse. Late in the afternoon I saw something half buried in the sand, and I stopped the horse and got off.

It turned out to be a giant piece of hammered brass, heavy and well wrought. I flipped it over and discovered it was a basin of some sort. It probably belonged to a merchant who'd found himself under attack and left in a hurry. It was too heavy to carry quickly, but it gave me an idea. We rode a mile or so out of the way to where I'd last seen evidence of water. We filled all of our containers and two wineskins and returned to the basin. I made a fire to heat the water and set the basin atop a little rise that offered the loveliest view of the sun as it showed off its ecstatic orange and purple streaks. The air turned cool and dim as Sophia watched my labors with a bemused look, but I kept at it until the basin was full of clean, steaming water.

We've become so used to modern plumbing we practically consider it a right to have a hot bath at the turn of the wrist, and it's easy to forget what a luxury it once was, but it was. I found a piece of soap in my saddlebag and handed it to her with some ceremony. It wasn't much of a gift, but it felt like the right way to send her on to her new life.

I was going to leave her in privacy, but I hated to miss her pleasure. "Should I go?" I asked her.

She shook her head. "You should stay." She took off her dress and underclothes without shame or shyness but without any coyness, either. I watched her set one foot, then two into the basin and shiver with delight.

I can make you happy, I thought.

I realized I was watching her with the knowledge of what was coming. I wanted to commit her to my memory more deeply and concretely than any other thing. I wanted to take in every bit of her so I could keep her with me for the long haul and so I could find her again. I studied her feet, slightly turned in, the pretty design of her rib cage, and the way she held her head forward. I knew her hair and her coloring and her shapes would be different next time, but the way she wore her body would keep on.

She slipped all the way in and dunked her head under. She came up smiling, and her skin was a lighter shade. She lay back in the tub and let the water settle and smooth around her, reflecting the colors of the sky.

"Come sit with me," she said, and I sat on a flat rock on the rise just above her. It was a beautiful view.

After she finished she ordered me into the bath. She watched me undress with proprietary boldness and scrubbed my back with deft fingers. I dunked my head under and felt only the silence and her hands. Each of these moments was a pearl on a string, one prettier and more perfect than the next.

"I wish you were in here with me," I said.

She gave me a long, full look. "There are many things I wish."

"We'll bathe together someday," I told her with a heave of contentment.

"Will we?"

"Yes. Someday you'll be free. Then I will find you and we'll be as happy as this."

She had tears in her eyes and suds on her fingers. "How can that be true?"

"It might take a long time, longer than you imagine, but someday we will."

"Do you promise me?"

I looked at her and made another fateful choice. "I do."

When I was clean she washed our clothes and laid them out to dry. We had no choice but to huddle under the blankets and cling to each other bare-bodied and -souled until the sun came up and our clothes were dry.

We ate the last of our food and rode out of our reverie and on into the village where she would begin her new life.

I didn't dare kiss her when we were naked under the blankets and burning with lust. I waited until we could read the shapes of the dusty village on the horizon before I stopped the horse and pulled her off. I held her for a long time. Even then I didn't mean to kiss her. I was too committed to preserving her lawful innocence. But then I saw that a kiss would serve her better.

It was a sadder, more tearful, and more serious kiss than it would have been a few hours earlier. I savored the feeling of her body for the last time with a heavy notion of what was to come. I knew what I'd taken. I knew what I'd get to keep, and I also knew the price I'd pay.

I LEFT SOPHIA in a tiny village where the houses were built into the sides of the hills. I put her in the care of an older woman, a widow, who was all too happy to take Sophia and call her niece. I knew this woman because she had been my mother once. I knew I could trust her. I left Sophia with money and what I hoped would be the safety of a new identity.

"I'll see you again," she said to me. Her face was resigned, but I saw tears, too.

I agreed sincerely and ardently, though I didn't mean it in exactly the way she did.

"You'll come back here someday."

"I promise I will."

By returning to Pergamum about a week later I knew I was taking a risk, but I didn't want to back down. I couldn't move away. I wouldn't become another person. There'd be time enough for that. I told my mother I would come back, and I did. I found my brothers. I settled them with her in her small house. I gave them each money and a few items that would be easy to hide and hard to steal. I did each of these things with a sense of finality, as I look back.

Leaving my mother's house on the third night, I can't say I was surprised by my brother's ambush. In hindsight, it would have been surprising not to see him following me into a dark street. It happened quickly.

I was prepared for a face-to-face confrontation, but he was angrier and lower than that. He struck from behind. He put a knife in my back and again in my neck, and I died painfully.

As I died, I felt the end of that life much harder than I expected. I found myself hoping my mother would never know what happened to me. I thought I was prepared for death, but I wasn't. Only as I bled away did I understand all that I was losing. I was losing Sophia and my family and myself, too. I would no longer be the person she trusted and loved.

I never had so much to lose. I never lived or died like that again. As much as I longed to get back to her, a part of me hoped that this, at last, would be the end of it.

IT WASN'T THE END, of course. It was, as Winston Churchill might say, the end of the beginning. I went back to that small village near Cappadocia to find her again. But I was eleven, traveling all the way from the Caucasus on my own.

I was just relieved to find her there. The widow had died, but Sophia was safe. She was kind enough to invite me into her little house and feed me tea and bread and honey. There was no sign of any husband or child, but there were lovely weavings on every wall and surface. I knew she had made them. I recognized our joint history in the flowering trees from the garden in Pergamum and the beautiful horse, the Arabian, on which we had ridden to this village.

She sat across from me at a little wooden table. The candlelight and the fabrics made it feel like the inside of a jewel box. I was with her and looking at her and also a stranger to her and missing her painfully. I saw her through old eyes and felt old things, and my child body didn't know what to do with them. Rarely have I felt a disjuncture between memory and body as confusing as that. I don't know what I wanted from her. She was the same person, and I was different.

She asked about me, naturally, and as I talked she was struck by me; I could see that.

"How do you know my language?" she asked me, puzzled.

"I learned it as I traveled," I said, but she didn't look entirely convinced.

I wanted to tell her more, but I couldn't. I didn't make sense to anyone. I knew that. It would make her instantly distrustful and remote from me, and I ached to be close in the old way.

She said I should stay the night and be on my way the next day.

The blanket she laid out for me was the same one we had slept under together when I was older and she was younger and she was my brother's wife. I was not equal to the smell of that blanket.

She sat with me on the little pallet and rubbed my back with great tenderness, almost like she could remember. Because I was eleven and lonely and holding far too many memories, I cried into my arm and hoped she didn't see.

When I looked upward in the morning light I saw the old curling piece of parchment pinned on the wall. It was the sketch I'd made for her of my baptistery mosaics. The garden and the apple tree and, of course, the snake.

"Who made that?" I asked her, pointing to it as she fed me a breakfast that must have used up most of her pantry. I always hated asking false questions, but I couldn't help myself.

She looked at the drawing thoughtfully. "A man I knew," she said, looking down.

"What happened to him?"

She shook her head, and her face contorted. She braced her chin to keep it steady.

"I don't know. He said he would come back here someday, but I am almost sure he was killed." The sadness in her face was as much as I could take.

"He will come back," I told her tearfully.

She shook her head. "I don't know if I can wait any longer."

I realized what I had done, and I was ashamed. I had given her false hope. She had believed in me, and I had disappointed her. She couldn't see the canvas as I could. It was selfish of me to promise her something she couldn't see.

"He didn't forget you. He'll find you again, but it might take longer than you thought."

She looked at me oddly. "That's what he said, too."

.   .   .

I WENT BACK to Sophia's village for the last time when I was
nineteen. I was bursting with intention to prove to Sophia who
I really was, that I really had come back as I'd promised.
I planned to live with her for the rest of our lives. I was ready and
armed to combat her every doubt and protest. I prepared the
words to convince her that the difference in our ages didn't
matter. I spent years and miles rehearsing these conversations
and dreaming of all the lovemaking that would follow.

But when I got there I saw that the craggy hillside was
blackened in places, and a new, larger house now stood where her
little house had been. Most of the village was newly built and
unrecognizable. I finally found the priest in his stone church,
one of the few familiar structures.

"We had a terrible fire," he explained to me.

I could barely listen as he told me how they'd lost most of
their houses and almost half of the villagers.

"What about Sophia?" I asked.

He shook his head.

I went back to the site of her house and found the new
occupants. "Was there anything left from the fire?" I asked them
desperately.

There was nothing. Aimless, I went into the desert, retracing
the route I had taken with her from Pergamum, but on foot and
alone. I felt the bending weight of my memory as I walked. She
was gone, and everything she'd touched was gone. Her weavings,
the blanket, my sketches. All of it was lost without a trace. It was
up to me to carry it forward or let it be gone forever.

DANIEL WAS TIRED. Too tired to change out of his hospital scrubs before he threw himself on his bed. He'd just come off a three-day shift during which he'd slept for a total of forty minutes in a chair with his head on a table and a TV blaring *The Newly-wed Game* a few feet away. There were regulations about how hard you were supposed to work a resident, but the VA hospital didn't pay them an excessive amount of attention.

He never complained about it. He liked being there more than he liked being home. He liked old people and he liked veterans, and because he was specializing in geriatric medicine, those were the kinds of people he spent his time with.

Home, in his present case, was a one-bedroom apartment in Arlington, Virginia, with a view of the parking lot. He always thought he would get himself a real house in a beautiful place. God knew he had the money. But he always got shitty, temporary places with month-to-month leases. This one had a full stove, but he hadn't turned it on yet. It had three closets, but two of them were empty. He had a big plasma-screen TV and a cable package that entitled him to see virtually every football, baseball, basketball, and hockey game played at every hour of the day. And other sports, too, but he wasn't as interested in those. Except tennis in the middle of the night when the Australian Open came along.

He'd skipped college altogether this time around. He'd skipped the first two years of medical school, too. He faked transcripts from both when he "transferred" to George Washington for his third year. That was about a month after he'd hoped to drown himself in the Appomattox River and failed at it. He was a sucker for more. He had too much to lose to commit suicide well.

GW had been happy to take him. It was remarkable what you could get away with if you had the audacity. He wouldn't have done it if he hadn't known he was reasonably prepared.

He had graduated from several colleges and universities in the States and in Europe. He'd gone through medical training more than once. Dozens of times, if you counted everything he'd learned about herbs and folk medicine through the late Middle Ages and the Renaissance. And those were surprisingly helpful to him. It was funny how the old practices always came around again.

It was the rhythm of human enterprise to invent and worship some new approach, to fully reject it a generation later, to realize the need for it again a generation or two after that and then hastily reinvent it as new, usually without its original elegance. Scientists hated to look backward for anything.

That was always a source of amazement to him, the blind devotion to making things new. People didn't seem to realize what a slender edge they stood on in human history and that every person before them stood on that same edge, thinking it was the world. If they were to look back they would see quite a landscape spreading out behind them, but mostly they didn't.

The building superintendent had taped a recycling poster to his apartment door, and it made him laugh. There was a burst of enthusiasm for recycling every so often, but it usually didn't extend to the heart or the mind. It was usually limited to tires or bottles. He was pro-recycling, all right. What if people knew *they* were recycled? Would that change anything?

There were a few basic things he sometimes wished he could tell people. Maybe he'd write an advice book someday. He'd educate them on recycling and also point out practical things, such as how every moment spent worrying about commercial jet crashes or shark attacks is a moment wasted.

DANIEL COULD NEVER fall asleep when he wanted to. No matter how tired he was. His brain would start to fixate in some direction or other. Usually in the direction of Charlottesville, Virginia, where Sophia was conducting her life in peace, he hoped—a peace he would surely not enhance by turning up in the lobby of her dorm, as he sometimes dreamed about.

Someday he would approach her again. He often fantasized about that moment. Someday he would know the right things to say to make up for last time. Someday he would call her with a quick question or send her a humorous e-mail or casually jot a message on her wall, and she would not be horrified by it, because by then the disaster of their last meeting would feel as though it was far behind them. Someday was the thing he had, because it was a lot harder to ruin than today.

Sleep was going to have to catch him unawares if it was going to catch him at all tonight. Hence the large TV and the cable package.

He hauled himself over to the couch, armed with his trusty remote. The Lakers were in a play-off series against the Spurs. It wasn't a deciding game tonight but still good to watch. He settled down into another episode of the Kobe Bryant show with a certain feeling of relaxation. He considered the story of Kobe. Not a brand-new soul but a young one, he could tell. Those often were the best athletes. They'd been around long enough to see the big patterns but not long enough to be encumbered by them. There were exceptions, of course. Shaq was fresh out of the box, and Tim Duncan, he was pretty sure, had been going on for centuries.

Somewhere around the end of the third quarter, during a long stretch of ads for cars and trucks, he started to doze off. When the picture shifted back to the game, he blearily tuned in again. The camera hung obsequiously on the big courtside celebrities for a few seconds. That was all right. That's what they did. His eyelids started sinking again, when he suddenly caught sight of something. He sat up. He blinked his eyes to clear them and leaned forward. He felt an awful tingle in his extremities.

There was a man just behind the courtside seats in the second row. He was tall, with a flashy jacket and a careful haircut. He might have been handsome if the look of him hadn't turned Daniel's stomach. He wore his body stiffly, like an expensive suit. He was in profile now, talking to somebody. He had glanced at the camera for only a second, but that was enough. Daniel felt the adrenaline hit his bloodstream so hard it felt as though his eyes were vibrating in his head.

He had never seen this man before, but he knew him well.

LATER, HIS BODY settled down. The agitation of the first sight gave way to a feeling of vague seasickness as he tried to process it. It wasn't just the sight of Joaquim or the reminder of their history that was jarring. It was the fact that Joaquim remembered it, too.

Having spent hundreds of years so sharply alone with his own memory, it felt bizarre for Daniel to be in any kind of proximity with another person who knew the things about the world that he did, who even remembered some of Daniel's early lives the way he did. If it had been any other soul, it would have been a comfort.

Daniel thought of the last time he had seen Joaquim, just a glance in a village square in Hungary in the thirteen hundreds. He'd already learned by that point that Joaquim also had the Memory, and he'd been on his guard, but Joaquim had shown no sign of recognizing him. Daniel kept expecting him to turn up much closer at hand—his uncle, his father, his teacher, his son, his brother again—as significant people often did. But unlike most things he dreaded, it hadn't happened. At first, Daniel expected, it was because his former brother's basic misanthropy held him up in death for long periods of time. If there was ever a soul that died apart—far apart—it was his. In lighter moments he'd pictured Joaquim zagging randomly around the globe, turning up here in Jakarta, there in Yakutsk.

Much later, Daniel had learned that Joaquim had begun to bend the rules of leaving and coming back. It was a chilling notion. Daniel didn't know how he did it; he'd learned it from a mystical soul, his old (*really* old) friend Ben, and how Ben came to know these things he never understood. But Daniel could well imagine that Joaquim wouldn't stand to wait his turn, or put up with starting again as a powerless infant. He wouldn't tolerate the impotence of childhood time after time. He was geared toward revenge, and he wouldn't leave the hunt for his enemies to chance, though he probably would have found them faster if he had.

It was a bitter thing to see him again after all that time. Daniel had been tempted to think that Joaquim's soul had finished, but of course not. He had too much hate to be gone for good. Daniel imagined Joaquim using his memory for the sole purpose of grinding out his vendettas over the centuries. Who knew how many he had.

It was grating to see him in a body he did not deserve. It was sick to think of how he'd done it and what had become of the man who did deserve it. Daniel had no way of knowing what Joaquim was up to. But he had a bleak sense that it was dangerous for him—and dangerous for Sophia, if he ever found her.

*A*t the turn of the tenth century, I was an oarsman sailing under the banner of the doge aboard a ship in the Venetian fleet. I hailed from the countryside to the east of Ravenna at the time, and like many boys in that part of the world, I dreamed of the sea. The Venetians were the finest sailors on earth, or so we believed, and we had good reason to. I joined my first crew at fifteen and sailed for twenty-one years on warships and merchant ships until I went down in a storm off Gibraltar.

We sailors expected and rather hoped to die at sea, so it was just a question of when. I had a fine, long run, and it wasn't a bad death, as compared to many others. I've drowned only twice, and the second time, with the novelty of it removed, I hardly minded at all, to tell you the truth.

Our routes took us primarily to Greece and Asia Minor, Sicily and Crete, and occasionally to Spain and the north coast of Africa. These were glorious places then, especially when you approached them by sea. As I've said, I keep the nostalgia minimal, but as the centuries pass, the brutality of that life falls away and I am left with the vision of sailing into the Grand Canal at dusk.

It was a fairly routine voyage to the Cretan port of Iraklion (or Candia, as we Venetians called it) that I want to tell you about. This was early in my career. I was still young and lowly in the naval hierarchy and suffered long shifts on the oars and more than my share of night watches.

From one voyage to the next you saw the same characters again and again, but there were always one or two new ones. In this case there was a sailor even younger than I, probably fifteen to my eighteen. I had noticed him not because of anything he said or did but the absence of either. He kept his mouth shut and did his job assiduously, but he watched and listened intently to everything around him. With him there was no ennui, no irony, no sass, no braggadocio—the staples of ordinary seamen. He had large, intelligent eyes, strangely complex in an otherwise innocent face. His name was Benedetto, but the men called him Ben or Benno when shouting orders at him or mocking him, and those were essentially the only times he was addressed.

The first few shifts we did not exchange a word. But I felt his heavy eyes on me when I talked to the other hands. I could tell how he listened. By about the fourth or fifth shift he was my only companion on the foredeck, and I was struggling to stay awake, so I started up a conversation.

"You're an Italian, no?" I asked in the low Italian vernacular we used on the ship.

He looked at me before he answered. "Yes. I was born south of Naples."

"Good wine country," I said irrelevantly. I've never been good at small talk and I'd never been to Naples, but he seemed tongue-tied and ill at ease. How little I knew.

"And you are Italian also," he said after a long silence.

"Ravenna," I said with some pride.

"And before that?"

"Before that?"

"Where did you come from before that?"

It was an odd question, and I wondered if he suspected I wasn't quite from Ravenna proper. I had more interest in status back then, I guess. "I was born three leagues east of the city," I said a little defensively.

He nodded. There was nothing urgent or demanding in his manner. "But before you were born three leagues east of Ravenna, where did you come from?"

I was struck mute. I still remember how the thoughts streaked around my head. I had been alive many times by that point. I knew how strange and even freakish I was. So much of my deeper life was conducted in the remote part of my mind, it never occurred to me that another person could get near it. Was it possible he was like me? Did he remember things? I was so accustomed to hiding these things that when I opened my mouth I literally could not put the words into the air.

Ben looked at me curiously. "Was it Constantinople? I know you must have spent some time in that region. Maybe that was earlier? Greece, perhaps?"

I tried out his words in different ways. Could they fit an ordinary interpretation? "I have not sailed to Constantinople . . . in this fleet," I said slowly.

"I don't mean as you are now, but before. I, for instance, was born in Illyria before Naples, and Lebanon before that."

I felt my breath catch short. I wondered if I was actually awake or even alive. Sailors loved to talk about enchanted stretches of the sea that made a sane man mad. I suddenly worried I was being tricked. "I don't know your meaning," I said slowly. My voice sounded so stretched I barely recognized it.

Ben had the least tricky face you've ever seen. "You must.

I have met only a few like you . . . like me . . . a very few. And I have come down on this earth many times. It is possible I am mistaken, but I don't think so."

"Like you?" I said cautiously.

"Like me in that you remember. It's rare, I know, for people to remember past their birth. With some it goes back only one life or two, and for others there are only bits and pieces. But yours goes deeper, I suspect."

I looked around to see that we were alone. I looked up at the moon and the stars to be sure of my relationship to them. "It does go deeper," I said.

He nodded. There was no triumph in his eyes. He never doubted it. "Half the millennium. Or more?"

"That's about right."

"Where did you start?"

"I was born first near Antioch."

"That makes sense," he said, gazing past my head to the east, where the sun was just beginning its climb out of the ocean.

"How so?"

He shook a thought away and refocused his eyes on me. "It's almost dawn."

What he meant was that our replacements would arrive at any moment. His face conveyed sympathy. He could see that it was worse torture for me to end this conversation than it had been to start it.

"How did you know?" I asked. "About me?"

"I can't really explain," he said. His eyes were no less direct. He wasn't meaning to be evasive. "I just . . . knew."

And that was my introduction to the extraordinary capabilities of Ben, and the near impossibility of getting at them.

.   .   .

BEN IS VERY OLD. I don't know how old. Sometimes I think he
is like Vishnu, holding the entire story of human experience in
his mind, but I'm not certain even he knows when he started. He
told me once that his first memory was the lapping of the river
Euphrates, but he is more impressionistic than factual in these
kinds of recollections. If he does hold our story in his mind, I'm
afraid it's been entrusted to a poet rather than a historian.

"It's all metaphor, finally, isn't it?" he said to me once in his
wistful way.

"Is it?" I asked, in my fact-craving way.

He is so old that his memory works differently from anyone's.
Even mine. Later he became a great fan of Lewis Carroll. (He
also loved the Upanishads, Aristophanes, Chaucer, Shakespeare,
Tagore, Whitman, Borges, E. B. White, and Stephen King, to
name a few.) One time when I was pestering him about how he
knew something that he couldn't possibly know, he quoted the
following line from Carroll: "It's a poor sort of memory that
only works backward."

He once told me he thought his first name had been
Deborah, but he didn't seem sure of it. I asked him if he'd like
me to call him that, knowing how important my name had
become to me, but he said no, he wasn't Deborah anymore.

Ben and I sailed three voyages together, one right after the
next, and had the opportunity to talk about a lot of things. The
third and final trip was to Alexandria, which prompted from
Ben a wealth of funny and fragmentary observations about Julius
Caesar, Mark Antony, and Cleopatra, as well as Ptolemy, her
pesky younger brother who was also her husband. I discovered it
didn't do any good to try to understand the mechanics of his past

or his memory in any literal way. A direct question never begat a direct answer. ("Tell the truth, but tell it slant" later became one of his favorite lines from Dickinson.) But to listen to him talk was a feast of odd and fascinating information.

He had the sunniest disposition of any sailor I knew and the keenest devotion to its lowly labors. I never saw a man more absorbed in tying a knot. Probably the worst experience of my life on the sea was hearing Ben beaten bloody by a couple of drunken spearmen on a dark reach out of Thira. He never had the right temperament for a sailor.

After that third voyage he disappeared, and it was several hundred years before I saw him again, but first we shared a conversation that has stayed with me even more than most.

On a slow night a hundred or so leagues off the coast of Crete, I began to tell him about Sophia. And once begun, there was not much I kept to myself. I began at the fateful beginning and told him about each of our meetings. I can't describe how thrilling it was to be with someone like me, and how little of myself I shared with most people. I dashed back and forth through my long history without having to make any explanations or apologies. I felt like a pianist who'd been forced to play on a few white keys in the middle, finally allowed to run his hands all up and down the keyboard.

I finished my story with our most recent encounter, with me as a child in her tiny cliffside house in Central Anatolia, but it was the part of the saga involving my brother, Joaquim, that Ben kept coming back to. He asked me to tell those parts again and again.

I got tired of it. I wanted to talk about Sophia, not my brother. But Ben wanted every tick of the story, starting with the feud in my first life and dragging me through each detail of my stabbing death more than two hundred years later. He closed his eyes as though he was seeing it for himself.

"Mercifully it's done," I said finally. "There's no reason to think of him ever again if I don't have to." Life was long for people like us. Long enough to smooth away the tragedies. That's what I thought at the time.

Ben was crouched over, his forehead in his hands. He was rocking, sort of; I didn't know why. He was acutely empathetic, I knew, but this was a bit much.

"Ben, it's not so bad. It's one life of many," I remember saying, ready to move on to a new subject. "We go along. We forgive and forget. At least I forgive and he forgets."

Ben lifted his head finally. He looked at me carefully. I was accustomed to this look, but it was darkened by something I hadn't seen before.

"Do you think he forgets?"

"What do you mean?"

"I trust you forgive, but are you certain that he forgets?"

"I'm sure he's long gone," I said quickly. "He's been dead at least a hundred years. I haven't run into him in a new life as yet, but I'm sure I'll have that displeasure sometime in the future."

I hoped my lightness would lift the troubled look from Ben's face, but it didn't. I was starting to feel uneasy. "What do you mean?" I said again.

"Are you certain that he forgets?"

"Everyone forgets," I said, almost combatively.

"Not everyone."

"Not you or I, but everyone else." I stared at Ben, desperate to see some sunniness return to his eyes, but I couldn't find it. "Do you know something?" I said, impatient and frustrated. "If you know something, tell me."

"I don't know, but I think," Ben said slowly. "I think about him, and I don't think that he forgives or forgets."

"Why do you think that? Joaquim gave no sign of it. He lived like a man with no history at all," I argued. "The Memory is rare, isn't it? In almost five hundred years you're the only person I've encountered with it. And you, who have no knowledge of him, think he has it?"

I think I wanted Ben to be angry at me in return, but he wasn't. I wanted him to argue, but he didn't. "Do you think anyone knows that you have it?" he asked. "Do you think your brother knows about you?"

I stood there with a growing sense of dread. Joaquim was present for those cataclysmic events of my first life. If I could trace my memory back to that time, why shouldn't he also have it? I didn't know what to say. I couldn't argue with Ben. I didn't want to think through what it meant for me and for Sophia, wherever she was.

"I hope I'm wrong," Ben said, and his eyes were compassionate. "But I think he remembers."

Often, over the years, I've hoped Ben was wrong. But unfortunately, as far as I know, he never is.

WHEN I THINK of my days as a sailor, I always think of a dog I once knew in Venice named Nestor. He was a street dog, a mutt, and I used to feed him between voyages. He was a smart dog. He always met my ship and greeted me, no matter how long I'd been gone. One time we brought him aboard the ship to eat rats on a voyage to a couple of plague-stricken ports in Spain, and he did his job splendidly. I really loved that dog.

He must have lived to an extraordinary dog age, because after I died I was born again, right in the city, and when I was six or seven years old, I wandered to the docks to look for old friends.

Who did I see there but Nestor. He was old and arthritic, but I knew it was him. And amazingly, he knew it was me. I am certain of it. He sniffed me. He wagged his tail so hard you would have thought it might come off. He licked me, played with me, asked for treats in the same old ways. That was one of the happiest experiences of my long life. I felt like a miniature Odysseus, remembered by someone at last.

Sometimes I find myself wishing that dogs lived as long as people do. I think my life would be considerably less lonely. But Nestor died not long after that. I went to the docks often as I grew up in that life, hoping I might see Nestor in his new body, as a new, young dog. But I was never able to identify him. By now I know that dogs, like most animals, don't have individuated souls. They have a group soul, if you can properly call it that. Bees and ants make a good illustration of the idea. They carry the wisdom of their kind with them, which is a privilege we do not have. But it makes it almost impossible to recognize them from life to life.

I sometimes think, and Carl Jung would probably agree, that an early version of man, maybe Australopithecus or Neanderthal, did have some kind of group soul. I think the true ascent of man, the moment when humans divided irrevocably from apes and other fellow creatures, occurred with the birth of the first distinct soul. And much unhappiness ensued.

CHARLOTTESVILLE,
VIRGINIA, 2006

HE WAS ONLY half on board with his plan but going along anyway. He feared seeing her. He hoped to see her. Hope was the thing
you picked to happen, and fear was the thing you picked not to
happen, and often with him they blurred.

Since he'd seen Joaquim on TV he'd been thinking about Sophia
constantly. Granted, he always did that, but it was her safety he
thought of now. Over the last two years he'd kept track of her
remotely, highly conscious of her whereabouts but stalling his
reapproach, afraid to get too close and cause more damage. Now he
needed to see with his own eyes that she was okay. One of his worst
fears was that Joaquim would somehow find her and do her harm.
One of his other worst fears was that Joaquim would somehow find
Daniel, and Daniel would unknowingly lead Joaquim to her. Daniel was torn between those two things, the desire to protect her
(and, admittedly, be near her) and the fear that his presence would
put her at greater risk.

Joaquim's cruelty forced a few limitations, it seemed. He had a
version of the Memory paired with a deeply grudging nature, but
he couldn't recognize a soul from one body to the next. "He can't
see inside people" was how Ben put it. But his cruelty also offered
Joaquim advantages—body stealing, for example—and Daniel
had the troubling sense that Joaquim was gathering these advantages over time.

Daniel parked near the hospital and walked up the lawn to the rotunda with a feeling of admiration. The place was old by the standards of this country, and bore the stamp of a mastermind. He wished he had been in the New World in the age of Thomas Jefferson. It was one of his favorite periods of history, but he'd been spending an odd, short life in Denmark at the time. Most of his lives suggested overarching coherence and some identifiable mark of his will, but once in a while he'd find himself somewhere like Denmark, among strangers.

He'd studied and read Jefferson's work extensively. He even thought he recognized the man once, in 1961, on a Freedom Ride down to Oxford, Mississippi. Daniel had bought an iced tea and a bag of peaches from him at a roadside stand. The man introduced himself as Noah. He was old and tired, working the same land, he told Daniel, where his grandfather had been a slave and his father a sharecropper. Daniel couldn't be sure it was Jefferson, because he had never seen the great man in person. He'd known him only from drawings and portraits, which weren't entirely dependable for distinguishing a soul, though much better than photographs. But Daniel felt it strongly and intuitively. You could still see some quality of him in Noah's eyes.

Noah was soul-tired by that point. It was probably the last of his lives, Daniel guessed, the final turn of his remarkable existence. It made sense to Daniel that as the lover of Sally Hemings and an ambivalent slave owner, Jefferson would come back as a black man before his circle would close. Noah never would have guessed who he had once been. And though Daniel had been tempted to mention it, he didn't. It was a strange source of loneliness, knowing things about people they didn't know themselves.

Daniel felt a drop of sweat go down his spine. The air was so humid you could smell it and hear it and touch it and see it and nearly chew on it. He hated to feel the sweat soaking into his best shirt, the white linen shirt she'd given him almost ninety years before when she was Constance. It had belonged to her grand-father, the viscount. He kept this shirt from one life to the next among his most treasured things, and wore it only rarely because he wanted to preserve it. When she'd first given it to him, it was too big for him, and he figured the viscount was a giant, but he'd grown so big in this life, it barely fit. He'd never been so tall before, as he was in this life. He'd worn the shirt today because he loved it and because he thought, in spite of it being a little stretched, it looked good on him. (He was rarely vain, but his body was twenty-one, and once in a while it got to him.) But the main reason he wore it was because he hoped, irrationally, that it might remind her of what he meant to her once. All these years later he could smell his old sweat and fever, and the smell of the great old house where she'd once lived, the polish and wax and a faint antiseptic hospital smell. And somewhere nested in all that was the barest, most fragile trace of her. Not just a representation of her but her. That was really why he loved this shirt.

Daniel suspected that smell was his only extraordinary sense in this body. His own version of a superpower. He was Smell Man, or maybe The Nose. His ears weren't extraordinary. He knew many songs and could play quite a few instruments, but that didn't mean his ear was always great. It had been good and even excellent in a few bodies and frustratingly bad in others. He used to think that over time he could overwhelm his body's limits with pure will and experience, but it didn't work that way. In fact, over time he became more convinced of the simple biology of talent. There were gifts only a body could offer, and a great ear for music was one of them.

His eyes weren't extraordinary. He could identify a huge num-ber of things by sight, but that was only because he had seen so much of the earth's surface under so many atmospheric conditions. He'd been a sailor in more than one life, crawling over the watery earth, minute by minute, in those places where time had the least effect. But his eyes weren't always very astute. He'd been a truly good artist only twice. A good eye was another thing you couldn't take with you.

Touch was a rudimentary sense, not so variable and not likely to get better with repetition. If anything, repetition made you feel a little less with each touch. As he saw it, anticipation and habit were two of the nastiest parasites of old souls and long experience. They fed on repetition and crowded out your eager senses over time until nothing felt new anymore. There were things he wished he could touch for the first time again.

Smell and taste, of course, were sister senses. More like Siamese twin sisters, with the first having most of the organs, including the brain. The second sister was built for pleasure and the occasional bitter warning. But it was smell that carried memory. He'd done enough work in neurology and even recent reading in neuro- science to know how simplistic his concept was, but that was still how he thought of it. Smell was like the wormhole connecting you to the other parts of your life. Memories of smell didn't fade, and they short-circuited your entire psychology—they didn't tunnel through endless experience or get loaded down by any part of your conscious mind. They stitched you instantly and fully to your other times, without regard to sequence. It was the closest thing to time travel on this earth. If he had to point to a place to explain his unusual abilities, it would probably be his nose. He'd had many of them over the centuries, and his gift of smell stayed with him through all.

He walked down Alderman Street, past the stadium and toward the dorms in Hereford College, where she lived. Here was where he might see her. This was where she lived and walked. His mounting adrenaline gave each of the sounds an extra boost. The drone of a mower. The rush of the trees. The trucks on a highway beyond his sight. This was her place, and the closer he got to Whyburn House, the more he imagined it was full of her. Her sidewalk, her pollen, her sky. The people in the direction of her building all wore her face for at least a moment.

It was hard for him, he realized, to picture her how she was now. He tended to picture her as Sophia and then let her image evolve in his mind as though in stop-motion photography. But she stayed on as a kind of amalgam, dissolving and resolving through different versions. It was hard to hold on to her as she would be right now if he saw her on the sidewalk. Her body was smaller this time, he thought, her bones lighter and softer. Last time, as an old woman, she'd had freckles and veins and spots on her hands, and now she was washed clean again.

He thought of the first time he saw her in this life, on the sidewalk with Marnie when she was fifteen and wearing those shorts. She was as radiant as if she had been chosen by the sun. That was before he'd moved to Hopewood, before she knew of him at all.

He thought of the time he'd watched her in the ceramics studio a couple of months after he'd arrived at school. He hadn't meant to stalk her. He'd gone to the art building to sign himself up for a printmaking class, and when he couldn't find the teacher he'd gone wandering. He was standing in the annex between two studios when he realized the lone figure at the kickwheel was her. He meant to say something and not just stand there, but he was paralyzed by the sight of her, and by the time he could think again he'd let too much time pass. She didn't look up. That was partly what caused his paralytic trance. Her foot urged the flywheel, the clay spun in a shifting mound, her hands moved in hypnotic symmetry, the sun was filtering down through dirty windows, and her eyes were focused on something he couldn't see. She had clay up to her elbows and all over her shirt and flecks of it on her face and in her hair. He was struck by how deeply absorbed she was in the moment and by the helpless sense he had that he couldn't reach her there. He was struck to admiration by the terrible state of her shirt.

He thought of that night at the high school and her in the light purple dress with the little purple flowers in her hair. His blood rushed high and low as he felt his hands holding on to her. She was certainly as beautiful as ever this time. Maybe it was just in his eyes, but her smile was a revelation. Although very young children were kind of homogenous, people pressed their souls into their faces and bodies fairly quickly in a life, and more and more deeply as they aged. A loving soul was always more beautiful over the long haul, but actual prettiness was fleeting. He used to think that fairness would dictate a conservation of physical beauty over the life of a soul, but it didn't work that way. Fairness turned out to be a human construct, and the universe had little use for it. Sophia had more than her share of beauty.

And today. What would he do if he saw her? It was a fantasy he'd played several different ways. Would she stop and know him? If she didn't, would he stop her? What would he say? Would it be enough just to see her? He told himself it would. He just wanted to look at her and know her life was marching along under the same arch of time and space as his. Even that would be a comfort, a kind of intimacy almost. Was it wrong that that could count as intimacy?

She lived with Marnie on the third floor of Whyburn House. He'd done the research to know that and not more. If he found out more he felt like a stalker, but if he did too little he'd wander around like an idiot. He didn't want to slant the knowledge too much in his direction. He didn't want one more inequality between them. Mostly he wanted not to know and to be surprised. Some sad part of him wanted it to be like a regular boy meeting a girl and falling in love.

She lived here in this red brick building. Her glass double doors, her nonskid floor covering. Her mail slot. One of them had to be. You could feel the giant air-conditioning system fighting its battle for her.

He'd lived in a dorm once, but he couldn't get used to it. It didn't have the functionality of a barracks or a monastery, say. It had the arbitrary and mildly coercive feel of social engineering. And this one was mostly empty, which underscored the impression. He greeted the guard at the desk and glanced down at the sign-in sheet. It had one name, not hers.

"ID, please," the guard said.

"Sorry?"

The guard turned down his buzzing radio. His tag said his name was Claude Valbrun. "You need to show an ID if you're not a resident, and you're not a resident, because if you were, I would know you." He wasn't the least bit unfriendly. He said it with evident pride.

Flustered, Daniel took out his driver's license. "I-I'm not—I wasn't planning on going in the building," he explained.

"Then what are you doing here?"

Daniel stopped. It was a good question, and he couldn't answer it.

The guard pointed to the phone on the wall past his desk. "Even if you just want to use the house phone, you still need to sign in."

Did he want to use that phone? Could he just pick it up and call her? He didn't know how to call her. Should he ask for her number? Would Claude Valbrun give it to him? And anyway, what was he thinking?

"You are looking for someone," the guard informed him sympathetically.

Daniel nodded.

"Who?" He wanted to help Daniel along.

Daniel felt like he was in therapy. Should he just tell him? He couldn't help himself. He was going to call her Sophia before he stopped himself. "Lucy Broward."

"Oh. Lucy." He smiled. "With the long hair. Third-floor Lucy. I like that girl."

Daniel found himself nodding eagerly.

"She gave me chocolates at Christmastime, and a little plant with red flowers for my wife. What was the name of that plant?" He closed one eye to help him think. "My memory is good for some things and not others." He closed the other eye. "What was the name of it? My wife knew."

"I don't know," Daniel said honestly. "Poinsettia?" He wished they could get on with it.

He opened both eyes. "Hmm. No. It started with a C, I think. Or a G. Just when you leave, I'll think of it. Anyway, Lucy is gone."

"She is?" His hopes fell so far and fast he had to realize how high he'd built them. He couldn't keep the disappointment off his face.

"Sure. Most of 'em are. May fourth was the last day of classes. It's quiet here until the summer students start showing up after July fourth."

"She's gone for the summer? She won't be back here?" Had he really thought he was going to see her just like that?

"She and that tall friend of hers moved out the end of last week."

"Marnie?"

"Right. Marnie."

"I don't know where she'll be living next year. Could be here. Could be someplace else."

Daniel nodded bleakly. Who knew if she'd even come back to

this campus? What if she did an exchange program or something? He hadn't found her at all.

Claude looked genuinely sorry for him as he handed back his driver's license. So much so that it was embarrassing. "Seems to me the school year ends earlier every year," Claude said philosophically, shaking his head in a way that gave Daniel a feeling of kinship. Here the man sat watching them go by, year after year, getting younger and further away from him.

Now was the time for Daniel to put his ID back in his wallet and turn around and walk out the door. Now, suddenly, he didn't want to go. He wanted to stay here with this nice man who liked Sophia. He wanted Claude to go back to trying to remember the name of the flower.

Daniel felt as though he was in a game of warmer-colder. This building wasn't so hot as he had hoped—it didn't contain Sophia anymore—but it was a lot warmer than it would be once he got outside, where the trail would be purely cold again.

He put his ID back in his wallet and his wallet back in his pocket, but he didn't turn to go. "What kinds of things is your memory good for?" he asked, trying to sound conversational and lighthearted.

Claude shrugged. He seemed happy to have company. "Faces. And names."

THREE BEERS MADE Daniel feel optimistic. Maybe she was staying in Charlottesville for the summer. Maybe she got a job here and moved off campus for a few months. Maybe she was waiting tables or wearing one of those Genius T-shirts, working at the Apple store. Maybe she would walk into this very bar if he sat here long enough.

"Another one," he said to the bartender, raising his glass. It took him several more tries to get the guy's attention. The bartender was enough in demand that he'd suddenly gone deaf and lost his peripheral vision at the same time.

"Thanks," he said when his fourth Bass ale finally arrived, knowing the futility of his maybes. He knew that he could have five or ten or fifty Bass ales and she wouldn't walk in here. She wasn't from the kind of family where you rented an apartment and pretended to earn money. She was from the kind of family where you moved home and actually earned money. He'd seen two kids from their high school already, one passing on the sidewalk and another spilling her breasts onto the table in the corner, and they were depressingly not her. None of this was remotely her anymore, and the more he drank, the farther away she seemed.

It was for the better, probably. What good did he bring her? But he just wanted to see her. That would satisfy him. That's all he'd come for.

He regretted wearing his best shirt, and looking at himself in the mirror that morning with so much pleasure and hope. What was he thinking? He wished he had a different shirt to change into. New bar smells and his new sweat and the perfume emitted by that girl over in the corner would get into the fabric and overwhelm the precious bit of her left in it. He hated that thought.

The guy sitting to his right had a double chin and soccer cleats and was getting drunk at a faster rate than he. There was something familiar and unappealing about him, which Daniel wasn't tempted to pursue.

The fifth Bass arrived around the time the girl from the corner table came over and sat on the stool to his left. He forgot that she might remember him until she remembered him.

"You went to Hopewood, didn't you?" she asked.

"For a while." She had very white teeth. People were always having very white teeth these days.

"I remember you. You were——" She had a bursting look, like the vodka was trying to do the talking and she was trying to stop it. "Never mind," she said mischievously.

He kept his eyes steady to the north of her neck. "Okay," he said, though she certainly wanted him to cajole her.

"Do you go here?" she asked. She had been on some kind of squad in high school, he recalled. He could picture her in one of those outfits with the very short pleated skirts, constantly being turned upside down.

"To school here? No. Do you?"

"Yes. Soon to be a junior."

She knew Sophia, no doubt. She started to emit a small glow of Sophia association. He resisted asking.

"Where do you go?"

He took a long swig of beer. "Nowhere. I work." He didn't feel like saying anything true.

This dulled the interest in her eyes a little bit. Or at least shifted it.

"Do you still see any Hopewood people?" she asked.

"No." He took another sip. It was hot in this place. "Do you?"

"Yeah. A lot. Like nine people from our class are here."

He nodded. Her glow intensified a little. He bought her another vodka tonic on the strength of it.

"Can I tell you something?"

He relented. "All right."

"We thought you were dead."

"Oh?"

"Somebody saw you jump off a bridge."

He tried not to wince visibly. It wasn't his best memory. "I guess they were mistaken."

She nodded and sipped her drink. "It's good that you're not dead."

"Hey, thanks."

She leaned over and kissed him just to the side of his mouth. He felt the slight moisture of spit and sweat that she left on his skin.

"So who do you still see?" he asked.

"From our class?" Her bracelets jingled with every gesture.

"Yeah."

He waited through the list until she got to Marnie, Lucy's friend.

"I think I remember her."

"Weird girl. Black-and-blonde hair?"

"She was friends with . . ." He felt stupid pretending to search for the name of the most important person in the world to him.

"Who?" She fixed him with a look that made him feel transparent. "You mean Lucy, right?" Her voice was flat.

Hungry as he was to hear one thing about her—that she was a drug dealer, a cross-dresser, a baton twirler, anything, so long as she was in his world—this was too stupid. He got up. "I have to piss," he muttered. He slapped down a twenty to cover the rest of his tab.

"I bet you don't remember my name, do you?"

He kept moving.

"Wait," she said. She jingled some more as she took hold of his wrist. "What are you doing after this?"

"Leaving. Going back up north."

"Wait, though," she said. "There's a party at the Deke house. Come with me."

His stupid reptilian mind wondered if Sophia might be there. "No. I hafta go." He could hear the fifth and sixth beers in his voice. He had to go back to his car and sleep until he wasn't drunk anymore.

"Are you sure? I'll order you another beer, and then you can decide."

He shook his head. If he had another beer, he wouldn't be able to keep his gaze from dipping into her blouse. And if he had another one after that, he would probably go back to her dorm room and roll onto her twin bed with her and take off her clothes with his eyes shut, because it wouldn't be her he was picturing. He'd done it before, and he never felt good about it after. She was probably an economics major or maybe a political-science major, and maybe she made great margaritas and loved her father and could hit a mean forehand and who knew what else, but she was also the kind of girl who got called another girl's name at the important moment.

"It's Ashley," she shouted at his back.

He peed a few beers' worth, and when he came out he noticed his barstool had been taken over by the very drunk guy with the cleats, who was leaning directly into Ashley's cleavage. Her manner had changed.

"What is your *problem*?" he overheard her say as the guy leaned so far over his stool it started to go. The guy was holding on to her with both hands when she shoved him off and his stool teetered and crashed to the ground. Ashley stood and backed away.

"Stupid bitch!" the guy called after her, getting up arduously. "Come here. Bring your tits back here." His words were a slurry of spit and gin.

Daniel strode back to the bar. He stood in front of the man as Ashley collected her stuff. The guy turned to Daniel. "What the fuck is wrong with you?"

Daniel looked at him, losing what little fun there was to his drunkenness. He looked carefully at the man's eyes and brows and shoulders and ears and pieced it together. He came up with a face in a bar not unlike this one. But in the winter in . . . someplace. Cold. St. Louis, it must have been. The face had waxy, smeary red lipstick, like girls used to wear back then. A flowery dress with a pair of terrible falsies creeping up out of the neckline. She'd told him she was a model and showed him her picture. It was an ad for a local car dealership. Oldsmobile, maybe. He remembered a lot of ass and leg, and not much face. She was very proud of that picture. She had heard he was interning at his dad's paper and called him there every day for a month. "I wanna be famous," she told him.

Don't say anything, he counseled himself. "I know you," he said.

"The fuck you do."

"I do. Ida. I definitely do. You haven't changed. You drink too much."

The guy was trying to decide whether to punch him.

"You like posing for pictures. I'm sure you still do. You still like your lingerie and your shoes. Lace and high heels and all. They're hard to find in your size, though, aren't they?"

Now the bartender was eavesdropping, and Ashley had floated back toward them to listen.

Had Ida been less drunk, he could have covered his astonishment and his discomfort better. Daniel didn't feel particularly honored knowing he was right. These were easy things to tell about a person. If you changed gender from one life to the next, it almost always meant you lived in some confusion in the middle. And exhibitionism was the kind of neurotic quirk that dogged a person from life to life.

"The fuck you do," the guy said again, but he had visibly shriveled.

The bar was quiet as Daniel left. He was ashamed of himself. He was disappointed and tired. He used to do that kind of thing. He'd punish people with the secrets and vulnerabilities they didn't understand. But he stopped many lives ago. They would forget the punishment, eventually, but he would carry it with him.

In his last life, when he was seven, he'd met a man in his uncle's office who was tormented by his need to have his healthy leg amputated above the knee. Everyone thought the man was deranged, naturally, including the man himself, and no doctor would perform the surgery. But Daniel remembered him from before, and he understood. Not everything, but just a little bit. He remembered that he'd been a soldier and that he'd lost his leg at the Somme when he was seventeen. Daniel told him everything he remembered. But that wasn't for punishment or retribution. That was mercy.

LUCY WAS ALONE in her dorm room early on a Friday evening
in October when the house phone rang from the lobby.

"Is this Lucy?"

"Yes."

"Hey. It's Alexander."

"Alexander? What are you doing here? Are you downstairs?"

"Yeah. Can I come up?"

"Marnie's not here. She's in Blacksburg until tomorrow."

"Can I come up anyway?"

Lucy glanced up at the clock. She glanced down at her pajamas.
She'd been planning an evening in her bed with Emily Brontë, but
she couldn't exactly turn Marnie's little brother away. "Okay. Give
me a couple minutes to get dressed."

He didn't give her a couple minutes. He was knocking on the
door inside of one minute.

She let him wait. When she opened the door he almost tackled
her in a hug.

"What are you doing here?" she asked him again when she got
loose of him.

"I'm college visiting."

"Really? Are you a senior already?"

"Yes, I'm a senior already." He might have looked hurt if he was capable of it. "I'll be eighteen in January."

"Does Marnie know you are here?"

He shrugged. "I might have mentioned it to her. I'm pretty sure I did."

"Well, that's funny, because she didn't mention it to me, and also she went to Blacksburg."

He shrugged again without looking the least bit rueful. She'd known Alexander since he was a baby, and he was probably the most well-meaning and least conscientious person she knew.

"Can I stay anyway?"

He had an absurdly appealing smile, and he always had.

"Do your parents know you're here?"

"Sure," he said, as committally as he said anything.

She laughed in spite of herself. "Okay, I guess you can stay." She'd barely finished the sentence when he'd thrown his bag on the ground and jumped onto Marnie's bed and lay back on it.

"You grew more," she said.

He nodded. "You stayed the same."

"Your hair grew more." He had wonderfully curly, sandy-colored hair. She and Marnie used to style it when he was little and they could get him to sit still.

He jumped up and went over to Sawmill's terrarium. "You still have that snake?" he asked incredulously.

Lucy sighed. At this rate it was going to live longer than Dana had. "Yeah, you want him?"

Alexander laughed. "Let's go out. Are there any parties? Can we go to a college bar? I brought my fake ID," he said eagerly.

Lucy cast a longing look at *Wuthering Heights*. It was raining out and damply cold, but she felt a big-sisterly obligation to show

Alexander the kind of college experience he'd no doubt been fantasizing about.

TWO PARTIES, one bar, and a pub later, Lucy was tired and very drunk. Alexander loved to dance, so they had danced. She saw how many of the girls watched him, and she found herself appreciating him in a new way. Two and a half years had seemed a bigger difference when she was ten or even sixteen.

Oh my God, what would Marnie say if she knew Lucy was looking at her little brother this way? She hoped he wasn't thinking this was a date or anything. She'd tried to encourage him to dance with other girls, but he hadn't gone for it.

"I'm hungry," Alexander declared, putting his arm around her a little sloppily. He was about a foot taller than she was.

He'd wanted to hold her and grind on the dance floor all night. She was getting used to the feeling of his body, and it didn't feel like such a big deal. There wasn't an awkward bone in him.

"Me, too. You want to get a slice?"

"God, yes!"

They walked in the rain to a place on West Main Street. The bright lights inside made her feel extra drunk. Alexander gallantly whipped out his wallet and paid for three slices of pizza, one for her and two for him. Outside, they sat on the bench and ate as though they were starving. Lucy wasn't cold anymore, but her sweater smelled like a wet dog.

"Do you remember when Marnie and I used to put ponytails and mini-buns all over your hair?"

He laughed. "Do you remember when Dorsey ate your birthday cake?"

"Do you remember when Tyler peed in your Mountain Dew can?"

He nodded. "When he handed it to me the can was warm. That's what made me suspicious." He chewed his pizza. "Do you remember when you babysat for me and made me pancakes with raspberries in them for dinner?"

"Did I do that?"

"You put raspberries in everything."

"No, I mean, did I babysit for you?"

"Marnie was supposed to, but she snuck out with a guy and you covered for her."

"I think I do remember that. Weren't you kind of old for a babysitter?"

"Yeah. I was fourteen. It was because my parents went to some resort for their anniversary."

"They went to the Greenbrier for the weekend. I do remember that."

"Can I confess something to you?" By the look on his face, she wasn't sure she wanted him to. "I climbed up the side of the house and watched you getting into the shower." He looked more pleased with himself than guilty.

"*Alexander.*"

"Sorry." He didn't look sorry.

She felt her face getting warm. "I can't believe you did that."

"It was wrong," he said. "But it was worth it."

She punched him in the stomach.

He was laughing. "It was. I'd do it again."

She tried to punch him again, but he grabbed her arms and started wrestling her. Before she could right herself he was kissing her.

"Alexander, stop," she said, laughing, trying to pull away.

He kissed her more. "Why? I don't want to stop."

"You're Marnie's little brother. I'm too old for you." She didn't really want him to stop, and he seemed to know it.

The rain started to come down harder, and he grabbed her hand. "Let's go back to the room," he said.

Out of the frying pan, she realized as they scurried along back streets to Whyburn House. She had not meant to go this far in realizing his college fantasies. *Don't do this,* she ordered herself. She reminded herself about being big-sisterly.

"It's late, and we're going right to bed. Different beds," she clarified as she turned the key in the door of her room. "Deal?" She looked up at him. Was he smirking?

He left her alone long enough to dry off and go to the bathroom, brush her teeth, and put on a pair of unsexy flannel pajamas. When she got back to the room he was lounging on Marnie's bed in a pair of boxer shorts like he owned the place.

"I'm turning out the light. You stay on that side of the room or you're going to have to sleep in the hallway, got it?" She turned out the light and got under her covers.

"You don't mean it," he said mournfully.

Not at all, she thought. "Yes, I do," she said.

She lay there in the dark. She could barely breathe, let alone fall asleep. She kept seeing the way his torso looked just before she'd flipped off the light. It was as if it was burned into her retinas. He started humming something.

What was her problem? So he was young. So he was Marnie's little brother. What was she waiting for? Here he was, presented to her in all his glory as though on a clamshell, and she was going to try to fall asleep? Daniel was gone. He was never a good excuse, and certainly not anymore. Daniel had always been an idea, a category where nobody else fit. Alexander belonged to a different category. But Alexander's was the category where life actually took place. Alexander was here and his mouth was warm and she wanted him in her bed in a way that didn't seem to involve any ideas at all.

"Hey, Alexander?" she whispered.

His head popped up. "Yeah?"

"Come here."

He arrived in her bed as though shot from a catapult. In a fraction of a second he was under her covers, kissing her, wrapping himself around her.

I can't believe I'm doing this.

"If Marnie ever finds out, I'll kill you," she whispered as he crawled down under the sheet. It was maybe not the most romantic thing to say, but he was undeterred. He nodded against her belly button.

He pulled off her pajamas with one hand, demonstrating the flair of a person who had done it hundreds of times. He probably had done it hundreds of times. He was sexy and charming and uncomplicated. Easily half the girls at Hopewood High School were in love with him, according to Marnie, and he loved them all right back. He'd probably slept with every unmarried girl between the ages of fifteen and thirty in the entire town of Hopewood. And he'd probably done it in a manner so good-natured that nobody thought any worse of him for it. It was a handy thing that he had a condom ready. He probably had them stashed in his pockets and in his shoes and behind his ear, just in case.

She had one other urgent concern as he took off her last sock. *Please,* she thought urgently. *Please don't ever find out this is my first time.*

．　．　．

"YOU HAVE TO GO," she informed Alexander when he woke up in the morning.

"Why do I have to go?" he said groggily. "I think you should get back in bed with me. I like college visiting."

"Because Marnie will be back before noon, and if she sees us, she'll guess what happened."

"No, she won't."

"Oh, yes, she will."

"Lucy," he complained.

"Get dressed, mister." She pointed to his clothes on the floor. "Come back another time. Anyway, when you go college visiting, aren't you supposed to visit classes and meet with the admissions people and stuff?"

He laughed, almost chastened but not quite. "Okay, fine, I'll go." He sat up in bed. "If you come back here for a minute."

"Alexander!"

She did go back there, for more than a minute. Then she marched him down to the lobby and sent him off. He managed to grab a full kiss on the lips before he got into his mother's blue Suburban.

"See you, Lucy," he said cheerfully.

On her way back through the lobby, Claude, the security guard, stopped her with a wink. This was her second year in his dorm, and she knew he wasn't going to let her get away without a comment of some sort.

"New boyfriend?" he asked.

It was pretty obvious Alexander had spent the night. She wasn't sure how brazenly she could lie.

"No."

"No? Good-looking young man."

"That he is."

"I liked the other one, if I may say so."

"What other one?"

"The young gentleman who came looking for you last year."

"Who was that?"

"Big like the one today, but dark hair. Nice face." Claude had a thoughtful look. "Sad face."

Lucy had been eager to run for the elevator and remove all traces of her night of debauchery, but something about the way he said it stopped her.

"That other one was very fond of you, I think," Claude added.

"I can't think of who he could be. Where was I?"

"You and your friend had just moved out for the summer."

"And he asked for me?"

"Yes. He was disappointed not to find you."

She tried to think who it might have been. "Has he been back here?"

"Haven't seen him since. Not on my watch. I've kept my eye out."

"Huh. You don't remember his name by any chance, do you?"

"He didn't introduce himself, I don't believe, but he did hand me his ID." Claude screwed up his face and thought for a minute. "I think his name was Daniel."

OF ALL THE nights in Lucy's life, this was going to be the one when she didn't fall asleep thinking about Daniel. This was the night when her body felt a little sore and a little as if it belonged to somebody else, and when her bed still felt and even smelled faintly foreign. This was the night she had every intention of falling asleep to vivid thoughts of Alexander: his generosity, his expertise, and the many weird and thrilling sensations she'd felt with him.

But as she bunched up her pillow and changed position a hundred times, her thoughts kept creeping down to the lobby and to the young man with the sad face who had come looking for her and who might have been named Daniel. And even on this night of nights, because of good Claude Valbrun and his uncertain memory, she found herself leaving her body behind and falling asleep yet again with the distant idea of Daniel.

*F*or a few hundred years I had been migrating slowly
westward, like the sun. I have an unconfirmed theory
that many of us do this. I'm not sure why, and not every soul lives
enough times to make that trip. Some souls live once. At least
one soul, Ben, has probably completed the entire circle. But if
the East strikes you as ancient and wise and the West foolish and
new, there probably is some basis for it.

I was born near Bucharest, in Montenegro, twice outside of
Leipzig, in the Dordogne. I picked up a number of languages
and skills along the way, as you might imagine. I seem not to dip
too far south or climb very far north. I've been born in Africa
only once, in the east, in what is now Mozambique, and never
have I felt more blessed or forsaken than in that beautiful,
remorseless place. I still dream of the darkness of my hands
sometimes; it's part of who I am. And then there was that one
cold life in Denmark. But otherwise I seem to track along the fat
haunch of the northern hemisphere.

I found Sophia only briefly at the end of a short, crushing
life in Greece. I had traveled to Athens from Montenegro on a
trade mission. I was a statesman and a merchant then, in control
of a large fortune. It was one of a spate of lives in which I amassed
power and money because I could, and because I couldn't think

of anything else to do. It took a half-dozen of those lives for me to recognize the difference between a means and an end.

I was pretty satisfied with myself at that time. I had a fat wife and two beautiful mistresses, one young and one old. I had a castle overlooking Dalmatia and hundreds of artworks I socked away and never looked at. I never forgot about Sophia, but the idea of her had grown dimmer in my mind.

So there I was on a street in Athens in all my finery, surrounded by an entourage of men who gasped at my wit and laughed at my jokes, when I caught sight of her. She was at the end of an alley, dark-skinned and black-eyed and huddled over a hunk of bread. She'd probably stolen it, because as I walked toward her she began to run. I ran after her, leaving my attendants in confusion. I was pretty fat and gouty myself at the time, and it took me several minutes to catch her. When I did she was crying. I reached for her, and she felt as though she was made of sticks and rags.

"It's okay," I told her soothingly in an array of languages until she seemed to understand. "I'm your friend." She was probably six or seven, but she looked much younger because she was starving. She didn't want to come with me, so I sat with her there. I wanted to buy her food and drink and clothing, but I was afraid to leave her, knowing she would disappear if I turned my head.

We sat there for a long time. I talked to her and told her stories about her and me until the sun ended and the moon began. I held her until she fell asleep. Her heart was skipping along so rapidly and her breathing was so quick, I put my hand to her head and realized she was burning with fever. I brought her back to the villa where I stayed and called the finest Arab doctor in the city. When we laid her on a bed we discovered that some grisly accident had befallen her. Her left arm was almost completely severed above her elbow. The wound was badly wrapped and gravely infected. I nursed her and sat with her and watched her die two days later. There was nothing to be done.

I didn't find her for a long time after that. Not for almost five hundred years. I was afraid that her soul had finished. The kind of life she'd suffered would be hard to rally from. You see, while some souls go out with the achievement of wholeness or balance, others end out of pure discouragement. As I've said, it's desire more than anything else that keeps us coming back for more. When your business is finished for better or worse, that is usually the last of you.

In my shameless heart, I've always hoped that Sophia and I would become whole together. I hate that phrase (along with the term "soul mates"), but I can't think of a better way to say it. I've always thought I could erase my sins and make myself a better person through her. I've had the gall to think I could love her better than anyone else could. I've always feared she would find completion without me, and I'd be around, stupid and unperfected, forever.

Finally, I came to England. On the last day of the nineteenth century, I was born in the English countryside, near Nottingham. I was fairly delighted to find myself there. Though the sun never set on the British Empire, I had not been her subject before. My mother took care of her children and her garden. I had three sisters, one of whom had been a very dear uncle to me in France and another who had been my wife, which was awkward.

My father worked in a textile factory, and as a hobby he raced pigeons. He kept a loft behind the house and raised them from stock that had been in his family for more than two centuries.

I wasn't interested in the racing or the hunting but was captivated by the flying and especially the homing capabilities of the birds. I was also fascinated by the prospect of flying men.

Percy Pilcher, the late glider pilot, was an early hero of mine, and when I was nine years old I remember excitedly following the progress of Wilbur and Orville Wright, begging my father to take us to Le Mans for the first public demonstration.

When the Great War began I fantasized about training pigeons to carry messages and medicine across enemy lines, and in fact the British and every side in that war relied on pigeons, but I was young and strong and came from the working class— ideal frontline fodder. I was a loyal subject of the crown and so eager to do my bit I would have enlisted as a powder monkey at sixteen if that's what it took, and probably gotten myself killed at Passchendaele or Verdun. As it was, I had to wait until 1918 to join up as an infantryman, and I didn't manage to confront death until the second battle of the Somme later that year. It feels very recent to me.

There's a lot I could say about that time, but I'll tell you I was both gassed and shot in that battle and left unconscious in the infamous mud, the closest I've come to death without quite dying. When I woke up I found myself blinking in sunshine, light streaming through a massive antique window. At the sight of my stirring—my first sign of life in several days, I was later told—a young woman in a white nurse's cap rushed over to me. I blinked and refocused to see a face hovering over mine of such loveliness and deep familiarity I thought I dreamed her. I would have believed I were in heaven, had I not experienced the actual afterlife (pre-life, inter-life) so many times.

She put her hand on mine, and somehow I thought that

meant she remembered me, too. "Sophia," I gasped blearily, my heart surging in confused ecstasy. "It's me."

Her look was not so much recognition as pity. I was half dead and disoriented but not so disoriented that I couldn't tell. "My name is Constance," she whispered to me. I could feel the tiny bursts of her breath on my skin. "I am glad you woke up."

It was her. It really was. Was she truly glad? I wondered. Was it possible I was familiar to her? Did she have any idea how important she was to me?

"Dr. Burke will be so pleased. We had another boy in your unit wake yesterday, and now you."

I was another boy in hospital, I realized. I was potentially one fewer death. I absorbed her pretty accent and her neat white smock. "Are you a nurse?" I asked her.

"Not a full nurse," she said, both modest and proud. "But training to be."

Her manner was so familiar and so sweet to me. I wanted to tell her so badly, but I didn't want to send her hurrying in another direction before I even really got to look at her.

"Where are we?" I asked. I raised my eyes to the large window and the elegantly coffered ceiling.

"We're at Hastonbury. Kent."

"In England?"

"Yes, in England."

"It looks like a palace," I said, unable to catch much breath.

"It's just a country house," she said. Her eyes darted downward and then back to me. "But it's a hospital now."

I realized I was breathless and my chest ached terribly. Other aches filed up to the surface. I tried to remember what had happened to me. In all the years I'd been involved in war, phosgene and mustard gas were not part of it. As elated as I was to see Sophia, I suddenly feared how she was seeing me. "Am I in one piece?" I asked.

She looked me over. "A bit banged up, but all of your parts seem to be in their proper places," she said. There was a hint of nervy good humor there, I felt almost sure.

"No burns?"

She winced almost imperceptibly. "Some blistering but no serious burns. You're very fortunate in that."

I tried moving my legs. It brought a wash of pain, but they were still under my body and still in my command. I could feel her hand on mine. No numbness or paralysis there. I started to feel hopeful. I had Sophia right there with me, and I wasn't dead or disfigured.

She put her hand on my forehead, and I felt that my skin was slick with sweat. Her tenderness gave me another kind of ache in the chest and the throat. Did she know me at all?

"Come, Constance. Get on with your rotation," said an older woman, probably a full nurse, who was nowhere near as pretty in voice, looks, or manner as Sophia.

Sophia looked up suddenly. "Patient . . ." She looked down at the chart. "D. Weston has woken, ma'am," she said eagerly. "Shall I tell Dr. Burke?"

The nurse didn't appear to find this news as exciting as Sophia did. "I'll tell him," she said, looking at me critically.

"Yes, Nurse Foster," Sophia replied.

I hated for Sophia to take her hand from mine, and I hated it when she walked to the next bed and put it on the forehead of the next boy in my row. My neck hurt too badly to turn it far, but that much I saw. I could hear how she spoke to him and how his spirits rose at the sight of her.

Indeed, I was another smashed-up boy in hospital, and she was the tenderhearted nurse in training who made us think of love and gave us all hope. She didn't know she was Sophia, and she didn't know I was me. But we were in the same place at the same time in our lives, and for that alone I was inexpressibly buoyant and a few hundred years' worth of grateful.

LUCY TOOK A few wrong turns, but ultimately she found it. It had been almost exactly a year since she had been there, and the roses were more abundant. The grass was longer. She knocked on the door to the trailer, but no one answered it. There was no car other than hers in sight.

Lucy couldn't just go home. She'd packed up her stuff and moved out of the dorm two days before. She'd spent the two nights at Marnie's summer apartment on Bolling Avenue, and now the car was packed to take her back to Hopewood for the next three months. This was her only chance. She got back in her hot, overstuffed car and waited. *What am I doing here?* She felt like a stalker.

How the mighty are fallen, she thought to herself. A year ago she hadn't had the remotest confidence in Madame Esme, and now she was staked out in front of her sad-looking trailer that didn't have any wheels, pinning her hopes on what Madame Esme might say.

Lucy leaned her cheek against the window and had almost fallen asleep when she heard a car pulling into the driveway. It was an old rusted red Nissan. It took Lucy a moment to decide that the girl who got out was the same girl who called herself Madame Esme.

Lucy got out of her car and intercepted the girl on her way to her front door.

"Excuse me? Sorry to pounce on you, but——"

The girl turned, and Lucy saw she was wearing a dark blue polo style shirt with the Wal-Mart logo in white thread. Her name tag said hi, her name was Martha.

"I came to see you once before," Lucy continued. "A year ago. You go by Madame Esme, right?"

The girl nodded slowly. She didn't show any obvious sign of remembering Lucy, nor did she look pleased.

"I'm sorry to just show up like this. You did a reading for me. I don't know if you remember. Probably not. You probably do a lot of these. So . . ."

The girl shrugged. Lucy thought the whole Madame Esme getup had been kind of silly, but in retrospect it had also been formidable and strange. Without it, this girl looked terribly young and small. Lucy noticed the bruise on her jaw and wondered about it. She found her hand floating up to her own jaw protectively.

"Listen, I've thought a lot about the things you told me. I was hoping I could ask you a couple of questions. Or if maybe you could do another reading. I brought money."

The girl was shaking her head before Lucy could finish. "Sorry. No."

"But, could you . . ." Lucy's voice was trembling. She didn't know what to do. Her arrival here was a desperate act. She who had disdained, doubted, and mocked Madame Esme had finally capitulated. Esme/Martha here was three parts nutjob, but Lucy needed her. Lucy had dropped to the bottom of sanity's barrel. She hadn't even thought of the further humiliation of getting turned down. Not with fifty bucks in her pocket.

"Could I just ask some questions?" Lucy asked. "You probably don't remember me, but you said a lot of really strange things, and as I said, I've been thinking about them. I didn't understand them at all, but I think—"

The girl was shaking her head again. Lucy realized the girl looked not so much uninterested as uncomfortable. She stared at Lucy carefully as Lucy kept talking.

"Are you not in the business anymore?" Lucy asked.

She shook her head. "It's not that. I just don't want to."

"You don't need the whole outfit and setup and everything, do you? I mean, I don't mind if you don't mind. And if you do need to get set up, I could wait. I could just—"

"You should go," Esme/Martha said in a low voice. She turned and walked to her door.

Lucy's distress was overwhelming. This was the last resort. What did you do when you couldn't even surrender?

"Please," Lucy said. "I'm sorry to ambush you like this. I realize how weird that seems. I don't mean to bother you, but if I could just—could I come back at a better time? I could make an appointment. I should have done that, but I don't have your number." Lucy held up her bag. "I have money," she said again, less confidently.

The girl was standing in her open doorway, looking over her shoulder at Lucy. Lucy saw compassion there but also wariness.

"My name is Lucy, but you called me Sophia. Do you remember me at all?"

"I have to go inside," the girl said.

Lucy couldn't do anything but walk herself to the car and get in it. There was nothing else to do. On one level, Lucy had hoped to find some answers. Short of that, she had hoped to prove to herself that Madame Esme was full of crap, clueless, possibly lucky, and driven by greed. She got less than neither.

She slumped into her car and cast a last hopeless look at the trailer. Esme/Martha was still standing in the doorway. She looked about as happy and comfortable as Lucy felt. Lucy was poised to close the door, but she saw the girl's mouth moving. She leaned out of the car.

"He's not dead."

"I'm sorry?" Lucy asked, astonishment dawning.

"I'm just saying. He's not dead."

Lucy was holding the door so hard her fingers were numb. "You mean Daniel?"

The girl didn't say anything more. She closed the door behind her forcefully.

I lived from one Sophia shift to the next. Breakfast porridge
was a delicacy when she brought it and tasteless slop when it
came from Nurse Foster or Jones or even the young, lumpy
Corinne. When Sophia touched my head or my hands or
administered medicine, I felt my entire body turning inside out.
There was nothing I could or would keep from her; I didn't have
the strength.

Sophia's purview was strictly shoulders up and wrists down.
The older nurses did the earthier duties, the bedpans and the
washing and the changing of dressings. They were rushed and
dismissive, and it frustrated me, honestly, to be at their mercy.
My head was so full of experiences, opinions. I had lived in
ancient cities and sailed across the world and read books on the
first parchment in the library of Pergamum, and I needed a
bedpan. They saw me for what I was: another eighteen-year-old
soldier with a ravaged body.

I wasn't used to being gravely injured. I had wounds and
aches in all my lives that dogged me, like anyone else. But the
serious wounds I died of. Medical science wasn't what it is now.
There wasn't usually a long transition or a lot of fanfare between
life and death, as there is now.

But apart from impatience at my own weakness, I confess that
it interested me. Huge advances were being made in medical

care, and I paid attention. It set the theme for my next few lives.
I have a natural bent for science, but probably the real reason
I turned to medicine is because the care I got in that hospital
came from such beloved hands.

Now that I was awake and no longer had the freshest of
wounds, I was moved to a room upstairs. It was a large chamber
with yellow walls and four other beds. It looked out onto a
garden. I could see a slice of green mixed with autumn red if I sat
up tall in my bed. The windows were large and let in a beautiful
leafy light, even when it rained. Somewhere under the smell of
antiseptic and ammonia, I smelled a faint trace of Sophia and
I held on to it, the thinnest thread of it, through my feverish
dreams.

At nights my fever was worst, but I didn't mind it, because
Sophia sometimes came to sit with me.

"Sophia," I murmured as she held my hand. It was the third
night in my new room.

"Constance," she whispered back.

I looked up at her. "Your eyes are blue now."

"They were always blue."

"No, they were once black."

"Oh?"

"Yes, and equally beautiful."

"That's a relief."

"Your hair was longer last time, and not in those . . . things
you wear."

"Combs?"

"Yes. It was darker, but your eyes were really the same."

"I thought they were black."

"Yes, different color but the same. Same in the important
ways. Same person when you looked into them."

She nodded. My fevers went so high that she humored me in everything.

"I saw you last when you were a very small girl. I think you were six."

"How could that be? You didn't grow up here in Kent, did you?" she asked.

"No, it was in Greece that I saw you."

"I've never been to Greece."

"Yes, you have. You had an awful time." My fever was like a truth serum. I felt tears filling my eyes, but I didn't let them go. "I tried to help you." I had a thought. "Let me see your arm." I closed my eyes and tried to picture it. "Your left arm."

She put it out reluctantly.

"Lift your sleeve. You have a mark there, I am sure. Right there." I pointed to the spot on the sleeve of her sweater.

She looked at me carefully. The patients weren't supposed to be asking her to show more of her skin, and she wasn't supposed to be doing it. But she was curious. She took off her cardigan sweater, nice English green wool, and lifted her cotton sleeve high up on her arm to show me. I was watching her so hard I made her blush.

On the delicate underside of her arm, a little ways below her armpit, was a brown birthmark laid out lengthwise along the curve. I wanted to touch it, but I held back. It is an intimate stretch of a person's skin, rarely out and about, especially for an English girl.

"How did you know?" she asked. "Did you see it before?"

"How could I have seen it before?"

She shrugged. "In Greece."

I laughed as much as my lungs allowed. "Yes. It was worse

then." I felt the tears again. A fever combined with a girl you've loved and haven't seen in five hundred years can just lay you bare.

"What happened?"

I didn't really want to tell her about it. "I hate to think. I don't know. You must have had a negligent mother, if you had one at all."

She was struck by that. "And now?"

"Your mother?"

She looked solemn. "No, the birthmark. Why do I have it now?"

"Well. It's a strange thing. With each birth your body starts out fresh and mostly blank, but then you print yourself on it, over time. You hold on to old experiences: injuries, injustices, and great love affairs, too." I glanced up at her. "And you hold them in your joints and your organs, and wear them on your skin. You carry your past with you even if you don't remember any of it."

"You do." She was giving me that same look of indulgence, but it was less confident.

"We all do."

"Because we live again and again?"

"Most of us."

"Not all of us?" Her face showed more signs of genuinely wanting to know.

"Some live only once. Some a very few times. And some just go on and on and on."

"Why?"

I put my head back on my pillow. "That's hard to explain. I'm not sure I really know."

"And you?"

"I've lived many times."

"And you remember them?"

"Yes. That's where I'm different than most people."

"I'll say. And what about me?" She looked as though she wasn't going to believe the answer but slightly feared it anyway.

"You've also lived many times. But your memory is just average."

"Clearly." She laughed. "Have you known me for all of them?"

"I've tried. But no, not all."

"And why can't I remember?"

"You can, more than you think. Those memories are in there somewhere. You act on them in ways you don't realize. They determine how you respond to people, the things you love and the things you fear. A lot of our irrational behavior would look more rational if you could see it in the context of your whole long life."

It was amazing the things I was willing to say if she was willing to listen, and she was. I touched the hem of her sleeve. "I know enough about you to know you love horses and you probably dream about them. You probably dream of the desert sometimes, and maybe of taking a bath outdoors. Your nightmares are usually about fire. You have problems with your voice and your throat sometimes—that was always your weak spot . . ."

Her face was rapt. "Why?"

"You were strangled a long time ago."

Her alarm was a mix of real and pretend. "By whom?"

"Your husband."

"Awful. Why did I marry him?"

"You didn't have a choice."

"And you knew this man?"

"He was my brother."

"Long dead, I hope."

"Yes, but bearing a grudge through history, I fear."

I could see by her face, she was trying to figure out where to put all of this. "Are you a psychic?" she asked.

I smiled and shook my head. "Although most psychics, if they are any good, do have some memory of old lives. And so do most of the people we consider insane. An asylum is about the densest concentration of people with partial memory you will ever find. They get flashes and visions but usually not in the right order."

She looked at me sympathetically, wondering if that's where I belonged. "And is that what you do?"

"No. I remember everything."

IT WAS A far cry from Madame Esme's trailer with the roses. This was an office in an actual office building off Wisconsin Avenue in Upper Georgetown. There was an actual elevator and a waiting room and framed diplomas on the wall. Lucy doubted Esme had gotten so much as her GED certificate, but this guy had diplomas from Haverford College, Cornell Medical College, Georgetown University Hospital, and a few other places, too.

When Lucy stopped to consider it, it was pretty strange to find herself here. After all of Dana's hideous experiences with psychiatrists, Lucy never thought she would go to one of her own volition. But maybe that's what made this feel different to Lucy. Dana had been committed, strapped down, drugged up, dragged in. She'd never chosen it.

In a way, Lucy had more evidence than ever for her own brand of madness, but turning to face it made her feel less crazy than running away from it. Rational or not, because of Daniel and Madame Esme she was beginning to suspect that these discordant images in her head corresponded to some reality, and she just needed to figure out how. She wanted information. She needed it. She hoped it would make some order out of the disorder that threatened at the edge of her mind. And besides, she didn't know what else to try.

When Dr. Rosen walked in, he looked as serious as his diplomas suggested. She stood up and shook hands, hoping she looked less young and desperate than she felt.

"So I gather from our phone conversation that you are interested in hypnosis," he said, gesturing to the sofa for her to sit down again.

"Yes. I think so."

"It can be helpful in cases of anxiety, as you've described to me, but it really works best in connection with therapy, and in some instances medication." He said these things almost as though he was supposed to.

"I realize that," Lucy said nervously. "But I live two and a half hours from here, and I can only afford one session right now. Can we start with hypnosis and see how it goes?" Lucy had done enough research on the Internet to know that Dr. Rosen had a reputation for being somewhat unorthodox in his use of hypnosis and willingness to work with good candidates.

He studied her. He nodded. "We can give it a go. Some people are more responsive to it than others. We'll see how you do."

He got out a tape recorder from his desk drawer. "Would you like me to record it? Most people want to listen to the session later."

She hadn't thought of that, but it seemed like a good idea. What if she'd had her session with Madame Esme on tape? "Yes, please."

He started by having her lie back and relax. He instructed her to focus on his gold pen until her eyes closed. He talked to her in a soothing voice for quite a while about being relaxed and listening to the sound of her breathing and that kind of thing. Then he said he was going to guide her through an image. He was going to lead her into a house, he explained, and she was going to tell him what she saw there. She felt herself settling into his voice until she felt a deep weariness come over her. The next thing she was aware of was walking down a hallway.

"And tell me what it looks like," Dr. Rosen said in his calm voice.

"The wood creaks under my feet. I don't want to make too much of a noise," Lucy said. She wasn't thinking so much as reporting.

"Why not?"

"I don't want anyone to know I'm going into his room again. I'm always creeping up there."

"Whose room?"

She wasn't sure if she didn't know or didn't want to say, so she kept going. "His room is right ahead of me. It used to be my room."

"But now it's not?"

"No. Because of the war. Now it's a hospital." Lucy was saying these things without really understanding what she meant or why she said them, but the oddness of that did not concern her for some reason.

"Do you want to go into the room?"

"Yes. I want to see him."

"So why don't you go ahead in," he suggested.

"Okay."

"Tell me what you see?"

She felt horribly sad all of a sudden. As though there was a terrible thing that she'd forgotten and now she remembered. She felt a painful swelling in her throat. "Daniel's not there."

"You're upset."

"There are three other soldiers. Not him."

"I'm sorry."

She felt the tears in her eyes and coursing down her cheeks, "Why did I think he would be there?" She was crying too hard to speak for a moment.

"You cared for him."

"I loved him. He didn't want to leave me. He said we'd be

together again. He said he wouldn't ever forget me, no matter what, and I have to try not to forget him. That's why I wrote the note."

"What note did you write?"

"I wrote a note to myself. For later. To make me remember. I hid it in the compartment behind my bookshelf in my old room. That's where his letter is, too."

"His letter to you?"

"Yes."

"In your old room?"

"Yes."

"Where is that room?"

"In our old house. The big house. Not the cottage by the river, where we live now."

She described the landscape around the big house, and the village of Hythe not too far away, and the river and the chicken coops and the old kitchen garden that had become a car park because of the war. She described the old gardens, the magnificent gardens from before.

"Before what?" he asked.

"Before Mother died. She was the one who made the gardens."

"When did your mother die?"

"When I was small, but I remember her."

At some point his slow voice walked her out of the house and back to the office where they were sitting. He talked more about relaxing and breathing. When he told her to open her eyes, she did.

She felt disoriented but not muddled or uncertain. She felt that she had been crying; she felt the residual sadness but not the real emotion. She tried to piece it together.

"Lucy?"

"Yes."

"Do you feel all right?"

"I think so."

"Do you remember what you saw?"

She thought back over it. "I think so. Most of it."

Dr. Rosen looked somewhat taken aback, she realized, as she focused on his face. "You went under quickly and very deeply," he said.

"Did I? Is that not how it normally is?"

He had an equivocal look. "There's not really any normal, I wouldn't say. But you were certainly responsive and . . . perhaps unusually clear about where you were and what you saw."

She nodded.

"Do you know what it meant? Was it based on some experience that was familiar to you?" he asked.

"Not an experience, no. But it felt familiar." She looked down at her fingers. "Would you call it a regression, do you think?"

He looked vaguely uncomfortable. "Could be. That can happen."

"I don't think it's any place I've been in my life. But do you think it could be . . ." She couldn't quite finish her sentence, and he seemed in no big hurry for her to finish it.

He let his breath out. "Lucy, our time is about up. That was a . . . dramatic experience for you, I'm sure. If you are feeling unsettled, you are welcome to sit in my waiting room for as long as you need to."

"I think I'm okay," she said. She thought it over again. It didn't feel as though it had happened to her, but it didn't feel as though it had happened to anyone else, either. Where was the house? Was it a place she could have ever been?

"Do you think any of it was real? Do you think I really left a note for myself? I don't remember anything like that." She felt oddly numb asking the question.

Dr. Rosen looked reluctant to offer any hypothesis. "You can expect that odd and incongruous things will come up in hypnosis. As they do in dreams. These pieces of information can be extremely helpful in terms of self-knowledge. But it's probably not wise to take them too literally. I think the wisest thing is to think of them as metaphor."

Lucy looked at him straight. "It didn't feel like metaphor."

LUCY LISTENED TO the recording of her hypnosis that night in her bedroom on a low volume with her door closed. The thing that struck her first and most powerfully was her voice. As she had pictured herself heading down the hall at the prompting of Dr. Rosen, she had stopped sounding like herself and begun sounding like an English girl. It was almost uncanny. She replayed that part three times, her heart pounding, to make sure she was hearing right, that it really was her speaking. And it was.

In real life, Lucy was terrible at accents. She'd played a Cockney in a school production of *Oliver!* in eighth grade with an accent that slid and scooted all over the map. It was worse than Dick Van Dyke in *Mary Poppins*. But her accent on the tape sounded eerily subtle and consistent. She couldn't have repeated it now at gunpoint.

She listened to her words as though they were someone else talking, but she remembered saying what she said and seeing what she saw. The voice, the images, were part of her but also not part of her. She remembered seeing the house, and as she closed her eyes and listened to the tape now, lying on her bed, she saw it again. The hallway, the door to the bedroom. Her old bedroom, the girl on the tape—she—said it was.

She was no longer under hypnosis. It couldn't last that long, could it? Dr. Rosen said he had brought her out of it. Since she'd left his office and gotten in her car to drive back home, she'd done many normal things and thought many normal thoughts. She'd pumped gas and bought a pack of Skittles. She'd cut a bunch of blue hydrangeas from the backyard and put them in a vase. She'd replenished Sawmill's water and fished another molted skin out of his glass box. She'd helped make and eat an early dinner with her mom. She'd heard her dad come home and helped him put away the Confederate uniform he wore in the living museum at Chancellorsville every year. She certainly hadn't continued speaking like an old-fashioned English girl. Her voice sounded normal again, and she felt, in spite of the strange and slow upheaval taking place in her head, more or less like herself.

But as she closed her eyes and listened to the tape, the things she saw under hypnosis she saw again. She pictured herself opening the bedroom door; she saw the room just as she had before. But in the recording the girl—she—was suddenly buffeted by emotion and stopped seeing clearly. Lucy didn't feel the pain she had felt then, so she tried to get a look around the room.

Keeping her eyes shut, she pictured the faint glow of the yellow walls, the green, leafy cast of the light coming through two high windows. She didn't feel as though she was making it up. She didn't know where the image came from, but she felt as if she was investigating, poking around something that was already contained in her mind in great detail.

There weren't three soldiers in the room. There weren't any, now that she looked. She could hold up a brief and fleeting image of the soldiers in there, but it didn't stay. The picture that stayed was an empty room with a tall, canopied bed, a heavy armoire, a bureau with a cloudy mirror over it, and a row of elegant bookshelves built into the far wall. She had the strange sensation that if she could get over to that shelf, she could see the title of every book on it. But the girl—she—hadn't gotten that far. She'd stood in the doorway, weeping.

Downstairs in her own house a door slammed and startled Lucy. She sat up, eyes open, back in her room, which also happened to have yellow walls. She closed her eyes and opened them again. She felt as though she'd come up through fifty feet of heavy water. Now, back up on the surface and looking down, the image she'd had was blurry and far away. She couldn't really see it anymore.

That night she dreamed of the yellow room—the other yellow room. She saw Daniel in it, which didn't surprise her dream-self in the least. He didn't look the same as the Daniel she'd known in high school, but she knew it was him nonetheless. That was often how it was in dreams. He wanted to tell her something. He had that same agonized expression as on the night of the senior party. He was trying to tell her something, but he couldn't make any noise. He had no air in his lungs. He tried and struggled, and she felt sad for him. And then she realized she knew what he was trying to say.

"Oh, the note!" she said, taking hold of his hands. "I know about that."

I could not believe I was dying. The good Dr. Burke knew it,
and at first I didn't believe him. I was absolutely certain he
was wrong, because fate could not be that cruel, I decided, even
though I had every reason to know that fate is not paying
attention on that scale. But as the days passed it was impossible
not to recognize that my lungs were deteriorating rather than
improving. I had died of tuberculosis before; I knew how it went.
And this time my lungs were already ravaged by gas. I was
perhaps the person in the world least afraid of dying, but this
time I could not stand it.

There had been so many lives I had been happy to leave, even
if painfully. So many times I had been eager to start again, to see
where a new life would lead with the hope that it would lead me
back to Sophia. And now I had her and couldn't stay.

How would I find her again? Fate might eventually drop her
in my lap again, but at what pace? Five hundred years? I couldn't
do it again.

I had the power to bring an end to my life. That was wrong,
maybe, but I did. Why couldn't I live if I wanted to? I should have
been able to. That's what I thought. I wanted to live. I'd never
asked my body for that before. All the stuff I knew, my head
packed so full of things, it should have made some difference. I
could speak Euskara. I could play the fucking harpsichord. That

should have bought me something. But it didn't. My body didn't care.

I knew Sophia could leave me behind. She could disappear for whole centuries, never knowing I even existed. I did the searching and remembering, she did the disappearing and the forgetting. I hated to be the one to leave her. I held on to those seventeen days as hard as I've ever held on to anything.

All I could think to do was love her. That's all a person can do.

SOPHIA MUST HAVE known, too. She had a sorrowful, questioning look in her eyes when she came into my room that evening. As if to say, *You're not really going, are you?*

The two other occupants of my room were gone, one released from his life and the other to a facility close to his family in Sussex. I can't say that I missed them. It gave our meetings, Sophia's and mine, a different feel.

"Can I tell you a secret?" she asked, looking around the room.

"Please."

"This was my bedroom."

I sat back against the pillow. "This was your *bedroom*?" I glanced at the yellow walls, the tall windows with the flowered draperies, the bookshelves along the wall. It was true that it didn't exactly have the feel of a hospital. "How can that be?"

"Before it was requisitioned."

"Really. You lived here?" It was clear from her accent and her manners that she was well born, but I hadn't realized quite how well. I considered this. "So I have been sleeping in your bedroom."

She nodded a little mischievously.

"I like that."

"Do you?"

"Yes. Very much. Where do you live now?"

"In one of the cottages by the river."

"Do you mind it?"

"Not at all. I'd be happy to stay, even after the war."

"But you'll move back here?"

"I suppose we will. If it ever ends."

"You don't want to?"

She shrugged. "It's not cheerful here anymore. It's far too big for just my father and me, and the gardens are all grown over."

The thought of her being born in this grand house made my claims on her seem a bit far-fetched to me. She was probably Lady Constance. She was back to being the magistrate's wife, and I was the barefoot orphan.

Once I knew her relationship to the house, it started to fascinate me. It was an old house and full of old things. Because I was dying, she brought me some clothes from a grandfather or great uncle and discreetly vanished while I struggled to put them on. Because I was dying, she agreed to take me on a walk through the upper floors and pointed out places where famous men and women had slept, sometimes together.

The next afternoon she brought me books from the vast library.

"If you've lived as long as you say, you've probably read all of these."

I studied the spines. "Most of them." I pointed to the Ovid. "I read this in Latin. And the Aristotle in Greek."

"So you read Latin and Greek, do you?" She could tell by my accent and my rank that I was not a product of public school. She had that challenging look, but it had a few parts of affection in it, too.

"How could I not, being around so long?"

"What other languages do you know?"

I shrugged. "A lot of them."

"Which ones?"

"Ask me one and I'll tell you."

"Arabic?"

"Yes."

"Russian?"

"Not the modern way, but yes."

Her nod was dubious but amused. "Right. And German?"

"Of course."

"Japanese?"

"No. Well, a little bit."

"French?"

"Yes."

She shook her head. "Are you being honest with me?"

"Absolutely. Always." My face was more serious than hers.

"It's hard to believe what you say."

I touched the curling ends of her hair, and she let me. I was happy. "Why don't you search your library. Try to find a book in a language I can't read."

She seemed to like the challenge. That night she brought me eight books in eight languages, all of which I read parts of and translated for her. She was able to test me a bit in Latin and Greek, and she knew enough Italian, French, and Spanish to be convinced.

"But these are easy," I protested. "These are all Romance languages. Bring me Hungarian; bring me Aramaic."

The look of teasing was gone from her face. "How do you do this?" she asked in a low voice. "You are beginning to frighten me."

·   ·   ·

OVER THE NEXT several nights she brought me artifacts from the house. Our second challenge after books and languages was musical instruments. Her great-grandfather had been a collector. And I was able to explain the origins of all of them and play most of them. I played an aulos made of bone and a panpipe rubbed with ancient wax, and blew into a buccina of a type I actually played at two points in my military career in Anatolia. They were too old to get a true sound out of, but at least I could demonstrate.

She could only bring the ones she could carry, but one night she led me out of her old bedroom, I dressed in her grandfather's riding breeches, to the harpsichord in the music room to play for her, which I did, and joyfully. My fingers were rusty and did not possess a great deal of talent to begin with, but the girl and the moment and my memory carried me.

Afterward, I wanted to kiss her so badly.

"You are extraordinary," she said. "How do you do it?"

"You wouldn't think I was extraordinary if you knew how many years I'd played. These fingers I have now can't quite keep up with me."

"You say that like you've had other fingers."

"I have. Hundreds. You need to develop the muscles and to have certain physical gifts to play really well."

She looked away, and I was scared I had gone too far with my hundreds of fingers. I came down from my high and realized I was tired and out of breath and felt frustrated by my stupid failing body. How was I ever going to kiss her?

"I honestly don't know how you can be so young and do so many things," she said softly.

"And nearly all of them are quite worthless, aren't they?"

"How can you say that?"

"What good does it do me to play an aulos or a panpipe? They are extinct. You have no idea how much time I wasted on each of those instruments. It doesn't add up to anything anymore."

"It wasn't a waste," she said passionately.

I couldn't help smiling at her warm, pink face. "You're right. They gave me a chance to try to impress you."

She regarded her ten fingers and then looked at me thoughtfully. "Didn't it give you pleasure to learn them?" she asked. "Didn't you like being able to play?"

"It was a long time ago, but yes, I loved being able to play," I answered.

"Then that's the good of them."

OUR THIRD CHALLENGE was nautical instruments. Another of her ancestors had been a collector, so she tried me on those. Not only did I know how to work each of them, but they were tremendously rich in memories. Each one suggested a story to me. Sailing the Cape of Good Hope in a storm, navigating the straits of fire under a providential ceiling of stars. I told her about massive typhoons, terrifying landfalls, pirate invasions, and many drownings, two of which were my own. She loved to hear about sailing in and out of Venice, and I told her about Nestor the dog. She took off her shoes and sat on my bed with her feet tucked under, listening for as long as I could talk. She leaned her head against my knee, and I prayed she wouldn't move it.

She sighed when the last lights blinked off in the hallway and she knew she had to leave. "How did a boy from Nottingham get so terribly clever at telling stories?"

"I am a boy from a lot of places. I'm just telling you things I remember."

She looked at me critically. "I am struggling against believing you. That was no trouble at first, but now it's become difficult." She studied my face carefully. "There is something about you that's not like any person I've met. You have a strange kind of confidence. Like you really are a man who knows the entire world. Or at least believes it."

I laughed, just happy that she let me hold her hand so long. "It's both, I suppose."

"Why aren't you famous? Why aren't the writers writing about you and the photographers taking your picture?"

I felt hurt, and I didn't hide it. "No one knows these things about me. I don't tell anyone. I don't want to be famous. And why would anyone believe me?"

"Because you can do extraordinary things."

"And so can many others."

"Not like you."

I touched the bandages on my ribs. "I want to live my life as serenely as possible. I don't want to be thought of as mad. I don't want to be thrown into the lunatic bin, where the other people with old memories go. I don't tell anyone these things."

"But you told me."

I turned to her. I felt grave, and I couldn't act otherwise. "God, Sophia. You aren't anyone. Haven't you heard anything I've said to you? You might think I'm another pathetic boy in your care, and I am. But you are *everything* to me."

I was sitting up and flushed, and so determined I could

barely feel my lungs or any other part of me. Sophia had dropped my hand, and she looked as though she was going to cry.

"Please try to believe me," I said. "This didn't happen by accident. You have been with me from the very first life. You are my first memory every time, the single thread in all of my lives. It's you who makes me a person."

LUCY SPENT THE majority of her days in solitary speculation. She stood behind the back counter at Healthy Eats, blending fruit smoothies out of mountains of ingredients for a seemingly endless line of customers, but she was so deep in her thoughts that she was essentially alone. The sound of crunching ice in the blender looped in and out of constant wondering. It was the soundtrack to her summer.

She hadn't told Marnie. She'd barely told herself. She was waiting for the right moment.

She wondered about Daniel most often. She didn't know whether to think about him as alive or dead, but she thought about him anyway. Inside her head, he was the one she could talk to.

She felt as though she understood his solitude better. She understood it so well that she felt as though she had caught it from him like a fever. Well, first she'd caught his craziness; the solitude came more slowly. When you knew you were different, when your interior world didn't make sense to anyone, including you, it naturally set you apart. You couldn't keep track of what normal people were supposed to think versus what you actually thought, and the gap between them widened. The simplest interactions were a little more strained, until maybe you gave up on most of them.

I think this might be called "mental illness," she said to herself on a few low occasions. *But maybe I am on to something true,* she would argue to herself. *Maybe a lot of crazy people are on to something true,* her self would argue back.

She'd long ago called it quits on finding a rational explanation. She was searching for the irrational explanation that best fit with all the things she had experienced. Internal consistency was as good as she was hoping for.

Some people thought you could access previous lives through hypnosis. Past-life regression, it was called. Of course, that meant accepting the premise that you *had* past lives, which was big, but she was putting that aside for the moment. She was accepting it in a probationary way, for the sake of conjecture. Conjecture was, after all, her constant companion, her new BFF.

So that would mean the English girl was her, Lucy, in a previous life. That, indeed, was a big one to swallow, but there it was. That would mean the enormous house really existed or had existed somewhere, presumably in England. That would mean she'd once had a mother who'd made gardens and died when she was young. That would mean that there had been a real boy she had loved who had died, whom she had called Daniel, whom she considered in her dreams to be the same person as her Daniel from high school.

That would mean there really was, or had been, a note left for . . . well, for her. That would mean there were these things in the real world and that she could, presumably, find them if they had not been lost or destroyed. It felt like quite a leap to connect these pictures in her mind to real things in the world, but that was what her hypothesis demanded. She wanted to find out. She couldn't let it go until she did. She was going to keep chasing her craziness; she wasn't going to let it chase her. If there was a real place and a house and a note, she was going to try to find them.

Her summer break really was turning out to be a vacation after all—a vacation from sanity. She thought fleetingly of Dana. She hoped she could make a safe trip back at the end of it.

She wanted to know about Sophia, so I told her. Not everything but many things. She listened with so much intensity that it was almost as though she was remembering it herself. That was what I fantasized, anyway, in the hours I had to spend without her.

"So what did we do when we rode into the desert?"

She was partly joking with me, still challenging me to see when I would run out. And she was deigning to believe me a little bit. She had begun, in spite of herself, to believe what I told her about my past. I could tell. But when she asked about herself, when I recollected her role in these adventures, she was still just playing.

"At first we were in a hurry. As I said, I needed to get you away from my beast of a brother as quickly as I possibly could."

"And then?" I loved it when she took off her shoes and got on the bed with me.

"And then we slowed down. The desert was utterly empty. We began to feel safe. You were hungry. You ate most of the food."

"I didn't."

"Oh, you did. Greedy girl."

"Was I five hundred stone?"

I shook my head, seeing her as she was in my mind's eye. "Hardly. You were as slender and beautiful as you are now."

"So I was greedy and ate all the food. And then what?"

"Then I made a fire and set up a very primitive tent and put our blankets under it."

She nodded.

"And then we both realized that the stars were extraordinary, so we moved out from under the tent."

"That sounds nice. And then what?"

"We made tender love with the open sky as our witness." I also loved to see the blush in her cheeks.

"No, we didn't."

I smiled at her. "You're right, we didn't."

"We didn't?" Now she looked disappointed, and I laughed.

"No." Boldly, I touched her cheek. "I wanted to."

"Maybe I did, too. Why didn't we?" She brought her knees up to her chest.

"Because you were married to my brother."

"The one who tried to strangle me."

"Yes. He was murderously jealous, because he thought I was betraying him and taking advantage of you. I didn't want to prove him right."

"He deserved it."

"Yes, he did. But we deserved better."

I could see the emotion in her face. "Do you think so?"

"Yes. The regrets stay with you. They distort you over time. Even if you can't remember them." I touched her feet through her socks. I was hungry to touch every part of her. "And anyway, we'll have our chance."

I DON'T KNOW what happened to Sophia that night, but when she came in the next morning, she was different. She was both solemn and urgent.

"Dr. Burke is wrong about you. You are going to be fine."

I couldn't lie to her.

"You are," she said combatively.

"Tell that to my lungs."

"I think I will." She put her arms around me and pressed her cheek to my chest. She had always seemed concerned about somebody else seeing us, but she didn't seem to care now.

She held me for a long time, and then she looked up at me. "I'm sorry for what you've been through," she said. "I can't stand to think of the pain you've been in. You deserve better."

"It's all right," I said quickly. "I've been through worse." Her eyes were full of sorrow, and I didn't want it for either of us.

"But that doesn't make it hurt any less, does it?"

"Yes, it does," I said forcefully. "Pain is fear, and I'm not afraid. I know I'll have a new body soon enough."

"You say that like your body is a room you can go in and out of." She had her hands on my arms. "But this is you."

I felt frustrated all of a sudden. I pointed to my chest. "This is not me. This body is breaking down, but I am not." I didn't want her look of sympathy. I hated to be weak in front of her. "I promise you. I will be healthy again, and I will find you."

Her expression was tender. She was quiet for a while, and it occurred to me that she looked older than she did the first day I woke up to her. "We deserve better," she said softly.

"We will have better."

"Will we?"

"Yes, we will." I looked at her with absolute seriousness. "I don't mind this. I can wait a little longer if I have to, because I know I will be with you again, and I will be strong again. I will take care of you and make love to you and make you happy."

"You make me happy," she said. She put her arms around

me, and I realized I was crying into her shoulder and I didn't want her to see. My fever was riding so high it was hard not to shiver in her arms.

"One thing, though," she said after a while, and her voice was lighter.

"What?"

"When you find me again, how will I know it's you?"

"I'll tell you."

"But what if I don't believe you? I'm a stubborn chit, you know."

I held her hard. "Yes, you are. But you are not hopeless."

ON THE LAST sunny day of my life, Sophia brought me her father's coat and led me outside. I can remember the effort it took to stay on my feet from one step to the next. We walked just far enough from the house to forget it was a hospital. She wore a bright blue wool hat and a fuzzy red dress that felt like contentment itself between my fingers. She didn't look like a nurse but like a lovely girl without a care on a stroll with her beau in the garden. That's how we pretended it was.

We found a patch of grass in the sunshine and lay down on it. I felt the warmth of the sun and the sweetness of her head on my shoulder, and I put my arms around her. I wished I could crawl into that moment and stay inside it without letting another one pass. In rapt silence we watched a yellow butterfly land on the toe of her boot.

"This was a butterfly garden once," she told me. "The most magnificent thing you have ever seen." She turned to me and smiled. "Well, maybe not the most magnificent thing *you* have ever seen."

I laughed. I loved the sound of her voice. I wanted her to keep talking, and she seemed to know it.

"There were thousands, tens of thousands, of them in all colors. And you should have seen the flowers. I was very small, but I would just lie here and let the butterflies land on every part of me and try not to laugh when they tickled."

"I wish I had seen it," I said, watching the slow flap of the butterfly's wings on her boot.

"My mother made it. She was famous for the gardens she made."

"Was she?"

"Yes. And for being beautiful. And reckless."

"Reckless?"

"She liked fast things. My father said she had jumpy legs, because she couldn't stand still even for a second."

We thought about that for a while. I wanted to be careful.

"And what about the butterflies? What happened to them?"

"They went after she died. My father didn't try to keep up the gardens after she was gone."

My carefulness hadn't helped me. I wished I hadn't asked that question. It cast us out of the shelter of that moment and back into the wash of time. Time was loss, and Sophia had suffered too much of it.

She didn't lift her head, but I felt the sadness of her body pressed against mine, and I was too weak to resist it. It filled me, too.

"I love you," I told her. "More than anything. I always have."

I heard the wetness in her breathing. I lifted my hand to her face and felt her tears.

"I love you," she said.

Those were words I had waited lifetimes to hear, but they gave me a deep ache. I wished she didn't. She had lost too much already. I wished I had died in the muddy valley of the river Somme and not made her lose one more thing.

FOR TWO DAYS I went in and out of feverish sleep. Sophia was there. I saw her when I opened my eyes and felt her when I couldn't. I wondered if she had been fired from her nursely duties, she was with me so constantly. I talked to her, and she talked to me, but I have only the blurriest idea of what we said.

And then I woke up. My body ached, I could barely get air, but my head was clear. Sophia was initially ecstatic when she saw me sitting up with my eyes open. The innocence of her response was both a joy and an agony to me.

But on further examination, she must have known that the color of my skin wasn't right. My breathing wasn't right. Dr. Burke said something to her in a low voice outside my door, and her manner changed when she came back in. Her eyes were full, and her mouth was pressed into a cooperative shape.

"Back again, are you?" I asked her teasingly, talking in a low voice to suppress an upheaval of fluid and coughing. "Haven't you gotten yourself tossed out yet for spending too much time with patient D. Weston?"

"They can't really toss me, can they? They can't spare an extra set of hands. And it's touchy, being that it is my house."

"But tell me the nurses are giving you a respectably hard time at least."

"I think they understand how I feel about D. Weston." She touched my ear tenderly. "All the nurses say you are the most handsome we've got."

I smiled because I didn't have the air to laugh anymore. "Is that what you talk about?"

She sat on my bed quietly for a while. Her face had turned solemn. "I want to go with you," she said.

I put my hands on her waist. "What do you mean, my darling?"

"I want to go where you're going. I'm not scared of dying. I want to stay together and come back together. You said that souls cohere. I want to stay with you."

"Oh, Sophia." I kissed her ribs through her sweater. I pressed my face into her abdomen. "You can't take your own life."

"Why not?"

"Because you're young and beautiful and healthy, and you can't. Anyway, rebirth comes from wanting to live. Suicide is rejection; it's the end. If death is truly what you choose, you might not come back after that."

"But I don't want to reject my life. I don't want to choose death—I want to live. I just want to live my life with you."

I took both her hands, and I looked in her eyes. "You can't possibly know how much I want to live my life with you. For now you have to try to live as fully and happily as you can. You'll become a nurse. Maybe a doctor. You'll fall in love."

"I've fallen in love," she said, and her eyes spilled over.

I kissed her hands. "You'll fall in love again. And maybe you'll have children and you'll grow old and die when it's time. And maybe you'll look back and remember me every so often. And when you come back again, I will be waiting for you. I will find you."

She was shaking her head. "But how? You say that, but how will you find me?"

"I just will. I always do."

"But I won't even know you, will I? I'll treat you like a
stranger. My memory is only average. I'm not even as good as
Nestor the dog." She started to cry, and I held her as close as
I could.

"You don't need to know me. I'll know you."

I felt her wet sobs against my chest. "I won't know me," she said.

IT TURNED OUT it was difficult to locate a young man named Daniel Grey (spelled both Grey and Gray the two times he was listed in the high school yearbook) about whom you thought incessantly but had no information. Lucy tried all the normal Internet searches and found a dizzying number of Daniel Grey/Grays. The only narrowing factor was his age—she didn't know his exact birthday—and that didn't help much. The school had no forwarding address and no record of him, but on the bright side, the morgue had no record of him, either.

She'd pressed Claude, the desk guard from Whyburn House, as hard as she'd dared for information about the mystery man who'd come looking for her, but Claude's initial certainty seemed to disintegrate under questioning. He wasn't truly sure his name was Daniel; it might have been Greg. He wasn't sure if his eyes were green. They might have been brown. "I'd know him if I saw him," he said apologetically.

It turned out, though, that it was easier to locate a young woman without a name who was long dead, based on a psychic, a hypnotist, and the contents of her mind, than a person she had actually known and kissed in high school. Hythe was an actual town in England, and of the handful of manor houses in its vicinity, only one had been used as a hospital during the war. She'd thought at first it was the Second World War, but the family who owned it had not been living there in the years leading up to it. It seemed that much more remote to extend her search back to the First War, but that's what she did.

And that's how she came upon the Honorable Constance Rowe. There was also a Lucinda Rowe, her older sister by four years, but as soon as Lucy saw the name Constance, she knew. Madame Esme had said the name, she was almost certain. Constance was the younger mistress of Hastonbury Hall, daughter of the lord, granddaughter of a viscount. The house was used as a hospital in both wars.

The English obviously loved their great houses, because there was a lot of information to be found on them, including the fact that Hastonbury was extant, though largely uninhabited this century. Lucy spent hours sitting in front of her computer looking at pictures of the house. She stared at the front gate, and she closed her eyes and she knew how the road curved beyond the reach of the photo. It was eerie how she knew the shadow cast by a giant stand of trees to the left and the way the meadow sloped down to the river on the right. How did she know? Maybe she didn't. Maybe she was wrong about them. Maybe it was just her imagination.

She felt as though she were living in *The Matrix*. She'd loved the movie. She and Marnie had watched it five times, but that didn't mean she wanted it to be real.

Every new picture she saw offered unnerving corroboration. She recognized the contours of the library from the arched mullioned windows along the façade, and then she found a picture of the interior to show it. She could point to the dining hall, the music room, the kitchen, from the pictures of the outside of the house. And then she discovered a floor plan with all of them marked, just as she remembered. She could clearly picture the way the staircase rose from the center hall. Eerie as it all was, it was kind of a fantasy to imagine herself belonging to such a world.

Lucy wondered what her father would say to this. He took pride in being a Southerner for seven generations. Forget the reincarnation, the psychic, the hypnotist, and all of that. What would he think of her having been a Brit so recently? It was probably worse than being a Yankee.

The more Lucy discovered about the short, tragic life of Constance Rowe, the less of a fantasy it seemed. In fact, as the days passed, she began to mourn her. Her mother, famous for her gardens and her reckless nature, had died in an automobile accident when Constance was a child (they'd had one of the earliest cars, and her mother had a passion for driving it) and her older brother had died in the war. She had fallen in love with a soldier in her care (for that part Lucy had not yet found corroboration) who died of war wounds and broke her heart. She became a nurse and traveled with a delegation of medics and missionaries to what was then the Belgian Congo. She died of malaria near Leopoldville at the age of twenty-three.

Lucy, manning her blender by day, found herself living inside a strange sorrow. She didn't mourn for herself—it didn't feel like that exactly—but the sadness of Constance covered her like a shroud.

Now her thoughts started to stray in yet another direction. She was sick to her very bones of blending smoothies. She felt as though she would cry if she had to cut one more blade of wheatgrass, but she needed to take on more hours. She needed enough to pay for a plane ticket and a cheap hotel and a rental car, and the pound wasn't in her favor. She needed to make enough money to get herself to England before the summer was over.

Constance was a real person. The house was a real place. Perhaps the letters she'd talked about were also real and waiting for Lucy to find them. Perhaps all the information she needed to find them was in her head.

There was a satisfaction in being right and a terror in finding so much evidence that the world didn't work the way you or most other people thought it did.

THE OLD ROOM, her yellow room, now had three new occupants. Their wounds were serious, and their spirits were low and they needed her attention. They didn't call her Sophia. They didn't speak or read Aramaic. They didn't tell her stories of riding her across the desert on horseback. Constance tried to take care of them anyway.

Daniel's body and his few things, including the shirt she'd given him, had been transported to his parents and sisters near Nottingham. He hadn't wanted to contact them before; she wasn't sure why. Perhaps because he'd known what was going to happen all along.

Constance had sat on the dusty back steps and watched the men load the truck. Daniel wasn't the only one. The little farm outside Nottingham wasn't their only stop. She'd watched them close the back and drive away. She watched it get small and watched the dust rise and then settle. She remembered when this car park was a kitchen garden and she grew cucumbers and tomatoes and lettuces and pumpkins.

He'd left her a letter. She couldn't read it for several days. She'd hidden it in her old hiding place, a compartment built into the wall behind the bookshelf in her yellow room. She felt guilty wishing that the sick, groaning men who were not Daniel would please get out of her room and leave her with her letter and her thoughts.

She tried not to be distracted, but she was. She tried to remember the names and the stories of these young men as though she cared, and she did care, but she couldn't make her mind stay with them. She thought of Daniel, and most obsessively and fearfully, she thought of her future self, who would forget him. *I don't want to forget him. How can I make myself remember?*

"Can you improve an average memory?" she'd asked him tearfully, two days before he died.

"If you want to badly enough," he'd said, "I think you can."

Well, she wanted to badly enough. If wanting was what it took, then she would succeed. But how did you do it? How did you shout to yourself across the years? How did you inscribe a message in your soul, deep enough so it would be sure to travel with you through death and loud enough to be sure to get heard? She wasn't asking to remember entire lives; she just wanted to hold on to this one thing.

I will leave myself clues. I will send myself dreams. I will make myself remember.

She thought of death more than life, and that was wrong in a place like this. Daniel had gone there without her. What was happening to him? Was he frightened? What if he didn't come back this time?

What if he finally stopped remembering? What if this was the death that would make him forget? Maybe in the next life they would pass each other on a sidewalk in Madrid or Dublin or New York City. Maybe they would stop and look at each other and feel some odd yearning, but neither of them would know why. They would want to stop, but they would be embarrassed, and neither would know what to say. They would go their separate ways. Who knew? Maybe that happened every day to people who'd once loved each other. It seemed inexpressibly bleak to have a tragedy you couldn't even recognize.

The idea of writing her own letter occurred to her in a morning dream. It was the kind of dream that was so vivid you kept thinking you were actually doing it. Like when you were cold and kept thinking you were getting another blanket. Or you had to urinate and you kept thinking maybe you'd gotten up to go, but you hadn't.

The letter was half written by the time she opened her eyes. She grabbed paper and pen and wrote without thinking, as though taking dictation. It felt promising, somehow, to have this conduit to her dream-self. Daniel once said that dreams were filled with images and feelings from old lives, and because he remembered the source material, he found his dreams less mysterious than most. Maybe this was a dream she could hold on to.

I don't know who you are, but I pray this letter will have gotten into the right hands. I pray that you will not scorn it for the strange notions it contains and will understand the ardent sincerity with which I have written it. I am Constance Rowe of Hastonbury Hall in Kent, near the village of Hythe. I am two weeks short of my nineteenth birthday. I was once called Sophia, and many other names, too. If this letter has reached its intended reader, then I am you, I believe, your past, an older incarnation of your soul. I know that sounds ridiculous and impossible to believe. I felt the same way. But please try to believe it.

Daniel told me some of the ways this works, living and dying and living again, but I don't understand it at all well. I know there are things about you/me that seem to survive every death. I would suspect that you have a birthmark on your upper-left arm. You probably have problems with your throat. You dream about the desert, and your nightmares are almost always about fire. Maybe you even dream about me and this house. I am hoping that you do.

I encountered Daniel here in the big house. During the war it's been turned into a hospital, though it belongs to my family. He was wounded at the Somme—the second, not the first—and I am a nurse's aide, and I cared for him. He died eleven days ago. I wanted to die with him.

Daniel knew me/you before, over many lives. He remembers everything. I don't know how he'll be when you see him, where he'll be from or what he'll look like, but he will be called Daniel. He will remember you if he finds you, and God, how I hope he will. He will want to call you Sophia and tell you extraordinary stories. You will be irritated, confused, perhaps even frightened at first. Get him to prove himself to you if you must. He's not much for showing off, but he can speak and read an impossible number of languages, and he knows how to work every kind of ancient instrument, whether musical or scientific. His mind is better than a full encyclopedia. He will know things about you: what you dream and how you think, and it will haunt you.

Please believe him. Keep your heart open to him. He can make you happy. He has always loved you, and you once loved him with all your heart.

Constance

LUCY RENTED A car at Heathrow and drove to Hythe, a quaint town with a long, pebbly gray beach on the Channel. There was so much salt and mist in the air that everything felt damp, even her clothes as she lifted them out of her suitcase. She had gotten a tiny room over a restaurant on the High Street. She'd thought it was going to be a pub, but it turned out to be a curry shop. Within a short while she was not only damp but smelled distinctly of curry.

In spite of the immense effort and expense to get herself across the Atlantic, and the weird lies she told her poor gullible parents about her dear friend Constance, the English exchange student, who was *dying* for Lucy to visit, Lucy was still reluctant to make the fifteen-minute drive to Hastonbury. She had the directions. She'd downloaded them and printed them out at home. All of the planning and the strategizing had been one thing, but now that it was time to face the real version of the house she'd been imagining for two and a half months, she was apprehensive. It felt to her as though every fear, every fantasy, every bad dream she'd ever had, would, from this time forward, have the potential to be real. Going to Hastonbury Hall felt like making a deal to live in a different kind of a world, and she didn't know if she could agree to her part of it. If she got really scared, she wanted to be able to put everything back in its place and go home. This, she suspected, was her Rubicon.

She had a cup of Earl Grey and two pieces of cake at a tea shop. She bought Marnie and her mother pairs of socks with ten separate compartments for the toes and the head of a different queen on each of them.

What am I doing here? she asked herself, trudging along the High Street. *I am getting fat and buying dumb novelty socks.* She seriously considered packing up her suitcase and checking out of her curry shop and just going home. She could go back to school and her regular life. She could go to parties and talk with real, living people. She could be pre-professional. She could leave this strange ghost life she had entered at any time. She could banish Daniel and Constance and Madame Esme from her thoughts.

She sat down on a bench and watched small cars go by. Could she really?

She got into her tiny rented car and unfolded the directions with shaking hands. She began the drive she had imagined so many times.

THE GATE AND the park leading up to the house were not exactly as she had pictured them. She realized, as she drove up to the front of the house, that she might actually suffer a different kind of torment on this trip.

She'd come here prepared to blow up the universe as it existed, pumped with adrenaline and ready to do the deed. But what if there was no point? What if the house wasn't especially familiar or resonant at all? What if she didn't find any letter? What if there never was one? What if her connection to the place was nothing special at all? Maybe it had been used as the set of an old movie she'd seen and forgotten. Maybe her knowledge of it could easily be explained. That seemed to her drearily likely as she drove over the silted, sad-looking river. That was no Rubicon. She parked the car and got out.

It looked the way she expected in its broadest outlines, but different in almost every particular. It didn't help that the place was practically falling down. It was hard to imagine the gardens had ever been magnificent. On one side of the house a farm stand stood, and a shop where you could buy postcards and teacups with a picture of the house on them. On the other, she knew, lived an old man. He was Constance's nephew, or something like that.

Lucy walked toward the shop. She knew they offered a tour of the house and grounds for a mere seven pounds, and she had come prepared.

The middle-aged woman running the farm stand was also in charge of the shop, it appeared. "How can I help you?" she called to Lucy, who stood in the door of the deserted shop.

"I'd like a tour of the house, please," Lucy said, walking over.

The woman shook her head. "I'm afraid our tour guide is out today."

"I thought there were tours between ten and three every day," Lucy said. "Should I come back tomorrow?"

The woman cast a long-suffering look at the other side of the house. "You can try. The truth of it is, he comes when he pleases."

Lucy had not anticipated this problem, but it turned out to be a boon. She opened her purse and took a ten-pound note in her hand. "I'm a student from the United States, studying English country houses." She held out the note. "I could just give myself a tour. I don't mind. I promise you I won't drag in mud or touch anything," she said.

The woman hesitated, but not for very long. "That's all right, then," she said, accepting the note. "I suppose there's no harm if you take yourself around. Just stay out of the rooms behind closed doors. And as you say, you mustn't touch anything."

"Of course," Lucy said. "I won't be long."

"Come back this way on your way out, will you, love?"

"Yes, I will."

She pointed. "The tour starts from inside the shop. Just go to the back and through the double doors."

"Thank you," Lucy said with a drumming in her head.

In the front of the shop Lucy noticed that alongside the postcards and gooseberry jam was an impressive-looking monograph on the history of the house and gardens. She ran back out to the farm stand and gave the woman another ten-pound note. "I'd like this, too, please," she said, holding up the book. She clutched it in her sweating hand as she walked back through the shop and into the house.

God, the smell. As Lucy walked into the house, the smell was enough to persuade her she couldn't have known it from a movie or a photograph. It was neither disgusting nor sweet, but old. There was no one identifiable element in it—it was probably a mix of hundreds of things over hundreds of years—but she knew it absolutely. It suggested a feeling, a mood, a strange sort of pain that came from a deep, unused part of her. She stopped and stood still for a while and felt grateful to be alone.

The interior of the house had been reconfigured a bit, she suspected, but she knew the way to the main staircase. She passed familiar rooms. She paused outside the music room. Her eyes trailed over a sort of miniature painted piano. *A harpsichord,* her mind supplied unexpectedly. Had Constance played that?

She knew she should make her way up to the room. She might need to take some time there, and she didn't want the farm-stand lady coming after her. She walked up the stairs, anticipating the give and creak of each step. There were the tapestries, faded by three centuries of sunlight and three centuries of gentle dust. A shaft of light wove feebly through a large window of dirty stained glass. She could imagine standing under it, watching the patches of colored light decorate her arms. Was that a memory?

She turned right at the landing. Now, this hallway was a place that looked exactly as she expected. The depth of the windows set in the thick plaster, the pattern of the floorboards. There were several doors coming off it. Hers was at the end. She recalled, standing in front of it, that she wasn't supposed to open any doors. She turned the knob and felt great relief when the door pushed open. She could see why it wasn't part of the tour. The walls were shabby but still the old yellow. There were a few pieces of furniture from the sixties or seventies, Lucy guessed, stacked up against one wall. There were some old, rusted lawn chairs pushed against another. The shape of the room was handsome and the ceilings were high, but it had been left to dust and spiders. She wondered if it had been used for anything but storage since the Second World War. Under a sheet was the armoire she'd pictured in her mind.

Now she turned to the bookshelves. Filthy sheets of plastic covered most of them. Without thinking too much, she went to the middle of the three units and moved the plastic aside. Just below eye level was a shelf with a couple of baskets and a few books. She slid the books aside. The compartment was behind them, just as she knew it would be. *Shit,* she thought. *Here we go.*

She put the monograph down. Her hands were shaking and black with grime as she turned the flat latch and opened it. She peered in, but there wasn't enough light to see. She was scared to put her hand in. Her fear that she would find the letter was almost perfectly balanced by her fear that she wouldn't. Both were unthinkable at this point.

She realized her throat was full and aching, and that she was barely breathing. She put her hand in. She felt nothing at first and experienced the worst kind of trauma. There was nothing there. Just rough wood and dust. What a waste. What a disappointment.

She put her hand in farther, all the way to the back, and the second trauma began. There was not nothing. There was something. Stuck against the back of the compartment was a piece of paper folded many times. Carefully, Lucy took hold of it and drew it out.

She held it for a moment. She closed her eyes, caught between two sets of perceptions, old and new. Remembering then and doing now. Was this the explanation for déjà vu? She had the sensation of both folding it up to hide it away and unfolding it carefully to discover its secrets. There it was. Yellowed, faded, but perfectly legible, written in a serious hand with little flourish or joy. She glanced to the bottom and saw Constance's signature. It felt momentous but not grand. She could almost feel the pen in Constance's fingers. It was the hand of a sad and determined girl. Whether she guessed it or remembered it she didn't know.

She sat down in the middle of the floor to read it. She wiped her eyes with blackened fingers as she looked at the first words.

She had to steady herself before she went on. She had to find her courage. This was the alternate universe. She was in it now, and she couldn't go back. This was a world where you could remember things that happened to you before you were born. This was a world where you could communicate with yourself long after you died and fall in love with a boy you didn't know again and again.

Please believe him. Keep your heart open to him. He can make you happy. He has always loved you, and you once loved him with all your heart.

CONSTANCE LOOKED OUT at the dim room from inside her fever. It swathed her closer and more comfortingly than the yards of insect netting. She dreamed that it was the same fever that had curled around Daniel and carried him away, and that it could somehow take her to where he was.

She heard her fellow nurses and nuns bustling around her, readying themselves for the day of mending limbs and saving souls, but she would stay where she was. They gave her encouraging looks as they left her. She wished she had as much hope for her life as they did. Sister Petra put a hand to her head and left her a glass of water. They'd tried the regular treatments. There wasn't much you could do at this stage for the kind of malaria she had.

Constance had been in Leopoldville for almost two years. She'd received her nursing certificate six months after the war had ended and left for Africa soon after, part of a delegation that included Nurse Jones and two of the doctors from Hastonbury. Some good souls had an insatiable appetite for healing and fixing, and she liked to count herself as one of them, but she suspected her motives were a bit more complicated. Here, at least until she'd gotten sick, she'd been occupied every moment of the day. There was the noise and bustle of neediness all around her in the hospital, and at night in her dormitory, a good soul sleeping on either side. She'd needed to get away from the multitude of ghosts at

Hastonbury: her mother, her brother, her grieving, deluded father. And of course, Daniel. She didn't think she could stand to stay home and lose any more.

Daniel would be ahead of her by three years, give or take. That wasn't much. It wasn't so bad to think of dying, knowing she wouldn't be far behind him.

She knew she shouldn't think like that. She was just twenty-three. It wasn't the full, happy life Daniel had encouraged. But loneliness had gotten its grip on her, and it wouldn't let go.

In her fever-dreams she often thought forward to the person she would be next. It didn't feel morbid to her but sort of exciting. Where would she turn up, and what would she be like? Would Daniel really be able to find her, as he'd promised? Would he be able to love her? What if she had warts on her nose and gas and bad breath and spat when she talked?

She thought of the note she had written and left in her old bedroom. How would she get herself to find it? How would she get herself to even remember to look? There had to be a way, and she would figure it out. She would not stay quiet inside her new self, whomever she was. She intended to give herself a very hard time.

She often thought of the very beginning. She tried again and again to pinpoint the mysterious thing that had happened in those seventeen days she'd spent with him. When he'd first woken up and called her by the wrong name, she'd pitied him and patronized him, as she'd done with many of the boys. Not out of meanness. But because there were so many of them and their needs were so vast and there was only one of her. She'd thought D. Weston was an exceptionally handsome and particularly addled version of the same, and that was all. He was too sick to be denied her indulgence. She'd listen to any madness that came out of his mouth and nod thoughtfully at the right times. She wished she'd listened more closely, less skeptically, so that she could remember it better now.

Because something happened. The addled things were true things. Too many of them to discount. And the way he said them, the odd way he saw her and knew her, cut to the very center of her. He didn't tell his stories like someone who read about them. His vision of the world was momentous, and it included her. Nothing in her small life could compare after that. In seventeen days her pity had turned into profound regard and overwhelming devotion. He was holding on to her, all of her places and parts, in a way she couldn't do for herself.

"Why do you always call me Sophia?" she asked him once, knowing how tenaciously he hung on to it.

"Because if I don't, I really could lose you," he told her.

SHE'D TRIED TO do what mattered after he died, by taking care of the neediest. For each sick, swollen child Constance sent on her or his way, she knew the child would come back something better. It couldn't be worse. *You, be a duchess,* she'd say to a tiny body. *Turn your nose up at the slightest error in fashion. You, be an MP,* she'd say to another. *Argue and bully the days away, and feed your fat belly on beefsteak and port all the nights.*

She'd done her best here, but some big part of the real, living, forward-leaning part of her died when Daniel did. She'd sensed it at the time, and she knew it now. Maybe the malaria sensed it, too.

She hoped that God, or whoever it was who ruled these matters, wouldn't punish her too grievously for it. *Please forgive me for not trying harder. It's not that I don't love life; I do. It's just that this one is too lonely.*

HOPEWOOD, VIRGINIA, 2007

SHE HADN'T BEEN back to high school since the disastrous
night of the Senior Ball, and she thought she might never go back
at all. But at seven in the evening, the day before Lucy was set to
go back up to Charlottesville to begin her last year of college, that's
where she went.

She went in a side door. There were maintenance people staying
late to get the school ready for the start of a new year. She'd seen
the mowers buzzing across the playing fields, two men painting
fresh white lines on the football field. In the halls they were fixing
mistreated lockers, scrubbing graffiti from the painted cinder-
block walls. *They should make the students do that stuff,* she found
herself thinking.

She watched it all with half her mind, watching herself watch
it, watching herself watching herself watch it, unsure of how to
think about the simplest things.

These days she took her body from place to place. She'd traveled
back from England, packed up her room at home. She'd retrieved
Sawmill from the thirteen-year-old neighbor who'd taken care of
him in her absence. (She'd begged the thirteen-year-old to adopt
him permanently, but the thirteen-year-old's mother said no.)
She'd shopped for school supplies. She'd even bought herself two
new shirts at Old Navy. She'd stood in the fitting room, staring at

herself in the mirror and not being able to tell who she was. She went around with a broken heart, and she wasn't sure who'd broken it. She thought it was herself, mostly.

She walked past her senior locker, remembering the pictures and notes she had pinned to the inside of it. She remembered the little pink-edged mirror in which she'd watched for Daniel in the hallway, sneaking longer looks in reflection than she would dare straight on. She could almost see him with his slouchy jeans hanging off his butt like every single other boy in the school. He was odd and far away, but he wanted to fit in. She could picture the shoes he always wore, tan suede Wallabees that looked like they'd been made in 1972 and came untied easily. She wondered things now that she hadn't thought of then. Who washed his jeans? Who cooked his dinner? Who gave him shit when he bombed a test? She thought maybe no one. But somebody had to have done it once.

She went into the chemistry room. She shut the door behind her and sank into a desk chair. She put her hands over her eyes. She was afraid the ghosts would come for her here, and when they didn't, she found herself wishing they would.

She didn't know what to do. She wanted to find Daniel. Beyond that, she didn't know what else to want or how to live. She hadn't set foot in a pottery studio in more than a year. She let her old garden go to weeds and blight; not even the raspberries were coming this year. She'd always had a drive to grow things and make things with her hands, but she didn't know how to make herself want it anymore. She wasn't sure how to care about her future. She was an adult; in nine months she'd graduate from college. She was supposed to be putting her life together right now, and all she could seem to do was throw grenades at it. How was she supposed to move on from him?

She remembered a dream she once had, where she was standing between two compartments on a train. It was dark, roaring along a curving track, and she kept trying to get into the compartment in front of her. She pounded on the door and kicked it and screamed at it, but it stayed locked. At last she gave up and went back to the compartment behind her, and discovered that it was locked, too.

She had wronged Daniel that night. She felt bad for it. What if she had just listened? It wouldn't have been that hard. She could have challenged him, argued with him, even asked him a question. That was probably what Constance had done. Lucy could have said, *Man, you kiss like an angel, but why are you calling me Sophia?* She hadn't given him a chance to explain himself, let alone prove anything. She had just raced away from him like a quivering hysteric.

Maybe because they got everything in the wrong order. They were practically devouring each other before they could introduce themselves. No *Where do you come from?* or *Do you have any brothers or sisters?* It seemed natural to get right into his arms at the time. It seemed necessary. She was hungry for him, and she now understood a little better why. She couldn't keep her hands off him, actually. Maybe that was not a good thing.

It was too intense. It was too much for her. The visions that invaded her mind made her think she was going crazy, and that was always her worst fear. She didn't want to end up like Dana. She'd always held on to her mind as tight as she could.

Maybe she feared a mind invasion because that's exactly what Constance was trying to do. It made sense now why Lucy was prone to out-of-place memories and dark dreams, why she was so susceptible in the hands of a psychic or hypnotist. Her consciousness was full of holes, and Constance was the one who'd poked them. Constance was dying to press her message through. She buried her treasure in plain sight and begged Lucy to find it.

Sometimes Lucy wondered about the other letter, the one Daniel had written Constance before he died. It wasn't in the compartment by the time Lucy got there. Maybe Constance had taken it with her to Africa. That's what Lucy would have done. But really there was no way to know what happened to it, and it frustrated Lucy to think of what little she knew, what few tiny scraps she had to hold on to.

Lucy was both frustrated at Constance for haunting her and sorry to Constance for having screwed it up. After all Constance had tried to do, the universe had finally blessed her with a moment alone with Daniel, and Lucy had let him go. *He can make you happy.* That's what Constance's letter said. You couldn't be too mad at her for wanting that.

Lucy was sorry to Daniel. She wished she could look him in the face and tell him she was sorry. If there was an hour she could cut from her life to redo, it would be that one. And though this new universe allowed for many extraordinary things, it did not allow for that.

You knew you loved him, though. That was offered by a small voice in Lucy's head, and it stopped her short. She wasn't sure if it made her feel better or worse. She had loved him. In a stupid, infantile, crushing way. But still. She had been onto something, hadn't she? She had known he was important to her. She was wildly attracted to him. She would have traded every object she owned for a word from him. She had wanted him, no matter how badly she'd bungled it.

If only she could be with him now. *This can't be the end of the story,* she thought desperately.

But either he was drowned in the Appomattox and it was her fault or he was alive and he'd given up on her. If he were alive, as Esme/Martha insisted, he could find her if he wanted to, couldn't he? She'd left out plenty of feelers. There was her listed phone number, her forwarding information at this school, her information in the university online directory, her parents' house, not to mention Facebook and a few other networking sites. *He doesn't want to find you,* she told herself. He may or may not have made a small stab at it once, but there was no evidence he'd really tried.

She thought of Marnie's old mantra: If he liked you, you would know it. The words gave her a funny nostalgia. He had liked her. Or at least he'd been pretty eager to kiss her. Or at least he'd liked her insofar as he thought she was Sophia. She paused in her thoughts. Did that mean Marnie was right or Lucy was?

That was another thing she wondered. Who was Sophia? When was Sophia? Was Sophia much longer ago than Constance? How much longer ago? She held her upper arm. There was a scar there, as Constance had predicted, but it was from a fishing hook; she hadn't been born with it. Was there any of Sophia left? How much did a soul really account for? Was there any part of Sophia still lingering in her memory and on her person? Probably nothing at all. Probably Daniel's devotion was the only thing she had left, and now she'd lost that, too. Once he figured out he loved a girl who no longer existed, he'd finally withdrawn it.

Daniel must have loved Sophia to have held on that long. It must have been painful for him to realize she was gone, replaced by a coward.

Lucy got up from the desk and wandered slowly back out the side door of the school. The sun was setting garishly by this time, creating a look of fire and oblivion in the direction of her house as she walked toward it. It was a walk she'd taken about a thousand times, but it didn't look the same anymore.

It was the letter. It was just an old piece of paper folded up in her purse, but it was powerful enough to break apart the world as she'd known it and consume her mind, sleeping and waking. But it didn't help her know what to do. It didn't create a new world in its place. It left her to wander around the rubble of the old one.

*W*hen I was a child growing up in the thirties in a suburb of St. Louis I built a pigeon loft on the flat roof of our garage.

I bought eggs from a breeder with old stock and raised them with enormous care. I designed training flights that were meant to be challenging, but my birds always got home before I did. I guess it was as close to fathering as I've gotten so far and probably will ever get.

I've always loved birds. I collected feathers from rare or beautiful species starting in an early life, and I still have most of them. Someday I'll turn them over to a natural history museum, maybe. Most of those birds are not just rare now but extinct, in some cases for hundreds of years.

I was always captivated by flight and aviation, and I had a child's worship for the Wright brothers. I was a child in England at the time of their first public flights. Later I realized that Wilbur had been around for centuries and Orville was brand-new, which always makes for the richest partnerships. (Think of Lennon and McCartney. Try to guess who is the old one.)

In this same life I went on an airplane for the first time, a Curtiss JN-4, "Jenny," just like the biplanes I watched overhead in the First World War. My father took me to a barnstorming show when I was eight and bought me a ticket to ride. I remember climbing up from the airfield, gazing down in a trance as the field became a small patch in a broad quilt and my father a small figure in the crowd. For the first time I swore I could see the curve of the earth. It was one of the moments when I felt the deepest respect for humankind. There have been a few moments like that. And many times I've felt the opposite.

My father also took me to the Lambert–St. Louis Flying Field to watch Charles Lindbergh return from Chicago with a cargo of airmail, one of the very first. I took flying lessons later in that life but hadn't yet gotten certified by the time I died.

When I think of that life, the thing I always picture is sitting among my birds at dusk every night, listening to the sounds of the neighborhood below, fathers coming home from work and kids riding their bikes and the voices on the wireless rising from living-room windows, satisfied to watch the world taking place below me.

I set up regular messenger routes for the pigeons to and from school. I once sent a note to a pretty girl in my English class that way, and another time sent in my history homework when I'd stayed home sick. Most of the times when I should have been paying attention to my lessons I gazed out the window and thought of the skies while my pigeons gathered on the sill.

One time I gave a pigeon named Snappy to my cousin in Milwaukee when the family came visiting at Christmastime. Snappy drove the seven hours in the car to Milwaukee and made her way back to my house in time for New Year's. I couldn't believe it when I saw her walking toward me across the front lawn. My cousin was disappointed, but I couldn't give Snappy away after that.

One night I was feeling lonely and wistful, and I wrote a letter to Sophia and attached it to the carrying capsule on Snappy's leg.

I sent her off expecting to see her back by dinnertime, but she didn't come. I waited for a week, and another. When a month had passed, I was miserable. I'd sacrificed Snappy to my hopeless errand, and I felt awful about it.

Years went by, and in lonely moments I sometimes imagined Snappy flying over oceans and continents, mountains, forests, and villages. I dreamed her eyes were mine. I pictured her in Kent, in London, flying across the Channel in the effort to deliver her letter. I pictured her perched on a rooftop of Hastonbury Hall, waiting for Sophia to come home. Sometimes I even fantasized that Snappy had found her and succeeded where I had not.

I kept track of time by the length of Snappy's absence and Sophia's advancing age. The day I graduated from high school, Snappy had been gone two years and three months, and Sophia was forty years old. On the first day of my residency Snappy had been gone eleven years and one month, and Sophia was just short of forty-nine.

When Snappy had been gone thirteen years and two weeks, and Sophia was fifty-one, I visited my father, who was ill, at our old house. I went up to the roof of the garage and sat by the old loft as the sun went down. I looked down and saw a grizzled pigeon walking up the driveway. With a familiar gesture, she spread her wings and rose to stand beside me on the top of the loft, where there hadn't been pigeons for years. I saw that she still had my old letter curled up in the capsule attached to her leg. She couldn't find Sophia, but at least she could find her way home.

*J*n the year 1968 I was forty-nine years old, almost as old as
I've ever been. I remember approaching this sort of
desolate-looking playground at an army base—Fort Stewart,
I think it was—in Hinesville, Georgia. The sky was gray, and the
equipment was sparse and rusted. I scanned the place, not sure
what to expect. There was one little girl swinging on a swing,
pumping her legs very determinedly, as though she had just
learned how. I looked at my watch, waiting for Ben to show up,
knowing I had a long drive ahead of me that night. I waited and
watched the little girl swing. She stopped pumping and slowly let
the swing fall still. She twisted the chains in her hands and
kicked her feet in the dirt.

"Hi, Daniel," she said. She waved in that open-handed way
kids have.

I walked over. "Ben?" I said, surprised.

"No, Laura," she said. She looked to be about six or seven.
"Did you get my letter?"

"I did. I didn't realize how young you were."

She nodded. "I wrote in my best writing."

"How did you find me?"

She shrugged. She kicked up some more dirt so her white
shoes and pink ankle socks were filthy. Even when I was a child
I carried much of my adult practicality. I didn't expect she would

tell me. I never knew how Ben found me, but it seemed he always could if he wanted to.

"Do you live here now?" I asked.

She nodded, pulling at one of the wooden buttons on her coat. "First in Texas and then in Germany and then here."

"An army brat, huh?"

She gave me a reproachful look. "I don't think that's nice."

I knew my old friend Ben was in there, along with many others, but it was difficult to see past this little girl. I smiled. "It's just an expression. I didn't mean you are a brat. You know that."

She shrugged again. Her nose was running, and she wiped at it impatiently without bothering with a tissue. Her knuckles and fingers were fat and imprecise, and I found myself staring at them in some wonder.

I never lived in my bodies like that. I always imposed myself on them. I named myself, and I tried to become the same man. I took on the same hobbies and tried to establish the same mode of life. I kept many of the same objects from life to life. I even wore my bodies the same way, same gait, same hair, same gestures, or as near to the same as I could.

"You are a hoarder," Ben said to me once. "You hate to let go."

"I am shipping out next week," I told her. "I'm not sure I'll be back here for a while."

"Where are you going?" she asked, starting to swing a little again.

"To Vietnam."

"Why are you doing that?"

"They need surgeons. I need a war zone," I said with a little too much lightness. I didn't believe in the war, but I believed I could save some lives and make some people more comfortable by being there. I hadn't managed to get myself killed in the civil rights movement, though I got arrested a couple of times. That would have been a death that meant something.

"Why do you need a war zone?"

I studied her eyes to see if I could find Ben in there. It wasn't easy. I don't think I could have recognized him if I didn't know. "Sophia is getting old," I said with a candor I would use only around Ben. "She must be about seventy. I haven't found her since the First World War. She disappeared. She must have gotten married and changed her name. I ran into a servant from Hastonbury Hall in the old days. He thought she had moved to Africa." I zipped my jacket against the cold. "It's getting time to start again."

She looked uncomfortable. She pulled at her button again. She got off the swing and walked over to the monkey bars. "I don't think you can be in charge of that kind of thing," she said as she climbed.

I felt frustrated suddenly. Ben was the only person in the world who could understand. I wasn't willing to give that up, no matter what body he was living in. "Ben, I know you understand," I said.

"I am not Ben." She shook her head as she launched herself onto the bars.

"I'm sorry," I said. "It's easier for me to hold on to the old names. I don't know how you do without it. I haven't been anything but Daniel for a long time."

She listened to me carefully. "But my name is Laura," she said. She climbed up to the top of the bars and perched there.

"Laura," I repeated, trying to be cooperative.

"You try to control things too much and you'll get to be like your old brother and you won't even die or get born anymore." She turned away as she said it.

I came closer to hear her better. "What do you mean?"

"You'll just take bodies that already have a soul in them, so you can be when you want and who you want, and that is just wrong." When she turned her face back, I could see there were tears in her eyes.

I was aghast. I was silent for a moment. "Is that what he does?" I asked.

She nodded with so much seriousness that I realized why I had been summoned. This was something she needed me to know.

"How does he do it?"

"He kills them first," she said simply.

I had never heard of that. I had never thought of that. I didn't know it could be done. "How do you know?"

This was a pointless question to ask her. The longer I knew Ben, the more extraordinary he became. He had recognition, precognition, and everything in between. He seemed to contain the omniverse, with or without the structure of time. And his knowledge wasn't limited to his experience in the world, as far as I could tell. Once I read a poem about a man with an imagination so great it became the story of the world, and it made me think of Ben. But you couldn't ask him how he knew things.

"Are you sure?" I asked, also pointlessly. "Maybe you are wrong."

She fixed her large, feeling eyes on me. "I wish I was wrong."

She'd said that before—when she was Ben. Then, as now, I wanted her to be wrong and had little hope of it.

"I haven't seen him in a long time," I said. "Not for six, seven hundred years. Even then he didn't recognize me."

"'Cause he can't see." She twisted around on the bars. "He can remember, and he can steal bodies, but he can't see inside."

"What do you mean? He can't recognize a soul?"

She shook her head. "If he could, he would have found you already."

For a while I watched her swing on the bars. She wanted to show me how she could swing all the way across like Tarzan the Ape Man, and she made me pay attention and not look at my watch or glance at the road behind me through all her tries until she finally got it.

As it got dark I walked with her toward her house.

"I have candy," she said. She pulled out a packet of Chiclets and unrolled the top. "You can have one." She pulled out exactly one tiny green Chiclet and held it out to me. Her hands were so sticky and snotty that I didn't want to eat it, but I took it anyway. "It's actually gum," she said with satisfaction.

I nodded. She reached up for my hand and held it as we rounded a corner.

"I live there," she said, pointing to a small one-story house identical to all the others on the street.

"Okay," I said. I watched her in pure wonder. How did she carry the story of the world, with all its troubles and pains, in her small head and still manage to act like a little girl? I didn't understand how she could be so much like an ordinary child.

She looked up at me, knowing my mind, as she always did. "I like to be ordinary, because that makes it easier for my mom," she said. I watched her tuck her Chiclet packet carefully into her pocket and run home.

DANIEL HAD BEEN able to find her latest and last housing placement online. In a couple of months her life would become unpredictable again. She would graduate, presumably. He didn't know what she would do next, and he wasn't in a position to ask her. It was almost sad, the joy it gave him to see her name in the little letters on his bright screen. It was absurd the amount of pleasure he had in copying her name and address on a piece of paper in his most careful handwriting. Not even her real name, just the one she had for now. It meant she was alive in the same world as him. She was where he expected her to be. She was safe.

It was sad in a different way from the anxiety and despondency he felt when he lost her again.

His life had become contemptibly simple, he sometimes felt. He was happy when she was on his grid, troubled when she fell off it. And she did fall off it—for hundreds of years at a time. Knowing where she was in the world, even if he never touched her, gave him a deep satisfaction, and he half despised himself for being satisfied with so little.

I could see her, he told himself. *I know where she is. I could find her easily if I wanted to.*

It was a wan reassurance. It was an aspect of himself he distrusted. Part of the danger of living so long, knowing you were going to come back and back again, was putting off your life until

MY NAME IS *Memory*   211

you never lived it at all. Just so it was possible. Just so long as you *could*, you never actually did. Just so you didn't ruin it.

That's why he drove by her house in Hopewood three different times over the past summer but didn't stop or knock on the door. That's why he sat on a bench outside her dorm last November, freezing his ass off for hours, but didn't call out to her when he saw her rush by. That's why at night before he fell asleep he checked her Facebook wall for a picture or any update to her status but didn't disclose that it was he who was her friend.

And though the piece of paper made him happy, it was not actually enough. He carried it with him for a week and a half before he got into his car and made the drive back down to Charlottesville.

He took a day off from work. He wore a fedora he'd kept from the nineteen forties. He wore a pair of sunglasses he'd picked up at a Target two days before. It seemed important to be invisible, but he realized he was more like a caricature of someone wanting to be invisible. He wondered if in fact he wanted to be noticed. If not by her, maybe by someone who might know her and say to her maybe that night or tomorrow: "Remember that weird guy from high school? Daniel something? I saw him on campus earlier."

What would she think about that? *Would* she think about that?

He waited for her on a bench on a path not far from her dorm. Judging from the map, it was the one she would use to get to most of her classes, and she had to pass by eventually. He held the newspaper and read not a word of it. He would have made a horrible detective, he decided.

The first dozen or so people to pass each triggered a jolt of possibility. After the first hour he had to calm down. If for no other reason than because his body had released all of the adrenaline it had.

Two hours later he'd begun to disbelieve in her very existence.

It was kind of remarkable, after all the millions of hours he'd lived, that two of them could seem so long. When she finally came, he almost missed her. She wasn't the way he expected. She wasn't with a chattering group of friends as she often was in high school. She was alone. Her head was down and her focus so inward he almost didn't recognize her as he watched her pass and walk away from him. It was her walk, linked in subtle ways to her earlier walks, and yet it was slower and less mindful of the world around her. The hem had fallen on the back of her dark red corduroy jacket. The lining drooped down, and little threads dangled. It made him sad to look at it.

He got up and walked after her at a reasonable distance. Her light, slippery hair was wound up in a rubber band. The part of her hair, in this life and before a line of certainty, now zagged here and there across her head. Her bag drooped off her shoulder. Somebody threw a ball across her path, and though he startled, she barely noticed it.

He waited outside Bryan Hall until her class was done and then followed her on a beautiful winding route through the gardens, past the rotunda, to the library. He followed her up to the second floor and tried to keep his distance as she made her way into one of the quiet study rooms, blocked by a glass partition. He could follow her there without her seeing him. And though he was tempted by that, some part of him held back. Her remoteness made it harder to barge in on her. The word rang a little in his head. "Remote" was the word people often used about him.

He passed rooms of students staring at computers. It was a lovely, crisp sky outside, about the best kind of weather that Charlottesville offered, and yet the windows were shaded and all these able-bodied young people, the flowers of the species, were hunched over their screens. For some reason his mind flashed to the olive groves in Crete during the harvest festival, a pulsing mass of young and beautiful bodies. He thought of the thrum of testosterone on the decks of ships returning to Venice, the number of babies conceived and diseases traded those first nights home. He remembered the campus of Washington University in St. Louis in the late nineteen forties and all the parties and blankets draped over the lawns on sunny days in September. He might have thought this generation was just more studious than those, but a quick survey around the room showed most screens devoted to Facebook and YouTube and various bloggy news sites. *You ought to get out more,* he felt like telling them.

He found a table off to the side where he could see her. She didn't open her bag and take out her books but sat hugging it on her lap, staring out through the glass. It didn't look as though she was staring at anything.

Evening came down around them as he gazed at her and she gazed at nothing. Her face was lovely to him in its sadness. He wished he knew what made her look that way. He wished he had any faith that his interruption could be a boon to her. He took the tentative steps of empathy. He could see they led a long way off, but he couldn't see exactly where.

He wanted to see her, and he wanted to be near her. He didn't want to lose track of her for a moment. But he had a deep insecurity about interacting with her. He wasn't good at it anymore. What could he offer her? A long and happy life? He'd never had a long life, so that seemed unlikely. Often he'd found ways to cut off lives prematurely, but even when he hadn't, he didn't last very long. And happiness? He'd had a little, mostly with her. He wasn't good at that, either. He could take happiness from her, but could he give any?

And what about children? They were a natural and sizable

ingredient in a long and happy life, and he wasn't any good at that, either. It's not that he wasn't good at sex—he was more than capable, maybe even good at it, though he hadn't had much practice recently. But he had been around for well over a thousand years, gotten to sexual maturity most of those times and had sex when he could, almost entirely in the era before birth control. He'd never understood why it didn't ever result in a baby.

Some people seemed to do it effortlessly and often. Think of all the times a guy got in the back of a car with a girl whose last name he didn't know, and suddenly, presto, he was a father again. Were those men worthy in some way he wasn't?

He used to tell himself he'd probably fathered a few kids and just didn't know about it. But he didn't really believe that anymore. Somehow he knew it wasn't true. He'd had too many chances where if it had happened, he would have known. It wasn't simply something he hadn't done. It was something he couldn't do. And he didn't know why.

Early on he figured he would eventually happen into a body with a couple of good working balls that made lively sperm. And by now he knew that he almost certainly had. The balls weren't the problem. It was him. It was some unaccountable impact he made on his body every time.

Maybe it was because of the Memory. What if it was inheritable in some way? Maybe God recognized his error and couldn't quite fix it but had taken measures to make sure not to repeat it, either.

He stood up and went to the glass that separated him from her. He put his hand against it, and then his forehead. If she looked up now, she would see him. She would probably recognize him. If she looked up now, he would go to her. If she didn't look up, he would leave her alone.

Don't look up.

Please look up.

He remembered the last night he saw her, at that hideous party. He remembered it with a feeling of shame, as always. He had caused her only distress then. Could he offer anything better now?

He watched her for as long as she sat there, until the windows were dark, but she didn't look up. He didn't go to her. He stood there with his own complexities.

He had thought a lot about her safety, but he had forgotten to think about her happiness.

FAIRFAX, VIRGINIA, 1972

*J*did manage to die a natural death in the battle of Khe Sanh in the spring of 1968. I was killed by artillery fire near the end of that bitter siege, just before Operation Pegasus reached the base in April.

I was next born into a family of teachers in Tuscaloosa, Alabama. We lived in a house near a large pond where the geese came for the winter. My grandparents, my mother's parents, lived right down the road.

In 1972, when I was four years old, we moved to Fairfax, Virginia. My father became superintendent of schools. I remember being sad to leave the geese and my grandparents, my grandfather Joseph especially, who loved airplanes as much as I did.

I shared a bedroom with two brothers, and I had the luck of being the eldest that time, so I got to set the tone for how much and how hard we beat each other up. One of them I had served with in the Great War, and the other was a fresh new soul. He was so hyperactive as to be a blur at the dinner table, but he was remarkably inventive, especially when it came to firecrackers.

My mother had been my first-grade teacher in my life immediately before, and I had loved her for her story voice and her juice and cookies. She read science-fiction novels and grew prizewinning dahlias, and she was a wonderful mother, one of

my very best. When she scratched my back or told us stories at
night, that's what I thought: *You are one of my very best.*

A sort of miraculous thing happened a few months after we
moved to Virginia. We were sitting in church, all five of us. I
remember my youngest brother was still a baby. I was staring at my
small loafers, which dangled about a foot and a half off the floor.
I paged through the prayer book and read some of the parts in
Latin. This is typically the juncture in my lives where I start to
remember and process my old lives at a rapid clip. I didn't
remember about knowing Latin until we started at that church,
because our old prayer books in Alabama didn't have the Latin.

There was a big space on the pew next to me, and on the
other side of that space was an older woman, about fifty, and an
even older woman on the other side of her. I thought by the way
they sat together that it was her mother. I looked at her carefully.
She had gray hair and a dark blue dress with a little belt. She had
stockings and practical, round-toed brown shoes. She was a bit
square-looking, and I remember being drawn by the web of veins
on the back of her hand, how they were blue and how much they
stuck out. I wanted to touch one, to feel if it was soft or not.
I moved a little closer to her.

My baby brother, Raymond, started making screeching
sounds, and the lady turned her head. I expected her to get the
frustrated look that people with gray hair in church often got
when babies started crying, but she didn't. Her face was pink and
not frustrated.

And suddenly I realized I knew her. I was only just getting to
the age of recognizing people from older lives, but I had already
started a couple of years before having my dreams about Sophia.

It felt as though there was an explosion going on inside my
head in very slow motion. She turned back to the front of the

church, and I desperately wanted to see her for longer. My
mother hustled to the end of our row with Raymond in her arms
and went out the back of the church to let Raymond do his
yelling outside with the cars and the birds. I slid closer to the
lady. I was practically in her armpit by the time she looked at me.

I remember my four-year-old astonishment. It was Sophia.
Her eyes were watery and sad, and her skin was loose and speckly,
but it was her. I thought of her when I had last seen her, when she
was Constance. She was so young and pretty then, and now she
wasn't, but I knew she was the same. Amid the astonishment was
also confusion, and it took me a few minutes to figure out what
was wrong. Thinking back to myself a few years before when I was
a grown-up doctor, before I died, I remembered expecting that
either she would be very old and still be Constance or she would
be very young—like me or even younger—and somebody new.
I didn't think she was supposed to be a person in the middle who
I was pretty sure wasn't Constance.

Are you still Constance? I wondered doubtfully. It was actually
easier for me to identify that she was Sophia than to ascertain if
she was still being Constance or not, but I was pretty sure she
wasn't. So I tried to figure out how it happened. As good as my
memory is, it is hard to make great use of it amid the disorder of
a surprised four-year-old mind.

When you are four it's easy to forget where your body is and is
supposed to be. As I was determinedly calculating, I had slid
myself against her. When I realized how much of myself I had
pressed into her, I looked up and saw she was still looking at me.
If I was confused, so was she. If I was calculating, so was she. At
the time I thought it was maybe because she knew me in some
way, but I think it more likely she was just confused to have an
unknown four-year-old worming his way into her armpit.

She was confused, but she accepted my presence. She put her arm around me. I realized my father was craning his neck toward us, looking confused as well. I saw her nod to him as if to say it was fine.

She squeezed me, and I felt myself relaxing into her. She put her hand over my round stomach.

I felt some disappointment. I was certainly aware of it. But because of my physical joy to be near her, I experienced it in an almost dutiful manner, for the sake of my previous older self and my future older self. That was something that always started early with me—a wordless feeling of loyalty to my old selves. Sophia was supposed to be young like me this time and not old and big, and I needed to figure out why.

"I guess you must have died young last time," I told her in her rib.

Of course there was disappointment. But I was four and she was holding me, and when you are four, the pleasure of the body is hard to puncture with the displeasure of the mind.

I touched the vein on her hand, which was indeed so soft it disappeared under my fingertip.

WE WENT TO the church in Fairfax for another year or so. I would find Sophia and scurry to sit with her every time. My parents called her my special friend and once invited her over for lemonade after church, and she said thank you but no, she had to take her mother home.

Eventually Molly, my mother, got tired of what she said were the sexist sermons at that church. She found a hippie church in Arlington where the priest sang his sermons accompanied by an acoustic guitar. I recall there were a lot of songs from *Godspell*.

I actually preferred the new service, but I was miserable not to see Sophia. I think my father was frankly relieved. He thought my attachment to her was weird. When I made a fuss about finding out her telephone number and calling her, I did not get much adult assistance. I called her Sophia, but when it came to looking up her number in the fat phone book, I realized I didn't know her actual name.

I took the bus to the old church when I was nine, but she wasn't there. I did it every Sunday for two months, but she didn't go there anymore. I didn't see her again until 1985, when I was seventeen.

My maternal grandfather, Joseph, from our old street in Alabama, was dying. Molly, my mother, decided to put him in hospice close to where we lived. She'd already lost her mother suddenly to a heart attack, and she wanted to be able to take care of him. I went with her to see him. I wasn't as much moved by my feelings toward him as by my mother's feelings toward him. Her grief was thick all over the house. I remember thinking to myself, *It's all right. It's not that big a deal. You'll get another one.* And yet somehow, even though it was the kind of thing I told myself all the time, it didn't seem exactly right. As long as I had been around, as much as I carried with me, I wanted to think I knew better than Molly, but I really didn't. I didn't know anything about love compared to Molly.

I kept thinking about Laura in the playground in Georgia, being ordinary for her mother. I was struck by it in a sad way, and I wasn't even sure why. I hadn't thought much about playing a role in anybody else's life. I was so eager to play myself every time; the others were just rotating through the bit parts. Because they forgot and I remembered. That's what I figured. They would be lost soon enough, and I would keep going. The best I could do was hold on to them after they forgot themselves.

Not that I didn't do my duty; I did. I made sure my mothers, all but the few who left me or died before I grew up, had food and basic comforts. I made sure they were looked after when they were sick or old. The money I stockpiled I used for them more than anyone. But I didn't think too much harder than that. In a life like mine, you get a lot of mothers, and you lose a lot, too. You don't so much appreciate the getting, but you mind the losing. After the first few losses I learned how to weather them better. *One mother out of many* was what I always told myself.

But I saw in my mother's grief how she loved her father. She didn't love him because he was her father, she loved *him*. She loved the kindnesses he had done her, the times they spent together. There was nothing abstract in the way she loved him or any of us. *You can get a new one,* is what I thought, but I guess in a deeper way, I knew she couldn't.

THE SECOND TIME I visited hospice, I inadvertently peered into a room a few doors down from Joseph's and saw a deteriorated lady propped up in a bed. I walked about twenty more steps before I realized I knew her. I retraced my steps and looked at her from the doorway. It was Sophia. Never had I seen her like this. She was the same as she was in our old church but older and sick. After I'd said good-bye to my grandfather, I went back to her room.

I sat with her for a while. I held her hand. She opened her eyes and looked at me. They were rheumy. I knew they were Constance's eyes and Sophia's eyes, but I resisted seeing them that way. Some part of me was staring down a big grief, and I didn't know what to do about it. I had the strangest sensation of lifting up and away, until everything on the ground got smaller and smaller and I could see the big patterns instead of the small, troubling pieces.

You won't be like this for long. You'll be young and strong again soon, I was saying to her over and over in my head. It wasn't for her sake but for mine.

I visited her twice more and sat with her and talked to her about all kinds of things. I think I might have done all the talking, but I also think she was happy to have me. An irritable orderly told me she asked every day, several times, if I was coming back. She had no children or grandchildren, he told me. I was about the only one who came.

One of the days she seemed more alert, and she kept looking at me in an odd way.

"Do you remember me?" I asked her.

She looked at me carefully. "I remember there was someone with your name."

"Do you?"

"From a long time ago."

"Someone you knew?"

"Not really knew, no. I was waiting for him. My mother said I was foolish, and I was."

"What do you mean?"

"I was a girl in Kansas City, before my father died and we moved east. We had a nice time then. Lots of parties and plans. I was a romantic soul, but my mother said I enjoyed my imagination more than any of the real boys. And that was a disappointment to her."

I could see, now, the loneliness that wasn't just from being old, and the reality of her began to sink in. All those years when I was trying to find Constance, picturing her getting old across an ocean, she was growing up like me, a couple of hundred miles away. I thought of Snappy the pigeon. I couldn't find her because she was dead.

I hadn't understood the full tragedy. I was a teenager, as selfish as a two-year-old, and there's no getting around that. I had always wished she would come back with me, and she had. At least she had tried. I was waiting for her and she was close by, waiting for me. In her way, she remembered.

Sophia's old eyes were watching me, and I hid my face from her. She didn't even know all we'd lost. "He was waiting for you, too," I said. I had disappointed her.

"I was always foolish," she said.

I stayed there as long as I could, my thoughts churning. I stayed until they kicked me out, sometime after ten that night.

I came back the next morning, and I told her about the old things. I held her hand for hours, and I told her about our ride through the desert. I told her about the Great War and her being a lady of Hastonbury Hall and how it had been turned into a hospital and she had taken care of me there. I called her Sophia and told her I loved her. I always had. She was asleep by then, but I needed her to know. I was scared I would lose her for good this time.

BY THE END of the third visit, I knew what I was going to do.

"Don't worry," I told her. "I'm coming, too. We'll come back together." That's what she'd wanted to do before, when she was

Constance, but I'd said no. This time we'd do it. This time it was her life that was spent and mine that was young and promising. I was the one who could see to the other side. That made it easier.

"This is going to be our chance," I said to her.

I was sorry to give up such a life. I was especially sorry for it because of my mother, Molly. She would lose her father and her son in one short stretch, and I knew—or at least I would have known if I let myself think about it—that it would be devastating to her. But I had a strategy for weathering the losses, and it didn't involve a lot of thinking.

I wished I could tell Molly that it was what I wanted, and that I would come back soon. I wished I could make her know it was all right. But another voice inside my head had a different idea. *She loves you,* it said. *She doesn't want to lose you, and it's not all right.*

I knew in my heart it was so, but I managed to ignore it. I was young and stupid, and in a big hurry to get to Sophia again. How else could I have done it? It's amazing the things we take for granted.

There was a big part of me that resisted Molly's love. I even had the effrontery to think I succeeded in it. It was hard enough to cling to one person from life to life. It was hard enough to have one person you loved forget you every time. Maybe Ben was capable of holding on to the love of an infinite number of people, but I could barely hold on to one.

I went to an infamous corner in D.C. on a winter night before my eighteenth birthday. I don't think of that night very often, but I confess I do think about what happened the night before. It was the first time in a very long time I thought enough about a mother's feelings to try to say good-bye to her. I won't attempt to describe the things she said or the way I felt. As Whitman wrote, they scorn the best I can do to relate them.

I'm not very good at living meaningful lives, but I try to make my deaths meaningful, when I can. I try to use them to benefit some person or cause in some small way, but that time I was too young and in too much of a hurry to think of a way to do it—other than scaring the shit out of a few drug addicts.

I went to this place near D Street, I think it was, near the 9:30 Club, where I used to go to hear music sometimes. I found my way to a room off an alley where the addicts went. Not the happy pot smokers but the serious users. I brought enough cash to make an impression. I found my druggie Virgil, a desperate woman in her thirties with an arm that told the tale. I promised I'd buy for her if she found me the best, strongest stuff. She had the idea it was habitual with me, and I didn't correct her. It was her needle, her excitement, her fingers tying the band around my arm.

That was the only time I ever took heroin, and it will be my last. I guess dying of it is no way to start. Maybe I angered fate by doing it. It wasn't suicide, but it was about the closest I've gotten. It was cheating, a way to avoid it on a technicality. I'd hoped my sheer fervency to reunite with Sophia would get me back fast, and thankfully it did. It wasn't death I wanted. That much was clear to me in my dying moment. I wanted life very badly.

But when nature offers you one of her true gifts, there's a special punishment for those who throw it away. I did come back again, but if you believe in these things, it probably explains the mother I was dealt in my subsequent life.

TYSONS CORNER MALL, VIRGINIA, 2001

The next mother I was born to was an addict. I was apparently an addict myself as a newborn. It seemed fitting. She was probably a newer version of some desperate character I had known in an earlier life, but I was too young to place her by the time she took off, which was when I was about three. I was found alone in the apartment by a neighbor. I think I'd been on my own for a couple of days, and I remember being very scared. When you are three it's harder to see the big picture.

I was held by the state for about a month before I was put into foster care. I remember meeting with the social worker the day before my placement. "So when am I going to meet my mom?" I remember asking.

I was put with a foster family near Shepherdstown, West Virginia. They had two regular kids and two other foster kids. They watched a lot of TV in that house. Both parents smoked constantly. I can't separate those days from the smell and the smolder of two lit cigarettes, and it gives me a sick feeling when I think of it.

I don't remember a dinner when we sat around the table. I don't remember a meal without the TV on. One of the foster kids, Trevor, was violent and prone to running away, so I was left mostly alone unless I got in the way during one of the severe storms, which I did a few times and paid a steep price for it.

It was strange living two such different childhoods back-to-back like that. My love for my old family and the pain of missing them was bound up close, and that was almost harder to take than the new people. With the new people at least, I didn't have to love anybody or be obligated to them. They weren't kind enough to require anything from me, and their unkindness I tried to leave unanswered. I was free of affection, living in my own world and doing things myself. I don't think I caused anybody too much trouble. I remember getting a look at my file later, during one of my periodic meetings with the social worker when I was about fifteen. "Attachment disorder" it said in big, sharp print at the top.

Sometimes I used to lie in bed at night and listen to some sports event on the radio pretty loud, though I could still hear the parents fight. I would think about Molly and my old family from before and wonder what they were doing at that moment. Sometimes when I missed them worst I thought, *What have I done?* But then when I got a little older and I didn't need a mother quite as badly, I started to think about Sophia again. It was the thought of her that kept me moving forward.

I was awkward in that body because it grew faster and bigger than my other bodies. I was not fast or especially coordinated, as I had been in my previous body, but I was strong, at least. The foster dad was no more than five and a half feet tall, and my size didn't make him like me any more.

I spent my time carving animals out of wood and reading books at the library and thinking about how I was going to find Sophia. I kept most of the animals hidden, but the foster mother once saw me putting the finishing touches on a goose. She looked it over carefully. "I'd say that's good enough to put in a museum," she told me, not like that was necessarily a good thing.

We went to a pretty dismal public school, but I had a few good teachers. I was obviously a capable student, so some good-hearted educator got it into his head that I was "gifted." They had me sit in a classroom by myself while everyone else was at recess and take one of those standardized tests where you fill in the bubbles with a pencil. I remember leaving every other question blank.

I had learned long ago that it was a dicey prospect to stand out very far. There was that one disastrous time in the early forties when my parents had my IQ tested. That was lesson enough. Needless to say, you've got to have a large and unusual mental capacity to remember a thousand years of largely insignificant history.

As soon as I got old enough I started to look for Sophia. I had some information to work with this time. I knew she must have died in late 1985 or early 1986, and I had seen her and talked to her in hospice close enough to her death to feel hopeful I had left a few influential ideas in her mind. I felt confident, almost by intuition, that she would come back somewhere nearby. She'd done it once before; I prayed she'd do it again.

My great stroke of luck came one afternoon at a mall in Tysons Corner when I was fifteen. I saw the girl, now called Marnie, at one of those nearly extinct photo booths just inside the entrance. It took me a couple of minutes to place her. Of course I didn't know her as Marnie at the time. I recognized her from the church in Fairfax in the early nineteen seventies. Her peaked eyebrows were what helped me out. She had the kind of eyes that gave you shit and wanted to trust you at the same time. She had been the old woman sitting with Sophia, Sophia's mother. She must have lived as long as her daughter. They had been close, I could see, and something about their way of relating gave me a strong conviction that they would come back close together.

You shouldn't try to control these things, I remembered Ben saying, as I followed Marnie from Tysons Corner. I followed her to the lobby of a building with a lot of doctors' and dentists' offices, where she met up with her mother and went down into a parking garage. I saw them get into a car together and drive off. I got the license plate number, and that's how I found my way to Hopewood, Virginia.

The first time I saw Sophia in her newest form was the following Saturday. That was a day worth remembering. I was nervous on the bus ride down there. You never know what you are going to find or if you'll find anyone at all. I went to Marnie's address in the morning and walked nervously up and down the block, not sure what my next move should be. And then I saw her. She was walking along the sidewalk toward me. It was pretty stunning. I can't really describe the way I felt. It was a lush spring day, and the sun was washing off her loose, light-colored hair as she bounced along the pretty sidewalk. She was wearing cutoff shorts and flip-flops and a green T-shirt. She was so young and so fresh-looking, after last seeing her old and dying in hospice. Her legs were long and strong and suntanned and skinny like a girl's.

That's a memory from my present life, just like anybody could have, but it's already been cataloged among my very best. When I think of it, I see her walking toward me in slow motion with a soundtrack in the background. The song I always think of is "Here Comes the Sun."

I saw such familiar things about her. The way she tilted her head when she laughed. Her wiry, capable hands. The crook of her elbows, the top of her ear poking through her long hair. She had a dark little freckle to the side of her chin.

I remember the feeling so well. *This is the beginning of something big. This is our time.*

I was kind of shattered in her presence, I realized. As happy as I was to see her, I was scared to talk to her for fear of beginning wrong. I was a stranger again. She'd be harder to approach, more suspicious this time, if anything. She was too pretty to presume upon. The life I was living was almost completely without love, and I was cut off and out of practice. I felt uncertain about being able to make her love me again.

But my hopefulness was the biggest thing. She was young, and so was I. I knew what she looked like; I knew where she lived. She was back on my grid, and she wasn't married to my brother or anyone else. This was the life we could finally, I hoped, spend together if I could just handle it right.

Sophia turned up Marnie's walk as I stood there stupidly. Marnie opened the front door, and I overheard Marnie's voice. "Hey, who's the guy?"

"What guy?"

"Across the street."

By the time she snuck a look back, I had turned and begun to walk the other way.

"I have no idea," Sophia said.

"Too bad," Marnie said. "He was very cute."

My heart soared to have any little thing. I was lucky to be cute, because I think I was pretty ugly in my last couple of lives.

But I knew I would have to be careful. This was the life for which I had sacrificed everything, and I didn't want to blow it. I was so used to getting a clean slate from life to life, a kind of do-over for any major mistakes I made. But inside of this life Sophia's memory would be just as good as mine. There were no do-overs. The whole thing felt fragile to me, and I was full of self-doubt. I didn't want her to think I was a madman or a stalker. Looking back, I wish I'd taken my own advice more to heart.

I visited her two more times in Hopewood over the next two years without getting up the courage to say a word to her. Once I saw her planting black-eyed Susans in her front lawn. Once I saw her and her sister, Dana, in a coffee shop on Coe Street. I remember being struck by the look of her and her sister together, Lucy's sweet eagerness contrasted with Dana's native jumpiness. Dana was familiar to me, probably from an old life but also because she had the ragged look of a deeply agitated soul. I recognized her as the kind that took her agitation from one life to the next, wreaking havoc as she went. I'm sure she tortured the people who loved her, made them worry about where they'd gone wrong, when probably they couldn't have made any difference one way or the other.

I waited until I was seventeen to make my move. I didn't want to cause any big trouble in leaving Shepherdstown. I wasn't worried about the foster family missing me so much as I was worried about causing headaches for my caseworker. I moved to Hopewood, rented myself a tiny apartment over an Indian restaurant, and entered Hopewood High School in Sophia's class.

HOPEWOOD, VIRGINIA, 2008

THE DAY AFTER her graduation from college, Lucy took a bus back to Hopewood carrying two bags, a scraggly philodendron, and Sawmill in his stupid glass terrarium. She'd shipped the rest of her stuff in cardboard boxes. She arrived home with no clear plans for her future beyond blending dreaded smoothies or selling underwear at Victoria's Secret. But then something strange happened. For twelve nights in a row she dreamed of a garden.

The first night she knew it wasn't a garden she had been in, but it was familiar even so, and naturalistic in a way that wasn't like a dream at all. The second night she was there again. She recognized exactly the things she'd seen the night before: the fountain, the little stone wall, the magnificent stands of peonies in pink and fuchsia and white. Most of all she recognized the scent. She wasn't sure she had smelled anything in a dream before, but this smell got into every part of her.

The next night she was joyful to find herself back in the same garden a third time. It was the same place in all its particular beauties, but this time she decided to investigate further. She went through a rustic pergola blazing with red clematis and found a low-walled garden surrounded by blooming pink dogwoods and populated by about a million butterflies beating their wings in slow motion amid daisies, snapdragons, zinnias, and cosmos. The butterflies came in every color, pattern, and size, and stood perched in their strange, stuttering suspension. And then all at once they took flight. They whirled around over her head, and she felt panic at the thought that she had scared them away. But then the flying spiral thickened and slowed until it was all around her and she was the center. She blinked her dream eyes, and all the butterflies went back to their slow-beating perches on the flowers.

The fourth night she investigated even further. By the fifth night she was so excited to begin dreaming that she went to bed at nine o'clock. It was still a little light out. She hadn't gone to bed so early since she'd gotten her tonsils out in sixth grade.

She was happy in the garden, happier than she could remember being since she was very young, long before the troubles started with Dana. She felt a kind of wonder there, which brought to her sleeping mind a deep, mysterious, inexplicable aspect of how it felt to be a child. Each night she lay in her bed waiting to fall asleep, scared she wouldn't go back to the garden, begging her waking self to please go back, and each night she went back. She wished she could swap her days for her nights, her reality for her dreams. Were you allowed to change from one side to the other?

She'd never slept so much in her life. Yet still she yawned through her days at the health-food store and yawned her way through dinner, longing to get back to bed and her garden.

The sixth night she dreamed she crossed a miniature bridge over a narrow stream and explored a new part of the garden. Most of the plants were unfamiliar, coarser and spinier, and the smells were different. It wasn't beautiful in the same way, but the air felt magical to her. Some of the plants were so distinctive she studied them for a long time, and as soon as she woke up, she got out a notebook and sketched them before the memory could fade. The next night she left her sketchbook and a set of colored pencils next to her bed, and when she fell asleep and went back to that part of the garden she studied more of them, seeming to know in her dream that she would be sketching them later. She recorded them as well as she could—smelling them and feeling the texture of their leaves. The next morning she woke early and spent the two hours before work on her drawings.

When she got home from work that evening, she took out her beloved *American Horticultural Society Encyclopedia of Plants and Flowers* and, with a thudding heart, tried to find real plants to match her drawings. It took a while, but she found some unmistakable matches. She discovered all of them came from one section of the book: the medicinal herbs. Feverfew, chickweed, goat's rue, blue cohosh, everlasting. This new part was a medicine garden.

It wasn't until the eighth night that she saw another person in the garden, over by the butterflies. At first she thought it was Dana, and she felt joyful, but she quickly saw that it didn't look like Dana and it clearly wasn't Dana. It was a woman in her twenties, it appeared, who had light gray eyes and freckles and shiny dark hair.

"I know you from somewhere," Lucy said to the woman in her dream.

"Of course you do, darling," the woman replied.

When Lucy woke she lay in bed for a long time, trying to hold the face of the dream woman in her mind. She knew her from somewhere, but she couldn't think of where.

When she got up she went into her closet and found the monograph from the gift shop at Hastonbury. She turned to the chapters on the gardens and stared at the photographs, incredulous. It was no wonder the dreams were so literal. This was Constance's mother's garden. This was the garden she had lived in as a little girl a couple of lifetimes ago. She shut the book again. She didn't want to supplant her dreams quite yet.

She spent the weekend making drawings of the garden in her dream and, when she was satisfied with them, comparing them to real pictures from Hastonbury. Her dream garden was far lovelier and more complete than in the photos in the monograph or the ones she found online, but hers matched them in every particular she could find. But it was the picture in the back of the book that stopped her heart. She'd glanced at it before, but she'd never really looked. Now that she did, she knew exactly who it was. It was the woman she'd dreamed in the garden. Of course it was. It was Constance's mother.

ON THE TWELFTH night the dream changed. The garden started to lose its borders. It extended farther and in new directions. She followed one path and she found herself in her own backyard before the blight that killed her raspberries. In another direction she found herself in Thomas Jefferson's gardens of the Academical Village at school, enclosed by the serpentine walls. She walked a different way and found, to her amazement, her swimming pool with the flowers up to the very edge, just as it existed in her drawings and in her imagination.

By the morning after the twelfth night she knew what she wanted to do. She found the application online and printed it. She spent the day filling it out and included the best of her schematic drawings from her dreams of the Hastonbury gardens and her sketches of the herbs. On a whim, she also included her three favorite drawings of her unbuilt swimming pool.

On the thirteenth day she put it all in a large envelope, brought it to the post office, and mailed it. On the fourteenth day she began to weed her garden.

·   ·   ·

TWO MONTHS LATER, on the night in August before she left home for real and for good, Lucy was packing up her room when she realized something. She couldn't take Dana's snake with her. Sawmill was apparently going to live forever, and she wasn't. Without giving herself too much time to think about it, she picked him out of his box and let him curl around her arm. He looked at her, and she looked at him. "I'm sorry we didn't enjoy each other more," she told him. "You were never my pet of choice."

She walked downstairs, through the kitchen, and out the back door, letting the screen door slap behind her. She walked across the yard and sat down cross-legged on the grass in front of her hydrangea bush. She gave Sawmill a last look in his snake eyes. She'd always thought that snakes represented evil and duplicity, and she'd always figured Dana had gotten him as one more badass parent-punishing act. But as Lucy admired his calm little head, she didn't think that anymore. She thought of his skins over the years, the spent versions of himself he'd left behind as he was constantly reborn. Maybe that was what he meant to Dana.

"Time to be free," she said solemnly. She put her hand down to the ground to see what he would do. He clung to her for a few seconds. But then he reached his head out courageously. He unspooled from her wrist by inches, reaching out and hovering over the unfamiliar earth. At last he dove down to the soil and slithered away inside the grass of her old pleasure dome.

CHARLOTTESVILLE, VIRGINIA, 2009

THE THING LUCY had once wanted to happen more than anything else in the world, that she had given up on ever happening,
did actually happen a little after six o'clock on a Tuesday evening
in January.

She was sitting outside Campbell Hall, the building that housed
the landscape architecture program along with the rest of the
School of Architecture, where she'd spent the previous ten hours in
the studio. Now she sat in a hungry daze, wearing her down coat
and brown wool hat, breathing the cold air and giving herself a
moment of peace before she rejoined the rhythm of the regular
world.

Marnie and her boyfriend, Leo, were making Chinese food for
dinner that night in their tiny apartment by Oakwood Cemetery.
They'd rented the apartment in August. Marnie was working at
Kinko's by day while taking an LSAT prep course and applying to
law schools by night. Lucy had expected to be working full-time as
a barista at the Mudhouse through the fall and early winter. She'd
gotten her application for graduate school in so late, the admissions officer told her she'd have to wait until January to begin the
master's degree program. But a space had opened up, and to Lucy's
exhilaration they had bent the rules and allowed her to start in
September. So she was working only ten hours a week at the Mudhouse and going deeply and calmly into debt to pay for graduate

school. She and Marnie had rented the apartment, just the two of them, but since then Leo had become the unofficial third nonpaying roommate. At least he was a good cook.

"Does it make you lonely now that Marnie has a serious boyfriend?" her mother had asked her a few weeks earlier. Lucy could tell it made her mother lonely. "Not really," she'd said. "I'm busy in the studio."

"You're not still waiting for Daniel, are you?" Marnie had asked her accusingly last Saturday, when Lucy had declined to go to a party with her and Leo.

"No," Lucy said. Marnie thought she was perplexingly celibate, and Lucy didn't correct her. She couldn't admit to Marnie that she'd slept with her brother, Alexander, four times over the past summer.

Lucy wasn't still waiting for Daniel. Not in her conscious mind. She'd made herself accept the fact that he wasn't coming for her this time around. But in her dreams she still longed for him. Her dream-self thought the story of her and Daniel was only paused; it wasn't over. *I can't wait for you forever,* she found herself thinking as she lay in bed most mornings, thinking about her dreams, waiting for her alarm to ring.

And now she was sitting on the bench in the winter dark, considering these things, when a young man walked up to her and said, "Are you Lucy?"

She looked up at him, expecting that she should know him. He was well dressed and clean-shaven, like an old-fashioned jock or a former fraternity boy. "Yes," she said. She didn't know him. He was probably in one of her classes, and she didn't feel like cultivating the association.

"I'm Daniel," he said.

She startled a little at the name, as though it had been lifted from her thoughts. "Do I know you?" she asked. It wasn't probably the most tactful thing, and if she'd thought to be polite, she would have phrased it differently.

His eyes were secretive in some way. "You might not think so, but you do."

She didn't want to play. Usually when she wore her clumpy brown hat pulled down over her face and huddled deep in her coat, she didn't have to. "And how is that?" she asked without curiosity or pleasure. She picked at the lint on her gloves. Maybe he'd been in one of her undergraduate classes. Maybe he was a friend of a friend who'd put him up to this because members of Lucy's circle thought she needed to get out more.

He bent down closer to her, like he was trying to get her to look at him again. "I know I look different now. I know it will be hard to make you believe it, but I am Daniel. The Daniel you used to know."

Now she did look up at him. "What are you talking about?"

"I knew you in high school. I knew you many times before that."

She stood up, both doubtful and beginning to feel electrified. "I don't understand."

"I'm Daniel Grey. From Hopewood."

She could barely keep herself upright. "You're telling me you are Daniel Grey?"

"Different, as you see. But yes, I am."

She stared at him, searching his eyes. "How can you be?"

"Do you want to walk with me?" He started walking, and she followed him. She felt dizzy, as though everything was at the wrong angle. She was shivering and also sweating in her coat. He had a long stride, and she took extra steps to keep up.

"I don't know how much you know about me," he said, looking forward, not at her.

She stared at the side of his face. Was this some kind of weird prank? He couldn't really be her Daniel, could he? It almost felt like her old longing was so fierce it had turned somebody up, whether or not it was the right person.

"I don't think I know anything," she said and immediately realized it wasn't true. "I mean, I might know something." She hurried along. What if it really was him? Maybe it was. She tripped on a curb and splashed her pants with mud and slush. "I know about Constance," she said quickly. "I know about Sophia." She wasn't caring about self-protection right now. She didn't care about whether she sounded sane or not.

"You know a lot, then," he said. His voice was sharper, different than she expected.

She wished she could look him in the eye again. How could it be him? If it wasn't him, why was he doing this? She was open to the idea of people coming back in different bodies, but this didn't make any sense. "I don't understand you," she said. "I don't understand how you could be Daniel. If you died at the bridge three and a half years ago, then you would be a little kid now, wouldn't you?"

In her fantasies of seeing Daniel again, she'd pictured running into his arms, holding him for hours at a time and telling him everything that she had learned and thought since the last time she'd seen him. This wasn't how it went.

"You don't understand, and I can't explain it all to you. There are mysteries no one understands. But when you're like me, you don't need to grow up every time. In rare cases you can . . . take over a body that has been abandoned."

"What does that mean?" She was in a wild and wilder version of the universe, but at least she was in a conversation with someone besides herself. "You can take *over* somebody else? Why would anyone abandon their body?"

"Usually it's not a choice. Sometimes it is. They abandon it when they die."

"But if they die, it's because it doesn't work anymore, isn't it?"

"Yes, usually. But people sometimes . . . How can I put it simply? They get out before they have to. They get scared and drawn away. It's tempting in that moment."

"Why is it tempting?"

"Because usually they are in pain, and it feels better to get out."

Lucy tried to read her own feelings, but beyond the pounding symptoms of shock, she couldn't. "And you take over?"

"The opportunity is extremely brief. And the body has to be salvageable, obviously."

Distantly, she wondered how this conversation might sound to a passerby. They were walking too fast to be overheard for long, and besides, she was too strained, too overwhelmed to really care. But what were these things they were saying? How could she even begin to accept it, and how could she not? Had she given up all expectation that the world would behave in the old way? "But what happens to them? What if they want back in?"

His look was unequivocal, almost demanding. "They don't." Was this a way that Daniel had looked? "I only take what's left," he said. For a moment he covered her gloved hand with his bare one. "And the soul that was there goes on to their next stage, whatever that is."

"Do they come back in a new body?"

He rubbed his cold hands together. "Most likely. Most people do come back."

Some part of her wanted to run away, and she felt disgraced by that part of her. She was so full of doubts; she always ruined everything. After what she'd learned, why couldn't she just try to believe him? The fact that she was having a conversation like this meant it had to be Daniel. Who else knew about these kinds of things? "So you just sort of . . . jumped into this person you are now. There used to be somebody else in there?"

"It's hard to fathom, I know. There is so much about birth and death and everything in between that ordinary people don't know. But you are beginning to grasp that, aren't you?"

She walked into a puddle. She barely felt the cold soak into her socks. "I think so," she said.

He stopped. He held out his hands, and she realized he held them out for hers. She gracelessly shoved her hands in his, and he squeezed them.

"Lucy."

She nodded. She felt the pressure of many tears behind her eyes, though she couldn't explain their nature. It made it harder to look at him.

"I am happy to see you. Are you happy to see me?"

The things she had imagined saying to him all these times, she couldn't say unless she knew it was him, and she still couldn't feel sure.

"It's hard to believe you are Daniel," she said honestly. She tried to look into his eyes, but he was busy pulling off her gloves. "Are you really Daniel?"

"I am really Daniel," he said.

She nodded again. She could believe him or not. If she didn't, and it was him, as it almost had to be, she would have blown her chance yet again. She didn't want to blow it again. "I'm sorry for last time," she said quickly. "I'm sorry I didn't try harder to understand." One or two of the tears made it out.

"I don't blame you for that. No one ever believes it. And it's probably for the best."

"But I wish I had tried."

"Right. I know." He was looking down. "There are things in the past you regret."

His expression was different from how she thought it would be. But then, what did she think it would be? Why did she pretend to herself that she knew him or had reason to expect or think anything? She didn't know him then, and she didn't know him now. Her only relationship, as Marnie had put it, was her relationship with her own imagination. And now she was trying to hold him to that?

"But we have the chance to start again."

She stared at him in some wonder. His words managed to penetrate her fight with herself. The problem was not the difference between this man and the old Daniel. The problem was between Daniel and her imagination. Of course, the actual Daniel was going to be different from the Daniel with whom she had spent so many hours in the privacy of her mind. It took the real thing to show you the size of your delusions. It made her think of when the Dominion power company couldn't get into her basement. They sent estimated bills for eight straight months, and when the guy finally read the meter he told her parents they'd been so far off they owed four thousand dollars.

"If you want to," he added.

They could start again? Could they just do that? Is that what would happen now if she let it?

This was Daniel. It didn't feel like it yet, because she was shallow and bound by her own fantasies, but it was. If she was really going to favor her delusions over the real person, then she should just get a lot of cats and shut herself in right now.

He looked different before, but now that she took a moment to think of it, she looked different, too. In high school, every time she saw him it was in full pose and pucker. She had a constant coating of lip gloss and her cheeks sucked in and her precise jeans and hair all going in one direction. Now she was distracted and absorbed by other things, forgetting to look in the mirror at all. She forgot to make her face for anyone's eyes anymore. She was lucky he didn't run in the other direction.

Her entire life had once ground to a halt because of him. Her sense of the world was blown open because of him. Would she really not take this chance? Her cowardice had kept her from him before, and it would stop her again if she let it. She was older now. She was on her feet. She could handle it now.

"Yes," she said. Another tear got out.

He smiled at her. It was a different smile from the one she expected. And then she wanted to punch herself. No expecting.

"I'm up in D.C. now, working at a marketing firm. I've got to go back for a business thing tonight. I didn't know I'd find you on my first try. If I'd known, I would have left myself all night. But I'll be back this weekend, all right? Can I take you out on Saturday? What's your favorite restaurant here?"

She was a little bit crestfallen that he was leaving already, but she was also frankly relieved. She could torment herself better on her own. "Yes. Okay." She named a place twenty minutes east. "I'll meet you there," she said nervously. She realized she didn't want him coming to her apartment. She wouldn't know how to explain him to Marnie.

"Great." He leaned in and kissed her cheek, catching the very corner of her mouth. He straightened up and strode away, calling good-byes over his shoulder.

She stood still, feeling the kiss sitting unabsorbed on her face. When he was very small and ready to disappear around the bend into a parking lot, she composed her face with the thought that he would turn around another time, but he didn't look back. *Shut up. You don't know anything*, she said to her own disappointment.

She began to walk. Without thinking, she ended up at the serpentine wall, where she climbed up and sat with her knees pressed to her chest and her arms holding her together. It was a hard world to know anymore.

What was wrong with her? Daniel had come. Why was she so weird and prickly feeling? Why didn't she throw her arms around him? *We have the chance to start again*, he'd said. What was her problem? What more had she wanted to hear?

This isn't how I thought it would feel.

Could she not get over the fact that he looked different? Was she really that superficial? It wasn't that he didn't look good; he did. He was plenty handsome in every objective sense. Maybe more so than before.

A stubborn, renegade memory of the fateful night with the old Daniel came to her. It gave an instant stretch and tingle to her abdomen. When he pulled her in that desk chair to face him. When they were knee to knee. When he kissed her. A four-year-old overworn memory had more punch than a fresh kiss sitting on her face.

Because you don't know this new version yet.

I didn't know the old version, either.

The old Daniel was the one Constance loved. And Sophia loved. That had made sense to her before. Why didn't it make sense now?

She put her hand to her mouth. She saw bits of icy lace on her dark glove and looked up to see big, uncoordinated flakes of snow drifting around her. It was a Virginia snow, where the sky didn't look like it really meant it and the flakes were out on their own.

Maybe it was she who had changed. Maybe that was the real problem. She was so much softer then, so much more willing to fall in love, or believe she was. She was colder now, more solitary, and her outlines were scratched in deeper. Maybe she wasn't capable of that kind of connection anymore.

But why not? Because of the things she'd learned from Madame Esme and Dr. Rosen and the falling-down mansion in England? Maybe she'd buried herself with the discovery of the old people she'd been. Maybe she'd lost that old self under the weight of them.

She felt sad, and she put her hands to her eyes. She wondered if it was really her he'd ever wanted.

He was different now, too, and maybe that was good. Not only in how he looked, she realized. For one thing, he called her by her name. He called her Lucy.

KOLKATA, INDIA, 2009

HE GOT THE CALL from the woman in Kolkata in early 2009. It was not too long after he'd seen Sophia in the library at the university. The woman introduced herself as Amita. She chattered to him in Bengali for a full minute before he could convince her he didn't speak it.

"How can you not speak Bengali?" she demanded of him in accented English.

"I . . . don't. How would I?"

"You've not lived here, have you? Hindustani? Do you speak that?"

"A little; not much. Can we stick to English for the moment?"

She laughed, and he realized she was Ben. "Ah, it's my old friend," he said in the extinct Italian dialect they used on the boat.

"Now you want to speak languages, do you?" she asked back in English.

"We have many in common," he said in Latin.

"Can you come for a visit?" she asked him gaily in English.

He knew to come when Ben summoned. "Yes. When?"

"Soon! Whenever you like."

She gave him an address, and he bought a plane ticket the next day. He had plenty of vacation days to use up at the hospital.

HE FOUND HER in a small apartment on the top floor of an old house in a crowded and shabby district of Kolkata. She was young, with a face constantly on the move. She wore a lovely peacock-blue sari and jingling gold bangles at her wrist. She embraced him immediately. She led him back to her small, old-fashioned kitchen, where she was cooking up a storm.

"You are very handsome, Daniel," she said, lifting her eyebrows flirtatiously.

"I got lucky this life," he said. "If handsomeness is lucky."

"Sometimes yes, sometimes no." She tasted something from one of her pots with her finger. "Delicious," she declared.

"I'm glad to see you," he said sincerely.

"And I am glad to see you." She moved toward him with a spoon in her hand and kissed his chin. "I'd like to kiss you more," she said. She gestured with her spoon to a small room behind a half-open door. "I'd like to take you in there, but I know you love another girl."

He laughed. He couldn't tell if she was serious or not, and regardless, he couldn't imagine getting into that unmade bed with Ben. First because she was Ben, and also because he'd known her briefly as Laura and several others. He could never let the old lives go. He couldn't with anyone, let alone Ben. The first time he met a person, if he was a man, Daniel had a complicated time being attracted to any subsequent version of him as a woman. He wasn't good at living in between.

"I am *Amita*," she said imperiously, reading his thoughts in the usual way.

"You are a shape-shifter," he said jokingly.

"No, this is called living," she shot back fiercely. "And what *you* do is not." Her eyes remained affectionate, but he couldn't help recoiling.

"Tell me about your girl," Amita said sweetly. She didn't want to be hurtful to him.

"I know where she is," he said.

"Why aren't you with her?" she asked.

You could always be sure that Ben would cut to the quick of it. Daniel was tired and he was in Kolkata and he needed to be honest. "I tried to talk to her a few years ago and I really fucked it up. I went too fast; I scared her. I don't think she'd want to see me after that. I'm giving her some time before I try again." His explanation sounded weak to his own ears. How much time was he going to give her?

"Maybe she doesn't want your time."

He rubbed his cheeks. He felt the sweat and grit of long travel. "I don't know what she wants." His voice drifted quieter. "But I don't think it is me."

Amita stood poised with her spoon, looking at him thoughtfully. "Oh, Daniel," she said finally. "You need to be loved. That's what you need. You are terribly out of practice."

He laughed. "Is that why you want me in the bedroom?"

"Love is love," she said.

He shook his head. Her flirtation was a mercy he didn't quite understand. "I don't think it's the right time to try again with Sophia," he said. "If I wait for a while, maybe I'll have another chance."

She looked sad. "And that's a thing you can keep forever." She slopped the spoon back into a pot and hiked herself up to sit on the counter. She put her chin in her hand for a few moments, thinking. "Maybe if you had approached her as herself and not someone else, you wouldn't have scared her away."

"What do you mean? I didn't approach her as someone else. I approached her as herself. I called her Sophia, but she is Sophia. Is it wrong to remember her?"

"Sophia is not her name. Sophia is a memory." Amita hopped down from the counter. She resumed her stirring. "I believe her name is Lucy."

"Same girl."

"Yes and no."

"What do you mean by that?" He sounded like a child to himself.

"You are a hoarder," she said. It was something Ben had accused him of several times before. "Love who you love while you have them. That's all you can do. Let them go when you must. If you know how to love, you'll never run out."

Ben sounded as chirpy as a self-help book, but still Daniel felt overwhelmed and strangely fragile. He didn't know how to respond, and she recognized it. She came forward again with her spoon. "Taste this," she said tenderly, holding it out to him.

He did. "God, that is hot."

She nodded and widened her eyes. "Isn't it?" She consulted her cookbook for a moment and then snapped it shut. "Since my husband joined the army, I cook and I read. Cook and read."

"Your husband?" He felt guilty for having gazed at the shapely brown region of ribs and stomach revealed by her sari.

"Yes. And when he comes back, I will amaze him with my dishes," she said, flourishing her spoon like a magician.

His mouth was burning. "You will. I am sure."

He watched her for a while. She stirred things and chopped things and scattered ingredients with abandon. She seemed to enjoy throwing her peppers into the pot, as opposed to just putting them there. "Sometimes you have to make a mess," she informed him merrily. She tasted the green stuff in a small brass dish. "Oooh," she said with a gasp. "Well, that is surprising."

"Really?"

"Yes! Perhaps not in a good way. Cooking is always surprising, don't you find?"

He hadn't found cooking surprising in four centuries, not since he'd cooked in the galley of a ship sailing the Adriatic for seven long years.

"I don't," he said honestly.

"Oh, but it is. It always is." She went back to her cookbook. "I don't have a mother or a sister to teach me, so I have to teach myself," she explained.

He was feeling subdued by this time. It was the jet lag and the tendency Ben had to push him into uncertainties. "How is anything new to you?" he asked her. "How do you still find anything surprising?"

She stopped for only a moment and looked at him. She stuck her finger in the green stuff and held it out to him. He took a lick, and it was shockingly horrible. Even poisonous. He relented. "You're right. That is surprising."

For some reason he thought of a thing she had said to him once when she was Ben and they were gazing up at the starry night sky on a long, quiet watch in the Aegean: "I don't see patterns easily."

DANIEL KNEW SHE would get to the point of his visit eventually, and it happened as they sat on the warm roof after dinner, chewing fragrant seeds and watching a large family reclining on beach chairs on the roof across the narrow street.

"The shape-shifter is not me," she said, apropos of nothing. "It is your old brother." She examined a seed and tossed it to the sidewalk below. Her face stayed still for only a moment, but she clearly meant to warn him.

"Is that right?"

"Yes. He steals bodies easily now. He has a dangerous friend."

"What do you mean? Who?" Daniel's mind raced through various characters he'd met or heard of over the years. There was the man who'd once approached him in Ghent who claimed to have been the archangel Azrael. The woman in New Orleans, Evangeline Brasseaux, and her bevy of followers who said she'd seen the apocalypse. There was a whole underworld of these people, and though he'd dipped into it a couple of times long ago, he'd mostly avoided it. Surrounding the ones with authentic memories were the hangers-on, the mythmakers, the rumor spreaders, and the out-and-out liars. He found it hard to keep his bearings among them. Only now he wished he'd taken the pains to know more.

She scratched her arm. Her bones were thin and definite, like a bird's. "He's been gathering his powers for a long time now. While you are not finding your girl, he is looking for her."

He felt a painful sting in his ears and throat, and he couldn't swallow it away. "He's looking for Sophia?"

She crunched loudly on a seed and picked it out of her teeth. "By finding her, he will find you."

"What do you mean?"

She thought for a moment. "Maybe he already has found her."

Daniel stood and walked. The terrible, albeit surprising, dinner was seizing up in his stomach. "How can that be? He can't recognize souls. You told me that yourself. Don't you remember?"

She joined him at the parapet wall and spit another seed. "It's possible he has help," she said again.

"How? Who? What do you mean?" He felt like an idiot saying

the same thing again and again, knowing it was the kind of question Ben would never answer, but he couldn't get his mind settled.

He paced, and for the first time she stood perfectly still. "How do you know this?" He was in agony.

She shook her head, but she must have seen his state. Out of pity she gave him an answer. "I remembered."

He watched her intently. "But it hasn't happened yet, has it?"

She flicked that away with her narrow, jingling wrist.

"I'VE BEEN READING Proust," she declared to Daniel as he helped her clean up the disaster in her kitchen. She didn't want to talk about Joaquim or Sophia anymore, and he had to accept it. He knew how Ben was. He gave you as much as you could process and not more.

"Is that right?" he said distractedly, wanting to be companionable.

"Yes. We have a fine library at the end of our street."

"Haven't you read it before?'

"I suppose." She laughed in a way that was remarkably ditsy, considering she'd lived forever. "I love it."

He nodded, wiping some sort of sauce from the ceiling. "What became of him?"

"Proust, you mean?"

"Yes. Did he have a memory?" If you caught Ben on a topic that interested him and was irrelevant, you could get odd bits of information to fall out.

She shook her head so her little gold earrings wobbled. "Not a stitch." She thought for a moment. "He's a housewife in southern Kentucky. A very competitive bridge player."

"Not a stitch?" he said, surprised.

"Not a stitch. And Joyce, you know, is gone."

"He's gone?"

"He only lived the one life. But he lived it brightly."

"Huh. No memory there, I guess."

"No. And Freud, neither. Did you know that?"

"I couldn't have guessed," he said.

"But Jung certainly did," Amita said animatedly. "And so did his mother."

"Really?"

"Of course."

He wound around to the question he needed to ask. "Does this . . . dangerous friend have a memory?" he asked slowly.

She shrugged in her carefree way, but her eyes shone with a complexity he couldn't read. "It isn't just us, you know," she said a little sadly.

AMITA WANTED HIM to stay the night. She offered him half her bed with a solemn promise not to lay a hand. The lift of her eyebrows made him laugh, which he might have thought was impossible at that moment. But he told her no. He had to get home.

She seemed sad when she hugged him. "You love your memory, but you need to love your girl," she said by way of parting. "You remember what is lost, and you forget what's right in front of you."

He knew what she was trying to say, but he couldn't be like her. "If I let go, who else is there to remember?" he said with unavoidable melancholy. "It will be gone."

She sighed. "It is gone."

DANIEL STOOD IN front of Campbell Hall. He looked at the windows where the lights shone and wondered if she was behind any of them. He'd come to Charlottesville three times in the last ten days, and he hadn't set eyes on her, but still he felt a sense of comfort. She'd graduated. She could choose to live anywhere in the wide world, yet she'd come back here. He had the address of her apartment on Oak Street, but he hadn't gone there.

In a few small ways he'd gotten warmer. He'd made friends with the guard who manned the entrance to the architecture studios. He'd spoken with a graduate student named Rose who was acquainted with Lucy and seemed to spend every waking hour in the studio. He'd made it sound to them as though he and Lucy were friends, and he felt a bit guilty for that. He hated to be creepy, and he didn't want to intrude on her, but his worries had become acute since he'd returned from India. He wouldn't bother her. He'd just make sure she was all right.

He hung around the entrance until he saw Rose, returning from dinner, he guessed.

"Hey, how's it going?" he asked.

"Good. You waiting for Lucy?"

"Yes, we were supposed to grab a late dinner," he lied. "You haven't seen her, have you?"

"No," Rose said knowledgeably. "She used to be here every

night until midnight, but she hasn't been staying late the last few nights." She took on a conspiratorial look. "The rumor around the studio is that Lucy has a boyfriend."

Daniel wondered if Rose had a cruel nature. "Oh, yeah?" he said casually.

"She was all dressed up when she left on Wednesday night. Nobody's used to seeing her wearing heels and makeup. She made a big impression."

Daniel found himself hating Rose. "Okay, well. Good for her. I hadn't heard about that." He had an uncomfortably fake look stamped on his face, and his only challenge was to keep it there. "I might have forgotten to leave her the message about dinner," he added lamely. He pictured Rose as a Stasi informant in her previous life.

So Lucy was suddenly a girl with a boyfriend. What a dumb term that was. He tried to remember when, in the history of the language, that had started up. He'd never be her boyfriend. *You'd be anything she wanted you to be,* a more honest part of himself countered.

As he walked away from Campbell Hall, Daniel felt immature and jealous, but he didn't feel alarmed. That was the one good thing. Lucy got dressed up. She went out with her boyfriend. There was no sign of Joaquim in any of that. It was depressing to think of her having a boyfriend, but he felt sure Joaquim couldn't get close to her in that way. If Daniel knew anything, Lucy would find Joaquim's presence deeply discomforting.

He trudged to his car slowly and with a craving he didn't often feel or, in any case, allow.

Without thinking, he drove north to Fairfax. He followed roads he'd learned as a teenager in the eighties. His mother used to let him borrow her red Toyota Celica, and he'd drive across the

Potomac River at night to see the Lincoln and Jefferson memorials glowing white against the dark sky. His father had discouraged it, but Molly almost always said okay.

He had an aching feeling as he drove up to the old house. He didn't really mean to drive all the way to the house and stop, but now he was here. He hadn't been here in twenty-two years.

If he could have left the world alone, maybe he'd live around the corner now. He could see Molly and his dad and his brothers all the time. Maybe he'd be married and well employed, using his huge experience for some good. Maybe he'd be a teacher like his parents. He could offer a unique perspective on history, that was for sure. Or maybe he'd just mow his lawn and whack his weeds and try to forget everything but the games on Sunday. Sometimes he felt sure that the key to happiness was a poor memory.

His old parents would be pushing seventy, assuming they were still alive. Did they still live here? He looked up at the front porch and squinted at the flowers. Even in the dark he knew they were dahlias, and that was his answer.

A light was on in the kitchen and a bluish TV light upstairs. He could picture the house as though it were his. It was his, once. Why couldn't it belong to him anymore? Why couldn't he belong to it? Because he gave it up. He held on to himself, and he threw the other things away.

He thought of his brothers, the three Robinson boys all cleaned up for church. His mother with her wintergreen Life Savers and stickers and coloring books to keep them quiet. And Daniel never needed them. He was always looking for Sophia. Did that hurt her feelings then?

She must have sensed she never really had him. That was a sadness of hers, he knew. She sat on his bed at night and tried to get him to talk to her, thinking she could get closer to whatever faraway thing it was he kept from her. She'd loved him as much as he'd let her. More than he'd let her; you couldn't control everything.

Then he'd disappeared without a reason, without ever giving her a moment of satisfaction. She didn't deserve that. There was a hole there still. He knew it if he was honest with himself. It was his as much as hers. He wished he could feel about himself now the way he'd felt then.

And here he was, sitting perfectly well and alive outside her house. But what good did that do her? What good did it do him?

I don't want to go forward, I want to go back. He didn't want to go forward, but he always wanted to get another chance. He was all starts and endings, where people like Molly lived in the middle as if it was all they had.

He found himself wishing that Molly would come out of the house. He thought of her crooked front teeth and her freckles and her fuzzy gray hair and he ached with missing her. But she didn't come out. Why would she? He sat alone in his car.

It wouldn't have been much different if he was dead. His memory made him invisible over time, even to the people he felt he knew and loved most. Not even they knew him or cared about him anymore. You could pretend you were in control of all the relationships when the people you loved didn't know you anymore.

He was more like a ghost than a person, watching people, waiting for people. Not to talk to them or hold them or build a life with them but just to remember them.

LUCY GOT A little drunk when she was with Daniel. He took her to nice restaurants, always ordered wine for them, and confidently paid the bill. She eagerly drank whatever it was. She was in a perpetual state of fuzziness with him.

Why do I do that? she wondered. She didn't do it other times. She liked to keep her wits close by. Why was she so eager to part with them when she was in his company?

Now came the end of dinner, melting chocolate cake somewhat romantically shared for dessert, and the bill was on its way. He must earn a lot of money at his job, she decided.

She looked at him across the table. She could hardly remember the old Daniel, she had worked so hard to conjoin the two faces. She felt a moment of boldness and let her mind wander back to an old conversation they had had.

"You used to call me Sophia," she said.

"When was that?"

"In high school. At that miserable last party. You can't have forgotten that."

He ran his forefinger along the clothed edge of the table. "You used to be Sophia."

"A long time ago, right?" She was definitely tipsy.

"Yes. Very long."

"Do you remember it?"

"Of course."

"How?"

"I just do. Some people remember a long time back."

"I wish I could remember."

"It's not all good," he said.

"Do you remember Constance?"

The pretty waitress came across the room with the bill. He examined it as he answered her. "Of course."

"How do you recognize someone? From one life to another? I don't understand how you do that."

He signed and stood up. "Let's go outside, okay?"

He didn't wait for her to agree, so she just followed him through the gauntlet of the coat check and the valet parking and all the tips she wasn't sure if she was supposed to pay. She usually tucked a few dollars here and there just in case.

Standing in front of the restaurant, he turned to her and grabbed her in one motion. His lips were on hers before she could equivocate. He always wanted to kiss her and grab her in public places, which was the opposite of what she wanted.

She tried to respond, but her body was shaking, her ribs and her knees and her shoulders. Her teeth were chattering too much to kiss. She pulled away to spare him.

"Will you come home with me?" he asked, putting a couple of fingers under the waistband of her skirt. "Please?"

Would she? She couldn't. She wanted to drink so much wine that she could, but she hadn't found that much yet. "I can't."

She remembered, with a flush, how eager she'd been to have his knee under her dress in high school, how she'd been kissing him before they'd exchanged ten sentences. She was beginning to wonder how much or little the soul really counted for.

The car arrived via the eager valet before he could get his hands into her tights. He drove a Porsche, which gave him things to say to the valet, and that was a relief.

"Why can't you?" he asked, sitting her on his lap on the hood of the coveted car after the valet had gone off to park an SUV.

"I have classes tomorrow. I have a studio crit. I'm supposed to finish a model."

He nodded acceptingly. He didn't seem to know that three excuses were as good as none. He thrust his hands under her coat and shirt, and burrowed them under her bra. He did know about some things.

His hands were cold on her. That's why she was still shaking.

"Next time?"

"Next time," she said. It was a ritual between them. It was always next time.

He lit a cigarette and walked her to her shitty car, which she'd parked at the edge of the lot. She was embarrassed to turn it over to a valet.

"Tell me about Sophia," she asked, her breath making a cloud. Her cloud was a white puff, and his was a gray twist. She wanted something to hold on to so she could believe in next time.

"Like what?"

"What did she mean to you?"

He drew his hands away. "She was my wife."

"Was she?"

"Yes."

"Did you love her?" It was the wine talking. It was next time talking. He wasn't even touching her and she felt the shaking and the chattering as though she was afraid. *I'm not afraid. What do I have to be afraid of?*

He looked at her. "Not as well as I should have."

"HE'S REALLY DIFFERENT NOW." Lucy was trying to explain her dinner with Daniel to Marnie. She had hoped Marnie would be asleep when she came in, but Marnie had been sitting on the sofa in their miniature living room, alert, with her computer in her lap, when Lucy eased open the door.

"How much difference can a few years make?" Marnie asked. Marnie, typically, was asking the right questions, and Lucy was copping out.

"Well, in his case . . . big." Lucy guessed they were talking quietly because Leo was asleep. She took a long time about her coat and hat and boots and socks.

"What do you mean?"

Lucy wanted to explain what she really meant, but how could she? Marnie thought she wanted to know, but did she really? She'd caused Marnie plenty of consternation already. Marnie missed the old friendship, when Lucy told her everything; she didn't understand what had happened to change it. Lucy missed the old friendship, too, but she couldn't get back to it. Nor could Lucy bring herself to tell Marnie the truth. Because the truth wouldn't be comforting and wouldn't bring them closer again.

"Just that . . . it's hard to explain." *How much do you really want to know?* was what she wanted to ask her.

"When are you going to bring him around? Are you hiding him? I want to see."

Lucy was absolutely hiding him. How could she possibly account for the fact that he bore no physical resemblance to the Daniel she knew? It had been painful enough dismantling the universe to make room for him. She couldn't bear to force all that on Marnie. "No. No. He'll be around sometime. He works in D.C. He's got a real job, and he's busy."

Lucy slowly unwound her scarf and hung it carefully on a hook in the closet instead of balling it up and tossing it on the hall table as she would have ordinarily done. She took her time looking through her bag for her phone.

"I think I'm different, too," she said into the hungry silence. "Definitely different than I was in high school."

Marnie stretched her legs out in front of her. "You don't like him as much as you used to like him is what you're saying."

"No, it's not that," she protested reflexively. "I was so stupid then, as you've pointed out." Lucy fiddled around with her cell phone charger. She didn't want to sit down in the chair across from Marnie, because then she'd have to be honest.

Marnie looked wistful. "Well, I liked you stupid. And anyway, I never said that."

"You know what I mean. I was just . . . slavering over him. I don't think I'm like that anymore."

Marnie looked particularly sober. She circled her slack computer cord around her foot. "Why aren't you?" She had to credit Marnie for keeping on asking, even as she must have feared what it would bring.

She held Marnie's eyes for a minute and then let them drop. Lucy was the coward around here. "Just older, I guess."

"Did you kiss him this time?"

"A little."

"How many times have you gone out with him?"

"I don't know. Seven or eight, maybe. Something like that."

"You kissed him *a little*? Are you twelve?"

"I have a crit tomorrow."

Marnie shook her head. "Is this the same Daniel?"

Lucy swallowed and nodded.

"You don't like him anymore."

DANIEL WAS DRIVING from the VA hospital to Charlottesville early one evening after a long, tiring shift, and when he saw the traffic backed up on the beltway he decided to take a different way.

He found himself thinking of his grandfather Joseph, Molly's father. He thought of Joseph not so much as he was when he was old and sick in hospice in Fairfax, but as he was when they lived in Alabama by the pond. There were geese in the pond through the winter, and they fed them bits of stale bread almost every morning. It wasn't easy to get a goose to trust a couple of humans, but they had succeeded. They didn't plan it, really. They were both early risers, and they showed up there. He could still picture Joseph's delighted expression in the center of a whirling globe of black heads with white chinstraps and gray wings and dark, squawking beaks. Geese paired up like humans, Joseph explained. Better than humans, because geese stayed true.

Daniel also remembered the days in the spring when the first flocks would go back up north to Canada or wherever they came from. He and Joseph would look up at the racing V overhead, a single thumping bird soul, and watch them with the excitement of travel and the sadness of being left again. Daniel remembered envying them their purpose and connectedness, and how they could just fly away. He collected feathers as a way to hold on to them. His grandma said they were dirty, but his mother secretly let him keep them.

Joseph dreamed of being a pilot, and he would have been if he hadn't had polio when he was a teenager, which left his leg weak. Daniel told Joseph that's what he would do, too, and he fully meant it at the time. After they moved, Joseph used to send pictures of the planes he thought Daniel should fly. Daniel felt sorry that he ended that life before he could do it.

HE WAS TWO miles out of town on a small road and heading south when he realized that the road was familiar to him, and it explained why he kept thinking of Joseph. He kept going for another couple of miles, looking for the cemetery on the left, where his grandmother Margaret and undoubtedly Joseph, were buried. Instead of keeping on, he surprised himself by turning left and driving under an alley of oak trees.

He was partly surprised because he almost never thought of graveyards. They meant so much less than most people thought they did. He remembered a woman from his old neighborhood in St. Louis driving fifteen miles to the cemetery every day to mourn her long-dead husband at a cold gray stone, while the husband was busy selling milk at the 7-Eleven just half a mile down the road from her house.

Daniel hadn't seen his grandfather since he'd died, though he had been keeping an eye out for him. They would likely be about the same age now. He'd thought they would have crossed paths, being as close as they were. But they hadn't, and it made him wonder if Joseph had lived his last life. It fit, as he thought of it, and it made him sad. Some chances you really did lose.

He parked the car and walked up to a hilltop. It was good to get out and walk a bit. He was drowsy, and his focus turned so deeply inward he half expected his body to stop breathing.

His grandfather's gravestone looked as he thought it would, except that it didn't have the bunches of dahlias he had pictured. He looked around and saw the familiar flowers a little way down the row, an armload of them, fresh-cut and deep pink. He was confused by that, and slightly alarmed. Was there a new death in the family? He hoped his brothers were all right. Curiosity drew him down the row to the decorated grave. He read the name twice before it meant anything to him. "Daniel Joseph Robinson, beloved son of Molly and Joshua."

It was possible he really had stopped breathing, as his breath came fast and painfully now. They'd engraved the name they'd given him second and the name he'd given himself first. There were not only flowers but two candles and a photograph in a frame. He didn't want to look at the photograph, but he reached for it anyway.

It was him, of course. It was him in his cross-country uniform, standing next to Molly. He was sweaty, the hair on his neck in wet spears. It was just after a race, and Molly carried the trophy. She wasn't holding it up for the camera, just dangling it in her hand. He won most of the races, and she knew he didn't care about the trophy.

He must have been about fourteen. He wasn't quite as tall as her yet. He was leaning his head against her shoulder. His eyes were closed, and he was laughing about something, not posing but really laughing. He knew why she kept this picture. Maybe there had been a moment or two of satisfaction for her.

He never looked at his own graves. He never wanted to see an old picture of himself. He had avoided those things, not knowing exactly why, and now he knew why. He sat down. He realized he held his car key in his hand and it was shaking. He put the key in his pocket.

He remembered the races. He remembered being fast, just effortlessly fast in that body. He remembered those autumn days and his favorite course that wound through the hemlock forest of the land trust. He'd never been so good at running before. No matter how much diligence and strategy you brought to a race, those legs were just faster than the others.

He thought of Molly tending this grave, bringing these flowers, lighting the candles. His impulse was to go and find her. "I'm fine," he wanted to say to her. "I still love you, and I think about you all the time. I'm not down there, I'm right here."

He looked at the photograph again. He looked down at his hands and remembered his old hands—the nail of his left middle finger, which grew in funny, his bony knuckles, his freckled skin. Those hands weren't here; they were down there. Or whatever was left of them. Those fast legs weren't here; they were buried, too. That was him, Molly's son, and he was under there; he wasn't right here. *That was me.*

He missed that body. He heard music so well in that body. His fingers were graceful and quick on the piano keys. It was a talented body, and it was a shame to throw it away.

As he looked at Molly's face in the picture, he knew he hadn't loved that body because it was fast and heard music well. He would have liked to think so, but he knew it wasn't true. He loved it because he'd been loved. Because Molly had loved him.

In this present body he hadn't been loved, and he found almost nothing to love about himself. He didn't want to give a mother that kind of power, but Molly had it anyway.

It was amazing how he thought he could take his whole self

with him to every new life, not remembering that when you left someone like Molly, you left a part of yourself behind forever. Sometimes he wondered if his memory for the important things was really very good at all.

He glanced at the photograph for the last time before he got up on trembling legs. He hadn't been able to see it or accept it then, but it seemed so obvious now. He'd looked just like her.

CHARLOTTESVILLE, VIRGINIA, 2009

ON THE FIRST Friday of spring break, after Lucy had turned in a research paper on Jefferson's "pet trees" at the Grove in Monticello and taken two exams in three days, Daniel showed up in the lobby of her building and called up on the intercom a little after noon. She was so surprised and anxious at the thought of him standing there that she went racing out of her apartment and down three flights of stairs without considering changing out of her sweatpants and T-shirt or putting on a bra.

He held out his arms for her, and she reluctantly went into them. Because she failed to look up, he kissed the top of her unshowered head. "I have a huge surprise for you," he said. He was obviously excited.

His being there, in the bosom of her life, felt like a huge enough surprise. She didn't know if she could take another one. She shuffled him toward the alcove with the defunct pay phone. She didn't dare take him upstairs, because Marnie and Leo were asleep up there. "What's that?"

He pulled some papers from the pocket of his long coat and held them out for her, not to take but to see.

"Plane tickets?" she asked.

"Yes. Well, not the actual tickets but our itinerary."

" 'Our itinerary'?"

"It's your spring break, isn't it? You said you didn't have plans. I'm taking you to Mexico for a week."

She didn't know what to say. She didn't know their relationship could contain this kind of thing. If somebody had told her a few months ago that Daniel would come back into her life, and furthermore, that he was going to sweep her off to Mexico for a week, she would have been ecstatic. But now she felt skittish and unnerved.

"I was going to see my folks for a few days. I told them I'd—"

"You've got two weeks off. You'll have time."

People straggled in and out of the lobby. People she recognized. What if Marnie came down just now? Lucy didn't want to prolong the discussion.

"We fly out tomorrow afternoon," he said buoyantly. If he picked up on her hesitance he didn't show it, and that, like so many things, seemed strange to her. "Go get packed. Do you want me to pick you up tomorrow or meet you at the airport?"

"Meet me at the airport," she blurted. "I'm totally out of your way."

"Great." He kissed her. "Let's meet at noon. I'll call you with the gate number."

She watched him go with an urgent feeling of relief. She wondered if she was going with him to Mexico for a week just to get him out of there.

DANIEL DID SOMETHING he promised himself he would not do. Late Saturday morning he drove to her apartment building. It wasn't enough to hang around spying on her any longer. He needed to get over himself and actually talk to her. He needed to find a way to warn her. He'd been in a state of anxious alert since he'd returned from India, but in the last twenty-four hours he'd been haunted—dreaming of her in the bare hour he slept and gripped by panic the rest of the time. He wasn't sure whether it was his experience at the cemetery that woke him up or some strange premonition in his dream, but the idea of waiting another moment to see her seemed unbearable. He found her name by apartment number 4D and pressed the intercom button. A familiar voice answered, but it wasn't hers.

"Is Lucy there?" he asked.

"No. Who is this?" it asked.

"This is . . . ah . . ." He felt desperate. "Is this Marnie?"

"Yes. Who is this?" she asked again.

"It is Daniel. Grey. From Hopewood." He felt stupid shouting into the intercom. "You probably don't remember me, but—"

"Oh, I remember you all right. You're in the lobby? What are you doing here?" Her voice was something less than friendly.

"I was hoping to see Lucy."

"What are you talking about?" Marnie was strident, impatient, even through the fuzzy speaker. "Aren't you two sauntering off to Mexico together? Lucy left for the airport an hour ago to meet you."

"I'm sorry?" His mind froze. He was polite if nothing else.

"I thought you were taking her to Mexico."

"Mexico? I was taking her? What do you mean?"

"She went to meet you! That's what she said. I don't understand what you are doing here. Are you really Daniel Grey, or is this some lame-ass prank?"

The churn of dread began somewhere in his lower intestine. "Can I come up and talk to you? Would you rather come down?"

"I'll come down," she said.

He watched the elevator fetch her on the fourth floor and bring her down. He didn't want a mystery. He didn't like to have Lucy far away where he couldn't find her.

"It really is you," Marnie said when the elevator doors parted. She was openly surprised. "Over here," she said. She led him to a tired-looking couch at the back of the lobby. She studied him for a moment before she sat down. "You don't look all that different," she said. "I'd say you look about exactly the same."

"What do you mean?"

"Lucy keeps talking about how different you are now, how she could barely recognize you."

The churn spread upward and down. Had she spotted him when he thought he was being invisible? Or was it something else? "When did she say she saw me?"

Marnie stared at him as though he was an imbecile and shook her head at him slowly. "All the time. Last weekend. The weekend before. Yesterday. You guys go out all the time."

"And she said I was taking her to Mexico?"

"Yes."

He realized that underneath her haughtiness, Marnie was spooked, too.

"And she's gone?"

"She's gone."

"You're sure."

"I know she packed and went someplace." Marnie's face was still hard, but she wanted to trust him. "She could have lied about who she went with. She could have lied to me about the whole thing." Under the peaked eyebrows, her eyes reminded him of when she had been Sophia's mother.

"But she said it was me, Daniel Grey, from high school?"

"Yes. Are you his evil twin or something? Because I don't know how this is a surprise to you. According to her, she has been going to every expensive restaurant in the state of Virginia with Daniel Grey from high school."

He shook his head. "I'm not a twin. If there's evil here, I don't think it's me." He needed to think. "Did she say exactly where she was going in Mexico?"

"A place on the Pacific. Ixtapa? Is that a place? I think she said they were flying to Ixtapa." She was intuitive enough to sense the depth of his concern. "You're going to Mexico? Right now?"

"As soon as I can get there."

"If she's not with you, who is she with?"

"That's what I need to figure out. You don't have any other information? Name of a hotel or anything?"

"Sorry, no. She packed two bathing suits. She's going to the beach. That's all she said."

"Would you give me her cell phone number?"

"Yes, but I don't think it will help. She said she wouldn't have service there." She told him the number, and he put it in his phone anyway.

"Okay. Thanks, Marnie," he said, feeling a moment of tenderness for her.

"You know, Daniel."

"What?" He was already halfway across the lobby.

"In high school, I never understood. Why didn't you love her then?"

He walked back to Marnie and looked straight in her eyes. "I did love her. I've loved her from the first time I saw her."

DANIEL GOT ON a flight out of Dulles bound for Mexico City that night and a connection to Ixtapa Zihuatanejo that landed midday on Sunday. He couldn't so much as read the newspaper on the flight. His fingers crawled and his knees bounced and his mind spun as he tried to figure out how this had happened. He suspected he was most likely walking into a trap. And in that case he guessed that the person he hated would probably be happier to see him than the person he loved. That was a bitter pill, but he had to go. There was nothing else he could do.

He felt as though he was trying to solve a problem with too many variables. How had Joaquim found Sophia? If someone was helping him, as Ben had suggested, then who was it and why? And what kind of memory did this person have? Or had Joaquim somehow gained the capacity to recognize people on his own?

By whatever means Joaquim had found her, he had probably discovered Daniel's proximity and also his remoteness, and thinking of that made Daniel feel stupid. Why had he stayed away so long? What, besides cowardice, was the point of that, exactly? Was he bowing to her fear or to his? By staying away, even while knowing what he knew, he left Sophia open to these weird machinations.

And this troubling thought ushered in the second category of variables. How had Joaquim been able to pass himself off to her as Daniel? What powers of persuasion could he have used to get her to believe that? And moreover, how had he gotten anywhere with it? Daniel, who'd loved her all her life, had sent her running for the doors, and Joaquim, who'd been nothing but brutal to her, somehow got to take her on vacation to Mexico. Daniel hadn't been able to make her believe anything, and somehow Joaquim had convinced her of . . . God only knew what. Maybe they were having a lovely and romantic time together. Maybe Daniel didn't know anything of human nature at all. "Fuck," he muttered to himself.

Joaquim wouldn't hurt her. Not yet, at least. That was the single benefit to Joaquim's pretense. As long as he was Daniel, he wasn't going to hurt her. When the real Daniel showed up, though, it would all be blown open.

The heat of the sun on his back as he walked off the plane in Ixtapa pressed on him like a weight. He stood in a snaking line of spring-breakers, already pink and drinking tequila out of paper cups. He was grim from his face down to the dark winter clothes he hadn't taken time to change out of. He was trying to think of something to say in his eighteenth-century Castilian to the customs official to get him to the front of the line.

It was impossible getting anything done in a town full of half-drunk tourists. Nobody else was in a hurry. It took him an hour and a half to rent a car. He was on the edge of giving up, but he knew he'd want it later. *Slow down,* he kept reminding himself. *He's not going to hurt her. Not yet.*

Once in town, it didn't take him long to find her. It wasn't a huge town, and there were only a handful of luxury hotels. If he had doubted whether it was a setup, whether Joaquim wanted to be found, he needed to look no further than the name he used to check them in to the Ixtapa Grand Imperial: Mr. and Mrs. Daniel Grey. Granted, Daniel was a little funny about his name, but still. It pissed him off.

The original, actual, and true Daniel waited in the lobby. He used the time to study the layout of the building until at last he saw a face he knew. It wasn't the one he wanted, but it was clarifying. And though he'd known who the imposter would be, it shook him anyway. The man from the Lakers game with the near-courtside seats and the good haircut and the rotted soul was more disturbing in person. There was something so deeply corrupt about his soul that it made him difficult for Daniel to recognize in the usual way, but Daniel knew it was him, and the passage of time didn't really make the feeling of revulsion less. This was the thing he hoped against and feared, but here it was.

"Do you sell cigarettes here?" he overheard Joaquim ask the concierge. Joaquim didn't bother to speak Spanish.

The man pointed him to the shop around the corner.

"You don't sell them here? Are you kidding me?"

"No, I'm sorry, sir. Just outside."

Joaquim strode out the door, and Daniel went up to the desk. "Mr. Grey's room, please," he asked in Spanish.

"I can't give you the room number, sir," the young man said politely. "But I can connect you."

"Yes, that's fine." He watched long enough to see the room number he punched in.

The attendant said a few words into the phone and put the line on hold. "Mrs. Grey is there, sir, but Mr. Grey is not."

He shook his head dismissively. "I'll call back later."

As soon as the attendant turned his head, Daniel took the stairs. He ran up six flights. It was hot in this place. If there was any air-conditioning, it was relegated to the rooms. He found room 632 and knocked.

"Yes?" He heard a tentative voice from inside the room, a voice he knew.

"Uh, room service," he said. If it had been a different day, he wouldn't have been able to say it with a straight face.

He fidgeted miserably as he waited for her to come to the door. *Please open it,* he thought. There wasn't much time.

What was she going to think when she saw him? For the first time in a long time he had the sense that he was walking into his life as opposed to just hanging around by the front door. That is, if she let him in. He hoped his face would not be completely unwelcome.

SHE WAS SITTING on the bed in a bathrobe with her arms around her knees. Daniel wanted her to keep the windows closed and the air conditioner laboring at full capacity, but he had gone out, thankfully, so she'd taken a fast shower, opened the big old-fashioned casement windows, and brought the breeze in from the sea.

She'd gotten through one night of this, but she wasn't sure she could get through six more. She couldn't sleep with him. Her nerves recoiled at the thought of having sex with him, and she literally couldn't fall asleep with her body next to his. They'd gotten in late the night before, and she had been far too agitated to sleep. She dozed off, finally, reading in a chair, and was startled awake long before the sun rose. As much as she blamed herself, it didn't change the way she felt. She'd made stupid excuses—she had her period, she was a heavy bleeder, cramps, and so on—stuff you said to put a man on his heels, possibly permanently. She was burning this thing down by now, but she couldn't help it. She couldn't sleep with him.

And he was frustrated, of course. You didn't take a girl to Mexico to have her sleep in a chair with her book. He didn't do anything hurtful, but still she felt strangely watchful around him. She sensed a volatility not far under his skin that she'd never picked up on in high school. He went out to buy cigarettes and she felt relieved, even just to have a couple of minutes to herself. She had a fantasy of sneaking out of the hotel and heading home. God, what was the matter with her? What would Constance say? How had it come to this?

I'm sorry, Constance. I tried to keep my mind open to him, I really did. But I don't think he can make me happy.

Maybe there was some mercy in this if she looked at it the right way. Before he'd found her, her life was at an impasse. She couldn't move forward without him. She thought she'd never get over him. But now that she was with him, she knew she could. Now that she was with him, her old romantic notions seemed ridiculous to her. She had more than gotten over him, in spite of the fact that she was stuck in a hotel room in Mexico with him for the next six days. She could eagerly and with a big dose of relief picture life without him. She was sorry to Constance and Sophia for not taking up her legacy, but she couldn't. As promising as this bold new world had once seemed, it was a disappointment. And maybe that was for the best. She could finally recommit herself to the old one without looking back.

When she heard footsteps outside the door, her heart sank. She didn't want him back so soon. She was surprised that he would knock.

"Yes?"

"Room service."

She hadn't ordered anything. Had he ordered something? She was frankly relieved as she walked to the door. She wouldn't open it for Daniel in her robe, but she wasn't afraid of room service.

She expected a stranger with a tray, and she could not take in what she actually saw. She looked at him and looked away and looked at him again.

"Oh my God."

"Hey," he said nervously, looking behind him, down the hall, and then back at her.

"Daniel," she whispered. He was an apparition, but he was also sweating and fidgeting and leaving dusty footprints on the dark rug.

"Do you remember me?"

"Oh my God." Her mind grabbed at different things. Had he somehow changed again? Got into yet another body? Got his old body back? How did it work? What was possible? But she saw his eyes and his chin and his shoulders and his shoes and his neck and his collar and his hands and she knew he was not, absolutely not, the same person as the one who left to buy cigarettes. *Oh my God.* It was him.

"I'm sorry to barge in on your vacation like this, but will you come with me?"

"Where?"

"Away from here."

He looked as though he was going to jump out of his skin. She understood that she had to hurry. "Just . . . like this?" She glanced down at her robe.

"Okay."

"Right now?" Her heart was ready to explode, her same old romantic heart.

There was the ding of the elevator reaching their floor.

"Right now."

She stepped quickly out of the room and he closed the door quietly. The elevator was down the hall, but you could hear the doors open. He took her hand, and she followed him, barefoot. They turned two corners. She heard footsteps not far behind and a key-card unlocking a room, probably hers. He stopped at a door just before the stairwell. He opened it and pulled her in. He closed it behind him. It was some kind of utility closet. He was able to lock it from inside.

They stood in the dark, and she tried to catch her breath. She realized they were still holding hands.

"Are we running away from the guy I came here with?" she whispered.

"Yes. Do you mind?"

"No."

"Good." He stood close, and she could hear them both breathing hard. "I'm sorry to be so surprising," he murmured.

She laughed. It was a strange sound to her own ears, as if she had never laughed before in her life. "You have no idea."

He smiled at her outburst but widened his eyes as though she had better be quiet.

The throb of her heart went up into her throat and down to the bottom of her pelvis. The idea that that other person she'd come here with was the same as Daniel was just so preposterous that she felt sorry for herself for trying to think it was so.

"I can't believe you are here," she whispered. "Are you really here? Are you still alive? Am I imagining you?" She'd stopped laughing, and now there were tears dropping out of her eyes.

"I think I'm really here."

HE WANTED TO put his hands on her, but he stopped himself. He had lost faith in himself. Last time he had followed his impulses off a cliff. He didn't want to make the same mistake again.

He was as old as a rock, and like a rock, he couldn't read her tears and he didn't know anything about love anymore.

"Are you okay?" he asked.

"Yes. I'm happy to see you." He watched her face, which was open and brave, and it made his chest hurt. Maybe he did know a little bit about love.

"Even after what happened last time?"

"That wasn't your fault. That was mine."

"No, it wasn't." His look was vehement.

There were two sets of footsteps outside the door. Joaquim's voice was shouting at a man who was answering in quiet Spanish. "I'm sorry, sir, but we can't help you with that," the quieter voice was saying. "You'll have to contact the police if you think something is amiss."

Daniel felt Sophia squeezing his hand. The sounds passed and faded.

"He said he was you. I knew he wasn't you. Why did he tell me that? What does he want from me?"

"It's a very long story," he whispered. "And possibly hard to believe. But I'll tell you if you want me to."

"Right here? In this closet?"

"No. I think the best thing is to wait here for a few more minutes and then go down through the kitchen and out that door. I'm parked in the alley. There's a place we can go to up the coast until I can arrange a flight out of here."

She nodded, both eager and bewildered, staring at him up and down as well as she could in the darkness. "You still have those shoes," she whispered.

He looked down at them and back at her questioningly.

"Those shoes. From high school. I remember them."

"Do you?" He felt absurdly happy about it.

He waited until all was quiet before he felt through the hangers in the back of the tiny room and handed her a dress-length, zippered smock like those the housekeeping staff wore. "You might be less noticeable in this," he said. He found a head scarf that went with it. "Keep your head down, okay? We shouldn't walk together. You go first, and I'll follow. But don't worry about me, just keep going. Go down the stairs to the right and then into the kitchen. Walk straight through to the metal door under the exit sign, which will take you outside. The car is a red Ford Focus with Mexican plates parked directly across the alley, and it will be open when you get there. Don't stop, and don't talk to anybody if you can help it. Okay?"

"Okay."

"Okay." He wanted to hold her. He wanted to touch her in some way. It was hard to keep his hands off her, but it was impossible to put them on her, too. What did she think of him now?

"Is he dangerous?"

"Yes," he answered. "But I won't take my eyes off of you."

She held up the smock.

He smiled in spite of himself. "Except for right now. While you change. I'll turn around."

She smiled, too, and he didn't want to turn around, but he did. He heard her fiddling with the smock.

"Done," she said.

He turned back around and the robe was on the ground and the smock was zipped up the front. She was packing her hair into the scarf. He put his hands in his pockets.

"What about shoes?"

"Right." There were shallow cubbies along the wall, in which he found a pair of pink foam flip-flops. He held them up to her.

"I think they'll work." She put them on.

He found a shelf of white linens and handed her a tall pile. "Here."

She took it.

He moved to the door and put his hand on the knob. He listened for a moment. "You ready?"

"Yes."

He opened the door. "Go. Keep your head down."

She went out into the hall. She took a moment to turn around and smile at him, and his heart melted some more. She made a beautiful housekeeper.

NOBODY TOOK NOTICE of either of them until they were in the car. A man in a bellman's uniform opened the kitchen door and started shouting at them, but Daniel was already steering out of the alley.

"He's taking down the plates," Daniel said to her, looking in his rearview mirror.

"What do we do?" she asked.

"We'll figure something out."

She kicked off her flip-flops and put her bare feet on the dashboard. "This is fun." She should have been scared, and she was, but it was hard to give the real world much notice when he was this close.

"If we get out of here it will be."

Daniel concentrated for a few moments on finding the road to take them northward. He kept glancing in the rearview mirror, and she guessed he was checking that they weren't being followed.

"Does he have a car?" he asked.

"Not that I know of. We didn't rent one. We took a cab from the airport."

"Good. That might slow him down a little."

"Are you sure he's going to come?"

"No. But I think he's going to catch up with us eventually. He's not going to give up now. We just have to hope it takes him a while."

She took off her scarf and studied the side of his face. It felt good to be with him, no matter what.

"Is this a good time for the story, do you think?" she asked.

He nodded, but his look was cautious, and she understood why. "It's long and strange, and you don't need to believe any of it if you don't want to," he said. "I'll tell you what. I'll tell you my version, and after that we can try to think of an explanation that actually makes sense."

His voice was light, but she felt deep compassion for him. He'd been alone with his version of the world for a long time. She wanted him to know she understood that. She had that and so much else to tell him, but she couldn't seem to get any of it out. Her ideas spun wildly in her head, and she couldn't slow them down or put them in a logical order. "It's okay, Daniel," she managed to say. "I understand more than you think I do."

He glanced from the road to her face and back. He was quiet for a few seconds. "What do you mean?"

She tried to calm her thoughts. She took a few slow breaths. "I mean I—I don't understand it exactly, but I believe—I think I believe the idea that we—our souls—live on in some way so that you can know people and remember things through more than one life."

He looked from her to the road and back several times. It was harder to have this conversation when they couldn't look at each other. She longed to connect with him in some way—not to grab him and kiss him, although she didn't want to rule that out, but to understand how he felt about her, to read his awkwardness better, to begin to break down five numbing years of uncertainty.

"What made you . . . think this?" he asked carefully.

"Well. A psychic, a hypnotist, and a few other things I don't believe in. That's another long story."

His posture was still. Both hands gripped the steering wheel.

"Do you know about me?" He looked as though he was scared to trust her.

"I only know a little bit. I know I've known you before. At least I think so." She plucked at her seat belt. "Can I ask you something I don't understand?"

"Sure."

"How come you are always Daniel, while the rest of us keep coming back as different people? Have you been alive for a very long time?"

She saw relief on his face. "Is that what you thought? That I was hundreds of years old?" He looked at her and smiled. "I think you've relaxed your standards for what's acceptable in a companion."

She laughed. "It's been a strange few years."

He let his breath out. He sat back in his seat. "I'm twenty-four years old. In a way I have been alive for a very long time, but I've died a lot of times, too, just like you."

"Then how do you stay the same from one life to the next?"

"I don't. It's my mind that stays the same. Because I remember."
She nodded.

"It's the only unusual thing about me. But it's very unusual."

"Huh." She took a moment with that. "And you remember everything? All of your lives? All the people you've known?"

He kept glancing at her, as though he wanted to be able to tell how this was going down. "My memory isn't perfect, but yes, I remember almost all of it. Except my birthday. I tend to forget that."

She heard the lightness in his voice, and she felt it, too. "You do not."

"I do. It seems like half the days of the year are my birthday. They sort of lose their punch."

"I can see that."

"And it undermines my belief in astrology."

"That's sad."

"Sad and happy." He looked happy right now.

"So . . . happy birthday."

"Hey, thanks." He fiddled with the radio and turned on some salsa. They were both smiling stupidly.

She drummed her fingers against her knee. "Is there anybody else like you?"

"A handful of people."

"Do you all know each other? Is it like a club?"

He laughed. "No. Not quite. No T-shirts or secret handshakes. But I know two of them and have met or heard of a few others."

"Like who?"

Daniel glanced at the rearview mirror. "Like the man who will soon be following us."

"I'VE KIDNAPPED YOU before, you know," Daniel told her as the sun tipped its pink rays into the car window and gave them both a kind of glow.

"Really?" she said. "And here I thought it was my first time."

He laughed. He was strangely relaxed, almost drunk on a cocktail of excitement, relief, and fear. The relief was because she knew about him, believed him, didn't run away from him or regard him with apprehension. It was remarkable, really, how she had worked these things out. What did it mean? What did he mean to her? And then the darker thoughts nagged to be let in. How could she have thought that Joaquim was him? How could she have come all the way to Mexico with Joaquim?

"So when was that?" she asked.

"A long time ago."

"What was my name?"

He looked at her in surprise. "It was Sophia."

"Sophia? That's the name you called me in high school."

"It was the first name of yours I knew. Last time we made our getaway on a beautiful Arabian, which was more romantic than the Ford Focus."

"I'm good with the Ford Focus," she said, and he laughed.

No matter how she'd ended up in this place, there was surprising sweetness in getting away from Joaquim, in being joined with her in a common cause and feeling that he could protect her. It was the one inadvertent good turn Joaquim had ever done him, or probably anyone.

She tucked her feet under her and looked at him more seriously. "Why did you kidnap me that time?"

"For the same reason and from the same man. I was trying to help you."

"Did I need helping?"

"Yes. Though by no fault of your own."

"What does he want from me?"

Daniel veered onto the road toward Los Cuches and got up to speed. "Now or then?"

"Let's start with then."

He nodded. "I'll start at the beginning, if you want me to."

"I want you to."

"Not the very beginning but the beginning of you and me and the man you came here with. His name used to be Joaquim, and I don't know what it is now. We know it's not Daniel, so I'll call him Joaquim. I'm kind of attached to the old names, as you probably noticed."

She nodded.

"It starts more than twelve hundred years ago in what is now called Turkey."

JOLUTA, MEXICO, 2009

THEY LEFT THE car in the parking lot of a brightly lit supermarket a few miles inland from the coast road. Daniel paid a young man a wad of pesos to drive them another half-hour to the ocean. He'd arranged for them to stay at a bungalow on a remote part of the beach, he'd explained to her, on an undeveloped bay between two rocky headlands.

The sun sat quietly over the water when they pulled in, as if it were waiting for them. Daniel thanked the driver and took down his cell phone number. "I might need to call you on short notice," he explained in his odd Spanish. He'd overpaid so dramatically, he seemed to know the young man would do what he could.

"Anytime," the man said.

Daniel found the key under the flowerpot, as he'd arranged with the rental office.

"How did you plan all this?" she asked. "How did you know what would happen?"

"I didn't. I hoped we'd get this far. I wanted to make sure we had a place to go if we did. I'm going to charter a plane out of Colima, probably, but we won't get out until tomorrow morning."

It was a whitewashed stucco house with a tile roof under a crown of deep orange bougainvillea. He unlocked the door and pushed it open. She felt the ocean air that filled the house. It had a big, high-ceilinged central room open to a terrace and the beach just beyond, with two fans spinning overhead. The kitchen was at the back, open to the big room. On either side was a bedroom, both of them simple and pretty.

As they wandered around the little house they kept looking at each other, and she wondered if his sense of disbelief could possibly match hers. What was the category of this adventure? Was he just looking out for her? Would he deposit her safely back home and go back to his life, and that was all it was? A part of her mind kept returning anxiously to the story he'd told her in the car about him and Sophia. He'd left her in a remote village and gone off and gotten killed.

A low wall surrounded the terrace, and without really conferring, they walked over to it and sat down on it side by side to watch the last of the sun. She was still wearing her ridiculous peach-colored housekeeping smock. He was still dressed for the Washington winter. They were both quiet.

She felt her thigh touching his. She couldn't help being aware that she was not wearing anything under her smock. She'd gone running out of the hotel room in a bathrobe. She had nothing to change into and no ability to think even a few minutes ahead.

Numbly, she stared at the floating dock about fifty yards out. She thought it would be fun to swim to it. That's the kind of thing they would do if they were on vacation together, she thought wistfully. But they weren't. She kept wanting to think it, but it wasn't so. This was a mercy mission to get her away from an old enemy. Daniel was just trying to help her. Maybe he just took pity on her. Maybe it was for old time's sake. *I hope that's not all it is*, she thought.

No matter how it felt to be near him, she had to keep her swollen heart in check. He could have found her long before this if he'd wanted to. She thought of all those years of yearning for him.

Why, if he had wanted her anything like the way she had wanted him, hadn't he come for her sooner?

When the sun dunked under the Pacific Ocean he went to the refrigerator and looked inside. "Can I get you something to drink?" he called to her.

"Thanks. Anything," she said. "No bourbon."

DANIEL HAD SOMETHING he needed to say, but he didn't manage to get it out until two ginger ales, a ripe mango, two sandwiches, and a bag of chips later.

"How did he manage to get close to you?" he finally asked her, as though it was the next logical line in a long and somewhat frustrating conversation.

"You mean Joaquim."

"I really didn't think he would be able to get close, because of what he did to you when you were his wife. I know it was a long time ago, but usually those feelings stay pretty strong. I thought you'd want to run in the other direction. But I guess I was wrong. Maybe the feelings do fade after a while. Or maybe I just don't understand the whole picture."

She put her glass down. She felt his frustration, and she sent some right back. "I did want to run in the other direction, Daniel. And I would have. I struggled to make myself sit next to him. I don't know how I did it. I felt like gagging when he kissed me. I felt guilty about that at the time, but now when I think of it I not only feel stupid, I want to gag some more."

"Did you . . . ?" Daniel had a pressing question, and he couldn't get it out. She knew what it was, and she didn't feel like helping him.

"Did I what?"

"Did you . . . spend a lot of time kissing him?"

"Not much. No."

He was embarrassed but stubborn. "Did it go further than kissing him?"

"Is that any of your business?"

"No."

"Daniel." She stood up. She felt like shaking him. "I didn't have sex with him. I wouldn't let him touch me. I couldn't stand it. Last night I slept in a chair. Is that what you were trying to ask?"

He nodded, with a look of chagrin. "But why did you go anywhere with him if that's the way you felt?"

"You know why. Because he told me he was you."

He shook his head. He was quiet for a moment. "And that seemed to you like a good thing?"

Her eyes were suddenly full. "How can you ask me that?"

He got up the courage to put a finger on her finger, a thumb against her wrist. "The last time I saw you at that party at the end of high school you ran away from me. I understand why. It was my fault, I know. But the last thing you did was to push me away from you. I've been trying to stay away, because that's what you wanted. I didn't want to cause you more distress. And I didn't know how to try again and make it right. I didn't want to ruin what little chance I might someday have with you."

She wiped at her eye before any tears could get going. "Everything changed since then. I was scared of the things you said, but I was more scared of the way I felt. I started having these . . . visions out of nowhere, and I thought I was going crazy. I kept thinking about them and about the things you said. I wanted to find you, but I thought you were dead. Somebody saw you jump into the Appomattox River."

He nodded morosely. "I jumped, but I didn't die."

"So I gather. But I didn't know that then. I looked everywhere for you. You have no idea how much I wanted to find you and how much I've thought about you these last five years."

His surprise was not the kind you could fake. "I had no idea." He was shaking his head slowly. "I wish I'd known."

"Well, you didn't know, maybe, but somehow he must have known how desperate I was to see you again. He came up to me at school saying he was you. I didn't believe it at first. But he knew these things he couldn't possibly have known otherwise. That's what I thought, anyway. I've learned such unexpected things about the world in the past few years, I don't know what is possible and what isn't. The same kinds of mysterious things you said to me at that party, he seemed to know. He said you'd died, which is what I already thought, and had come back in a new body. He even explained this complicated thing of how he went from an old body to a new one."

Daniel's face was pained. "That was the only part of what he told you that was true," he said.

"Is it?"

"Yes."

"He said he didn't hurt anybody with it."

"He hurts people with it," Daniel said.

She closed her eyes. "I didn't know that. I didn't know anything. It scares me the things I told myself. But I would have told myself almost anything, because I wanted to believe him."

"Why?"

"Because I wanted to be with you."

THEY WENT DOWN to the sand to put their feet in the surf. It was dark, but the moon was full and bright. The water was calm and practically calling out to them, and Daniel really wanted to go for a swim. He sensed she did, too, but he felt awkward about making the suggestion. He could strip down to his boxers, but she just had that housekeeper dress and very possibly nothing under it.

Thinking of that, he thought of the way her body looked in it, and then he thought of the way her body looked under it. And then he pictured her unzipping it to go into the water, and then he realized it would no longer be a good idea to strip down to his boxer shorts. He sat there tangled up in his own awkwardness, and the most he could finally do was reach out and hold her hand.

"What happened to you?" she asked, looking at his arm where his sleeve had bunched up.

"What do you mean?"

"These scars."

"It's nothing." He put his sleeve down again.

She lifted it up again. "It doesn't look like nothing."

To his astonishment, she bent her head and kissed the burn marks, each of the three, slowly and deliberately. He stared at her. As much as he'd wanted her lips on him, he wished she would leave that part alone.

"I had a tough set of foster parents," he said quickly. "The mother was a smoker with a bad temper."

She looked horrified. "Your mother did this to you?"

"She wasn't my mother. She was just the woman I lived with when I was a kid." His voice was so dismissive it was rude, but he couldn't help it.

"Who was your mother, then?"

"The woman who gave birth to me was a heroin addict. I haven't seen her since I was little. I was too young to really remember her." He sounded impassive, and he was.

She kissed his arm again. She was sadder about it than he was, and he wished he could make her see.

"It doesn't matter," he said to her. "I've been through worse. I didn't care about her. She might have thought she could hurt me, but she couldn't."

She lifted her head and looked at him. "How can you say that? How can you say it doesn't matter? You were a child, and she hurt you. She burned your skin and left scars. Of course it matters. That's why you hide them."

He shook his head, suddenly irritated. "I don't hide them."

"You do! I don't care how many times you've lived or what you remember, it still hurts. It does matter."

"Not the way you think." He felt angry at her. This was not what he wanted to talk about, and he wished she would stop. "I'm different from you, Sophia. That's the thing. I'm different from everybody. You don't get that."

"Oh, I get it, all right." Her eyebrows came down. "And by the way, I am Lucy. I am right here, and I am Lucy. You are you, and you are not as different as you think. You are *this* man right here." She held his arm with two hands. "With this skin and these scars on your arm and your fucked-up mom. That is who we are."

"You're wrong." He glared at her. "We're more than that."

She looked mad, and that was fine, he told himself. He would rather she be mad than sympathetic. She provoked him, and he hated her in that moment, but he hated himself most. God, maybe she would run away again. Maybe he'd blown it again. Maybe for a lifetime. Maybe for all lifetimes. It wasn't meant to work with them, was it? He didn't know if he could try anymore.

She stared at him for a long time. She was tough when she wanted to be. She put her hands on his shoulders, and he half expected she was going to start shaking him, but she didn't. She leaned in very close until he could feel her warmth. He felt shaken, and he couldn't breathe right.

"You know what, Daniel?"

He held his breath. "What?"

This was where she said good-bye and walked out. He didn't know where she would go, but he felt sure that's what was coming. He hoped at least she would let him help her get somewhere safe.

"If it doesn't matter, then this doesn't matter." She turned her head to the side and put her mouth to the hollow at the base of his neck and kissed him long and slow. He could feel the moisture. He could feel her tongue.

He was too shocked to respond. He was frozen. He didn't know what to do. His body was suddenly a mass of throbbing nerves, and his brain didn't even work.

She pulled away and looked him right in the eyes as she began to unbutton his shirt. In astonishment he watched her as if it were happening to someone else. She pulled the shirt off his shoulders and left it in a pile on the sand behind him. He was breathing hard, but he didn't dare move.

"If that doesn't matter, then this doesn't matter." She leaned down to his chest and kissed it.

His hands were clenched. He drew in a sharp breath.

"And this doesn't matter." She slid her hands around to his back and came up to kiss him on the lips. She kissed him hard, and in a rush like a tide he kissed her back. He didn't think about anything. He kissed her with all he had, because he couldn't help it. He couldn't hold back if he tried. His hands were making their hungry way around her hips when she pulled away from him.

She held him away and looked at him, and his whole big, stupid body just hurt. He physically could not stand to be apart from her any longer. Once started, there was too much to feel. He couldn't help that, either. He was drowning.

Her eyes were unflinching on him, but they were filled with tears. "Does that not matter?"

She was going to cry, he realized. She was going to cry for him, and he didn't want her to.

He closed his eyes.

"Daniel, tell me. Does it not matter? Because if it doesn't, I'll stop."

He didn't want to open his eyes. He felt a tear escape under his eyelid. He couldn't lie to her. He never had, and he couldn't now. "Don't stop." His voice was barely a whisper.

"Why not?"

He felt as though he would die if he couldn't touch her. "Because it matters."

When she kissed him again he was crying, too, for the good and the bad. They were down on the sand, a wet blur of kissing and tears. He didn't try to make sense of it anymore. He didn't try to organize it or record it for the long future. This was what he had. It not only mattered, it mattered the most. He kissed her with everything, because loving a person was all you could do.

HE DIDN'T KNOW how long they'd been kissing in the dark sand or the things he said to her. There was nothing that separated him from her anymore. At some point, without really thinking, he lifted her from the sand in his arms. He wasn't thinking, he just let his body do. He was long past fighting it anymore. It was a strong body, and it lifted her with ease and walked her into the house and into the bedroom. It parted the mosquito netting and put her on the bed.

Time lost its meaning. The regular sequences he kept such careful track of were gone. If anything, the circle of his long existence clicked back to the start and made him new again.

He unzipped her housekeeper smock with aching tenderness and found her naked under there with a burst of unexpected wonder, even though he knew that's how she would be. He felt as though he'd never seen a woman's body before, and when he put his hands on her, he felt as though he'd never touched anyone before. He discovered every part of her with his fingers and his mouth as though it was new. He went up every so often to kiss her wet face and look at her eyes and make sure she was still with him. She gave him everything unstintingly.

"I love you," he whispered to her, and if he'd ever said it before, he couldn't remember.

After he'd found every part of her, she wound her legs around him and pulled him inside. She clung to him. She held his neck and kissed him damply and fiercely.

He could lose himself in her forever, he thought. He might never come out. She was right here, and she was Lucy. He was this man in this skin, and that was all. Lucy was right. That was all they were.

At last he came and came and came inside her. It was just raw senses. It was a moment big enough to scatter all memory of before and after. Maybe he wouldn't get to keep it, and that was the thing that always scared him most. But he felt a delirious joy in setting his burdened mind free. He let it all go. The rest of the world and all record of everything that had ever happened to him. He pressed his sweaty body along her beautiful, sweet skin. He curled around her, and he was as raw and new as if he had just been born.

SHE WOKE TO a sound. Not his breathing or occasional sighing, which she incorporated pleasurably into sleep, but a sound she wasn't sure of. Regretfully and carefully she unwound them, his leg back to him, her arm back to her. He'd gotten up to pee a little while before and had put on his boxer shorts.

There was a faint light of dawn making its way into the room. She crept quietly out of bed. She found the housekeeping smock in a ball on the floor and pulled it on, zipping slowly so she wouldn't wake him up. She turned to the window. She could barely make out the leaves of a mango tree. She stood, alert.

She heard something again from the same direction. It was probably a bird or some other little animal. The landscape was tropical and busy around here. She walked along the edge of the room toward the window, trying to tune her eyes to the dull light.

"Daniel!" She screamed his name before she had time to think it. There was something there. She couldn't make out a face, but she was almost certain she could make out the shape of something in the half-open window. She tried to make sense of it. Was it a gun?

Several things happened at once and without any perceptible order. He sat up at the sound of her voice. She ran toward him as fast and as hard as she could to push him out of the way. The gun fired and she screamed and Daniel was suddenly on his feet shouting.

She didn't know what was happening. He was holding her and

yelling like crazy. She saw blood, and she was scared that he was shot. He pulled her off the bed and carried her out of the bedroom to the big room. She heard another shot behind them. She was crying. "Are you hurt? Are you okay? Did it hit you?" She wasn't sure what she was saying and what she was just thinking.

He was running through the house, out of the house, onto the beach. He was running with her across the sand, and she heard a third shot. They were going to die. Where could they go? They couldn't go back to the house. They were easy targets on the wide-open beach. Ahead of them was only water.

There was blood on his chest. Oh, God, was he hurt?

He ran with her down to the surf and pulled her into the water with him. It wasn't until she was trying to swim that she realized she could barely move her arm. Distantly, she heard another shot. "Take a big breath," he ordered her. They went under together and he pulled her along and she swam as best she could. It dawned on her that her shoulder hurt. Had she injured it somehow? He was swimming so powerfully for the two of them, it made her think he couldn't be badly wounded. He pulled her up for a breath and then down again.

When they came up for the next breath she saw the floating dock right in front of them. *This is what we would do if we were on vacation,* she reminded herself incongruously. He swam her around to the other side, pushed her onto it, and quickly scrambled up behind her.

She was aching for breath. She put a hand to her shoulder. She saw the figure on the beach with the gun. Joaquim was what Daniel called him.

She felt Daniel's arm supporting her, his other hand unzipping her smock. He pulled it gingerly over her shoulder, and it hurt. He was taking off her dress, and they were both going to die at any moment, and she felt oddly calm about it all.

"We'll be easy to kill out here," she said, trying to catch her breath.

"If he wanted to kill us, he would." He was studying her shoulder, and she realized for the first time that she was the one who was bleeding.

The gun was trained on them. "You think he doesn't?"

"I think he would have already if he was in any hurry to."

"Did I get shot?" she asked incredulously.

"Your shoulder caught the edge of a bullet that was not intended for you. You jumped right in front of it, my girl, and scared the shit out of me." She couldn't believe he was smiling at her, but he was. "There's a deep scrape but not a bullet. We got lucky there."

"Who was it intended for?" She cast another wary eye at Joaquim and his pistol on the beach.

"It was intended to intimidate us and get control of us but not to hurt you. Joaquim might not have minded shooting me, but it would have been an anticlimax. He wants to put me at his mercy. That's the kind of person he is. He wants to do to me what I did to him—to take you away from me and have me know that you are in the world, but I can't have you. He probably thinks you still belong to him. I'm not saying he won't shoot me or both of us as a last resort, but it's not what he wants to do."

"Why not?"

"Because then he loses us again. He's got us in this life but not the next. He can remember, but he can't recognize souls."

"He can't?"

"No. He couldn't in the past, anyway."

"You can?"

"Not perfectly but yes."

"So then what's going to happen now?"

"I don't know, and neither does he. When he brought you here I think he probably hoped that I would show up, but he didn't expect me to succeed in running away with you. I am almost sure this was not in his plans. He knows we have no options right now, but neither does he. Besides shooting us both dead, all he can do is stand there and wait to see what we do. He can't leave us and get a boat. We'd be gone by then. He can't swim in after us."

"So what do we do?"

"For now, it's a stalemate. We're all going to wait."

"We are?"

"Unless you have a different idea."

"I'll get to work on that," she said. She realized he was pulling at the bottom of her smock, and she sat up. "Is this really the moment for that?"

He laughed. "I wish it were." He was examining her hem. "Listen, I know you haven't got a lot to work with, clothes-wise, but do you mind if I rip off the bottom couple of inches? I want to tie up your shoulder." He gestured to his wet boxers. "I've got even less to spare."

"I think we should use yours," she said.

"All right, then," he said. He stood up and started to strip, and she couldn't help but admire his beautiful body up and down.

She was not in her right mind. She'd been too drunk with happiness to sober up properly. She suspected he felt the same. The world wasn't big enough to contain the magnitude of what had happened between them last night. There was no way it was big enough to contain this, too. She didn't want to sober up.

"Stop. I'm kidding. You can rip my dress. We don't want to be totally naked out here."

"Don't we?"

"Not with our audience."

He expertly tore the bottom few inches straight around the hem. He snuck a peek under it. "You are driving me insane in this thing."

She laughed. "It's not the outfit I would have picked for our reunion, but I admit it's easy to get in and out of." She couldn't quite believe that they were still lusting after each other.

He carefully and expertly bandaged her shoulder to stop the bleeding.

"You seem like you know what you're doing."

"I'm a doctor. Did I mention that?"

"No, you are not."

"Yes, I am. A few times over."

"You're too young."

"I'd been to medical school already. I skipped ahead a bit."

"A bit? A lot."

"Okay, a lot."

"Do you work in a hospital?"

"Yes." He tied off the bandage, kissed her breast, pulled her smock back into place, and zipped her up. "You'll be fine, ma'am."

"Another scar for my collection."

"You have many bullet wounds?"

"I mean the kind you gather over lifetimes, that stay with you after you die. Like this one, right?" She pointed to her upper arm.

He tipped his head. "How do you know about that?"

"From Constance."

"How do you know about Constance?"

"I was Constance."

"I know, but how do you know that?"

"I read a letter she wrote to me."

He glanced briefly at Joaquim on the beach and back at her. "And how did you do that?"

"I went to Hastonbury Hall in England and found it in her old bedroom."

He shook his head in disbelief. "You are kidding me. I don't know what to say."

It was fun, having this to tell him. "Remember the hypnotist I told you about? I did a regression under hypnosis and went right back to Constance. She was desperate that I find her note. And she's been badgering me and making me remember things ever since."

"Unbelievable."

"She is."

"I was wrong, you know."

"About what?"

"When you were Constance I told you your memory was only ordinary. Now I see I underestimated you."

"Because that girl would not leave me alone. She would not be happy until I got with you."

Daniel laughed. "Is she happy now?"

Lucy laughed, and she also felt as though she was going to cry. "She's very happy now."

DANIEL LOOKED UP at the sky. He felt that he could see the sun arcing across it, and he really wanted it to slow down. He heard the slap of the water against the float. He felt a silky strand of her hair tickling his armpit. He felt as though he'd smoked a whole lot of pot. He knew he had no right to be happy with a gun trained on the two of them. He knew he should feel anger and outrage, but he couldn't quite help it. Fear almost always trumped joy, but not today.

"I should be coming up with a plan," he said, twisting a strand of her hair between his fingertips, "but all I can think about is how you look under that dress." He rolled onto his elbow. "I can't take it."

"Maybe we should do the deed right here and now," she said. "That would show him."

"That would probably get him mad enough to shoot us both dead."

"But we'd come back together, wouldn't we?"

He sat up and looked at her seriously. "If you love me even a tiny fraction of how much I love you, then yes. I am almost certain we would."

"Then we would," she said simply. "Because I do." She thought of a darker possibility. "Maybe us together is exactly what he doesn't want."

"I suspect he doesn't."

"Maybe we won't give him a choice," she said. She sat herself between his legs and pressed her back against his chest. "There's no way he's getting you without me. He's not that good a shot."

"I don't know how I feel about that," he said.

She shook her head. "You're not going anywhere without me." She might have sounded like she was kidding, but she wasn't. "Wherever we are going, we are going together."

He frowned at her.

"Seriously, Daniel."

He held both her hands and rested his chin on her good shoulder.

"So besides both of us getting shot, what are our other options?"

"We could swim in to shore and take our chances."

"And what chances would those be?"

He pressed his lips together. "I don't know. Probably end up at Joaquim's mercy. That would be his option of choice."

"And what happens then? He takes me hostage? He hurts me in some way, and you have to watch? He forces you into some humiliation and then he ends up killing you anyway? That's the kind of showdown he's looking for, isn't it?"

"I'm almost sure it is."

"He doesn't care about committing murder, does he? He can just skip to another body if he ever gets caught."

Daniel nodded.

"That is the worst of all worlds. Are those the kind of chances we are looking at?"

Daniel closed his eyes for a moment. He didn't want to enumerate what would happen, but he couldn't stop her from doing it.

"Is there anywhere we can swim to? Can we try to swim around the headlands and make our way in?"

"He'd get there faster."

"Do you think anybody ever comes here?"

"It's not impossible, but I think this is a pretty remote spot."

She thought about that. "Daniel?"

"Yes."

"If by some miracle we can't think of, we do get out of this, what then? Is there anywhere we can go or anything we can do where he won't find us?"

"Probably not for long."

She looked discouraged, and who could blame her? "Daniel?"

"Yes."

"Did you ever think we were meant *not* to be together?"

Her face was serious, but he couldn't help smiling. "No. We are meant to be together. We are just meant to want it very badly."

She smiled at his smile in spite of herself. "I'm running out of ideas. Are you holding something back? Do you have an idea here?"

He lay his head back and looked up at the sky. "I have the idea of being with you a little longer."

"ARE YOU SCARED of dying?" she asked him.

The sun was rapidly making its way to the top of the sky. He lay on his back and she was curled up against his side with her head on his chest. He felt remarkably relaxed.

"No. I've died many times. I've only made love to you once, though, so that's the miracle I'm focusing on. Joaquim can't take that from us one way or another."

"Do you think we're going to die?"

He breathed in and out, in and out. He'd never felt the warmth of the sun so purely. "Lucy, I don't want to have to think about it. I just want to think about you. But if I have to, I guess I think it is likely that either we are going to suffer or we are going to die. I'd rather die, and honestly, I think I can die happy now."

"You can?"

"Yes."

She lay back beside him. "Did you call me Lucy before?"

He turned his head to look at her and shielded his eyes from the sun so he could see her well. "It's funny, I look at you now, and you are all I can see."

She shook her head. "We're on a float in the middle of the water. I'm all there is."

He laughed and pulled her on top of him and hugged her. He kissed her neck and then her lips. "Lucy," he said. "Lucy." He shrugged. "I don't know. I think that is a perfectly good name." He kissed her chin. "Lucy. That's you."

.   .   .

BY THE TIME the sun was stretched overhead, Lucy's skin was turning pink and she was getting thirsty. She could tell he was, too, but neither of them wanted to say anything about it.

"I'm seeing a problem with the waiting," she said.

"Tell me." He pulled her onto his lap.

"I'm going to get burnt to a crisp, and we're both going to get very thirsty, and it's not going to feel good. I'm going to try to be brave, and you're going to start worrying about me, and then you are going to do something you'll regret."

"You are right." He kissed the side of her face. "So maybe we should undress each other and enjoy what we have left."

"I don't want him to kill us."

"I don't, either."

"And we can't just wait forever."

He nodded. He didn't want to mention that he didn't think Joaquim would let this stalemate go past sunset. He'd never been a patient man.

She was quiet for a while. He wrapped a hand around each of her feet. "Can I ask you something?" she said.

"Anything."

"What kind of a death is drowning?"

He looked at her in surprise. "What do you mean?"

"I mean, how is it? Does it hurt? Does it take a long time? Is it worse than, say, getting shot to death?"

"Well." He thought it over. "I've done it twice. That was a long time ago. I've gotten shot twice. That was more recently. I would say drowning is, overall, better."

She rubbed her hands together. She licked her dry, chapped lips.

"Then that's the worst that can happen, right? And I grant you it's pretty bad, but it's better than giving him the pleasure of taking our lives. What do you say? We'll just jump off this thing and start swimming." She gestured out to the open sea. "Either we'll make it to China or we won't."

He squinted toward China.

"So what do you say?"

"I say there's weather coming in."

"What do you mean?"

"There's a storm out there, and it looks like it's coming this way. I don't know if that's good for us or bad."

"How could it be good?"

He thought about that. "Less sunburn. Less thirst if we could catch some of it."

A shot rang out, and it startled them both. "I think he's getting tired of waiting," Daniel said.

She curled herself tighter around him, and he knew why. "I think we should make our move," she said. "Come on. I know you don't want to give him the satisfaction."

He was in a daze. He wanted to touch her and talk to her and smell her smell and watch her laugh. He didn't want to die. He didn't want this to end. But he had to shake himself out of it. He didn't care very much about what happened to him, but he cared about what happened to her.

"Is this really what you want to do?" he asked.

"Yes." She put her feet over the edge, and he followed her. He noticed she was staying very close to him, touching some part of him all the time.

"Are you willing to choose this? Do you really believe the things I've told you so completely that you are willing to swim to China?"

She looked him in the eyes and checked him. "Yes."

She wasn't kidding around. He had to contend with that, and it forced him to have to be serious, too. "Stop for a minute, Lucy. Think it through. I'll let him shoot me, and you go back to him in peace. Maybe that would satisfy the bloodlust for a time. Maybe he wouldn't hurt you. You could head back to the States and go back to some regular kind of life. That would be the most sensible thing to do."

"How can you even say that?" She twisted his big toe, hard. "I could never let that happen. Anyway, do you really think he'd leave me alone? Do you really think he'd let me go back to a regular life?"

He wasn't going to lie. "No. I don't. But there's a chance."

She chewed on her bottom lip. "I like that about as well as I like the rest of our chances. Anyway, I'm not going anywhere without you. We're swimming to China together. And if the worst happens, I'm dying with you before I'm living without you."

"You said something like that once when you were Constance, and I talked you out of it."

She looked at him ominously. "Fool me once, Daniel." He heard her Virginia twang.

She put out her hand for his. "Ready?"

"I don't want this to end," he said.

"It's the beginning," she said, with a certainty he envied.

They pointed themselves west. He leaned over and kissed her. "To China," he said.

She nodded. Her chin quivered, and he could see that she was afraid to open her mouth for fear she might cry.

"I love you," he said.

She gave him one last look, a teary smile. She held his hand so tight his fingers went numb, and when she jumped he jumped, too.

.   .

ANOTHER SHOT RANG out as they plunged in. He wanted to keep holding her hand, but he knew it made it hard for her to swim. He thought about her shoulder. They swam with a sense of purpose, but he knew they wouldn't last very long.

The sun was still shining down into the water, but he saw a bolt of lightning in the distance and presumed that would be the end if it didn't come before. He watched her pink legs in the water, the scraggly smock. He was still holding off on the reckoning, but it was starting to come after him cruelly.

A part of his mind was back on Joaquim. The waves were getting bigger and frothier, which would make it difficult to target them from the shore. A few hundred yards farther out and they would be out of his sight and out of range. He was calculating, as Joaquim would be calculating.

Joaquim could try to go after them in a boat, but the weather would make it difficult. No reasonable boat owner would agree to let a craft out in a storm. Maybe Joaquim already had a boat. Maybe he'd steal a boat. But if he left the beach even briefly, he'd be giving up his command of the shore. He must have believed they would come in at some point. He knew they had no other option. The one thing he couldn't control was their ability to die. He couldn't chase them where they were going.

They'd made it another quarter-mile or so when he saw that she was out of breath, and he feared she was in pain. He slowed down and bobbed for a minute. It took work not to get buffeted. "We can take it easy," he told her. "China isn't going anywhere."

"He can't shoot us from here, can he?"

"Not likely. I can't even see him anymore."

"It's just us, then." She was shivering.

"Just us." He put his arms around her. "How's the shoulder?"

"I'd say it's the least of our problems."

He nodded. He wished they could skip over this next part, because it wasn't going to be fun. The water was getting colder, and it would slow all processes down, including death.

"What happens if we don't get there?" she asked breathlessly. "How do you die?" She didn't look frightened so much as determined.

"You don't give yourself to it," he said. "You let it take you. You just keep going until it takes you."

"Does it last long?"

He didn't want to go into the biology of drowning. It would only scare her. "A few minutes. You're strong and your body will struggle, but I promise you something."

"What is that?"

"At the worst possible moment, the most painful, darkest moment when you can't take it anymore and you are afraid, that is when a feeling of peace and comfort will come over you, and it's like nothing you've ever felt."

She looked hopeful. "Does that happen to everyone?"

"It will happen to you."

THERE WAS A strange stillness that came over them through the next stretch. They did their swimming underwater, coming up for fewer breaths. He stayed close to her and watched her. He felt almost hypnotized by the slow beauty of her body under the water. He fought with himself about whether to try to support her and give her a rest or not. He didn't want to drag it out. As terrible as it was, there was something lovely about the way the waves surged around them and yet the sunlight continued to filter through. He thought of his first life in Antioch, as a five-year-old lying in the river through an earthquake. He thought he saw eternity then, and he wondered if he would see it again with her.

She was remarkably strong. Her body was giving her a great burst of energy, and he could see it in her legs and her face. He knew she wasn't feeling pain anymore.

And then slowly, in time, she began to falter. Her movements slowed. Her strokes were less precise. It was happening to him, too. It didn't disturb him in himself, but it hurt him to watch her. He didn't want to watch, but he wasn't going to spare himself, either. He had dragged her into this.

And then came the moment, unexpected though it had to come, when she stopped laboring. Under the water, in the speckled sunlight, she turned her face back to look at him. It was not a smile but like a smile. It wasn't a face of fear. It was an expression of faith more than anything. She had faith in him and the things he promised her. She trusted him.

This was what it felt like to be loved. Instead of warding it off as he used to do, he let it sink in. He tried to open up every part of himself to take more of it in.

And then, to his horror, she lifted her arms over her head and began to sink. He watched it as though in slow motion. The sun was streaming down in shafts, fluttering around her. Her hair was a slow golden cloud, and her hands were open.

She was sinking. He saw the back of her head, her open fingers sinking down past the level of his chest. She was pulled down by the hungry darkness of the bottom. She was leaving the sunlight and leaving him, and he was frozen by the sight of her.

You have to let her go.

Why? A voice in his head was bellowing at him, waking up the rest of him.

Because this is how we save ourselves. This is what we chose. This is what we've been waiting to do all these centuries.

What were all those centuries? They were days and years and months of memories. They were nothing. They were thoughts in his mind and nothing more. Could he really be sure of any of it? Did he have any real, tangible reason to know he had ever come back from death or ever would? She believed him. But did he believe himself? Was he so confident he was willing to sacrifice her?

Because maybe he was crazy. Maybe it was as simple as that. He belonged in a mental institution with all the other people who shared his views. Why did he think he was any better? Just because he was good at keeping his crazy ideas to himself?

How could he be sure there were any lives before this one? He couldn't. How did he know there would be any lives after? He didn't. What if he'd invented this memory as a way to contend with a life of abandonment and abuse? Damaged people did strange things. How did he really know he wasn't crazy? He didn't. It was easily possible that he was living one long delusion and he'd dragged her into it.

It was all just stories, he knew that much. But what if they weren't true stories? Could he take that risk? Could he really let her go on the strength of that?

Thoughts were nothing. Memories were nothing. They were nothing you could touch. They took no time. You could fit them all on the point of a pin. You could bring your entire world into doubt in a span of a few seconds.

He watched the cloud of her hair sink to the level of his knees. *Don't drag it out. Don't make her die a longer death.* Her larynx was going to seal off, and her heart and her lungs and her brain were soon going to start their involuntary struggle, and him holding her or interfering with her wasn't going to make it any easier.

This was the girl he loved. This was his strong, beautiful girl.

He'd made love to her in the most exquisite moment of his life and kissed every inch of her body just a few hours before, and now she was dying in front of his eyes.

No. There was one word in his head, and it spread through him quickly. It galvanized every muscle and nerve. *No.* She wasn't leaving him. *No.* He wasn't letting her go.

No. With the word came a memory. He had watched her die once before. He watched her die because he had killed her. He had burned down her house and watched her die, and he'd thought of it and dreamed of it with pain every day since. *No.* He was not going to watch her die this time.

We have no choice. We have no options.

No! If you didn't have a choice, you had to make a choice. If you didn't have options, you made some. You couldn't just let the world happen to you. He'd done that too long.

He didn't see eternity. He saw this girl and this moment and one slim chance. His body broke out of its strange freeze. It knew what it wanted to do. It was pure brain voodoo and bodily torture to hold back from her any longer. He dove down and reached for her. He grabbed her around the middle and pulled her up to the surface. This was his body, and it was a good, strong body. It loved her as he did, because it was him. It wasn't any more or less.

He held her and treaded water. Her head fell on his shoulder. Her limbs weren't moving. A surge of adrenaline filled his body as he felt her neck and her chest for signs of life.

She wasn't dead. She hadn't taken water into her lungs, but she had sealed them off, and it was a crippling moment of suspense until she opened her throat and started breathing again.

"You are not going to die," he told her. He felt the emotion breaking his voice. "I know I said I'd let you, but I can't."

HE PUT HIS arm around her chest, under her armpits, the way he'd learned in a lifesaving class in Fairfax, and towed her along. He swam into the storm, because there was nowhere else to go. The sun disappeared, and the rain came down. He prayed the lightning would keep moving up the coast and away.

He swam as hard as he could. He didn't know where he was going or what he would find besides water and rain. He felt the current pulling him north, and he fought it at first, but then he swam with it. How did he know which way to go?

In moments of tremendous stress he used to picture the world as it would look from high above. But now he saw them down here, two tiny white faces bobbing in a wide, stormy sea.

His lungs were raw and his limbs were starting to ache, but he wouldn't slow down. He wouldn't give in. *You are not taking her,* he wanted to say to the indifferent ocean as much as to Joaquim. *I am going to keep her safe.*

He didn't know how to keep her safe other than to keep swimming. He had to fight. That's all he had. Not memories, not experiences, not skills. He had a will. And his will was to fight until he couldn't fight anymore.

THE SUN WAS cast over by storm, and so it set without much bother. He knew it must have set only because the air was suddenly dark and hard to see through. He had long since stopped feeling anything from his body. His legs were numb. He knew his arm was there only because it was still clutching Lucy and towing her along. He knew his body was trying to conserve oxygen for his brain and his vital organs, but even those were badly depleted. His brain had entered the phase of slow blur. He should have drowned already. In his blurry mind he almost envied the times when he'd just been able to drown in peace.

When he looked back at Lucy he suddenly discovered that her eyes were open wide and disoriented. Her limbs weren't moving. She let herself be pulled along.

His face was so numb he could barely make his mouth open or his tongue work. "Hey, baby," he choked out. He wished he could make his voice sound normal enough not to scare her.

She blinked a few times. "What are we doing?" she asked. Her voice was barely audible.

"We're not dying," he said.

She leaned her head back. "It's raining," she said.

"I know."

"Are you sure we're not dead?"

His mouth loosened up a little. "I really fucking hope not," he said.

THE THUNDER RUMBLED, but the lightning stayed away. The wind blew the waves up and over them, and with each one he glanced back to see her sputter and breathe again.

What have we done? he thought.

His heart was swollen to bursting. It was all puffed up to start with, with love and lust, and now add hypothermia and myocardial infarction. Usually you lost consciousness before your heart exploded, but he was clinging pretty hard to consciousness. His thoughts were getting dim and disorderly, but he tried to keep alert and out loud for her. *Don't you go yet*, he begged his heart.

Her head was back. Every so often the clouds let through a bit of moonlight, and she watched it. The planes of her face, turned up to the sky, were lovely in the moonlight. She trusted him enough to die, and apparently she also trusted him enough to swim hopelessly and endlessly in a stormy ocean.

He thought he heard something besides the wind and the toil of the storm, but his brain was too slow to process what it was.

He heard Lucy say something, but he couldn't quite hear her.

He willed his dead arm to pull her a little closer.

"Is this the darkest hour?" she sputtered.

He realized his teeth were chattering uncontrollably. His body was shuddering. "W-why do you ask?"

"Because look." He followed her eyes up to the sky. He saw a flash of white through the rain and heard the sound again. He stared at it stupidly. Ideas were clamoring to be thought, but he couldn't quite get them started.

"Do you see it?"

"I-it's a gull."

It circled them a couple of times, probably wondering whether it could possibly figure out a way to eat them. Daniel saw the direction it went, and he followed. He couldn't make the thoughts go, but his body seemed to know that gulls did not stray far from land, especially not in weather like this. They did not fly this far out to sea without some place to land.

Daniel doubled his efforts. Blindly he knew he had to follow the gull. He couldn't let it out of his sight. The bird soared and stuttered and twisted through the rough air, and the pain of envy woke Daniel up a little. *We weren't made for water or sky,* he thought. *How are we supposed to follow you?*

"It's gonna land somewhere," he choked out.

"How do you know?"

"I-I—I just know."

She stared at him, and concern broke the calm. "How can you

be doing this?" She was shouting at him over the waves. "How can you still be moving, Daniel? I don't understand."

He didn't know. He wasn't sure he was still moving. He was glad if his legs were still kicking, though he couldn't feel them. *We have to live,* he wanted to tell her, but he didn't have the breath left to make the words.

He was having trouble seeing. He kept his eyes open, but they could barely make out even big shapes. He was lucky she had her eyes open.

"Daniel, I see something," she shouted.

He looked back at her. He tried to focus his eyes.

"It's there, ahead of us. It's a dark shape coming out of the water. It's like a big rock. Do you see it?"

"I-I don't know."

"Can you keep going? It's so close!" She tried kicking, too, to help.

It was practically looming over him; he was practically crashing into it before he could make it out with his eyes. With a last breath of pure exhaustion, he heaved her up onto the rock and watched her legs scramble up the craggy surface. He had only enough mental energy left to feel a slow rush of relief.

He put his hands against the rock to lift himself. He closed his eyes. *I'll just take a little rest,* he thought. *Just catch my breath.*

She was screaming before he knew what had happened. "Daniel! Daniel, get up here!"

He'd drifted a few feet away. A current had hold of him. *I'll just rest another minute,* he told himself blearily, *before I go over there.*

"Daniel! *Daniel!* Open your eyes. Look at me. Come back. We're going to be okay! Do you hear me?"

I'm tired, he thought.

"I'm getting back in the water if you don't get over here!" she shouted at him. "I'm not kidding. We're gonna go right back to drowning if that's what you want."

He blinked his eyes open and shut. He saw her white limbs climbing back down off the rock. Why was she doing that? *Why are you doing that?* he tried to ask, but his mouth didn't open. In his confused mind he thought it was a bad idea. He tried to push himself toward her. *Don't do that.* He got to her and found his hand on her ankle. "Y-y-you're g-g-gonna drown." His voice was slurred, and his brain was so slurred he barely knew what he was saying.

"Get up here, Daniel, or I swear to God I am going to drown right along with you." She had her hand wrapped around his other wrist. He could feel it there. She placed both of his hands on a flat spot. "You ready? Stay with me! I'm counting to three. Ready? One. Two."

He felt his eyelids dropping closed again.

"Daniel!" She squeezed his arm so hard he opened them again.

He could see her eyes clearly now, right in front of his face. "One, two, *three!*"

With a heave and a thunderous groan, he pulled himself up on the rock. Like an inchworm, he folded himself together and pushed himself higher on the rock. He inchwormed one more time until all but his feet were clear of the water, and that was the moment his body gave up. It just collapsed and possibly died, and he couldn't have asked anything more of it.

PETACALCO, MEXICO, 2009

SHE RUBBED HIS back and waited for the morning to come. Every so often she prodded him or felt his chest to make sure he was still going. Every so often he let out a satisfying groan.

There was enough dawn that she could see the shape of their rock. It had three peaks and several gullies where the rainwater had gathered. She was desperate to drink it, but Daniel was collapsed across her legs and she didn't want to wake him yet. The rock was red in some patches and black in others. It had a few tenacious vines growing at odd angles and a whole lot of bird shit. A handful of gulls were complaining and gossiping on the other side. The air was clear and the light was coming on fast now, but there was no land in sight. Daniel had swum them a very long way.

It was chilling to think back to the night they'd spent. She would take it on in pieces, she decided. Just one thing at a time. The first feeling she thought of was falling down through the water. She was willing to die, but he wasn't.

She didn't know how he'd done it. For hours, many hours, after she could no longer move, he was still swimming. Not just himself but the two of them.

They were going to make it. She hadn't been able to think how they would, but because of him they had. There was water enough to drink to keep them for a couple of days. The sky was clear and the water was calm. Somebody would have to pass by. They would get picked up eventually.

And then what? What would happen to them then?

He stirred and turned over onto his back. She leaned down and kissed his mouth. The rock surface was not comfortable. The backs of her legs were all scratched from it. You'd have to be half dead to actually sleep on it, which in fact he was.

She wondered if he was having bad dreams, because a look of pain crossed his face and his body shook and then stiffened. His face compressed in terrible anxiety before it opened again. She rubbed his stomach and chest with the lightest fingertips. She wished she could do something to take the nightmare away.

The early sun rose high enough to stick a ray in his face and pry open his eyes. His eyes closed and opened a few more times before he could focus on her. "It's you," he said.

"It's me." She kissed the center of his forehead and both temples.

"I'm happy. Where are we?"

"We followed a seagull to a rock. Do you remember any of that?"

He thought a minute. He squeezed his eyes shut and opened them. "No."

She shook her head and smiled at him. "You're losing your magic, baby."

He smiled weakly.

She smoothed his hair sympathetically. "I bet everything hurts," she said.

He nodded.

She gently pulled his head onto her lap and cradled it. "Honest to God, Daniel. I don't know how you got us here. I think your memory used to be your magic power, but I think you lost it and got a new one, which is a special kind of swimming power."

"It hurts to laugh," he said.

"We'll talk about sad things, then."

He nodded. He reached up and touched the zipper of her smock. "I remember that dress."

"You mean smock?"

"Yes, I love that. I love taking it off."

"That's not sad, though."

He shook his head painfully. "That's the best thing that ever happened to me."

She leaned over him and kissed him upside down on the lips. When she lifted up, his eyes were open and his face was serious. "I need to tell you something."

"Okay."

"Do you know what I did the first time I saw you?"

"No."

"I was a soldier and I burned your house down."

"When was that?"

"Five forty-one A.D."

"I don't remember."

"You died. I'm sorry." He pulled her head down to his and buried his face in her neck. It was almost fifteen hundred years ago, but she could feel his raw shame, and she wasn't about to disregard it. His breathing evened out, and he let her head go. "That's the main thing I wanted to say. I think about it all the time. I've been wanting to tell you for so long."

She rubbed his chest tenderly. "I'm glad you told me."

"Are you?"

"Yes, because now I can tell you that it's okay."

"How can it be okay?"

She looked down at her hands. "What Daniel taketh away, Daniel giveth."

"What do you mean?"

"You gave more than you took, my love. We're all square. You're allowed to forget it now."

HE WAS SITTING up next to her a couple of hours later when he heard the drone of a motor over still water. "It's a boat," he said to her just before it came into view.

It was a fishing boat and coming in their direction. They both stood up and waved their arms. It turned out Lucy could do a taxi whistle. It hurt his ear, but he couldn't help but admire it. "Will you teach me that?"

The boat captain saw them and steered over. He had two crew and a smelly net full of catch. He immediately invited them on. Daniel forgot how odd they looked until he saw it in the strangers' faces.

"We've had some trouble," he said in his stilted Spanish.

"I see that," said the captain. "Are you all right?"

"Yes. Would you mind dropping us up the coast?"

"Of course not. We can leave you at Petacalco. You can go from there to Guacamayas or Lázaro Cárdenas."

"That would be fine. Thank you very much. I wish I had money to pay you."

The captain looked at him in his boxer shorts as though he might laugh. "I can see you travel light."

They sat at the back of the boat. The captain lent Daniel his cell phone, and by the end of the hour-long journey to Petacalco he'd arranged a car to drive them to Guacamayas, a rental car in Guacamayas, and a chartered flight from Colima to New York, leaving that evening.

She, who did not speak Spanish, looked at him in disbelief. "You have no money, no credit card, and no ID. How did you do that?"

"All you need are the card numbers and a decent cell connection."

"So how did you get the numbers?"

He pointed to his head. "I remembered."

JOHN F. KENNEDY INTERNATIONAL AIRPORT, NEW YORK CITY, 2009

HE SAT FOR two hours on a bench facing the wall in the United terminal. He made travel arrangements on a newly bought cell phone while Lucy slept with her head on his lap. After he finished, he waited for her to wake up and then took her to a bar in the next terminal over, where they could sit by the window and watch the planes take off. He ordered them each a bourbon for old times' sake.

She was dressed in jeans and a flowered shirt and a sweater and a down vest and socks and boots and proper underwear now. She had a suitcase full of clothes they'd bought in the last few hours. Kennedy was like a miniature shopping city, though not a very nice one. He made her promise and swear she would save the housekeeping smock forever and wear it for him when he saw her again.

He handed her a folded piece of paper. "I wrote everything down, okay?"

She nodded. It wasn't the first time he'd said it.

"I put all the numbers you'll need into your phone."

"Right."

"Have you thought of what you want to say to your parents and Marnie?"

"Still thinking," she said.

He nodded. "Your tickets, your itinerary, your passport, your travelers checks, and your money are all in the envelope."

"Your money," she said.

"Well, I gave it to you, so it's yours." The cash he'd given her was the least of it. He'd spent an extraordinary sum securing two black-market passports in Mexico the day before.

"Are you rich?" she asked him.

"Yes."

"Very?"

"I've had a long time to save up for a rainy day."

"I wouldn't have guessed that about you in high school."

"I'm glad. Why not?"

"Because if you were rich, I would have thought you would have gotten a new pair of shoes."

He laughed. He pictured those tan suede shoes in the bedroom of the bungalow in Mexico, where he'd kicked them off in a frenzy of desire. "You know, I was sorry to see those go. That's another thing I'm going to take up with my asshole former brother."

She took his hand and brought it to her cheek. "Daniel, I don't want to do this."

"I know. I don't, either. I don't want to be apart from you, and I'd do anything to avoid it, but this is the only way."

"I think I'd rather drown together."

He took her two hands and kissed them front and back. He kissed the tender part of her wrists and each of her fingers.

"It's beautiful where you are going. And I promise you will be safe."

"How do you know?"

"Because it is one place in the world Joaquim would never dare to set foot. They would see through him instantly there."

"So why won't you come there with me?"

"I will. When I've done what I need to do, I will come and get you. And then we can live wherever you want. You can finish up graduate school in Charlottesville, we can move to D.C., we can live in California, Chicago, Beijing, Bangladesh. We can move back to Hopewood and live in the room next to your parents."

She laughed in spite of herself.

"We can go anywhere we like."

"And what else?"

"We can do anything we like. We can get married. We can not get married and live in sin. We can get jobs. We can not get jobs. We can loaf around. We can live at the top of a skyscaper. We can live in the middle of the water in a house on stilts. We can make love every day."

"Twice a day."

"Three times a day."

She lifted her eyebrows. "Three times a day?"

"We've got a lot of making up to do."

She nodded. "We can get old together."

"That's what I wish for."

"Maybe have a baby or two."

Her face was so rapt in the fantasy that he hated to let her down. He knew his expression was hard to read. "I don't know if that's in the cards for me," he said.

He could tell she wanted to ask him why not, but the loud-speaker blared and they were suddenly calling her flight.

He picked up her bag and they hustled down the terminal to the last gate. First class was most of the way through boarding.

"This is you," he said.

"This is first class."

"So's your ticket."

"No, it's not. Is it?"

"The big Mexico swimming vacation I took you on wasn't very comfortable. I was hoping to improve my record."

"I'd rather be uncomfortable if we could stay together."

"I know. We will be together soon. I'm going to start making plans for our first real vacation. I'm going to take you to Budapest and Athens, and then I want you to see Turkey again. I don't think you remember it as well as I do."

She shook her head.

"We're going to stay in a palace in Istanbul and then go back to Pergamum, and you are going to get a tour like nothing you ever imagined."

She nodded. There were tears in her eyes, and he put his arms around her. "Once he is gone, Lucy, we can do anything in the world we want. But until he is gone, we will live like prisoners and we can't. I don't want to wait around for things to happen anymore. I've spent too long doing that. I get defeated or discouraged, and I die because I figure there's always a new life and it will be better. But nothing can be better than this life, because I have you."

She held him hard. He felt her sniffling in his armpit. "Where will you go?"

"I'm going to find him. I'm going to destroy him before he can destroy us."

"How do you destroy someone like him? Is that even possible?"

"I think it is. I'm sure it is. I need to figure it out, but I have a friend I think can help me."

She lifted her head. "It scares me to hear you talk like that. He's vicious, and you're not. It makes me scared you aren't coming back."

"I am coming back."

"In this life."

"In this life."

"But how can you be sure?" She was crying openly now. They were down to boarding the very back of the plane.

"Because I've got something to live for, and he's only got vengeance. Because I can see and he can't."

"Yeah, but he's probably got ten guns and five bombs and a whole set of knives."

"So I'll get that, too. I'm smarter than him, Lucy. If I have the time to think it through, that will be my advantage. I'm bigger than him, and I won't be the victim any longer. I won't be running from him."

"What if you don't come back? I feel like Constance and Sophia and all the others who got left with a broken heart."

"It was me with the broken heart, Lucy. I carried it longer than anyone."

She looked at him thoughtfully. "Can I ask you a question?"

"Of course."

"Did we ever . . . you know . . . do stuff before?"

He loved the blush in her face. "You mean like hook up?" he asked her teasingly.

She smiled. "Yeah. Did we ever hook up before this?"

"No. Never."

"Never?" She wiped her eyes with the back of her hand.

"I think I'd remember."

"Not once in all those thousand years?"

"Not once."

"I don't just mean actual sex, but not even like, you know." She had to stop because she was laughing. "Third base?"

"No. Not even. Not even like, you know, second. Barely first."

"Well, there. We've got something to be proud of, don't we?"

He laughed and picked her up off the floor. "If that's not enough to keep me alive and coming back for you, Lucy, then there's nothing in this world that is."

THE LANDSCAPE WAS more beautiful than he had promised. The monastery was laid out on a remote hillside over the Paro River valley in the Eastern Himalayas. Every morning she looked beyond the valley to a far line of peaks so stunningly high and deeply faceted and glittering white she counted them more as sky than earth.

Lucy was treated by the monks as a most honored guest, and she understood that was because her arrangements had been made by an Indian woman, a close friend of Daniel's, whose name, oddly enough, was Ben.

She understood why Daniel wanted her to come here. The devotion to the spirit was more pervasive than anything she'd experienced, and their belief in reincarnation was fundamental. They picked their highest lama not by any hereditary line but by searching for the boy the old lama had reincarnated into. She understood why Joaquim would not come here.

She'd had a few small adventures. With her eager guide, Kinzang, who was all of twelve, she'd visited the capital city of Thimphu and gone to an archery contest and the weekend market. She had made treks through the valley and seen things she'd never thought to see in her life. Terraced rice paddies, orchards flowing down the mountainside, a monastery called the Tiger's Nest perched on a cliff.

She'd worked alongside the monks in the monastery garden and learned the names of dozens of unfamiliar plants in Dzongkha. She'd begun to learn weaving from a local woman in the village, and she'd taken to it quickly and eagerly. She'd begun wearing the traditional kira.

But mostly she stayed within the confines of the monastery, reading, writing letters, weeding in the garden, and learning to meditate. The monks were kind to her and patient to teach her, but they spoke very little, and she couldn't understand what few words they said. She was cut off, and she was lonely. She missed her parents, and she missed Marnie. She'd told them she'd been awarded a last-minute fellowship—an opportunity she couldn't possibly turn down—to study Himalayan gardens and could be reached only by letter.

More than anything she missed Daniel. The ache of missing him hung on her like a cloud and followed her everywhere she stepped. It got into her eyes and her nose and her mouth and her ears and changed the air around her.

She read each of his letters hundreds of times, trying to wring out every feeling, every scrap of information, every possible smell or molecule of him that might have traveled with it. She lingered for hours over the list he'd written for her in the airport. It was just a stupid list, but he'd spilled a drop of his drink on it as they sat together in the bar, and now she put her finger on the brown blurring dot and felt as though he was real.

She'd begun to feel sick to her stomach after the first month. She thought it was the yak meat or the butter tea or the vast number of chilies that turned up in every dish. The food was mostly delicious, but it just didn't agree with her, she thought. She'd tried to eliminate various ingredients from her diet until she was barely eating at all, and that made her stomach feel worse. By the second month she realized she hadn't gotten her period since before Mexico and put the evidence together.

And then she began to feel scared. A baby was the one thing Daniel had not dreamed up for their life together. It was the thing he didn't want. She didn't know why, and she didn't know what to do about it. She couldn't tell him. She tried, but she couldn't. She was twenty-three years old, unmarried, and alone in a strange world. She couldn't have a baby, but she had no idea how not to. She wrote him letter after letter intending to tell him, but she didn't tell him.

At the beginning of her third month in Paro his letters stopped. She continued writing to him every day, but with diminishing hope as the days passed that he would ever read them. She thought of him with a deepening anguish.

Time stretched out horribly, but comfort came from three unexpected places. First were the letters from Marnie, full of questions and doubts Lucy couldn't answer, and yet overfull of uncomplicated, unstinting love. It was a miracle, almost, how Marnie could love even when she didn't understand. It was a miracle and a lesson.

Second were the letters from her father. He described his latest Civil War reenactment with humor, his concerns for her safety with intimacy. In an age of cell phones and e-mail, she'd never realized this was his métier. As rigid as he seemed in person, he was oddly demonstrative in ballpoint pen. She found herself wondering whether he'd ever written a letter to Dana.

Third, as the weeks passed, was the heaviness in the bottom of her abdomen. It turned every taste and smell sour, and yet it provided an odd sense of companionship. She wasn't quite alone. It was hers and his together, no matter whether he wanted a baby or not. She prayed it wouldn't be all she had of him.

You promised me, she said to him in her thoughts every morning and night and a thousand times in between. *I love you. I won't give up on you.*

Dearest Lucy,

*I may not be able to send this letter today or even tomor-
row, but you are in my mind and my heart every minute. I
won't try to describe exactly where I am. But I am safe and
will tell you everything when it is done. There is a lot to say
that can't be written or even thought right now.*

*I've begun to see what this adversary of ours can do, and it
is beyond what I imagined. This thing I am trying to do has
to be done. I know that even more urgently now. To kill him is
not enough. I've learned to think on a big canvas, if nothing
else. I know what I have to do and how to do it.*

So what do I do for fun, you ask?

*I think of you. I think of you wearing a kira and digging
your hands in the dirt of the garden they have there. I think
of you taking off your shoes and socks and dunking your feet
in the fishpond. I think of you putting your hair behind your
ears. I think of you drinking tea. I think of you sleeping.
(Seriously, I do. That's my idea of fun, and I don't care what
you say.) I think of all the different parts of your body—and
no, not just the ones you think I'm thinking of. I picture the
scar on your shoulder, and I picture me kissing it as though
that's going to help it heal right. I picture us together. I picture us making love three times a day. (You promised.) I*

*picture you lying in my arms for hours and hours after all
this is done, and me telling you everything that's happened.
It's quite a story, and by then it will be a better story, because
I'll know how the ending goes.*

*I don't want to say more now. You are with me, my Lucy, in
every idea, every calculation, every lust, every stumble, every
triumph, and every grief. What I see, I see with your eyes, too,
and with you I am more determined and better than I could
ever be without you.*

*I know this letter is devoid of any real information, and I
apologize for that. You can punch me for it later. But I realize
I write it as a kind of prayer. I pray that even without getting
it (or the letter I wrote you last night or the one I will write
you tomorrow and tomorrow and tomorrow) you will know
what's in it: that I am safe and above all that I am with you
wherever I am, that there is no force on this earth or length of
time that will keep me from you. I will come back. My love
for you is truer than anything I have known in this long, very
long, life.*

*Love demands everything, they say, but my love demands
only this: that no matter what happens or how long it takes,
you'll keep faith in me, you'll remember who we are, and
you'll never feel despair.*

Yours forever,
Daniel

ACKNOWLEDGMENTS

With love and thanks, I acknowledge Jennifer Rudolph Walsh, my muse
for this story. I thank my editor, Sarah McGrath, for giving her immense
talent wholeheartedly. I thank my two most enthusiastic readers and
advisers, Margaret Riley and Britton Schey. I am deeply indebted to
Tracy Fisher and Alicia Gordon, both great champions of this book. And
with warmest appreciation, I acknowledge the entire outstanding team
at Riverhead and Penguin, including Sarah Stein, Stephanie Sorensen,
Geoff Kloske, and Susan Petersen Kennedy.

I thank my wonderful, inspiring parents, Jane Easton Brashares and
Bill Brashares. Last and most, I thank my beloved family, Sam, Nate,
Susannah, and Jacob. We are five good trampoline builders.

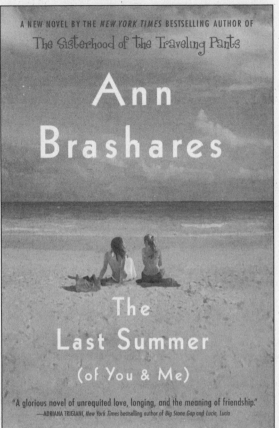